HAPPY ENDINGS

HAPPY ENDINGS

Stories by Australian and New Zealand Women

1850s–1930s

Edited by Elizabeth Webby
and Lydia Wevers

Allen & Unwin/
Port Nicholson Press

A&U
PNP

First published in 1987
by Allen & Unwin New Zealand Limited in association with
the Port Nicholson Press, 60 Cambridge Terrace, Wellington

Published simultaneously in Australia by Allen & Unwin Australia Pty Ltd,
NCR House, 8 Napier Street, North Sydney, NSW 2060, Australia

ISBN 0 86861 419 X

Cover Painting: 'Study: Girl with Poppies' by Grace Joel
Cover Design: Missen & Geard
Typeset in Bembo by Graphicraft Limited, Hong Kong
Printed by SRM Productions Ltd, Malaysia

Contents

Introduction

The literatures of Australia and New Zealand can claim many similarities, and in the colonial and immediately post-colonial periods particularly the commonly accepted notion of Australasia indicated the degree of identity felt by the two countries. Because the basis of their shared experience was gender as well as geography and cultural origins, Australasian women writers can suggest both the similarities and the distinctions.

The difficulty for colonial writers is always that of accommodating the new in the conventions of the old; the least successful stories are those in which convention has a stranglehold on experience and uses it simply as exotica. A great many stories in the period from which this selection comes, mid nineteenth century to post World War One, abound with New Zealand and Australian place names, references to Maoris, or to Aboriginal customs and legends. But it is the dead hand of the 'storiette' writer that handles them and little sense of a living country comes through. This can be ascribed partly, but not entirely, to lack of talent. Among other things, local writers had to cope with public taste and the demand was for escapist literature. In her *Reminiscences* Sarah Selwyn remarked: 'We had enough of the real thing, and wished for a different atmosphere from travels in the bush, and settling, and sheepruns and squatting etc. etc.' Nevertheless, a sense of literary identity does fitfully emerge from colonial writing in this part of the Pacific, and it is the root that eventually branches into distinctive national literatures.

Australian writing began earlier than New Zealand's and, partly as a consequence of a larger population, produced a greater quantity, but there is a sense in which colonial writers of both places saw themselves as part of the same literary environment. This is evidenced in a number of ways. For one thing, all European writers in Australasia at the time, male or female, saw themselves as essentially belonging to another culture, and used the conventions, styles and expectations of that culture while writing from another place. The point is not that this happened but that it was unquestioned. Consequently the strong similarities in style and particularly in types of story written by late nineteenth-century Australian and New Zealand women are attributable to the prevailing literary tastes of Victorian England; stories of courtship and society, love and money, class and honour dominate the periodicals and literary society collections. This reflects not only the demands of public taste but also the way in which women writers defined themselves. Their unquestioning acceptance of cultural identity led to a distinction between 'lady' writers and pseudonymic writers. What was proper for a lady writer to produce, both in subject and mode, could be acknowledged directly; but stories that were more closely related to the local environment were generally written within a masculine narrative tradition, from a male point of view, and under a pseudonym that implied a man. If you didn't want to write within the courtship mode, then you wrote, as Mrs Edith Lyttelton did, under the pseudonym G.B. Lancaster, and wrote stories of engineering in the bush, farming, horsemanship, bravery, mateship and honour, all from a male point of view, and reflecting a developing male literary convention in the new society; the glorification of certain essential colonial qualities and the kind of manliness with which they were associated.

With the exception of Lady Barker (who is not, strictly speaking, writing fiction), that distinction persisted until the emergence of writers like Katherine Mansfield, Blanche Baughan and Jean Devanny in the early twentieth century. It is characteristic of the effects of powerful Victorian social and literary modes on the new literatures of Australia and New Zealand. Every so often New Zealand periodicals would be graced by a lengthy serial by a writer such as 'Alien' (Louisa Baker) who, having visited New Zealand, wrote a voluminous story of predictable romantic complication and moral worth, and set parts of it in a whare on the West Coast where the characters behave as if they are in a shooting lodge in autumnal Scotland. As a model for local women writers it could not have been more restrictive, yet this was the wars that New Zealand experience was commonly used in the writing of the period.

Literary conventions and cultural expectations, then, are the basis of a broad sense of similarity between Australian and New Zealand writers generally, and women in particular in the nineteenth-century. There is also narrative evidence to suggest that the Tasman boundary was not much more significant than the state boundary between New South Wales and Victoria. Characters in New Zealand stories frequently had some kind of Australian background (though the reverse is not necessarily the case). There is, particularly in nineteenth-century publications, a strong sense of Australia lying behind New Zealand as part of the same journey, an earlier stage of the colonial voyage. In Clara Cheeseman's 'Married for his Money', published in the *Australian Ladies' Annual*, the visiting baronet takes quantities of surreptitious notes on colonial society, and subsequently publishes a 'valuable' work on the 'Australian Colonies'.

It is not only fictional characters who moved untroubled over the Tasman Sea. At least two of the writers in this selection are claimed by both literatures. G.B. Lancaster is better known in Australia, where she was born, as a novelist. She spent her adult life in Australia and elsewhere, but her New Zealand writing dates principally from her early life which was spent there. Jean Devanny, whose early small-town life in New Zealand is reflected in her story 'The Perfect Mother', moved to Australia in 1929, where she wrote a large number of novels including the well-known *Sugar Heaven* about the 1935 Queensland canefields strike. A number of New Zealand writers also published in Australian journals, particularly the *Bulletin, Australasian, Lone Hand* and *Town and Country Journal*.

Certain narrative settings are held in common, particularly by male writers: gold-digging stories come from both countries and are a feature of nineteenth-century fiction, as are the demotic stories of mateship under duress. Such descriptions of the kind of society generated by 'life in the bush', of which G.B. Lancaster provides many examples, eventually led to the distinctively Australasian voices of Henry Lawson and Frank Sargeson, each seen to herald a new growth of national self-consciousness. It is in considering the way-stations in the growth of these distinctive male voices that one realises how much the early women writers conform to a gender-based definition of their interests and influences that has little to do with their geographical locations as writers. When the move away from love stories begins (slightly earlier in Australia), a wealth of other styles, subjects and interests emerges, as well as, in Katherine Mansfield and Jean Devanny in particular, some pointed and satirical variations on a theme.

A number of minor New Zealand women writers around the turn of the century display a great interest in Maoris, both as a subject for fiction and more generally as a race who appear conventionally in the literary landscape. Marie Stanmore's story 'In Wellington Was Consolation' is an example of the latter; it is well within the usual convention for lady writers, but the traditional tale of courtship is given an edge by the young man's sweetheart being a Maori. Stories featuring the indigenous population are much more common in New Zealand than in Australia, reflecting perhaps the relative accessibility of the Maori people to European settlement. To some extent though, the Maori presence in colonial writing is merely exotic and decorative. In the hands of numerous contributors to the *New Zealand Illustrated Magazine*, the use of Maori characters does not disguise the immutable predictability of the story. Blanche Baughan's story is one of a number written from a Maori point of view. But, by 1912, writing of an individual Maori woman, with strong characterisation and attention to details such as Maori vocabulary, Baughan manages to suggest some of the effects of European colonisation – in the generation gap between Pipi and her granddaughter for example, and in Pipi's attitudes to Pakehas. We are given a sense of the changes taking place, and see the beginning of a literature specific to its time and place and not merely an outpost of a distant culture.

Both Baughan and Mansfield rise magnificently out of the conventional limitations of the immediate colonial past, though there are indications of what has been left behind in Mansfield's later stories such as 'The Garden Party' with its class distinctions or the ironic portrait of Aunt Beryl in 'At The Bay', cast directly from the mould of the love story heroine. Like Blanche Baughan, the early Katherine Mansfield is remarkable for her witty observation of what lay around her and her attention to its detail. In 'A Woman At The Store' there is almost a documentary eye at work within the powerful narrative, noticing the heat, the physical landscape ('wave after wave of tussock grass'), the utilitarian clothing ('a blue galatea shirt, corduroy trousers and riding boots'), and the food ('fly biscuits and apricots by the side of a swampy creek'). The story is a portrait of murder that has its origins in the nature of colonial existence. It is perhaps an indication of the lessening extremity and privation of settlers that Katherine Mansfield can write this story in 1912; conditions in G.B. Lancaster's 'Our Lady of the Plains' are just as extreme, but we know far less about them.

The numbers of women writing short fiction and non-fiction were surprisingly large, and the establishment of a regular monthly outlet in the form of the *New Zealand Illustrated Magazine* in the 1900s tapped a constant supply of contributors. Few of these women were more than occasional writers and one suspects the activity of writing to have been a necessary escapism quite as much as the reading of it.

The large number of women writing short stories in New Zealand in the post World War One period is reflected in the first collection to appear, *New Zealand Short Stories*, printed by J.M. Dent in London in 1930. In his introduction, O.N. Gillespie worried that 'to many, it may prove disappointing because the stories, particularly by contrast with those from Australia, lack any national outlook or distinctive atmosphere'. He was, perhaps, anticipating the reactions of those English readers who had already enjoyed the exotica of *Australian Short Stories*, published in the same series two years before. Its editor, G. Mackaness, had deliberately excluded 'stories which have no Australian, or in its wider connotation, Australasian touch about them'. Today, the most striking contrast between the two collections is the much higher percentage of women writers in the New Zealand one. Gillespie prints thirty-two stories; more than half of them, eighteen, are by women. Mackaness prints thirty stories, ten by women. (Nettie Palmer's *An Australian Story Book*, also from 1928, has the same proportion of women.)

Gillespie attributes the lack of distinctiveness of his New Zealand stories to the close ties between England and New Zealand and the prosaic, unromantic nature of New Zealand life and history. He opines that 'Any distinctive national characteristics will be long in making their appearance.' (Frank Sargeson was just around the corner!) But Gillespie has not been included here merely as a caution to writers, and readers, of introductions. There does seem to be a link between perceptions of national identity in Australia and New Zealand and attitudes to women writers. In Australia, for example, a distinctive literature was thought to have emerged in the 1890s, associated with the work of Henry Lawson and other writers for the Sydney *Bulletin*. Lawson's stories, in particular, were seen as models of their kind; they established a tradition of story-writing, as Sargeson's were later to do in New Zealand. So anthologies of Australian stories compiled between 1928 and 1980 were dominated by stories set in the bush, either realistic or broadly comic in mode, usually centred on male characters and concerns, and written by men. Writers like Christina Stead, whose stories broke all these rules, were persistently overlooked.

In the last few years, however, women writers, especially Elizabeth Jolley, Olga Masters, Helen Garner and Beverley Farmer, have become prominent in the production of short as well as longer Australian fiction. And critics have begun to reassess the work of earlier decades. In selecting stories for her anthology, *Australian Short Stories* (1983), Kerryn Goldsworthy deliberately chose ones which, whether by men or women, emphasised women's experience. She also included two stories by Stead and two by Ethel Anderson, another excellent but rarely anthologised writer.

One disappointing feature of Goldsworthy's anthology was her decision to begin with the first chapter of Catherine Helen Spence's novel *Clara Morison* (1854). This, as well as denying the distinctiveness of the short story as a literary genre, appeared to suggest that no women were writing stories in nineteenth-century Australia. It is true that Australian women writers have tended to prefer the longer forms of fiction. Among the many reasons for this, an important one is the economics of the publishing industry. Many women, particularly in the earlier periods, took up writing as one of the few professions open to them. More money could be made from novels; they have always sold better than collections of stories.

One of the few Australian women to specialise in the short story, the still mysterious 'W.W.' of the *Australian Journal*, wrote hundreds of stories in the second half of the nineteenth-century, as well as a few longer serials. The first of her 'Detective's Album' series appeared anonymously, as 'The Shepherd's Hut; or, 'Tis Thirteen Years Since: Being Memoirs of An Australian Police Officer', in the first issue of the *Australian Journal*, 2 September 1865. Her stories were still appearing regularly in the 1910s. In the intervening years, there was hardly an issue of the *Journal*, published weekly till 1869, then monthly and the most popular Australian magazine till the rise of the *Bulletin*, without a contribution from her. She tended in later decades to concentrate on her detective stories – she was probably the first woman in the world to write them – but wrote many others, not using a male persona, as 'Waif Wander'. Though 'W.W.' was the most prominent, the *Australian Journal* had many other women contributors. Indeed, at least half the original fiction it published appears to have been written by women.

It is, unfortunately, very difficult to be exact about the number of women contributing to newspapers and magazines, particularly in the nineteenth century. The majority of stories appeared either anonymously, or signed with initials or a pseudonym. Sometimes editors provide a clue, as with 'Waif Wander' or the 'M.E.' who contributed four stories to the *Goulburn Herald* in the 1840s. But usually identification will only occur if the writer has gone on to make a name for herself. Even when, by the end of the century, signed contributions became the rule, women often used male pseudonymns, like Henry Handel Richardson, or, like Blanche Baughan and Mabel Forrest, their initials rather than their first names.

For most of the contributors to newspapers and magazines, the step from periodical publication to the more lasting (at least in bibliographic terms) fame of a book was never possible. Authors who produced books in nineteenth-century Australasia usually did so at their own expense, or that of their friends. An occasional alternative was publication in parts. Mary Vidal's *Tales for the Bush* (Sydney, 1845), the first collection to appear in Australia or New Zealand, was originally issued in sixpenny numbers. Her stories were carefully considered for this collection and rejected with some regret. Like most of the earlier stories included here, they are filled with shrewd and often surprising glimpses of colonial life and also contain some delightful character studies. Unfortunately, they are also full of

Victorian religiosity and class consciousness and, like many from this period, are over-long. Ellen Clacy's 'An Agreeable Mistake' is a welcome exception. It also displays the sharp eye for local detail seen to best advantage in her *A Lady's Visit to the Gold Diggings of Australia* (1853).

Like Mrs Clacy, all of the nineteenth-century writers included in this anthology, and many of the later ones, had their books published in Britain. For Clacy, who paid only a brief visit to Australia, this was perfectly natural. Others, like Ada Cambridge, suffered the disadvantages of living on one side of the world and being published on the other. In the days before airmail it was, for example, impossible for authors in this situation to correct their own proofs. (Sometimes as with Miles Franklin's *My Brilliant Career*, 1901, considerable liberties could be taken with manuscripts.) The need to publish in England and/or America was clearly one reason why so many of the earlier women writers from Australia and New Zealand spent much of their writing lives overseas. Most of the better-known writers in this collection were expatriates. There has, of course, also been a clear correlation between overseas success and local recognition.

With the exception of Barbara Baynton, the better-known of the Australians represented here made their name through their novels, but all published at least one collection of short stories. Rosa Praed produced three such collections, though two were of interlinked stories, and marketed as novels. 'A Happy Ending' was the final story in one of these, *Stubble Before the Wind* (1908). It had only the most tenuous of links with the earlier stories; in a passage removed for this edition, the reader was told that its heroine's 'remote not wholly accordant Australian associations' had resulted in friendship with the narrator of the previous stories. In 'A Happy Ending' Praed has some gentle fun at the expense of the romance conventions which were the staple not only of her own work but of many other women writers, particularly those, like Callie Griffin or Praed herself, writing to support themselves and others. During the 1880s a Sydney magazine, *Australian Century*, ran a short story competition. Prizes were awarded according to readers' votes. All the prizewinning stories were by women; all were sentimental love stories with happy endings.

Magazine stories, particularly in the nineteenth century, can be divided into three broad types: love stories, either happy or unhappy; mystery/adventure tales; comic anecdotes and tall stories. Women writers tended to produce more love stories and fewer comic ones, a tendency reflected in this collection. At least half the Australian stories would fall into the love category, though few are of the standard 'courtship and marriage' type. Those that are closest to this genre, by Praed and Ada Cambridge, both play on the conventions. Praed's lovers are neither young nor beautiful, but distinctly comic; Cambridge's story turns on a very unromantic illness: seasickness. Seasickness also plays a role in 'Barren Love', a story by 'Tasma' which, besides its other virtues, brings sharply before us the sights – and smells – of the long sea voyage from Europe to the Pacific. Many of the writers of these stories, and their original readers, had this experience in common: it was an inevitable part of being a colonist. Given its title, it is not surprising to find 'Barren Love' anything but the conventional 'happy ending' romance. Surprising is, however, the only word for its technical sophistication – the fine control of tone and manipulation of point of view – particularly as it appears to be Tasma's first published story.

Two other largely forgotten writers, Myra Morris and Mabel Forrest, make interesting and original uses of bush settings and stereotypes as well as of the conventions of the courtship story. Morris appears to be writing one of the 'city girl goes outback and finds romance' type, perhaps, as this is a story from the 1920s, in its more modern variant, 'frustrated spinster discovers nature and sexuality'. But 'Sun' is not a love story with a happy ending. Nor is Forrest's 'The Housekeeper', which plays even more elegantly with the reader's expectations. Forrest's story is also notable for what she does with the stereotype of the feckless and luckless Irishman, one of the staple characters of nineteenth-century Australian fiction.

Even more than Forrest, Sumner Locke is concerned to work with, and subvert, characters and settings established by male writers. The stories in her *Mum Dawson, 'Boss'* (1911) offer a woman's version of Steele Rudd's selection stories which became enormously popular in the 1900s. While 'Mother' is a shadowy figure in Rudd's stories – it is 'Dad' and 'Dave' who have become part of Australia's folklore – 'Mum' is very much at the centre of Locke's. Her stories, particularly 'When Dawson Died', also seem much blacker than Rudd's, which rely more on slapstick humour. Beneath the comic surface there is, one feels, a version of the bush remarkably like Barbara Baynton's. Grotesquerie is even more pronounced in the work of another of the few women writers who went in for comedy. The fantasy of Mary Simpson's 'The Salvage Sale' is, indeed, rarely found in any stories of this period. Though the narrator's comparisons are with big-game hunting and detection, this story can also be read as a suburban version of Australian exploration epics.

The stories by the three most frequently anthologised Australian women writers of this period, Barbara Baynton, Henry Handel Richardson and Katherine Susannah Prichard, all fall outside the popular fictional conventions of their times indicating, perhaps, one reason for these writers' pre-eminence. (Compare the situations in Forrest's and Baynton's stories; in 'Billy Skywonkie', 'housekeeper' is a very thinly-veiled euphemism for 'mistress'.) Richardson's was her first professionally published story, appearing in the *English Review* of 1911, just after her novel *The Getting of Wisdom*. It is reproduced here without the fairly minor revisions made for its reprinting in *Two Studies* (1931); the most significant was a change in title from 'Death' to 'Mary Christina'. Mary Richardson's death from appendicitis in 1896 clearly provided the impetus for this story; the detailed diary kept by Henry Handel Richardson during her mother's illness is now in the National Library, Canberra. 'Death' reminds us that Australasian women writers often set their stories in other countries, though the bias of this selection has been towards the local. It also reminds us that stories as well as books were published abroad, though systematic searching of British and American, let alone European, periodicals has so far only been carried out by bibliographers and biographers of major figures like Richardson and Mansfield.

Both Baynton's 'Billy Skywonkie' and Prichard's 'Happiness' have outback settings, though Baynton characteristically stresses the nightmarish features of the bush, Prichard its unexpected loveliness. Both also tell their stories from the perspective of women characters who usually figure, if at all, on the fringes of earlier fiction. Baynton's heroine is half-Chinese, or supposed so by the other characters; hence she is subject to the racial as well as the sexual indignities of late nineteenth-century Australia. She is still, of course, a cut above the Aboriginal, usually seen in Australian stories of this period as either a bloodthirsty savage or a comic caricature, in neither case fully human. Even today, one would not expect to find an Australian equivalent of 'In Wellington was Consolation', where the heroine's race occasions no comment or surprise. In the 1830s a Sydney critic firmly pronounced that 'the aborigines of Australia are not the children of romance'. Katharine Susannah Prichard was one of the first to challenge this long-held belief. 'Happiness', like two of her other major works, the novel *Coonardoo* (1929) and the play *Brumby Innes* (1940), was inspired by a period spent on a cattle station in Western Australia. Prichard, coming into close contact with Aboriginals for the first time, found many of her stereotypes overturned. In 'Happiness' she attempts to do the same for her readers, suggesting that happiness is more likely to belong to the old Aboriginal woman, sitting in the dust with her offal, than to those living in the big white homestead. Today we may feel that Prichard, in elevating 'nature' at the expense of 'civilisation', was merely exchanging one set of stereotypes for another. Equally, Blanche Baughan's Pipi may now appear perilously close to a caricature of the Maori trickster. But both portraits, particularly given their times, are sympathetic ones, reminding us of the longstanding tendency of women writers to draw a society's attention to its outcasts, whether they be the negroes of Harriet Beecher Stowe's America, the workers of Mrs Gaskell's England, or the dispossesed of Australia and New Zealand.

Much more could be written about these stories, the links between them and the differences, how they relate to stories from other colonial and post-colonial societies and to those of the parent culture. But the longer the introduction, the fewer the stories. We hope that this bringing together of the known and the unknown will inspire readers from both countries, and elsewhere, to make some of the links, fill in the gaps and go on to many more discoveries of their own.

Elizabeth Webby, Sydney
Lydia Wevers, Wellington

Ellen Clacy

An Agreeable Mistake

1854

Have any of you, my readers, ever seen a copy of the *Melbourne Argus* – that oracle of the diggers? If so, you could not fail to observe the peculiar social phenomenon which distinguishes it from any and all of our English papers, morning or weekly – its column for 'Missing Friends'.

There, W.S. is informed (whether the information will please him it does not say) that 'his disconsolate wife has just arrived in Australia in the hopes of finding him, and begs for his address'. 'T.H. is earnestly requested to return to England immediately, as his father is dead, and his mother left alone in the world.' 'L.R. informs her sister that when she lands in Melbourne, she is to proceed to — —.' 'Caroline T. acquaints the world and her friends that she is married, and will be happy to receive visitors and congratulations after the — inst., at her new residence, Love Cottage, St Kilda.' And so on, *ad infinitum* – each few lines, perchance, the germ of a romantic history, or, at all events, the record of hope, joy, or despair.

It was in the middle of July, 1852, that a young man sat alone in a wretchedly furnished little room in the suburbs of Melbourne, skimming over with a listless eye the *Argus* of that morning.

He had only arrived a few days previous, without much money, and no friends, except a married sister and her husband, who lived somewhere in Victoria, but the exact locality he could not recollect. He had addressed letters to every possible place that he could think of, in the hope that one might happen to reach them; and, in the mean time, he was working as storeman in a warehouse, every day expecting tidings from his sister, and every day doomed to fresh disappointment.

As he now ran his eye down the columns of the paper, the idea struck him – why not advertise? Hundreds were doing it, why should not he? It might catch the right person's attention, and would cost but a shilling or two.

No sooner said than done. The advertisement was drawn up, taken to the *Argus* Office, in Collins Street, and a few days after, the following appeared:

'John Dean has just landed in Victoria in a state of great friendlessness. His father died suddenly before he left England. He earnestly requests his sister, Anna Johnson, or her husband, to communicate to him at —, — Collingwood.'

Several copies of the *Argus* of this date found their way in the course of time to the diggings, and one fell into the hands of Mrs Johnson, whose husband kept a large and profitable store at Bendigo, not far from the Creek.

'Bless my heart alive! what's got to my good woman that she doesn't come?' exclaimed Johnson, impatiently, as he saw a store full of customers, and only himself to attend to them, 'Here, Hann! Hann! why, what be you after to-day?' he added, as, with swollen eyes and distressed countenance, Mrs Johnson made her appearance.

'Father's dead,' she began, breaking forth into fresh sobs, and utterly unconscious of the staring people around; 'and poor Jack be come to Melbourne without a friend.'

'There, there, lassie, don't her cry; we'll do summut for Jack; who telled her on it?'

Mrs Johnson produced the paper.

'Ay, ay,' after spelling out the advertisement; 'Pearson be going down to town to-morrow, he shall see about him. Think you the lad understands figures, and could gie me'd hand in the store?'

'Oh! yes; Jack was sharp in them things, but – ' and here Mrs Johnson paused. She could not find in her heart to say, 'Don't bring him to live with us,' though certain far-from-pleasant reminiscences of his quarrelsome and dictatorial disposition came back upon her memory. But she held her peace, and the next day Pearson took with him a sisterly letter to John, with an order on a Melbourne bank for £50, and a request that he would accompany the bearer back to Bendigo.

As some weeks had elapsed since he had put in the advertisement, our hero was beginning to despair of its having been seen by any one, when the arrival of Pearson put a pleasant termination to all his speculations on the subject; and delighted was he to obey the wishes of his sister, and set out for the diggings.

The style of life and travelling pleased him; and, as they neared the world-renowned Bendigo, his excitement and pleasure were extreme. It was towards evening that they approached it. The men were leaving their work and returning to their various tents – their tools slung across their backs; some were whistling, some were too tired out to do ought but swear or grumble; whilst others, of a more joyous temperament, joined in some of the favourite digging songs.

As they slowly walked on beside the dray, in the direction of Johnson's Store, snatches of the following came to their ears. We give it nearly entire, as a genuine specimen of Bendigo poetry:

In bush attire let each aspire,
With noble emulation,
To gain the digger's chief desire –
Gold – by wise regulation.

With spades and picks we work like bricks,
And dig in gold formation;
Then stir our cradles with short sticks,
To break conglomeration.

This golden trade does not degrade
The man of information,
Who shovels nuggets with the spade
Of proper conformation.

What mother can her infant stock
View with more satisfaction,
Than we our golden cradles rock,
And love them to distraction.

Let those who dare try thwart our care
At our gold occupation;
Then in bewilderment they'll stare
At golden incubation.

We dig and delve from six to twelve,
And then, for relaxation,
We wash our pans and cradles out,
And turn to mastication, etc. etc. etc.

They now stopped outside the long wooden building, with the significant flag flying above it, which John Dean rightly concluded to be his brother-in-law's premises. Pearson entered, leaving our hero alone, and uncertain whether to wait there or go inside in search of his sister.

At this moment a crowd of little ones ran past, romping and shouting to the highest pitch of their voices. It was such a pretty sight, and altogether so different a scene to any his imagination had pictured of digging life, that he felt tempted to move a few steps from the store, so as to be enabled to watch them.

On they ran – the little girls with their sun-bonnets hanging down their backs, and their hair streaming in the wind; whilst the boys, with their blue serge over-shirts, their leather belts, and tiny wide-awakes, looked for all the world like a miniature race of diggers. On they ran, and poor lonely John kept watching them, till he heard a few distant childish screams, and saw the children rushing to and fro in consternation.

He paused not a moment, but rushed to the spot, and then perceived a little girl, of about nine years old – whom he had looked upon as the sort of queen of the merry troop – struggling in the water.

Without a minute's delay, John had plunged after her, and, being a bold and good swimmer, without difficulty brought her safely to land. She was frightened and exhausted, so he carried her in his arms.

'Where does she live?' he inquired of some of her companions, who, pale and cast down by the accident, walked calmly by his side.

'She's Polly Johnson; her dad keeps yon store.'

'My niece, perhaps,' thought John, as he scrutinised her features; but there was nothing in her round fair face that at all resembled his dark sister Anna.

Before they could reach the store, they were met by Mrs Johnson in a state of distraction, and anxious to learn the fate of her child. In the joy of seeing her alive, she looked upon John as little short of a good angel for having saved her.

John followed her into the building in a state of mystification; for, if this was Mrs Johnson, she was not his sister; and most impatient was he to unravel the mystery. But the accident to little Mary – she was an only child – caused such a commotion that it was some time before they again even so much as noticed his presence. When, however, Mary had been safely put to bed, and was in a comfortable sleep, Mrs Johnson repeated her thanks, and pointed him out to her husband as 'the young man that had saved Polly.'

This elicited some inquiries respecting himself, when, suddenly, Mrs Johnson exclaimed, 'Sure you're not the John Dean that telled me in the *Argus* as father was dead?'

John signified assent.

'Why, man,' laughed out Johnson himself, 'we tooked you for her brother Jack; but it's a pleasant mistake, any how.'

Poor John at first felt very disappointed, whilst Mrs Johnson was equally pleased — first, that it was not her father who was dead; and, secondly, because she found that her domineering brother was most probably still in England.

Had she been his sister in reality, instead of only bearing a similar name, he could not have experienced greater kindness from her. Johnson made him clerk and chief manager of the store, and soon after took him into partnership.

John Dean is now considered a rising man in the colonies, and as such receives very kind looks from some of the newly arrived unmarried young ladies; but he always declares that he is keeping himself in reserve for little Mary Johnson.

W.W.

The Evidence of the Grave

1870

'Most of you remember the robbery at Gardner's Store, and all the queer and horrible events that arose out of it,' said John Somerton; 'and as I happen to know a good deal of what happened behind the scenes, and with which the law had nothing to do, I'll tell you the story as my share of the evening's entertainment.

Gardner's Store was on old Jeffries' Creek diggings, as you all know, and was one of the best stocked country stores that I ever saw in the country. The post-office was there too; and as the old diggings became gradually almost deserted, and the small population crept farther and farther away up the hill, people used to growl awfully at having to go all the way to Gardner's for their letters, or to post one they had written. But honest Gardner had a friend at court, and used, it was said, to keep the hand of the said friend pretty well greased for the retention of his billet; and now you may guess that the said influential friend was "our member", if you like.

At any rate, it was all in vain that petitions were got up and applications made to the proper authorities, the post-office at old Jeffries remained at the old store; and king and kaiser from the creek had to ride or tramp to Gardner's for his letter. Once there, it was impossible for the needing to pass by the great bargains to be had at the old store, and Mrs Gardner was so quiet and so obliging, that a customer once got was sure to be retained.

I often wondered at the patience of that woman. She was so young too – barely two or three and twenty, I should say – to have such a load of responsibility and work on her back. They had no children, and a blessed good job it was, for what sort of father John Gardner would have made it would not be hard to guess.

He made a precious bad husband at any rate, and to the most patient wife a man ever had. Not that Mrs Gardner was wanting in spirit, or hesitated to show it at times, but the way she worked to clear him out of some difficulty into which his folly had brought him, and the untiring way in which she returned again and again to stop up the breach his intemperance had made in their business connection, was something wonderful and admirable.

For John was dreadful intemperate, you know, and in his cups would offend the best customer he had without the slightest hesitation. If it is true that under the influence of drink a man's true nature comes out, then John Gardner's nature must have been a particularly bad one.

This is how it used to work on him. When perfectly sober, he was as sulky-looking and surly as a bear – that's what he was. He was as jealous of his wife as any fool who had no occasion to be ever was, but a few extra nobblers turned him into a bragging, patronising gentleman, who would shout for the very man he was most jealous of, until he himself had reached the stage of violence to which an increase of indulgence invariably brought him. Oh, he was a nut to crack, was John Gardner, drunk or sober.

Well, you know that the camp was right behind the store, just on the rise of the hill, and that it was no uncommon thing for us troopers to drop down there of an evening and have a yarn with one or other of the chaps that were sure to be there on post-office business. And, as it happened, I was there the very evening previous to the robbery; and so was young Hastings, as you shall hear.

Now Hastings was John's suspicion for the time being, and it was as good as a play to see his thundery looks when business brought Hastings to the store. He couldn't be even civil to him, and used to sit in the corner and smoke furiously; and if Hastings stopped long, he generally wound up by getting outrageously drunk, and making a bigger fool of himself than nature ever intended him to have been.

I am as certain as that I sit here that Gardner had no more cause to be jealous of Ned Hastings, than I have to fancy that the Czarina of Russia will fall in love with my own handsome face. For one thing, Mrs Gardner was not an attractive woman by any means. She was entirely too sensible to flirt with any man; or, maybe, as I often suspected, her thorough knowledge of her precious ass of a husband had lowered her estimation of the sex generally, and she looked down upon the whole race of men with unutterable contempt.

On the day in question, a waggon load of new goods had arrived at Gardner's – drapery principally; and when I lounged in during the evening, the counters were piled up with rolls and bolts and pieces of soft goods, among which Mrs Gardner was busy putting away on the shelves, and sorting, in her own peculiarly quiet manner. Gardner was pretending to help, and watching from under his heavy black brows, and Ned Hastings lounged against one of the half-empty cases, smoking a cigar and chatting unconcernedly.

"Hallo!" said I, "ye're going into it heavy here. Why, ye have enough to stock the Monster Clothing Company's place down in Melbourne, let alone a country store. Good evening, Gardner. What do you call that stuff, Mrs Gardner?"

"Merinoes," replied she. "I never had a finer lot in the store – the colours are very good. But Gardner is putting up something more in your way. Look at those tweeds."

And so we began to examine and price, and the upshot of the matter was, that Hastings bought ten yards of gray French merino, while I was suiting myself with the makings of a pair of trousers of Geelong tweed. "But what on earth are you going to do with a dress-piece?" asked Mrs Gardner, smiling. "There's no missis at your place."

"There ought to be, then," said he; "and it won't be my fault if there isn't soon. You like gray, Mrs Gardner, eh? I notice that you often wear it," and Hastings's roguish eye twinkled in the direction of Gardner, to see how the insinuation agreed with him; for Hastings, as well as every man in the place, knew of the poor fool's jealous weakness.

Gardner didn't like it, that was plain to be seen, for the scowl on his face grew deeper, so that I was positively glad when I saw him go to a decanter and pour out a glass for himself. I knew it would put him in a good humour, but did not think he was on the way to indulge, as he did afterwards. A something unusual thing with him too at so early a stage was, that he asked me to drink with him, for he was generally as stingy as an old miser, but I think he did it to slight Hastings, by leaving him out, as much as anything else.

Well, one and another dropped in, and with one and another Gardner had a glass or two, until he got so drunk as to be incapable of even bragging. Finally, he deposited himself in a case half filled with hams, and there he snored like a man on the verge of choking.

"I'm going to Clunes to-morrow," said Hastings to me as he said good night. "I bought that merino for my sister. What an ass that Gardner is, to be sure," and the hearty young chap turned a look of infinite disgust at the rolled-up storekeeper.

At length I thought it advisable to go, as bed time was approaching, but just as I was passing out, Mrs Gardner asked me to help her to put Gardner into bed. "I know how 'twill be," she said – "he'll waken up, half stupid and frozen, and the first thing he'll face to will be the bottle again. Goodness knows, there isn't such a beast of a man within twenty miles."

It's not a very pleasant job at any time to get a man who is helplessly drunk into bed, but when he happens to be of a quarrelsome disposition, and doesn't like being disturbed, it's the deuce and all. First he doubled up as we tried to lift him out of the case, and then he opened one eye and gave me a kick in the chest that nearly demolished me. Then he caught hold of a coil of windlass rope that happened to be near, and we were absolutely obliged to carry rope and all into the bedroom, for not an instant would he lose his grip of it.

"If I was you I'd lock the store door," says I to Mrs Gardner as I was going. "If he gets more in the night, it'll make him mad outright."

"Oh, leave that to me," she replied; "believe me I'll see to it. And I'll let every one of the horses out of the stable too, for he'll be for galloping, like a cranky fool as he is, through the whole country tomorrow."

I got up, bright and early, next morning, for I had a notion of getting in a few loads of firewood for the camp, and old Bill, the camp horse, had been turned out for the last fortnight. I knew he wasn't far off though, for he was a regular old forager, and came home regularly for his feed.

The sun was barely visible as I went down the hill, and I thought I was dreaming when I saw Mrs Gardner in front of the store rolling a quarter-cask into the middle of the road. In the name of all you ever heard of, what do you think she was doing? Divil a less than starting the cask and letting the spirits run out of it into the dust; and there was such a smell of drink on the air as I'll make an affidavit never was on the old creek before, drunken a place as it was well known to be.

"What in the name of Christianity are you doing?" said I, as I stopped in front of her with my mouth wide open. "Are you doing that on purpose?"

"That's the last, thank God!" says she. "And if ever another drop comes into this store I'll know the reason why. There was five of them, and I haven't even left him a drop of wine to poison himself with. What do you think he did in the night? Got in the kitchen window, and so to the store. When I missed him this morning he was lying on the floor with the brandy tap running at his head. And there he lies yet – just come in and look at the beast."

"But couldn't you have got rid of the drink without throwing money on the road that way?" I asked, as I followed her to the door.

"He wouldn't believe I meant it," she answered; "but, maybe, he'll believe it now," and she looked behind her at the puddle in the road.

You will remember that there were no windows in the store – indeed, there are few stores on the back diggings even yet that are supplied in that way. Gardner's was in the old style, and dependent upon the wide, two-leaved door for its light in day time. As a natural consequence of the said big door being only slightly ajar, the interior of the store was almost dark to one entering from the broad daylight outside.

Mrs Gardner pushed open one of the halves of the door, and while she was doing so I took a few steps inside, to look for the miserable object I expected to find on the floor. A something strange in the appearance of the place as Mrs Gardner let in the light, however, stopped me, and I called out to her, "What have you been up to here? What's all this? Are you going to shift?"

"How? What is it? Good lord!" cried she, in a breath, as she looked round and discovered the cause of my astonishment.

The long and the short of it was, that the drapery shelves, that had the previous night been almost bending under the weight of the new goods, were almost empty, and heaps of things were lying in disorder upon floor and counter.

The poor woman looked around her in the greatest bewilderment. Some idea that her drunken husband was in some way accountable for the extraordinary position of things at first entered her mind, but it could not but die out as she recollected his helpless condition. As for myself, it did not take long for me to decide that the store had been robbed.

Yes, an entrance had been forced by the back door, and the thieves had, it would appear, gone to work in a most deliberate manner, for matches that had been used were scattered about the floor, and all the most valuable goods had been selected, while the discarded ones were tossed anywhere out of the way. All the splendid new merinoes were gone, and they had even selected from bales of made up goods, leaving behind the most conspicuous in pattern, as likely to be more easily sworn to.

"The store has been robbed," said I. "Here's a pretty to-do, and Gardner in that condition. You may depend upon it the thieves, whoever they were, knew he went to bed drunk last night."

"Serve him right!" she cried. "I wish they had found him under the brandy cask, and given him a sound kicking. And I never to notice it when I was taking out the casks! What is to be done?"

"I must go up and waken Cross till we have a hunt for tracks. Why there must have been some conveyance in it, they have taken such a swag."

I left Mrs Gardner examining into her loss, while Cross and I followed up what traces were to be seen, and they were but few. The ground at the back was hard and stony, and among the many wheel tracks on the dusty road, who could discover the one which might have been left by the vehicle or vehicles that removed the stolen goods? We might have hunted ineffectually until doomsday had it not been that Mrs Gardner alighted upon a ticket, from off some of the drapery, at the edge of the bush right at the back of the camp, which, if it had not been purposely placed there to mislead, might be received as an indication of, at least, the direction they had taken.

Mrs Gardner was one of the most thoroughly energetic women I ever saw, and while Cross and I were maundering after traces, she saddled a horse and galloped off for a black tracker that put up at a diggings about twenty miles off. "I'll be back before dark," she said, as she gave me the key of the store, "and do you have a look after that beast, and see he doesn't set the store on fire."

So I mounted guard over the place, while Cross went off to make inquiries; but I didn't open the door until I thought my hearty Gardner would have slept himself sober. It was between four and five o'clock in the afternoon when I disturbed him, and he opened a pair of the blackest eyes you ever saw, and stared at me as I stooped down to rouse him up.

"What the devil is up?" he asked, as he sat up stupidly; but his first look encountering the empty stands where had lately rested the precious barrels, he got altogether on his feet, and looked from them all around the half empty shelves, and then at me again. "What, in the name of the devil, is up, I say?"

"It's time for you to ask," I said, "although I don't see that asking will do much good, as it's rather too late. Don't you see the store has been robbed?"

"Robbed! Who robbed it? Nonsense! Do you think I'm a fool to believe a pack of lies because I've had a glass too much?"

"Oh, very well; any way you like, mate," I replied, seeing very little utility in arguing with a man not more than half recovered from a beastly fit of drunkenness. "Perhaps you'd better lie down again and have another sleep."

"Where's the missis?" was his next question, as his eyes wandered over counter and shelf, in the vain search, as I well guessed, for a bottle.

"Oh, she's off, and taken every drop of grog in the place with her. You're regularly done for now."

There was something perfectly villanous in the scowl he gave me as I concluded, and he could see that there really was not anything in the shape of drink to satisfy his craving with.

"Look here, mate," he said, "if you don't tell me the plain truth, I'll make a hard try to get that jacket pulled off your back. What's happened to the store, and where's Mrs Gardner?"

"The store has been robbed while you were drunk," said I, "and your wife is gone to look for a black tracker. As for pulling my jacket off, mate, two can play at that game, and you'd better get sober before you try."

"Black tracker, be d—!" he roared, becoming perfectly outrageous, as all his efforts to discover a nobbler were ineffectual.

"As you please, mate," I returned.

And as I spoke, two or three of the customers dropped in to examine for themselves into the report that the Post Office Store had been broken into and robbed.

"Is all this yarn about robbery and abduction, and what not, true?" asked Hastings's mate, Larkins. "I couldn't get away soon, on account of Hastings going off this morning. Hallo, Gardner, what's to do with you?"

"Is Hastings gone off?" asked the fool, with his teeth set.

"Yes, break of day this morning."

"By —, I could have sworn it!" he thundered, bringing down his fist on the counter in a manner that rattled all the glasses and bottles that indicated the previous night's spree; and grasping a new hat that lay handy, he dashed out at the back door like a madman, as he undoubtedly was.

A loud laugh greeted his departure, for there was not a man in the whole neighbourhood unaware of his absurd jealousy of Hastings.

"I lay you anything he's off to hunt up the runaways," observed Larkins.

And, sure enough, a few minutes brought Gardner back booted and spurred, and with a long-lashed hunting whip in his right hand, that, I have no doubt whatever, he fairly itched to lay about the shoulders of the unconscious Hastings.

"There's no use humming or hawing about it," he cried; "you may as well out with it at once, for I know that fool of a woman is off with Hastings, and has robbed me for his benefit. But we'll see! By —, we'll see who wins! Can't you tell me where I'll get a nobbler, man?"

This last characteristic inquiry was addressed to me, and, seeing the man's absurd determination to go off on a wild goose chase to be genuine, I began to reason with him in the way I thought most likely to be effectual.

"Don't be making an ass of yourself, Gardner. Didn't I tell you that your wife is gone to look for a black tracker to try and trace the goods. As for the grog, the long and short of it is, that she emptied every drop of it into the road this morning; but I've a bottle up at the camp, and if you'll give up that foolishness of yours –"

"I'll see you — first!" he interrupted, almost foaming with rage, as he dashed out once more, and began to mount the horse he had already saddled.

"You'll break your neck, man. Why, you're no more fit to back that horse than –"

But the remainder of the sentence was drowned in the clatter of his black horse's hoofs as he dashed out of the stable yard.

And now comes the queerest part of the whole story. Mrs Gardner returned that evening, having been unsuccessful in procuring the services of the black tracker; but two days elapsed and not an appearance put in either Brown or young Hastings. If Gardner had not gone, no one would have troubled that Hastings did not return as he had promised; but, knowing the violent jealousy of the foolish storekeeper, the absence of his mate created great uneasiness in the mind of Larkins, and he went over to Hastings' sister's to make inquiries about him.

The tidings he got there was not calculated to ease him much. Hastings had left for home on the evening of the second day, driving a spring cart he had borrowed for the occasion, and Larkins returned full tilt to me to consult what we had best do.

"We don't know what way to turn at this time of night," I said. "It would be pitch dark by the time I could get my horse in, and what could be seen then in the bush? But, heaven bless you, Gardner is most likely stuck in some shanty or other boozing; and as for Hastings, why, 'tisn't every day a young chap gets a chance to go and see his sweetheart. He may have one that his sister knows nothing of."

Even as the last words were leaving me, an unsteady figure darkened the door, and Hastings himself staggered into the room. His face was white as chalk, and it was with the greatest apparent difficulty that he reached a seat, into which he fell, with the air of one completely exhausted.

"Give me a glass of brandy, for God's sake," he gasped, "for I'm as nearly cooked as ever a fellow was in the world."

"What, in the name of wonder, has happened to you?" we asked, as I complied with his request. "You do look like a man in a bad way."

"It's no thanks to Gardner that I'm not dead. He shot at me in the bush, the precious scoundrel, and left me for dead on the ground."

"Tell us about it when you are able," I said. "You and Gardner have been giving us enough to do these couple of days; but I didn't think he would go so far as to try and murder a man in the bush."

And this is what Hastings told us as he found himself able:

"I was coming back from my sister's yesterday, as you know, and had got about half way to the creek when I met Gardner riding, like a madman, through the bush. When he recognised me, he pulled up, and without giving me time to think, he roared out,

'Where's my wife, you — scoundrel? Where's my wife?'

"I thought the man was mad, and I suppose he was, with the drink.

'I know nothing of your wife, you fool,' I said, 'and if you don't get out of my way, I'll drive over you,' for he had reined up his horse right on the track.

"With that, he pulled out a revolver, and let fly at me; but the minute he did it I was in the act of urging the horse I drove to run him down, and the result was that Gardener's bullet went through my horse's head instead of my own. The animal reared and fell dead, pitching me out head foremost, and I knew no more until I came to my senses, and saw the stars peeping through the dark branches above me.

"I must have lain a long time insensible, and the Lord only knows how I came this length. I crawled on a hundred yards or so at a time, and thought I should have died twenty times over."

"The scoundrel!" I said. "A man like that has no business to be at large at all. How far is it from this, do you think? We'll have to go and hunt up the place for the spring cart. By Jupiter, Bray's horse will be a loss to some one."

"It'll be a dear horse to Gardner, that I'll swear," said Hastings, bitterly. "You know the blind creek, back of Bell's Station. Well, as near as I can guess, the spring cart is about three miles from that; on the back track."

And to that spot Cross and I made our way on the following morning, taking with us the old camp horse to bring back the spring cart. We found the place with little difficulty – the dead horse, with a ball in his brain, lying among the broken harness and smashed shafts, just as Hastings had said, and we succeeded in taking the spring cart back with some little trouble.

Well, day after day passed on, and neither tale nor tidings could be heard of either Gardner or the robbers of the Post Office Store. Mrs Gardner carried on the business as usual, and there were those who said that she didn't care if her husband never came back; and, indeed, why should she? A man for whom the police were everywhere in search, on a charge of attempted murder, was not a great acquisition to any woman.

There were many different opinions as to the whereabouts of the storekeeper. Some said that he had come to his senses when he saw Hastings lying insensible on the ground, and that he had bolted from the country. Others smiled and pictured to themselves Gardner still besotting himself in some out-of-the-way corner, and utterly unconscious of the flight of time, or the trouble he had got into in one of his mad fits. But among all the gossiping, there was not one who dreamed of anything approaching the reality, or of the dreadful fate which had closed the career of the miserable drunkard.

It was nearly three weeks after the robbery of the store that I was in camp alone, one evening, about eight o'clock. I was rubbing up my carbine, when a knock at the door arrested me, and a man followed my summons to enter by showing himself inside the door.

A more pitiable-looking object you can scarcely imagine. His clothes hung in almost tatters around him, his wiry gray hair was flying in every direction from under a wretched old hat, and as for his face, it was dirty and cadaverous looking to an extent that was painful to contemplate.

"What's up?" said I.

"This is a police station, isn't it?" he inquired, looking around in a wild, unsettled way.

"Why, you can see that without asking. What do you want?"

"I've been lost in the bush for the last four days," he explained, "and the life was barely in me when I dropped on to

Bell's Station at last. I fell across a dead man in the bush, and I thought I was in duty bound to report it at the first camp I came to."

"Of course you were. What sort of a man was it, and whereabouts did you see the body?"

"Ah, that's what'll puzzle me. You see it was while I was lost that I came across the corpse, and that was three days ago. I know no more than a fool where it is, only, of course, it is somewhere between this and Kerr's Diggings, where I started from."

"But surely you took some notice of the landmarks? Was there no hill, or creek, or anything that could guide you back again?"

"I'd know the place well enough if I saw it, to be sure; besides, I put up some saplins in a way that you couldn't mistake, but whether it's one mile or three from this, I can't say no more than the child unborn."

"Was it at this or the other side of Bell's?"

"At the other side – the Kerr side; but as I was wandering for two days after I saw it, the Lord only knows where it is."

"You can describe the body?"

"It was a dark, middle-sized man, dressed in a suit of gray tweed, and he had a lot of dark whiskers. But, to tell you the truth, I didn't like to stay too long, or look too close. You can guess why."

"What's the matter with you?" I asked, as I noticed the increased trembling and wildness of the man. "You look as if the very recollection of the sight wasn't good for you. Sit down."

"I'm as weak as water," he answered, taking advantage of my permission to seat himself. "I don't think I'll ever get over it."

"Over what? The sight of the corpse?"

"No, no; the starvation and thirst while I was wandering. I didn't see a face for the four days but one man, and he directed me wrong. That was the second day after I left Kerr's. I wonder if that man knew anything about it?" he added, suddenly lifting his head, and it was as if he was trying some experiment on me, and anxiously, as well as cunningly, watching its effect on me.

"Knew anything about the body, is it? Did you see anything about that made you fancy there had been foul play?"

"I tell you I didn't look too close – oh, no! But that man had a suspicious look about him. Could you oblige me with a drink of water, if you please?"

"I tell you how it will be," I said, as I handed him the drink; "you'll put up at the camp to-night. We'll want you to go with us to-morrow to try and find this dead man you talk of, and it would be awkward for you to be out of the way. I'll make a shake-down for you."

A look of the most perfect terror came into his face as I spoke.

"You don't mean to take me in charge," he gasped, "for coming out of my way to give you information?"

"Who's talking of taking you in charge? I'm offering you a night's lodging, and, to a man in the way you say you are, I should think the offer ought to be very welcome, especially as it will include feeds. If, indeed, you were to refuse to go and point out the spot to us, that would be another matter. My duty then would be plain enough."

I had nothing in the world against this man now, but the expression of his face, which was never, at its best, anything but a bad one, but I determined not to let him out of my sight until I knew more about him.

As for the body he had described partially, it corresponded with the missing Gardner so plainly, that I had scarcely a doubt of its identity. He wore such a suit of tweed when he rode off like a madman on the day we last saw him, and he was middle-sized, and wore large, almost black whiskers.

When Cross came in I gave him instructions to keep his eye on the newcomer, who, by the way, called himself Jack Lawson, and I went out to organise a search party for the following morning.

As may be guessed, there were plenty of willing men among the diggers and reefers, who did or did not affect the Post Office Store, to accompany Cross and myself on our bush search. Foremost among the volunteers was poor Hastings, who had quite recovered from the effects of his fall, and who, to do him justice, had quite forgiven Gardner the attempt on his life, looking on it, as did many others, as the act of a man unaccountable temporarily for his actions.

I returned to the camp at an early hour, and I found Cross busy preparing a lair for the man, who appeared, under the homely influence of my mate's free manner, to have quite got over his suspicions, and to be enjoying himself and Cross's pipe; and in a short time we were all apparently buried in sound repose.

Nevertheless, there wasn't a "wink in my eye", as the saying is, for I had a fancy to examine the pockets of our visitor. What I anticipated finding there, it would be impossible for me to explain. Who can account for the one-half of the strange impulses that guide the most of us through life.

Mr Jack snored hideously, but I was proof against the loudest and most ear-torturing of snores. As a policeman, you know, I was intimately aquainted with what is technically called foxing, and I was prepared for any amount of it in the present instance. But I was agreeably disappointed. Mr Jack's snore was genuine, as a close inspection soon convinced me.

His apparel, as may be guessed, was not of the choicest. One might readily credit that the old tattered and patched moleskins, into the pockets of which I dived, had indeed wandered through many a mile of scrubby bush, and that the coarse, but warm, jumper he wore over a stout Guernsey had been exercised in a similar manner. Nothing whatever rewarded my search, save an old tobacco knife and a small scrap of tobacco wrapped in a bit of newspaper. Even the bushman's friend, the pipe itself, he seemed destitute of ; and so I was fain to replace the knife, and to content myself with the bit of newspaper, putting a similarly-sized piece in its place.

Since that shooting case, which you all remember, where we convicted, through a scrap of paper used as wadding, I never neglect to take notice of printed or written bits that I may find in the possession of any suspected individual; and so I stowed away Mr Jack's wrapping paper, and got into bed again, only half satisfied. Nevertheless, I fell asleep quickly enough, and slept so soundly that it was only the fall of a stool, or something, at my very nose almost, that aroused me. Of course I had put out the light which had served me in my search of Jack's belongings, and the room was in utter darkness.

"What the devil's up?" was my question as I heard the muttered curses of my mate, who was trying to strike a light.

"The devil himself, I think, to kick up such — rows" (poor

Cross was not very choice in his language when excited) "in the middle of the night! I've broken my shins over that — stool. What the —'s the row?"

This latter to Jack, who was revealed, by the light Cross almost poked into his face, sitting bolt upright in his bed, with his eyes about the size of saucers, and his hair standing up straight on his head, quite in the legitimate manner of persons under the influence of horrid terror.

"What the —'s up, eh? What are you kicking up that — shouting for? I'd gag you for two pins!"

"Oh! was I shouting? Is there nobody in the place ? Are you sure there's nothing in it?"

"There's a — fool in it – that's what's in it!" cried Cross, bundling into bed again; "and what's more, he's got a — bad conscience too! Well, I'll leave it to you, Somerton, as the best sleeper within any distance of yourself; bedad, they'd better be civil to you down below, for you're worth any money as a policeman, anyhow. You remind me of O'Brien, although he had a better excuse than you for sleeping through the deuce's own racket."

"Well, I'm wide awake now, at any rate, and you may as well tell me how O'Brien slept," I said, lighting my pipe, and keeping my eye on the man, who still sat bolt upright, glaring about him like a maniac. "Why don't you lie down, mate? What's the use of staring that way at the wall? Did you see a ghost?"

"I must have been dreaming," he said, with a shudder. "I could have sworn he stood *there* – just where the spot is on the floor."

"Who stood there?"

"The dead man in the bush."

And he shrunk down again, and covered his head up in the blankets.

"Um," *thought* I. "Well, about O'Brien?" *said* I.

"There was one of the greatest storms seen for years passed over where he was stationed, about five years ago. Houses were carried bodily away, and as for the biggest trees, why they had no chance at all. Well, among the rest, every inch of roof was torn off the camp, and, as it was of corrugated iron, you may fancy it didn't fall without making a taste of a shindy.

The morning broke, calm and beautiful, just like a baby that had cried itself to sleep, and if it did, up gets me hearty O'Brien, and comes outside, feeling, and looking, as he mostly did of a morning, devilish seedy; and he reached up his arms and gives a big yawn, while he was on the spy to see if the store beyant was open, till he'd get his morning. And it wasn't; so he turned his face to the camp, and at last ketches a glimpse of the state the roof was in."

'Be jabers, the roof's off!' ses he, and to this day 'tis a byword against the same O'Brien.

"Now, go to sleep, and be — to you!"

And that was my precious mate, Cross, for you all out.

There was an early muster at the camp on the following morning, and twelve of us in all, mounted, at last made a start in the direction of Bell's Station, at the other side of which, toward Kerr's, we were to begin our search. Jack we had accommodated with the use of our old camp wood and water horse, and so satisfied ourselves of his safety, for the poor old fellow wouldn't have run away with his rider had he been ever so well inclined to escape.

As the leader of the party, however, I took especial care to keep the man close to my elbow by way of a guide as it were; and when we had at length passed Bell's, and made our arrangements as to signals, etc., we separated, Jack and I going on in company, examining every denser spot of bush, and rounding every belt of scrub we came in contact with.

Meanwhile I was watching him closely, and noticed the twitching lips and anxious looks, that increased as we went on and on through the forest; and at last I saw him start as plainly as ever a man started in the world, when the figure of one of our mates came into view riding in a direction to intercept us.

"That's Hastings," I said. "I expect they've found the body."

"I was just thinking that I knew the place," he spoke hesitatingly. "That there looks like the place I cut down the saplins I told you of."

And he pointed in a direction to the right, with a hand that I noticed trembled like that of a man who had been drinking very heavily.

I noticed something else, too, which recurred to me later in the day. I noticed that a piece was torn raggedly out of the bottom of his jumper, that became plainly visible when he lifted his arm to indicate the saplins. The jumper was of a coarse woollen material, and much worn, and the piece I missed might easily have been caught and torn out by a branch or broken bush.

"Well," I inquired of Hastings, who now rode up, "have you found anything?"

"About a hundred yards out there is a spot where *something* has certainly been. We hunted a dozen crows away from it, and there are evident signs of the something; but whatever may have been there is there no longer."

I looked at Jack. There were beads of perspiration standing on his face, and he looked at me fearfully, but there was no astonishment in his eyes, I noticed that, only inquiry and alarm.

"Of course you'll know if it's the place. Come on," I called, as I turned to follow Hastings's lead.

A few minutes brought us to the spot, around which were gathered several of the party, some remaining on horseback, and some having dismounted and busily engaged in examining the place indicated.

"Is this the place?" I asked of Jack, as I followed the example of the others and got off my horse.

"Yes," he said; "there's the saplins I put up; but he's gone. That chap must have buried him."

"What chap?"

"The fellow I met when I was lost."

"You seem to have quite made up your mind that the chap, as you call him, was a murderer, eh?"

He didn't evidently like the keen look I gave him as I made this observation, and I was sorry I made it the moment the words had escaped from me, for they might put him up to my suspicions, and render him more careful of both words and looks.

Partially under the shelter of a cluster of young trees, a spot in the grass looked polluted and damp, as if indeed carrion had been lying there long enough to leave a loathsome imprint. In one spot was a dark, large spot that might have been blood, but which the weather had dried and discoloured until it told no tales; and that was all that a careful examination revealed.

"What's that in your hand, Cross?" was a question induced by seeing my chum drawing out and smoothing a bit of something he held in his fingers.

"Only a bit of newspaper. I got it among the grass there."

I took the paper he handed me, and two or three looks satisfied me that it had once formed a portion of the very bit I had abstracted from Mr Jack's pocket. For the life of me I couldn't help the sudden look I shot at that gentleman, but I turned it off by asking if he had noticed the paper when he saw the body.

"No," he said: "he might have had a pocketful of sovereigns. I wouldn't have gone near him to touch one of them for any money."

As I have already told you, there was an imprint of something which had disappeared on the grass, and the grass in the partially shaded place of interest to us was rather long. A sort of trail marked upon it, close to the spot and a good bit from it, was the next thing that attracted our notice; and from it, in some unaccountable manner, the eyes of both Hastings and myself wandered, to rest upon a partly withered branch of gum that was tossed upon the ground not far from a fallen tree that lay rotting upon the grass.

Jack Lawson was standing with his face half averted from our party, and the branch I allude to was on his left, at about the distance of twenty yards. I could see that he was watching me furtively, and that his eye followed mine as it caught the trail and the branch beyond it, and there was a gleam in his eye and a compression of lip that assured me of a knowledge of something connected with the matter beyond our ken.

"If anything *has* been removed from this, I should say it had been dragged over there on that branch. And look what clusters of flies and ants are all along the trail," said Hastings.

"It looks pretty like it," I replied, leading my horse toward the place, to which I was closely followed by all the party, including Mr Jack Lawson, who brought up the rear.

"I'll lay anything you like that there's a plant of some kind here," was the next remark made by Cross, as he put his foot upon a spot of ground close to the log.

It was fresh-looking, and not far from the branch, and pieces of fresh-looking bushes were sticking up from the earth in a manner that indicated no attempt whatever at concealment.

"Whoever planted there wanted some one to find. And now, how are we to unearth whatever is hidden?"

"I've a tomahawk at my saddle," observed one of our friends, "and we can make a good shape to root out that loose place."

During the exciting few moments that followed I was too much interested to watch Lawson very closely, but I noticed that he kept aloof, and that his face was as white as the face of a coward.

The tomahawk and half a dozen sticks, procured on the spot, soon rooted out sufficient of the loose earth to expose the buried bushes which we had observed. When this had been accomplished, half a dozen hands seized portions of the branches, and in one instant they were dragged off, and with them the superincumbent soil; and there, lying stiff and distorted, with bloody and clay-soiled face, with torn and discoloured clothes, and with matted hair in a gaping and hideous wound in his forehead, lay the corpse of the wretched John Gardner.

Although the sight was only what we anticipated, I may say it momentarily paralysed us. The very strongest minded and most careless cannot but shrink from the decomposed clay of poor humanity; but when it is that of one with whom you have been on terms of intimacy, and whom you have been wont to see in full vigour, and thoughtless of death, the feeling is doubly painful.

There was not a spoken word for some seconds. All gazed down upon the fearful sight, incapable, as it were, to remove their eyes from a scene that shocked them too deeply for utterance; but at last, with muttered ejaculations of horror, one and another dropped back from the offensive neighbourhood, and left Cross and me alone bending over the body.

The limbs were distorted, as if from the agony of a painful death, and the stiff hands were clenched and bloody. In one of them was grasped a something, which appeared to me like a bit of flannel, and, with the greatest difficulty, I dragged it carefully from the tenacious grip. Picture to yourself my satisfaction at recognising the piece I had observed to be missing from the jumper of Jack Lawson.

"The cursed scoundrel!" ejaculated my mate, as I in a whisper explained the thing and gave him his instructions; and then we both stood up and turned toward our silent party.

"Come here and see if this is the body you spoke of," said Cross to Lawson.

There he stood, about a dozen yards off, with his white face and quivering lip, but I don't think he had any idea of the evidence against him we had discovered in the grave.

He came forward, hesitatingly; but, as if mustering up a desperate courage, he walked the last few steps rapidly, and stood on the brink of the grave for a second, holding his hand over the lower part of his face.

To give you an idea of how the next incident occurred, I must tell you that directly behind us was a close belt of young trees, and that during our examination of the body, a horseman had ridden around this belt, upon the soft grass, without being either seen or heard by any of us. When Lawson lifted his eyes, with a terrified shudder, from the fearful face of the dead, they fell upon the stranger, who was standing at the other side of the log, holding his horse by the bridle.

Had the man been supernatural, the sight would probably not have had half the effect it produced upon the miserable wretch. With a wild cry, he raised his arms, as if to grasp at some support, and then he fell heavily forward into the open grave, and right upon the unconscious and polluting body of poor Gardner.

Of course, we hauled him out as quickly as we could, and carried him to a tree at a little distance, leaning against the trunk of which we placed him, to recover himself. He had not fainted, or lost sensibility in any way, but temporarily paralysed by the unexpected sight of the man he had most cause to dread in the whole world – by the only man who could prove him the murderer of John Gardner.

"There's the man!" was the first gasping assertion of the wretch, as he partially recovered, pointing a palsied finger at the stranger, who now approached, leading his horse. "I'll swear to him – that's the man!"

The man indicated was clad tolerably well, and there were

the remains of some far-off decent days in his haggard face; but dissipation and evil of many kinds had left deep imprints in his dark countenance. He walked straight to me, or to the three stripes on my arm, and, touching his hat, said,

"I've been at the camp to give myself in charge, and to give information of a murder; and hearing the errand you were on, I followed you. Since that terrible night" – and he pointed toward the open grave – "I haven't slept an unbroken hour – God help me! – the man's dead face is always before my eyes."

"Do you mean to say you were an accessory to the murder?"

"Thank heaven – no! I'm bad enough, but not that," and he shuddered visibly. "It was Lawson there that murdered him; but we were mates in the robbery of the Post Office Store."

The miserable object sat there, propped up against the tree, with a cheek as colourless as clay, and starting eyes that he was probably unable to remove from his accuser. He tried to speak and get on his feet, but the words seemed to die on his trembling lips, and his limbs refused to obey his wishes. It was not necessary to prevent any attempt at escape, for he was utterly incapable of making one; and, besides, he was surrounded by the horrified party, who listened with anxious faces.

"We robbed the store," went on the strange man, "and camped in what we thought a safe place in the bush; but, late at night, who should ride down to us by accident but Gardner himself. We had plenty of grog in the cart, and plied him with it, intending, when he should be incapable of following, to remove our booty. As the poor chap's evil luck would have it, however, he recognised some of the goods which Lawson incautiously exposed in a search for a fresh bottle, and swore he would have us in the lock-up in a couple of hours.

"Lawson there was always a devil under drink, but I never expected that his propensity to evil would carry him the length of murdering the unfortunate storekeeper. I went to look for the horse that we had turned out, and when I came back Gardner was weltering in his blood, and Lawson standing over him with the axe in his hands. 'He'll not inform now I don't think!' he cried, with drunken glee, and then he lay down near his victim, and slept.

"No sooner was I certain that he was really unconscious than I harnessed the horse to the conveyance, and left him and the dead man alone in the bush. I was glad to put miles between us, but I carried the dead face wherever I went."

It was easy to guess Lawson's idea of revenge. On waking up and finding that his mate had levanted with the goods as well as the secret, he had conceived the idea of trying to sheet the murder home to the absconder without implicating himself. He was ignorant, too, and superstitious, and the haunting fear of that bloody corpse had followed him even to his dreams. As he afterwards confessed, it was days before he dared to cover him up out of his sight, during which he wandered around the spot, terrified to leave the bloody evidence in the light of day.

Lawson suffered the extreme penalty of the law. As you will remember, the evidence of his mate in the robbery being, firstly, borne out by the portion of his jumper I rescued from the grasp of the dead, and, lastly, by his own confession. As for the informer, his sentence was a lenient one – perhaps, more lenient than it ought to have been; but who can account for the inconsistencies with which our laws are administered?

I have only one bit more information to give you about the affair, boys, and you can draw any conclusions you like about it, or from it. In less than two years, Mrs Gardner married young Hastings, and that same gentleman is now the proprietor of the Post Office Store, on Old Jeffries' Diggings.'

Mary Anne Barker

The Shepherd's Story

1872

'Things are very different now,' said Bob, 'all over the country, though it is not so many years ago, not more than six or seven perhaps. We did not think much of Sunday in the early days; we didn't exactly work, such as digging or such-like on that day, but we did other jobs which had been waiting for a spare moment all the week. We used not to think any harm of breaking a young colt on Sunday, or of riding over to the next run with a draughting notice; or if it was wet we lay in our bunks and smoked, or p'raps we got up and sat on a bucket turned wrong side up, and mended our clothes. As for Christmas Day, we never thought of it beyond wondering what sort of "duff" we were going to have. That's colonial for a pudding, ma'am, you know, don't you? If we had a couple of handfuls of currants and raisins, we shoved them into a lot of flour and sugar, and we put a bit of mutton fat into the middle, and tied it all up together in the sleeve of an old flannel shirt and boiled it, and it used to come out a first-rate plum duff, and we thought we had no end of a Christmas if we could manage such a pudding as that.

'But we could not always get even a holiday on Christmas Day, because of the shearing. Shearers were too scarce in those days, and wages too high to miss a day's work, so it often happened that we had to work just as hard, or harder on Christmas than on any other day of the year. I was working then up at Mr Vansittart's ('Vans-start's', Bob called his master), and we had hopes of getting finished by Christmas Eve, and having at all events a good lie-in-bed on Christmas Day; but as ill-luck would have it, a mob of wethers bolted from the flat where Tom Duckworth was watching them, and got right away into the hills at the back of the run. *He* said it was because his dogs were new and wouldn't work properly for him, but I knew better – he done it a-purpose. Tom's sheep were always coming to grief. He couldn't cross 'em over a river without losing half the mob, and never a week passed without his getting boxed. That's mixed-up, ma'am,' explained Bob politely, observing a puzzled expression in my eyes. 'We calls it boxing when your sheep go and join another mob feeding close by, and you can't tell one from another except by the brand or the ear-mark. It's a nasty business is boxing, and *werry* trying to the temper. Even the dogs get out of patience like, and nip the stupid sheep harder than they do at any other time.

'Well, ma'am, as I was saying, Tom Duckworth let a fine mob of young wethers get away the day before Christmas Day, and started to look for them with his precious dogs. They were the very last mob which had to come up to be shorn, so, as he couldn't find 'em – I never expected he could, – there was the skillions standing empty, and the shearers lounging about idling when Christmas Day came; and a werry beautiful day it was, just like this one. The boss, that's Master Vans-start, he was at his wits' ends what to do. He knew right well that if the wethers wasn't in the yards that night, the shearers would be off across the hills to Brown and Wetherby's next morning first thing. You couldn't expect men who had their two pounds a day waiting for them to lose many days, especially as Brown and Wetherby's was an "open shed", where any shearers that came were taken on until there were hands enough, so they knew they might lose the job if they didn't look sharp. The boss managed to keep them quiet on Christmas Day, by pretending he always meant to take a spell on that day. He got the cook to make a stunning duff, and he sent a boy on horseback across the river to Mulready's for some beef; he knew Mulready always killed a bullock about Christmas and he served out some grog, so in that way he kept the shearers well fed and rested all Christmas Day. He never let them out of his sight, not even down to the creek to wash their shirts, lest any of them should slip away.

'I didn't come in for any of these good things: so far from it, quite the contra-*ry*;' and here Bob paused and took a pull at his pipe, resting his hands on his knees and gazing straight before him with regretful eyes, as the memory of his wrongs rose freshly to his mind. 'Tom Duckworth did, though, the stupid fool! He laid in his bunk on Christmas morning and had his snooze out, and then he got up and eat the best part of a cold leg of mutton for his breakfast, and he came in for the duff, and the grog, and all the rest of it afterwards. But I'll tell you how I spent my Christmas Day, ma'am, and I hope I'll never have to spend another like it.

'As soon as ever it was light, the boss, leastways Master Vans-start, he came into the kitchen where I was sleeping, and he says, "Bob, I must have that mob of wethers by tonight, and that's all about it. They're quite likely to have gone up into the back ranges, but unless they're gone up into the sky I'm bound to have 'em in the skillions tonight." You see, ma'am, when Master Vans-start put it in that way, I knew that mob had got to be found before nightfall, and that he was going to tell me off to find 'em. So I lay there and listened, as was my dooty to. "Bob," says Master Vans-start, "I'll tell you what it is, I'll give you a fiver," – that's a five-pound note, ma'am, you'll understand, – "yes, Bob, a fiver, over and above your year's pay when I draws a cheque for your wages next week, and you can go down to town and spend it, Bob, if you bring me in the whole of that mob of wethers by sundown. Take any body you like with you and the best of the dogs, only you bring them in; for if you don't, I shall be three hundred pounds short in my wool-money this year, and I've got too heavy a mortgage on this run, Bob, to be able to afford to lose that much, and all through Tom Duckworth's sleepy-headedness."

'Well, ma'am, when the boss spoke so feelingly, and put it to me in that way, I knew it had to be done, so I said, "Right you are, sir," and then he only said, "I looks to you, Bob, for them sheep," and he went away. It was barely light enough to see your hand, and I knew that the *mistesses* (that was the way Bob pronounced mists) would be hanging about the hills for a good time yet, so I reached out my hand and I got my pipe and a match and I smoked a bit, whilst I considered which way I should go and who I should take with me. Men, I mean; I didn't want to know what dogs I should take, for if Sharp and Sally couldn't find 'em, all I could say was, they wasn't to be found. I'd a good mind to name Tom Duckworth to come, but I meant to give whoever went with me a pound a-piece, and I didn't want to tip him for giving all this bother; besides, he was just as likely as not to sit down under the lee of a rock and smoke the moment he got out of my sight. No, I wouldn't take Tom, but I'd take little Joe Smelt, who was as active as a kid on the hills, and Munro, who, although he belonged to the next station, knew every yard of country round, and who had the best head on his shoulders of any man I knew. Besides, Munro had always been a chum of mine, and was such a decent well-spoken fellow, it was a pleasure to have any dealin's with him.

'By the time I had settled all this in my own mind, I thought it was about time to get up, so up I got and I lighted the stove and put the kettle on to boil, and a whole lot of chops on to fry, and I got the pannikins out and the tin plates. I remember well I was so anxious to have a good comfortable breakfast ready before I called Joe and Munro, that I even cleaned up the knives and forks for 'em. How did I do that, is it you want to know, ma'am? Oh, very easy: I just stuck 'em into the soft ground outside the back door, and worked 'em up and down a bit, and they came out fine and clean. Well, as soon as I had got everything ready, I went into the men's hut, and I got out Munro and little Joe Smelt without waking up any of the others; and when they got on their boots and moleskins, saving your presence, ma'am, they come into the kitchen, and I showed 'em the breakfast all ready and smelling uncommon good, and I told 'em what the boss had said, and I lays it before 'em whether they likes to come up the hills with me and earn their pound a-piece, or whether they'd *pre*-fer to loaf about the station all day, whiles I goes out by myself and sticks to the whole of the fiver.

'Munro, he goes on eating his breakfast quite quiet-like – for that matter we was all pegging away pretty tidily – and then, after a bit, he says in his peaceable way – I've told you he was a very well-spoken man, ma'am, haven't I? – he says, "Well, Bob, I don't mind if I do come;" and then Joe Smelt says, as well as he can speak for a mouthful of damper, "The same here;" so then I knew it was settled, and I enjoyed my breakfast with the rest. We didn't dawdle too long, though, for it was getting light enough to see, though them mistesses was still too low to please me, but I thought we might be making our way up the river-gorge and smoke our pipes as we went. The sheep had gone up that way, I knew, and there was no way out. Besides, sheep don't like crossing the water oftener than they can help. Nine times we had to cross that there river on that there blessed Christmas morning. Get wet! I should just think we did: leastways I took off my Cookhams and worsted socks at each ford, because I knew right well that if I went up the hills and walked all day in wet things, my feet would get that blistered I'd feel like a cat in walnut-shells. Joe Smelt found that out to his cost before the day was over. He started werry cocky and turned up his trowser-legs and walked right through the water, saying he couldn't be bothered to stop and take his boots off and on at each crossing. Munro, he walked through all nine fords in his boots; and then, when we had done with them for that day, he sat down on a big stone and took off his socks and his boots and drew out a nice dry pair of worsted socks and put 'em on; then he poured the water out of his boots and shook 'em up and down a bit and put 'em on again, and laced 'em up werry tight. But still, long before the day was done, his feet was smartin' and his boots was all out o' shape, and wringing him awful. Joe and I couldn't have managed that way if it had been ever so, for socks wasn't plenty with us in those days. We just used to get one pair at a time from the nighest store, and wear 'em until they got into one big hole all over, and then we chucked 'em away and got another pair. Now, Munro, he had a nice little Scotch wife up at his place, and she was always a-spinning and a-knitting for him, and kept him as comfortable as could be. But Joe and me, we hadn't neither wives, nor socks, nor anything nice about us, but we just pulled through as well as we could.

'Well, ma'am, to come back to that Christmas Day. It was as beautiful a morning as you would wish to see, and not too hot, neither; the sun just beginning to shine, and drinking up them mistesses as if they was grog, till there wasn't one to be seen, and Munro's glass showed him every sheep on every hill within sight as plain as you see your hand now. Lots of sheep there were too, and werry cheerful it sounded their calling to each other, and werry good feed there was for 'em on those hills. But they was all too white for what we wanted. They'd all been *shored*, 'twas easy to see that, and the mob we wanted was still in their wool, and would have looked dirty and much larger among the fresh-shored ones. We could track 'em easy enough by their footmarks up to the head of the gorge, but there we lost all trace, and though we spent a good hour hunting. We felt sure they'd all keep together, for they'd be frightened at the sight of all their fellows so white and so bare, and likely as not travel away from 'em. They wasn't anywhere on the low hills, that was certain; there was no use funking it, we had got to separate and go carefully over the back ranges, and a long hot climb we had before us that Christmas morning; and, not to be too long about it, ma'am, a long hot climb we had if ever there was one in this world. I sent the dogs many and many a time after what I thought might be a part of the mob; but though I hunted as close as ever I could, never a sheep did I see, no, nor a sign of one. Well, ma'am, it was very disheartening, you'll allow that, and I was so vexed I couldn't feel properly hungry even long after dinner-time came, and I kept thinking whatever I should do if they wasn't to be found. You see, I had chosen the most likely place to search in myself, as was but nat'ral, so I never thought that if *I* couldn't find 'em anybody else could. There's where I deceived myself; because when I had worked all round that blessed range and come upon Davis's hut – that was the out-station where we had settled to meet some time in the arternoon – what should I see but Munro and Joe Smelt a-lying on the shady side of the hut as cool and comfortable as you please, smoking their pipes, and the whole mob of sheep lying quiet and peaceable on the little flat, with Munro's dog watching 'em. Not that they wanted any watching just then, for sheep always take a good spell in the afternoon of a hot day, and lie down and go to sleep, maybe, until it gets cool enough to make it pleasant to wander about and feed before dark.

'As soon as ever I see that sight I flung up my hat and danced for joy, and I felt desperate hungry all of a minute. I can tell you, my mates, I didn't lose much time getting down that hill, though I come pretty quiet for fear of scaring the sheep.

'When I comes up to the men, before I could speak, Joe Smelt says, first thing, "Munro found 'em; I haven't been long here." And Munro smiles quiet and pleased-like, and says, "I had a mob once served me the same trick, and I thought I knew where to look for 'em, and sure enough they was there, reg'larly hiding; I had to bring 'em down uncommon easy, for it was a nasty place, and I didn't want half of 'em to be smothered in the creek."

'Well, of course I meant to ask and to hear all about it, but I thought it would keep until we had had a bit of dinner, for it was about two o'clock, and you must please to remember, ma'am, that we had breakfasted somewhere about five, and likewise that walking up and down them back ranges is hungry work at the best of times, besides being wearing to the boots. "Where's Davis?" was my first words. "Davis must have gone away altogether for a bit," they said, "for the hut is locked and fastened up until it can't be fastened no more, and unless we reg'larly break into it, we shall never get in it."

'"Drat the fellow!" I cried, "there ain't no bushrangers about. Why doesn't he just lock his door and hang the key on a nail outside where anybody can see it, as I used to do when I was a back-country shepherd, and wanted to go away for a bit." But it was no manner of use pitching into Davis, not then, because you see, ma'am, he wasn't there to hear himself abused, though we did that same and no mistake. It *was* aggravating – now, ma'am, wasn't it? There was we three, and the dogs, poor things! as hungry as hungry could be; and we knew there'd be flour and tea and sugar, and likely a bit of bacon (for Davis was a good hand at curing a ham of a wild pig), inside the door, if we could only open it. Not a bit of it would stir, though, for all our kicks, and Joe Smelt ran at it with his shoulders until I thought he must burst it open; but no, the lock didn't give one bit. "Tell you what," said Joe, rubbing his shoulder after his last attempt, "Davis has gone and barred this 'ere door up on the inside, and then got out of the window and fastened it up outside afterwards." When we came to look, it seemed quite likely, for the shutter was driven home and kept in its place by good-sized nails; but we got a big stone, and we used our knives, and Munro worked away that patiently that at last down came the shutter, and we had the little bit of a window open in no time after that. We made little Joe get through first, and we laughed and said we felt just like real housebreakers, but we thought we'd keep our jokes until we had had something to eat. Before Joe had well unbarred the door – for it was fastened up as if it was never meant to be opened again – Munro and me had settled that he should make some flap-jacks as soon as ever we could get the fire to burn; that is, supposing there wasn't any bacon or mutton lying about.

'The minute Joe opened the door with a cheery, "Here you are," we looked round us like so many hungry wolves, and the first thing we see is a fine big shoulder of mutton on the floor. Well, it was easy to see how it had got there, for there were marks of rats' teeth and feet too, all over it. Davis hadn't been long gone that was easy to see – not more than a few hours likely, though he plainly intended to be away for some time by the way he'd fastened up everything; but still it was very neglectful of him not to have flung that shoulder of mutton outside before he went, because you see, ma'am, in a day or two it would surely be very unpleasant. A neat man was Davis – a very neat man – and when we'd prized open his cupboard made out of old gin-cases, we found his couple of tin-plates and pannikins, and his tea and sugar, and his flour and his matches, and his salt, all as tidy as tidy could be, and there was a big packet of "Vermin Destroyer" too, open and half used. We gave that a wide berth, however, as you may fancy; but we had some sticks in the fire-place and the kettle on to boil before you could say "Jack Robinson". We found half a loaf of bread also in the cupboard, which we concluded to eat, lest it should get stale by the time Davis came back, and we told Munro we'd have his flap-jacks for second course. "Here's a capital Christmas dinner after all," said Joe; and he picked up the meat carefully off the floor, and blew the dust off, and we sat down to the table with that shoulder of mutton before us; and all I can tell you, ma'am, is, that long before the kettle boiled – and it had a good fire under it too – there wasn't a scrap left on the bone. Cooked! in course it was cooked; you don't think we was going to eat raw wittles on Christmas Day. No, no, ma'am, we weren't such cannibals as that! Davis had baked it as nice as could be, but it seemed uncommon funny that he should have taken so much trouble for nothing. However, there it was, or, I *should* say, there it wasn't, for we had eaten it up, every bite; and we told Joe Smelt to get the tea out of the cupboard, and throw a couple of handfuls into the kettle, which was beginning to boil. Joe got up, saying, "I haven't half done yet; I'm just as hungry as ever I can be;" and he went to the cupboard and began to rummage among the things in it. "Don't give us any pison by mistake, Joe," said Munro, joking. Just as he said the words, Joe turned short round, his face looking as white as death underneath all the sunburn and freckles, his very lips white, and his eyes open wider than I thought mortal eyes could open; and he said in a dreadful voice – a sort of whisper, and yet you might have heard it all over the place – "That's where it is, we're pisoned!" With that Munro and I jumped up from the table, and we gasped out, "Pisoned, Joe!" but we needn't to ask – we couldn't speak if we wished. Joe pointed to the bare mutton bone, and held out the half-used paper of the poison in the other, and never a word did he say but, "Rats."

'We guessed it all then. Davis must have been fairly bullied by the impudent hungry critturs, and he had taken the trouble to cook for 'em, as if they had been Christians, and then he'd quite likely as not rubbed an ounce or two of strychnine into that shoulder of mutton, and left it where the rats could get at it, and we'd been and eaten it all up instead o' they. Yes, ma'am, it's all very well to laugh,' said Bob, taking his hat off, and wiping his head with the handkerchief stowed away in its crown, looking into the hat afterwards as if he saw the scene he was describing pictured there – 'it was the werry roughest moment of all *my* life. To be pisoned like a rat, and in a lonely gully, where no one would ever pass. Most likely we shouldn't even be found before Davis came back. It was lucky Davis didn't come back, though – not at that moment, I mean – for I'm certain that if he stood in his own doorway just then we'd 'a set on him and killed him without so much as saying "with your leave or by your leave." We couldn't have been whiter than Joe, not if we'd tried; but we was white enough no doubt. Munro was a good man, so he was the bravest of the lot, and he said, or he tried to say, for he couldn't speak very clear, "The will of God be done, my poor Jeanie!" and with that he threw himself down on Davis's bed and hid his face.

'I don't rightly know what poor little Joe did, for I felt desperate mad. I caught sight of half a bar of soap stowed away at the back of the cupboard, and I seized it as if it had been a life-buoy, and I'd been a drowning man. I couldn't have gripped it harder or held it tighter if it *had* been a buoy,' said Bob, shaking his head meditatively. 'And I runs down to the creek with it. I don't know why I went there, unless it was to be handy to the water to gulp it down with. Well, ma'am, I had picked up my knife off the table as I passed, and I cut great junks of that bar of soap, and bolted 'em, whole. I seemed to remember having heard some one say that soap was good as a hemetick: and so I found it; for by the time I had swallowed half the bar I felt desperate sick, and joyful I was to feel it, I can tell you; but still I wasn't bad enough to please myself, so I drank some water and had three or four slices more, and that about finished me, and I lay down among the tussocks by the water side; and what with the fright, and the early rising, and the long walk, and the heat of the sun, joined to the murmur-like of the creek, I went off into the comfortablest sleep as I ever had, and it wasn't till the sun had got right behind the high hills to the westward that I woke up. I reckon it was the barking of Munro's dog that woke me, for the poor beast found he had more than he could do to manage the mob of sheep. They must have been feeding some time, and now wanted to be off up the hill to their camping ground; for you must know, ma'am, that sheep never settle for the night on low ground. They always travel up as high as they can conveniently get, and camp on the top of a hill.

'The poor beast seemed quite joyful to see it was me coming to help him, as he thought, but I couldn't give my mind to the sheep, not just yet. I was rather empty and a bit weak, but as well as ever I felt in my life. I remember I took off my hat, and looked up to the sky and I thanked God in my own rough fashion for saving my life all along of that bar of soap, and I give you my word, ma'am, I meant it, even when I found out my mistake. I thought I'd look up Munro and the other little chap, but I was more than half frightened to go and see about 'em, for at that time, you see, I thought I was wot you may call the sole surwivor. However, the others were surwivors too, and a very good job for 'em *that* was. Munro had pegged away into a bag of salt until he must have reg'larly *cured* his inside in more senses than one, whilst Joe had hemeticked himself by shoving his fingers down his throat. Poor Joe! he must have been desperate bad too. Well, they'd been to sleep as well as me, and there we stood staring at each other, awful pale and haggard-looking, but still safe and well so far.

'Munro was the first to recover himself, and he said, "Them

sheep'll be off before we can count ten," so with that we went to help the dog, who was barking hisself off his legs. Joe Smelt hung back a bit at first, for he said he'd heard as how exercise caused pison to work, but Munro called out, "Do your duty, Joe, and never mind the pison."

'So we got the sheep together, and we brought 'em down to the homestead, and right glad the boss was to see 'em. When I told him the story of the shoulder of mutton, he went nearly as white as we did, and he said he'd send for the doctor and tell him to bring proper hemeticks along, but we felt we couldn't stand no more not just then, and Joe says, says he, "It wouldn't be no manner of use, sir, not till we'd had some supper." With that the boss laughs and tells the manager to give us each a glass of hot grog; and very comfortin' it was. That's all, ma'am,' concluded Bob, getting up from his hencoop and making me a bow.

'No, no, Bob,' I cried, 'that isn't all; I must know the end.'

'There wasn't no more end than that, ma'am; leastways when Davis turned up, which he did by chance next day, at the home station, we werry nearly made an end to him when he lets out that there never had been no pison on the shoulder of mutton at all. He said he'd cooked it, meaning to take it in his swag for his supper that night, and was fine and mad when he found he'd forgotten it. Mr Vans-start, he said we ought to be downright thankful to Davis when we found he hadn't let us in for his pison, but we couldn't see it in that light no how, and we give Davis, one and all of us, a bit of our minds, and Joe Smelt offered to fight him the very next Sunday for five pounds a side. Poor Davis! he made us mad by the way he laughed, and he tried to comfort us by telling us that if the "Vermin Destroyer" did us as little harm as it did the rats, we needn't to have cried out. "Why, they thrive on it," he said. "I lets 'em have it pretty often, and they comes about more than ever arter a dose on it."'

Bob's story took a long time in the telling, for he told it very deliberately, and enjoyed a long word, or any pet expression, such as his life-buouy, so intensely that he repeated it over and over again, rolling the words in his mouth as if they were good to taste. By the time he had finished, the valley was in deep shadow, and the delicious crisp feeling in the air, which always follows a summer's day in our New Zealand hills, made us feel inclined for a change of occupation. The quoits were got out, and the iron pegs stuck in the ground, and some of the shearers were soon hard at work pitching the heavy circlets through the air. Another group were putting the stone or the hammer, whilst a few made themselves very hot by running races or having hopping matches. The constant open-air exercise, keeps men of all grades in New Zealand in such good condition that, even in such rough primitive sports as these were, I have seen far more surprising feats of strength performed by athletes who had had no other training than their daily hill-walks and frugal, wholesome fare, than in the *champ-clos* of a fashionable arena in the old country.

But to-morrow's work must begin with the dawn, so whilst there was yet light to see their way home across the rolling downs which stretched like a green sea before us, the good-nights were said. I stood in the porch and shook hands with each guest as he passed, though the performance of this ceremony entailed deep blushes on the part of my stalwart company. 'Here's wishin' you the best o' luck, mum,' was the general adieu; but when they all got to the bottom of the paddock, they consulted together and gave a ringing hearty cheer, which woke up the valley's quiet echoes, may be for the first time since it emerged from the water-world. 'One more for Old Father Christmas,' were the last words I heard, as I turned indoors, leaving the joyous sounds to die gradually away into the deep perfumy silence which hung over that lonely valley of the Malvern Hills.

Tasma

Barren Love

1877

Only two veins standing out from a woman's neck – that was all! The cynic told himself he was a fool, and telling himself so, walked away to the farther end of the deck. Blue veins starting up from a young throat! There was nothing, after all, in a phenomenon of the sort – nothing, that is to say, that could not be explained on physiological grounds. The cynic was accustomed to look at manifestations of pain from a point of view purely scientific. Thus, when you cut off the head of a dog-fish, the monster squirms with the agony. Like the evil it typifies, there is a hold-fastness in its grip of life. But you know, or you believe you know, of how much account is all this resistant wrestling with death! What softer sensation do you have than one of animosity towards the dog-fish for dying so hard, and for giving you such a world of trouble to get your blunt knife through a neck like animated indiarubber?

The cynic admitted a difference between the throat of a placoidian and the throat of a young girl. But to watch the one gasping its death-gurgle from a bleeding gash, and the other, distorted, working against a sentimental grief, might not of itself be a process provocative of intensely differing emotions. The cynic, holding it as a theory that softening of the heart and softening of the brain have meanings almost synonymous, pooh-poohed his maudlin fancies, and walked resolutely back to his old post by the bulwarks. Those obtrusive veins annoyed him! In thirty or forty years' time they might ride up, if they chose. Everything should be smooth in youth, even to the trunk of a tree. Nature had given these veins a semi-opaque covering, smoother and softer than the blossom of an arum. In their normal condition they obliterated themselves behind it, or only started into the faintest show of self-assertion when their home was unsettled. And here they had risen like blue weals, raised by the lash of an inward thong!

The cynic, feeling justified in his irritation, looked up from the demonstrative neck to the face above it – and immediately walked away. This time it was for good. He felt about as much ashamed of himself as if he had torn open the girl's dress and asked her where she was smarting.

Not that the cynic was unacquainted with the nature of tears – 'a limpid fluid secreted by the lachrymal gland,' &c. If you come to tears, nothing can shed them more profusely than a seal. The soft-eyed creature wails and cries on the score of her outraged maternity. She plants her unwieldy body in front of her little one and asks for mercy with streaming eyes. Tears, therefore, are nothing in themselves! Sterne shed them by the bucketsful, with much maudlin satisfaction to himself the while. The cynic loathed Sterne, and despised the sentimentalist for his perpetual flourish of handkerchiefs in the faces of his readers. But on the present occasion he came very near to despising himself. He wondered just when he would forget the strained eyes – every gleam of self-consciousness washed out of them – nothing but an intelligence of suffering left. He did not require to be told that from among the departing boats, fast turning into mere buoyant dots in the distance, one more than another must have magnetised the hopeless gaze.

Looking half-way across Plymouth harbour, by the light of a sudden burst of yellow sunshine, he could discern the outline of a man standing upright in the foremost boat of all.

The cynic was so quick in connecting the dejection of the man's attitude with the crushed aspect of the girl, that he would have despised himself with a fresh access of vigour if it had occurred to him to think about himself in the matter at all. Somehow, he forgot at the moment to make proper sport of his own show of human interest. The fluttering of a handkerchief in the boat called forth a curious corresponding signal on the part of the girl. Her hands, trembling all over, like the rest of her body, tugged at her collar-fastening and extracted a hidden white envelope. They carried it to her lips – she was past all heed of curious bystanders long ago! The passionate kissing of the unheeding paper – the stretching of it out towards the boat, as if so frantic a gesture might stay even the stolid Plymouth boatman – the effort that she made to restore it to its place and lay it as a sort of healing plaster against her gasping throat – all this might have been grotesque if it had been only one shade less humanly real. The cynic found a characteristic outlet for his unaccountable sensations by glaring with an expression of appalling severity at any unwary waif who might venture within three yards of the desolate girl. Long after the boat was out of sight she continued to stand in the same spot, stonily indifferent to the scene before her. For the last English sunset was sending the ship on her way in a rose-coloured light. People on the Plymouth pier saw her in a haze of burnished mist, moving airily away under gilded sails.

CHAPTER II

The cynic, who was not called Mr Cynic, however, by those on board, but Mr Ralph Grimwood, or Mr Grimwood only, was very sea-sick. Between the intervals of his degradation he thought about dog-fishes and seals; he thought about the affections too – those perplexing equivalents in the sum total of the disturbing influences that control us. On principle, he execrated the affections – officious meddlers in the sound mechanical functions of the body. On principle, he was antagonistic to love, the mere display of which would have been nauseous if it had not been so ludicrous! But sea-sickness, it would seem, had rendered him illogical. As he lay in his bunk, careful not to look at the swinging port-hole, a mere glance at which seemed to heave him up into the watery clouds and drag him down into the watery depths, he fell to picturing what his life might have become if he could have changed personalities with the vague outline in the boat. Being weakened by so much diminution of bile, he was fain to indulge the fancy. He had never known what it was to be light-headed as yet. Instead, therefore, of controlling his impulse, according to his stern creed, he was constrained to let his impulse control him. And it controlled him utterly!

Now he could see the boat racing after the ship, while he himself was urging it on! Now he could see himself climbing up the ship's side, clothed always in the shadowy form he had distinguished. How soon he had kissed back into their white hiding-place the poor swollen veins! He had separated the helpless hands twisted into each other for their own support, and put them round his strong, surly shoulders. His lips had closed for one instant the heavily-weighted eyelids, that he might see the grey eyes open again with such a look as his touch would have restored to them. It need not be pointed out that the light-headed fancy was running riot through his brain.

Meanwhile a wind had set in that was driving away all traces of tears from the emigrant's cheeks, and blowing a fresher brininess against them instead. The ship, at the outset, swayed timorously along, like a child in leading-strings. The wind pushed her about, slapped her alternately on either side, tilted her forward, and hitched her back, till she jerked like a gibbing horse – finally took her by the hand and pulled her smoothly along across the Bay of Biscay. Then Mr Grimwood came on deck.

The passengers up above were proudly displaying their newly-acquired sea-legs. They strutted along uncertainly, after the manner of ducks, – very much pressed for time to get nowhere at all. Mr Grimwood watched them stumping past him, the same strained expression peculiar to landsfolk at the outset of a long voyage, stamping them all; the rims of their eyes reddened by the wind.

The deck was a flush one, and amid-ships was a balustrade dividing the spaces allotted respectively to the first and second-class passengers. As it is always easier to lower one's social status than to raise it, on board ship as in the world, passengers from the first cabin were allowed the run of the space paid for by passengers from the second cabin. None of them, however, with the sole exception of Mr Grimwood, seemed in any especial hurry to snatch at their privilege. Probably it was one of the cynic's eccentricities to like whiffs of a mixed character.

On the second-class deck the nostrils conveyed food to the mind in the shape of a hundred conjectures. For instance, on the weather side, it was impossible, after a few enforced sniffs, to abstain from speculations as to the state in which the fowls might be kept. On the lee side, the speculative mind might find a still wider range and lose itself in dwelling on the odoriferous origin of ship's grease. It is not certain whether these inducements allured Mr Grimwood from the quarter-deck. If neither fowls nor ship's grease attracted him, it may be inferred that the people were worth a glance, albeit not from Mr Grimwood's point of view – a cynic always sees a crumbling skeleton behind the most life-warm flesh.

They were of all varieties – the needy family man whose olive branches would have borne pruning, the runaway defaulter who looked even at the horizon with suspicion – the willing-to-better-herself spinster, who knew to a nicety how many of the ship's officers were married, and could have told off each mate to his watch on deck with less hesitation than the Captain himself. In none of these classes would you have included the one solitary passenger standing by herself on a coil of rope, with arms leaning on the bulwarks and eyes directed to the impalpable boundary-line of the sea. Neither would you have found her counterpart more readily among the first-class passengers. In the quiescence of her present attitude, as in the mute storminess of her grief, she seemed absolutely to ignore all human surroundings. Andromeda, chained to a rock, with foam leaping over her white limbs, could not have been more oblivious of the impression she was conveying than was this plaid-enveloped girl.

Mr Grimwood had cultivated art even before he cultivated cynicism. To a stirring of the ancient art-impulse within him he sacrificed his reflections anent dog-fishes and seals. With such a model for an Andromeda, his cynicism might all have spent itself on the Dragon. Who can say? It is certain that some of his bile had spent itself already. Andromeda would not, perhaps, have worn a black felt hat or a green plaid shawl; but could even Andromeda's hair have been blown back into softer, silkier rings from whiter temples; could Andromeda's eyes – always granting that they were of the same transparent grey – have been hedged in by longer lashes; could Andromeda herself have shown a purer profile, or – now that the mutinous veins were laid to rest – have displayed a more rounded throat? Mr Grimwood, gravely parading the second-deck, must have known all this by intuition. It was soon after his excursive walk along the hen-coops that he was seen in conversation with the Captain.

That same afternoon, the second-class steward, who was washing second-class plates in second-class slop, was half-deafened by a call from the Captain himself. The steward was to fetch him the young woman in plaid – Miss Leighton by name – and to look sharp about it.

The Captain was a sort of typical tar – one of a race not quite extinct; still to be met with on old colonial wool-ships, despite the new genus introduced by steam. He did not think about Andromeda when he saw Miss Leighton, but it partly occurred to him that it was a blank shame such an eternally fine girl should be spooking about the world by herself. It seemed that he had summoned her to give her a cheering piece of news. It appeared, according to the Captain's story, that a letter and a deposit had been put into his hands at starting which, by some remarkable oversight, had never been opened until to-day. The letter bore no signature – over this part of his story the Captain blundered unaccountably. Somebody, about whose appearance the Captain was by no means clear, had entrusted the letter to his keeping. In fact, only as regarded the instructions, did the Captain express himself with anything like clearness, and on that head he was more than explicit. Miss Leighton was to travel as a saloon passenger, the deposit being sufficient not only to defray the cost of her passage-money, but to give her a cabin to herself. Here the Captain attempted an apology for his delay in imparting the news. Somehow, he blundered again, and stopped suddenly short.

Certainly Miss Leighton's mind must have been given to travelling on its own account. All the time the Captain was speaking, it seemed to be journeying back from some dreary distance, until it shone through her great abstracted eyes. Their lost, desolate look made way for the light that a warm sense of surrounding care brought into them. It was no longer Andromeda with the horror of the Dragon's presence in her white face, but Andromeda with uplifted eyes watching the glittering pathway of her deliverer through the air.

Poetical justice should have awarded Mr Grimwood a seat next to Miss Leighton at the dinner-table, but poetical justice was not embodied in the head-steward – a ginger-hued little man, upon whom devolved the arrangement of the passengers' places. A constant suspicion that some outrage upon his dignity might be meditated had caused the little steward's eyes to protrude. His exalted position was a bar to his making any confidential friends. He was on speaking terms only with the cook, and spent his life with one eye upon the lazarete and the other on the look-out for a slight.

The cynic's post at the dinner-table was exactly in front of his cabin. When his eyes travelled along a row of ungainly noses on the same side of the table as his own, they invariably stopped at a small Greek profile, standing out like a cameo from among the irregular heads that flanked it. There was something embarrassing in looking down a column of strongly-defined nose-tips. The cynic waited until the regulation plum-duff was put into its place; then he took a rapid glance to the rear. Out of all the assortment of heads, there was only one that could possibly correspond to the profile – a stately little head, very black and shining, perhaps a shade too upright, as if the knot of heavy hair on the nape had pulled it ever so slightly back.

And through all the swinging about in the Bay of Biscay, Mr Grimwood continued to take his daily glance. It was not, perhaps, so fruitful of consequences as a nearer approach to the Andromeda might have proved itself. Sympathies have declared themselves on board ship between young men and women in proximity at meal-time, which otherwise must have been everlastingly ignored. What will not a constant adherence to black-currant tart in two young persons of different sexes engender? How steel yourself against a growing interest in the possessor of a plate that accompanies your own with such unswerving fidelity?

Only that the cynic was like nobody else on board ship or elsewhere, he would not have sat daily with an afflicted dowager and a failing octogenarian on either side of him. He would have found means to install himself in the place of one of the nondescript spinsters who enclosed Miss Leighton. But being unlike anybody else in any respect whatever, it was entirely consistent with his character to make a point of avoiding her. As to analysing his motives, that is another thing. It is not pretended that any man's intimate feelings are open to dissection.

There have been natures sufficiently high-flown to set a flesh-and-blood statue on an ideal pedestal, and to shrink from seeing the statue come down to its regular meals. There have been natures, high-flown too, to whom the quintessence of beauty lies in the bloom which covers it. Perhaps, in the cynic's eyes, the mystery surrounding the luxury of Miss Leighton's position was the bloom that covered its solid good. There are yet other natures, and these are not necessarily high-flown, who argue that only one passion can move a woman to so intense an agony of grief as that of which the cynic had been witness. Were such a passion immediately transferable, at what value must the new recipient place it in the sum of human emotions? Its sweetness might be just as transitory as its grief – all a piece of unconscious play-acting. Now the list of possible reasons is quite exhausted, it is hardly necessary to repeat that the cynic was unlike anybody else. As for the present of the cabin, there have been precedents in this direction. Amelia Sedley played on the piano Dobbin had restored to her, with something of the feeling that comforted Miss Leighton when she closed her eyes in the new cabin that the George Osborne of her dreams had chosen for her.

CHAPTER III

If Mr Mantalini had ever been in the doldrums, he might have added to his experience of 'demmed moist unpleasant bodies'. A ship constrained to loiter there breaks out into a cold sweat. Everything she carries becomes clammy. In this respect there is not much difference between the animate and the inanimate bodies that she holds – unless it be that the first are pervaded with a warm stickiness, and the last with a cold stickiness. The most sanguineous of people assume the consistency of dough before it is kneaded. As for the spare folk, they look as if the scant supply of blood in their veins had turned to London milk. Then simple practical suggestions on the great question of 'demand and supply' occur to those unversed in the rudiments of political economy. The balance between the internal and the external moisture must be maintained; in maintaining it, panting passengers are reminded of 'Fair-shon's Son' –

'Who married Noah's daughter,
And nearly spoilt ta Flood
By drinking up ta water.'

'Which he would have done,' adds his sceptical chronicler –

. . . 'Had the mixture been
Only half Glenlivet.'

In emulation of the patriarch's convivial son-in-law, passengers only temper their drink with the tepid water served in regulation quantities to all on board. It is calculated that a little tepid water is very satisfying. Niggards, who depend upon it entirely, not using it as a tempering medium, but as a pure draught, are not taken into account on board a sailing-ship. They cannot even act upon Mr Barlow's sage advice, and only 'drink when they are dry.' For they are always dry, and there is nothing to drink.

Under all ordinary and everyday circumstances the usual lot of the niggard at sea would have fallen to Miss Leighton's share. The Turkish bath atmosphere had wrapped her round, as it had enveloped her fellows. The cynic could see that his marble Andromeda was fast turning into an Andromeda of alabaster. Alabaster needs more tender handling than marble. The deposit placed in the Captain's hands seemed to have become self-fertilising like an oyster. How else could it be that a friendless young woman, who had come on board with nothing but a second-class ticket, a pair of strange grey eyes, and a Grecian profile, should find all her wants guessed at and gratified, before she had had time to acknowledge them as wants at all? The pompous little steward 'put himself in four' (as the French say) on her behalf. The easiest of easy-chairs was always in waiting for her, in the shadiest patch on deck so soon as the top of her straw-hat could be seen in the saloon beneath the skylight. While simmering dowagers wiped their faces, palm-leaf fans lay ready to hand, to beat away the too bold air resting in heavy heat on her pure cheeks. She could no longer look in the direction of the damp decanter with its freight of rusty warm water. So sure as she did so, the steward's eyes goggled at her meaningly. A moment later, in spite of all her laughing, wondering protestations, she was assailed with a whole battery of bottles. For peace's sake she was constrained to make choice from among the cool effervescent drinks drawn up before her. She was like Beauty in the enchanted palace, whose sensations were responded to as soon as they were born — but where was the BEAST?

The mystification gave rise to the sweetest of day-dreams. Whether the mysterious guardianship was exerted, like an electric wire of love, from the home she had left – whether it was held by some loyally-loving soul on board, she could not so much as conjecture. It was always there – like a soothing magnetic influence. Sometimes she fancied it must be very close to her – only there was nobody exactly like the Beast on board. The cynic, to be sure, in his aloofness from his kind, had something of the untamed beast about him; but then he never came to her to be stroked. He spoke rarely, and his rare speech was only exchanged with two persons – the Captain, who was 'boss' on deck, and the steward, who was 'boss' down below.

By the time the ship had passed through the Tropic Belt most of the resources in the way of amusement had been exhausted. The Trades, in rescuing the vessel from the doldrums, had been so much in earnest, that before long they would launch her into the 'roaring Forties' south of the Line. They had not quite abandoned her yet, but took her up and dropped her capriciously, treating her very much after the manner of a sovereign to a court favourite.

The cynic did not as yet admit to himself that he was well content they should drop her thus. He would never have allowed that, of his own accord, he indulged in the ridiculous visions that forced themselves upon him as he stood night after night intently watching the heaped-up glories in the west. Mad visions of finding the ship converted into a love-laden *Flying Dutchman* everlastingly sailing over such a glowing sea as this, to such an impalpable shore as the landscape in the clouds. With only one passenger, whom he would have chosen! The rest were for the most part sensible, prosaic folk, who would have looked properly disconcerted had it been suggested to them that, instead of sailing direct to Melbourne, they should make tracks for airy cities built up of glittering hues.

CHAPTER IV

The cynic did not drivel in the morning. It was his wont to wake himself early and think over a subject he had in his mind to write about. The subject was to bear upon the futility of giving the reins to the indulgence of the weakness called sentiment. He had his arguments all ready before coming on board. The perplexing part of it was, that although he was as much convinced of their soundness as ever, he did not see his way to putting them as clearly as he would have wished. He woke himself up on purpose to think of them at such an early hour, one morning in particular, that his ideas respecting sentiment were rather confused. They were mixed up with a sort of apathetic wonder at the noise of the swishing of water overhead. He supposed, lazily, that the middies must be washing the deck earlier than usual.

He felt no curiosity, however, about the change of time, being in the condition of sleepy receptiveness which makes everything indifferent to us. Neither did he trouble himself so far as to open his half-closed eyelids, even when a sort of red glare pervaded the darkness before them. Half-raising them at last, he saw – always with the same dream-like stolidity of gaze — that the sunrise seemed to illuminate his cabin in bursts of crimson light, and that the calm sea, lying tranquilly before his port-hole, was stained a deep carmine. He would have shut his eyes again on this phenomenon, if his sight had been the only sense appealed to. But a vigorous call was suddenly made upon his hearing and smelling perceptions as well.

Through the tarred planks over his head came the discordant sound of a woman's agonised scream – through the chinks and crannies of his cabin came a sickening scent of burning. Away went the thread of his argument against sentiment; away went the fag-end of his meaningless dream! As he bounded on to the cabin floor, a hundred trembling wretches, waking to so cruel a mockery of the morning sun, shrieked and raved to the Captain and the Omnipotent to save them from the flames.

Mr Grimwood's cynicism ensured his keeping a cool head. One glance at the deck was enough to convince him that in a very few hours the ship would be nothing more than a flaming tar-barrel. The fire, he could see, must have been working in an underhand way in the hold, from the mouth of which it was coming up now as from the bottomless pit. There was something so sublime in its greed of prey, as it rolled up in scorching volumes of transparent blood-colour, that he stood watching it for a few seconds, unheeding the yells of the passengers.

There was a show being made of keeping the triumphant flames at bay, whereat they crouched like a panther preparing for a final spring. But Mr Grimwood could see through this pretence from the first. The real work of the moment lay in the getting out of the boats for escape. But two of the boats were already useless, and the others could never have held the souls, all counted, on board. The cynic's theories about sentiment were strangely revolutionised as he went below and passed the open cabin-doors. Of all the distorted faces that he saw, how many would ever shape themselves into a laugh again?

The one cabin-door that he stopped at was ajar. In his hurry he hardly made a show of knocking before he pushed it open. Already there was a thin smoke spreading itself over the saloon. Inside the cabins the air was unnaturally warm. The cynic knew that all this was real. He knew that he had no more proprietorship over the girl he had come to save than he had over the ship itself. Yet it would have been just as easy to tell the upstart flames overhead to lie down and lick at empty space as to tell his own foolish heart to stop beating with unreasonable, exultant joy while he edged his way into the little cabin. He had hungered for it so often in his dreams – for just what had come to pass now! Only, as a dying man, he might speak without attuning his voice to a pitch of artificial coldness – he might look without dreading lest the love-light in his eyes should betray him. He had forced his way through with the one thought only uppermost in his mind. The sinister glare from above – the crackling noise of the flames as they ran around the mainmast – the ugly chorus of screams overhead – screams of vitality that will not be tortured out of being, and protests against surrendering itself: all these were ministers to his absorbing passion. Now that he had passed into the cabin, pity and tenderness for its occupant swallowed up the egotistic triumph.

She was crouched on her berth like one waiting; partly smothered up in the worn plaid shawl, an old-fashioned covering of modern date, invested with all the grace of ancient drapery in the cynic's eyes – partly wrapped round by layers of brightly-dark hair, that lost itself somewhere in the blankets beneath her. Through all the terror in her drawn face, there was a something of expectation in the startled eyes – a vague trust that the guardianship she had taken refuge in would not forsake her in this pass. It could not be that the unknown power so quick to divine her wants, to forestall her fancies, to humour her passing whims, should leave her here, until her white skin shrivelled away with the heat and her voice was strangled by the smoke in the middle of its prayer for help. She had not so much as uttered one cry as yet. When Mr Grimwood made his way in she broke into a sob of relief.

'I knew you would come,' she said. 'You are come to take care of me!'

Perhaps if the goggle-eyed little steward had come in she would have said the same thing. Any one appearing at this crisis must be the embodiment of the invisible love that had cherished her. Only it is doubtful whether, even at this supreme moment, the red light could have transformed the perky expression of the little steward as it had transformed Mr Grimwood's. Women's rights' champions are without doubt altogether right. They have no end of solid grievances to redress. Let them bring about – if they can – social, intellectual, and muscular equality between the sexes. There is a certain sentimental instinct they can never do away with – the blind, unreasoning sense of comfort a trembling, frightened woman feels when a strong, earnest man takes her under his protection in a moment of danger.

There was such a volume of father-like, lover-like tenderness in Mr Grimwood's tone as he came closer to reassure her – if the fire had curled itself round her doorway as the faint wreaths of smoke were beginning to curl she could not but have taken hope. He did not even hurry her unduly, though he knew that every second lost was a chance of life gone. He kneeled down by her berth – she had held out her hands to him as he came in – and holding her hands he spoke.

'She should go in the first boat,' he told her; 'the sea was so calm that the journey would be an easy one – they were within a hundred miles of Cape Town – he knew she was a brave girl and would do as he told her – he guaranteed to save her, but she must dress without loss of time – never mind what she put on – he would bring her a cloak and wraps from his cabin – in a minute he would be back again for her – only she must not lose any time.'

He was happier than he had ever been in his life as he scrambled together the coverings in his cabin that were to protect her from the chill sea-air. He dived into his trunk for a small treasure-box filled with his money and valuables, and carried it out with the wraps. When he returned to Miss Leighton's cabin the saloon was already dusky with smoke. She was waiting for him, dressed as when she came on board, and held close to his arm as he piloted her through the tumult below to the deck.

She could not help clinging to him afresh, with a gasp of horror, when she saw the scene above. It is all very well for people to die when they are let down to it by long illness or age! To be forced out of life so summarily – to be whipped into the green deep water, from which all your body shrinks, by the tingle of an unnatural smart against your flesh, is enough to make you shriek and protest. To see your own belongings in the same plight is enough to make you blaspheme. As for the sense that your kind is suffering along with you – there is not much comfort to be got out of it. Companionship in the search for glory is quite another thing. Warfare is as much a preparation for death as an illness without the bodily attenuation. A company of soldiers incite each other to mount a breach. On board a burning ship there is no glory to be gained – no predominant feeling for the most part, but a frenzied desire to save self. Nothing but a system of discipline can prevent the weak from being sacrificed to the strong.

There was just so much discipline on board, that the Captain's roaring order to call up the women and children was attended to. They were wailing as they were hustled into the boat. No mother set her foot in it until every child belonging to her had been tumbled in before her. Wives were in a sad pass. They clutched at their husbands and smuggled them into the boat at the risk of upsetting it.

Just as it was about to be pushed off, Mr Grimwood's peremptory voice was raised high. 'Stop a moment!' he called loudly; 'another lady!'

At the instant of Miss Leighton's leaving him he put his small strong-box into her hands. She remembered afterwards that he had spoken quietly, but with wonderful quickness and clearness, as if these few last sentences were the outcome of a whole world of thought he had been fain to conceal. She seemed to read in his face that he looked for nothing but death after she had gone from him, and that as death only it would not be loathsome to him. She would have thought herself contemptible if at such a moment she had fettered her demonstrations by any apprehensions as to the after-construction that might be put upon them. She raised her face to his, put both her arms about his neck, and kissed him on the lips, as if in tearing her body away she were leaving her soul in his keeping. Then it was that he said what was on his mind.

'I can't help myself, darling! It's just as well that I should be going out of the world. We couldn't have made things square, I know! I only want you to remember that I would rather die like this than live as I did before I saw you.'

If he had more to explain, there was no time for it.

The sad boat pushed off, and already a wild fight for the means of salvation was raging all round him. The cynic watched the little boat so long as it remained within sight. It was cheering to see it pass out from the ghastly red influence of the ugly flames, into the sweet gold-scattering light of the morning sun. When it was lost in the brightness of those wholesome beams, the apotheosis of the cynic had begun. Who will say he was to be pitied? A barren life is not such a boon that any, save the timorous, need cling to it. But it is worth living even through a barren life to know an instant's unalloyed happiness at the last. What if the happiness involve the surrender of all your finely-constructed theories? – if it prove that you have been blundering from the beginning? What if the discovery come too late for you individually? You could not have made such a discovery without incorporating yourself so far with humanity as to die Christ-like – hoping for all! For to know the rapture of merging your spiritual being into that of another is dimly to conceive the possibility of an after-fulness of content for all that part of your nature which is not entangled with the bodily mechanism. That is why – since materialists logically maintain that the heart is nothing more than a muscular viscus, and the brain a whitish viscus, and tell us that the dissolution of these two means the annihilation of the keenly-conscious self – we, being unable to gainsay in truth a single reason advanced by materialists, may find an aimless life atoned for by an unreasoning flash of hope at the last. No matter how it is brought about, to die while you are in possession of it is to rejoice that you were born. Who would refuse the alternative?

Perhaps Miss Leighton, finding the cynic's money heavy and cold compared with the cynic's love, wished in after-years that she had flung it into the boat and stayed behind herself, to share in a hope-crowned death. Perhaps the shadowy outline in the Plymouth harbour developed into a prosaic husband, who liked modern cooking better than Greek art. Perhaps his wife thought sometimes of a tranquil southern sea, all aglow with a lurid stain – a sea ready to take into mysterious depths of changing colour two tightly-locked bodies that should never have been separated. Perhaps she dreamed all this after a futile fashion of her own. It is one thing to poetise about going to the bottom of the sea when in a cheerful sitting-room with a bright fire, and another thing to be brought face to face with it on a flame-shrouded ship a hundred miles from land.

As for deciding whether the cynic's fate or the girl's was the better one – it is for each one to judge according to his lights.

Clara Cheeseman

Married for his Money

1878

I

Those persons who were fortunate enough to be acquainted with the Repton family, wondered how they lived. Mr Repton could not be exactly described as having no visible means of support; for he received from a grateful country the pension of £200 per annum; but it is well known that such an income is quite inadequate to supply the wants of a fashionable family.

Auckland is supposed to be a cheap place; but even there, to provide several young ladies with three-button kid gloves, and prunella walking shoes alone, without reckoning other equally indispensable articles, is no joke; and then they have also to be taken out to every entertainment of the day, and be present, as a matter of course, at the vice-regal and other balls. All must acknowledge that their parents have managed well if they find their accounts balance at the end of the year. This small sum, however, was all that the Reptons had to depend on, and they contrived to keep their footing in society, or thought they did, which nearly amounts to the same thing. If Mr Repton was sometimes troubled with little bills, or seen in company with a professional money-lender, who had the reputation of charging higher interest than any of his Auckland brethren, it was nobody's business; and if anyone deserved blame it was the niggardly New Zealand Government, whose miserable pittances were not sufficient for the support of a respectable family.

At the time of which we are about to write, Mrs Repton was engaged in projecting an evening party. She very seldom entertained her friends; it was so much cheaper to go out than to receive company in her own house; so the unusual event required considerable thought and preparation.

'I think, my dear,' she observed to Mr Repton, who lay on the sofa, reading a new novel ('A Struggle for Existence'), 'that we had better order the refreshments from Candytuft's this time. You know you have not paid Joffee yet for the last affair.'

'Well, how was I to pay him? I am surprised when I succeed in paying anyone. Thank goodness we are going to get one of the girls off at last! I suppose that Simpelson will come down with something handsome.'

'Don't allude to it so heartlessly,' said Mrs Repton, making a great show of her pockethandkerchief. 'If it were not for our unhappy position, I should be spared the humiliation of seeing my daughter marry beneath her.'

'I see more cause for rejoicing than humiliation, about it. A man with £40,000 does not turn up every day. If you could contrive it, Emily, it would be as well for him to bear the expenses connected with the wedding. I could not borrow another penny now, if I were to tramp Queen-street from morning till night.'

'I have arranged that already,' said Mrs Repton. 'He is a good-natured young man, and easily led. It is quite a charity to relieve him of some of his superfluous cash. Those men who have become suddenly rich are never happy, except when they are spending, and he seemed quite pleased when I just hinted how he could assist us.'

'So much the better; he may please himself in that way as long as he likes. One blessing is that he is fairly presentable, and, so long as he does not open his mouth to say anything, may pass for a gentleman. Give him a hint, if you can, not to wear so much jewelry.'

'I will see about that,' said Mrs Repton, 'but we cannot be too careful. You offended him, you know, last night, by remarking on it. He is improving fast, and after all is not so bad, considering his former station. I was very glad to hear that both his parents are dead, and I cannot learn that he has any relations here. It would be dreadful to have a crowd of vulgar people all claiming relationship with one.'

'I should prefer them to a crowd of debt collectors, my dear,' remarked her husband. 'I believe – yes, there is Simpelson walking down the road. Now, if he is coming here, you might get an advance, you know. If he is going to pay for everything, I don't see why he should not begin to do so at once, and then I will settle with both Candytuft and Joffee, and give something to Pinchbeck, to stop his mouth about that silver service you bought for Mrs Raymond.'

'It is an expensive habit, giving those wedding presents,' said Mrs Repton. 'I wish it would go out of fashion. Simpelson is not coming here, after all.'

Which was true, the object of their hopes did not enter the Repton residence. About a mile further on, he stopped before a very neat little house, with an orchard and vegetable garden attached.

Here, lived a family named Landon, who were not in Mrs Repton's set; Mrs Landon being a dressmaker, and her husband a market gardener. Mrs Landon, however, and her daughter Milly, had sometimes the honour of making the Misses Repton's dresses, and generally waiting a year before they were paid for their work.

On this morning Landon was in his garden, promenading the walks, armed with a large pruning knife, as sharp as a razor, with which, whenever he saw a tree or a shrub presuming to grow too luxuriantly, or not according to orthodox fashion, he immediately cut it down without mercy.

Evidently he was somewhat excited, and did not very well know what he was about, for he kept muttering fiercely to himself, and occasionally, with a more vehement gesture than usual, would savagely brandish his knife, and lop off the greater part of some offending plant.

When he observed Mr Simpelson at the gate, he scowled at him, and retreated to the back of the house. 'I won't speak to the fellow,' he muttered, 'though I should like to have the pleasure of kicking him. A good riddance for Milly, I say,' and a little apricot was cut down almost to the root.

Mr Simpelson looked very downcast as he came up the path to the door. He knocked gently, and was admitted by Mrs Landon, whose greeting was of the shortest and most unassuring kind. Evidently Mr Simpelson, though he might be worth £40,000, was no welcome visitor here.

He was shown into the room where Milly Landon sat at her sewing machine. Now, Miss Milly was a very pretty girl indeed; with hair and eyes as black as jet, and being well skilled in her trade, and very tasteful (which all dressmakers are not), was always the perfection of neatness and good taste in attire, and looked what Mrs Repton would have called 'superior to her station'.

She had been engaged to Simpelson for four years, during which time he had been an unsuccessful searcher for gold at Hokitika. He would have starved there, had it not been for the pecuniary assistance of the Landons, who had forwarded him, from time to time, enough support till something should turn up.

Something did turn up; a rich old grand-uncle was considerate enough to die, and wishing to disappoint his nearer relatives in England, left his property to Simpelson, whom he had never seen. Simpelson became a personage of importance, and wedged his way into higher society than that of the Landons. He was very affectionate to them, at first; but soon began to think that it would be as well to marry into a more stylish family. Milly was very nice-looking and lady-like; but fancy, having old Landon for his father-in-law, a mere market gardener, and who had, worse than that, even been a milkman! The idea was revolting to his noble soul, and when he became acquainted with the Reptons, who quite charmed him by their gracious condescension, the superior acquirements of Miss Blanche Repton decided the question. With such a wife, he might hope to rise in the fashionable world, and then after all, it would be very much better for Milly to marry some one in her own walk of life. She was not fitted to be the mistress of a large establishment, such as he intended to have, and ought to thank him for having discovered this fact.

But these convincing arguments did not seem to give him confidence, when he was in her presence. He looked woefully embarrassed, and presented a most ridiculous appearance. Mr Simpelson had, since the arrival of his fortune, indulged in a style of dress resembling that often affected by lucky diggers, and other suddenly-enriched mortals. Although it was only eleven in the forenoon, he was in full evening costume; his black suit was of superfine cloth, his new boots creaked with every step he took. The jewelry that the misguided young man wore would have realised a small fortune; coral and gold studs, and sleeve links, a gold watch with a guard that was nearly thick and strong enough to be used as a dog chain, and from which were suspended various ornaments, while six rings studded with enormous gems, adorned his fingers. He sat down when invited to do so, and feeling uncommonly nervous, mopped his face with an embroidered cambric handkerchief that diffused a fragrance throughout the room.

Deep silence prevailed. Milly would not speak first, but gazed at the bedizened figure before her, with something like contempt.

At last, Simpelson, having composed a speech, said, 'I suppose you know the object of my visit, Miss Landon?'

'I think you fully explained in your letter,' said Milly.

'I did; but I thought it my duty to call, to thank you, and Mr and Mrs Landon, for what you have done for me, and to make some return. I was afraid you would not understand my motives, and think me ungrateful.'

'I believe we perfectly understand them, Mr Simpelson.'

'Good gracious, Milly!' said the unhappy Simpelson, again mopping his face, 'don't look at me in that way. I am sure I have done all for the best, yet your mother looked at me as if I was a houtcast' – Mr Simpelson occasionally murdered the Queen's English, though he had wonderfully improved, in that respect, since his introduction to the Reptons – 'and your father would not speak to me at all. But I'm willing to forgive anything, and I feel sure we made a great mistake. We are so unsuited to each other in every way.'

'I quite agree with you, Mr Simpelson, and feel grateful to you, for having made the discovery in time,' said Milly, her eyes fixed on the gigantic watch-chain.

'But I hope, really now, you'll allow me to do something for you. I've not forgotten how your father helped me at Hokitika. If you will give him this, and accept this for yourself, Milly, I shall be very happy, and you may always depend on me as a friend; I hope you will always think of me as one.'

Milly had been very cool and contemptuous up to this point; but now she flushed scarlet with anger, and wounded pride, as the magnanimous Simpelson drew from a bulky pocket-book, two cheques. One was for the amount that her father had lent him, with interest added, nicely calculated up to the very day, the other was payable to Miss Landon, and for the sum of 200 guineas.

'No, thank you,' she said rising hastily. 'We are fully repaid already, Mr Simpelson, for what we have done for you. All that I desire is, that you will return my letters.'

'I will send them up to-night,' faltered Simpelson. 'I am very sorry, Mil – hem, Miss Landon, that you take such a wrong view of the matter. You are very unjust to me. I – I – I think I'd better be goi – .'

'Wait a moment, if you please.' And Milly swept with dignity into the next room, where she was heard pulling open drawers, and rustling among papers. She returned with an apron full of a most extraordinary collection of articles, and in her hand a parcel containing the jewelry that Simpelson had presented to her, in the first excitement of his newly acquired riches, and before he had been captured by the Reptons.

In the parcel, were seven brooches and lockets, four pairs of earrings, three bouquet holders, six bracelets, and a dozen rings at least.

'I ought never to have taken them,' she observed, handing him the parcel; 'I never should, if I had not been blind and foolish. As for these,' and she indicated the contents of her apron, a mass of lace and silk ties, collars and cuffs, gloves, fans, and many an ill scrawled and spelt letter of Simpelson's, 'I shall dispose of them more easily;' and she threw them passionately into the fire, where they blazed up with such flame and thick black smoke, that neighbours concluded the Landon's chimney had caught fire, and some officious persons rushed to ring the fire-bells.

I fear that Miss Milly's conduct cannot be excused, it was both ridiculous and unladylike, and Mr Simpelson felt more than ever convinced of his wisdom. Miss Blanche, he was sure, would never have behaved in such an unbecoming manner. He ventured to press his cheques on Milly again, who took them this time, and added them to the blazing pile. And then he retired, as quickly as possible, taking the rejected jewelry with him. It would come in very nicely for presents to the bridesmaids, Mrs Repton having already given him a hint of what would be required in that way. As for Milly, she returned to her work, and stitched away very composedly at Miss Blanche's wedding dress, a splendid garment of white satin and lace.

II

That day week, Simpelson dressed himself with unusual care, and repaired to the Reptons. It was the evening of their party, and Mrs Repton had brought together a very select company.

Her intended son-in-law was improving so rapidly in manners and dress, under her tuition, that she did not fear presenting him to anyone.

As, however, the house was small, and the number of guests limited, she displayed great skill in securing the attendance of those whom she considered the very cream of Auckland society.

She had invited Sir John Jennings, Bart., then travelling in New Zealand. He had only been two days in Auckland, but Mrs Repton had heard of him, and determined he should grace her party with his aristocratical presence. It was a pity he was not a Duke, or Earl at the least; but those characters do not come round every day, and in default of something better, a Baronet would do very nicely. Besides this gentleman, also came the Hon. John Sanders Sanderson, Mrs and Miss Sanderson. Mr Sanderson was a member of the Legislative Council, and chiefly remarkable for a golden silence, generally preserved both there and everywhere else. There was also Alexander Rufus Marchmont, Esq., and the Misses Marchmont. He was a Canterbury run holder, and supposed to be immensely wealthy, and having been on a visit to the Lake district, was taking Auckland on his way home. Also there were two M.G.A.'s, a Colonial judge, a distinguished lawyer, and various members of their families; Mr Scampion, and old colonist, whose antecedents were rather shady, but were thickly gilded over by his money, with his showy wife and daughters. Mr Layman, a high and mighty Government officer, and Mrs Layman; and a few bank clerks and young ladies of the neighbourhood, added chiefly on account of their extraordinary dancing and conversational powers.

Mr and Mrs Repton received their friends with that politeness and urbanity of manner so natural to them. Simpelson behaved very creditably, and followed Mrs Repton's delicate suggestions, by leaving most of his heavy jewelry at home. Miss Blanche was radiant, and exquisitely dressed, and she and Simpelson looked so well, when they stood up together in the first quadrille, that Mrs Repton thought that after all, her daughter might have done worse.

As she never had an opportunity of doing otherwise, perhaps this reflection was unnecessary. The evening was perfectly charming. Simpelson had been practising dancing with all his energies for a fortnight before, and acquitted himself very well. In fact, he presented such a distinguished appearance, that Mr Scampion, who had heard there was to be a baronet at the party, imagined he must be the great man, and persisted in addressing him as Sir John.

At length the company repaired to the room where supper had been laid. This was the kitchen; but the bare, unlined walls, and the whitewashed chimney, and cooking stove, had been so skilfully concealed with ferns, green boughs, and great masses of white clematis, then in bloom, that no one would have suspected the fact. The supper was sumptuous; for Mr Candytuft, having been paid in advance, was so surprised and gratified at the unusual promptitude of the Reptons, that he had done his very best. Mr and Mrs Repton were beaming with delight, on their assembled friends, when there seemed to be some disturbance in the entrance hall, and voices heard in high altercation.

'Now, just stand out of the way, my good fellow. I know he's in here and it's strange if a man can't speak to his own brother.' Great scuffling followed, then the door was burst open, and in walked a dirty, rough-looking man, without coat or waistcoat, his tall felt hat perched on the back of his head, and his muddy boots leaving many fine impressions on the spotless floor.

On he strode, right up to Mr Simpelson, grasped that gentleman's reluctant hand, and wrung it heartily.

'Well, Jack, my boy, right glad I am to see you! It's sometime since we set eyes on one another, I was working on the railway down at Dunedin, when I heard of your stroke of luck. Thinks I, there's shares for you, Bill Simpelson, Jack won't grudge his brother a slice. You're in good quarters here, old boy, risin' in life I should say.'

All this had not taken five seconds. The Reptons were paralysed, and could not have uttered a word, had it been a matter of life and death. Mrs Repton stared at the intruder with fixed and glassy eyes. Simpelson was as white as a sheet, and attempted to gasp out a faint denial.

'My good fellow – er – look here, you must be mistaken, you know; you take me for someone else.'

'Well!' exclaimed Mr W. Simpelson, 'if ever I heard the like of that! Ain't you afraid of the earth opening, and swallowing you up? Oh Jack!' he added, with real emotion, 'I never thought you'd deny your own brother.'

Meanwhile, the others had been making remarks on the occurrence.

'How extraordinary!' said the Hon. J. Sanders Sanderson.

'It reveals the hollowness and corruption of colonial society,' observed the baronet, who was surreptitiously taking copious notes. They were afterwards inserted in his valuable work on the Australian colonies.

'I shall faint soon,' said Miss Theresa Sanderson, 'if that horrid man is not put out. Why don't they put him out, Mr Cashman?'

'Why,' said that young gentleman, a rising bank clerk, 'I suppose they don't like to turn out their future relations.'

'Delightful!' said Mrs Scampion, 'it is evidently the first scene of a charade. What perfect acting! Mrs Repton always has something new and original at her parties.'

'Just look at old Repton,' sneered Mr Scampion, 'I'll bet fifty to one he's thinking how he's to explain it all. Simpelson don't seem over pleased to see his brother again!'

'It serves them richly right,' said Mrs Layman, who before the announcement of Simpelson's engagement, had patronised him most indefatigably, 'I detest such fortune-hunting.'

Mr Repton saw the smiles and glances of his guests, heard some of these remarks, and the suppressed laughter of the bank clerks and young ladies. His indignation was at boiling point; he rose and was about to thunder forth some sentences, when suddenly his countenance changed, he smiled blandly, and said, 'Poor fellow! I see it all. Ladies and gentlemen, you must excuse this little interruption of the harmony of the evening. Simpelson, I am delighted to find that you have such a near relation as a brother living! I hope he will permit me to offer him some refreshment. We require no introduction; Mr William, I think;' and Mr Repton actually extended his lily white hand, which never in all his lifetime had done a hard day's work, and it was grasped in the rough and horny palm of the railway navvy, with a vigour that made him repent his cordiality.

'Any friend of Jack's, sir, is one of mine. Your health, sir; and glad I am to know you!' and the wine-glass was set down again emptied.

Mr Repton now said a word or two in Mr Simpelson's ear. He had been unable, after his last effort, to do anything but sit still, and stare at his brother; but now he rose and whispered something to him.

'Well, Jack,' replied that person audibly, 'I don't care if I do. I'm not exactly of your friends' sort. You have risen to a higher spear, old fellow. Good evening, ladies and gentlemen,' and with an awkward bow, that sent the Misses Marchmont off into convulsions of laughter, he suffered himself to be led from the room.

Mr Repton followed them, but returned after a few minutes. He came in smiling. 'A most laughable affair,' he said, 'if it were not for the sad fact that the poor fellow is a lunatic.'

'A lunatic!' exclaimed Mrs Repton, taking up the cue at once, 'I thought so! His eyes rolled frightfully.'

'I knew it at once, and so thought it best to get him out of the way quietly,' continued Mr Repton. 'He escaped from the asylum this morning, and thought he recognised his brother in Mr Simpelson, who really resembles him very much.'

'So he does,' said Mr Margin, the lawyer, who prided himself on his penetration. 'I saw it as soon as he entered the room.'

'Mr Simpelson,' said Mr Repton, 'had the good sense and presence of mind, after the first shock, not to contradict the assertions the unhappy man made in the aberrations of his intellect. He deserves our thanks; had he lost his temper, as most men would have done, the maniac might have been provoked to some desperate deed. I tremble to think of what might have happened!'

'It is just like him, so unselfish!' said Mrs Repton, 'I can breathe freely now;' which was quite true.

'Really, Repton ought to be in the General Assembly,' whispered Cashman to his next neighbour, 'did you ever hear a more plausible account? It won't do, though, too transparent.'

'Disgraceful,' said Mrs Layman. 'I am perfectly astonished at the effrontery of these people. Not all the gold in the universe would tempt me to admit that Simpelson to my house!'

It was very sad for the Reptons, but the charm of the evening was gone, never to return. Very glad were they when it was over. When their friends had gone, Mrs Repton broke out with, 'I knew it all. I felt sure something would happen of this kind! After this Blanche cannot disgrace herself by marrying such a low fellow. That brother of his would be everlastingly appearing.'

'Mrs Repton,' said Repton, solemnly waving his cigar, 'you are a goose, to use a very mild expression.'

'Of course I am, whenever I do not agree with you,' answered his wife.

'My dear, don't lose your temper. A woman never should; it induces premature age.'

'I know I look old, Mr Repton, living as I do, with all the care and trouble of the family dragging me down.'

'Listen to me,' said Repton. 'This Simpelson, so far as I can make out, taking him all in all, is a very decent fellow. He is steady in his habits; his manners are not amiss; and better than all, he has £40,000. Money, my dear, is of great importance to us. It is not of great importance what our friends who were here to-night, think. Simpelson can give his brother three or four thousand, he will never miss it, and stipulate he is not to show himself again. What can be easier. I thought you were a sensible woman, Emily; now, to-night, if I had not had the spirit to get up that monstrous fib about the asylum, I believe you and Simpelson would have allowed that man to say and do exactly as he liked, and ruined everything.'

'And what good do you think you did? Not one of them believed it.'

'What does that matter?' rejoined her husband; and then, bursting into a loud laugh, he exclaimed – 'It was perfectly splendid to see Simpelson wither up when the fellow came in! What does Blanche think of it?'

'Blanche,' said her mother, 'will never suppose that he really was an escaped lunatic. I shall take care of that.'

About three weeks after this, a fashionable wedding took place, at which several clergymen assisted one another, and a numerous crowd of bridesmaids attended the beauteous and richly-attired bride.

Blanche Repton became Mrs Simpelson, and received congratulations and costly presents from more friends than she was aware she possessed; for it was as well to be on good terms with a young couple who started in life with £40,000.

Milly Landon was acquainted with all the fine doings at the Reptons, and saw the hundredweight of bride cake borne triumphantly to the house, uncovered to the vulgar public eye, in a common baker's cart, for which negligence Mrs Repton sharply reprimanded Mr Candytuft.

Milly was even present at the wedding, in a quiet corner of the church, unnoticed by anyone, and did not seem remarkably heart-broken at the spectacle. There is now a Madame Blanchard, milliner and dressmaker, who has a stylish establishment in Auckland. I think that the elegant and polite Madame very much resembles Milly Landon, and she certainly speaks English with great correctness, considering her foreign extraction. There is also a M. Blanchard, and he is very like a certain young Frenchman, a working jeweller by trade, who used to be intimate with the Landons, before Mr Simpelson's frequent visits threw him rather into the shade.

As for Simpelson, he flourished more and more, and so did the Reptons. Mrs Repton always speaks of him in a most touching manner, and declares that he is the best of husbands to her dear Blanche, and that she herself looks upon him with as much affection as if he were her own son. And so she ought, for Simpelson paid all the bills when he became one of the family, and has continued to do so ever since. Mr Repton takes care that he does not waste his money, and as Simpelson has been troubled no more by his affectionate brother, nothing has occurred yet to disturb the happiness of this united family.

Mrs Simpelson has money without end to spend as she likes, is always beautifully dressed (she is the chief customer of Madame Blanchard), and is perfectly happy. She firmly believes that her husband's talents would have raised him to a high position, even had he never inherited forty thousand pounds.

Ada Cambridge

The Wind of Destiny

1889

The yachtsmen of the bay had been jubilant for months: this morning they were simply in ecstasies. Aha! it was their turn now. The sporting landsmen, magnates of the Melbourne Club and the great stations, who had had all the fun of the fair hitherto, were out of it this time. Oh, no doubt the new Governor was fond of his 'bike', and of a good horse, and of golf and polo, and the usual things; and, of course, he would be pleased with the triumphal arches and many gorgeous demonstrations of civic welcome and goodwill. But it was here that his heart would be – here, on the blue water, with the brethren of his craft. The country might not know it, but they knew it – mariners all, with their own freemasonry – they and he.

Every yacht of any consequence had been on the slips quite lately – as lately as was compatible with having paint and varnish dry. One or two of the newer models, wanting extra depth for their bulbous keels, were all but too late in their desire to be spick and span for the great occasion, but happily got a west-wind tide to float them up in time. And here they all were, scores and scores of them, as smart as they could be, with their beautiful sails going up, burgee and ensign flying in the breeze of the loveliest morning that could possibly have been provided for a national festival depending wholly on the weather for success. Yesterday it had been cloudy and gloomy, threatening rain; and to-morrow the north wind was to blow a sultry hurricane, opaque with dust; but to-day was heavenly. No other adjective, as Fanny Pleydell remarked, could describe its all-round perfection.

She was putting on her new white drill with the blue sailor collar, and her new straw hat with *Kittiwake* in gold letters on its new blue ribbon, and joyously addressed her brother through a passage and two open doors. He shouted back that it – the day – was 'ripping,' which meant the same thing. The only doubt about it was whether there would be wind enough.

There is always that doubt in yachting forecasts – that and the lesser fear of having too much; without which, however, yachting would be no fun at all. The *Kittiwake* (once the property of Adam Drewe, Esq.) was one of the crack boats, and Herbert Lawson – familiarly 'Bert' – was skipper and owner; and he had no mind to make himself a mere St Kilda decoration, as the land-lubbers in authority desired. Let the others tug at moorings if they chose, like wild birds tied by the legs, for hours and hours; the *Kittiwake* intended to fly when she opened her wings – weather permitting – and not submit to be treated as a slab in a canvas wall. She was going to meet the *Sunbeam* on free water, halfway down the bay, which, with any sort of wind, she could easily do, and still be back in time for the landing ceremony. And so Captain Bert kept an eye on tree branches and the set of anchored craft, while giving keen attention to his toilet, arraying himself in ducks like the driven snow and flannels like milk, waxing the curly points of his moustache till they tapered smoothly as a ram's horns, trimming his nails, and choosing a silk handkerchief to foam out of his breast pocket, as with a view to being inspected at close quarters through a strong telescope from the *Sunbeam's* deck.

But he was not dressing himself for the eyes of his vice-sovereign lady. It was for the sake of Lena Pickersgill and Myra Salter that he took such pains to render his handsome person as attractive as possible — and he did not quite know which.

Let me briefly explain. Old Lawson had died not long ago, leaving Herbert master of a good business in Melbourne, a good old family house at Williamstown (with the *Kittiwake* attached), and a most comfortable and even luxurious income for these post-boom days. Sister and brothers were sufficiently provided for – the former married, the latter studying for professions – and there was no widowed mother to take care of and defer to. Herbert was a man of domestic instincts, and turned thirty, and an arbitrary housekeeper bullied him. In short, every circumstance of the case cried aloud to him to take a wife, and he was as ready as possible to do so. But, of course, he wished to be a lover before becoming a husband, and fate had not yet clearly indicated the object he sought. He was a particular young man, as he had every right to be, and much in dread of making a mistake.

To-day he had arrived at the stage of choosing Lena and Myra, out of all the girls he knew, as the only possibles. Before night he hoped to have made up a distracted mind as to which of the two was the right one. Chaperoned by young Mrs Pleydell, both were to be guests of the *Kittiwake* for a long, fine day; and surely no better opportunity for the purpose could possibly have been devised.

Miss Salter was a Williamstown young lady, a schoolmate of Fanny Pleydell's, and was to embark with her hostess early. She was Fanny's candidate for the vacancy in the family, and rather suffered as such from the advocacy of her friend. Miss Pickersgill, belonging to a somewhat higher rank of life, lived in town, and was to be taken off from the St Kilda pier. Fanny had not wanted to have Lena asked, and for that reason Bert had firmly insisted on it. For that reason also he was inclined to promote her to the place of honour, rather than a girl whom he felt was being thrust down his throat.

But when he presently met the latter, and helped her into his dinghy with the tenderest air of strong protection, he thought her very sweet. She was a fair, slim thing, shy, unaffected, and amiable, and looked delicious in her white garb. All the ladies on board had to wear white to-day, to harmonize with the pearly enamel of the boat and her snowy new Lapthorn sails; and Myra had the neatest frock, and the prettiest figure to set it off. And, moreover, as he very well knew, *she* did not run after him when she was let alone.

He rowed her and his sister to the yacht, on which a numerous white-uniformed crew had made all ready for the start, and he sent the dinghy back in charge of his brother to pick up three more lady guests. These three were nobodies as regards this story – a homely aunt and two plain cousins, who had a family right to the suddenly valuable favours at their kinsman's disposal. They made up the number he thought would fill the cockpit comfortably – three on each side.

Mrs Pleydell, as soon as she had gained the deck, plunged below to investigate the matter of supplies; Miss Salter sat down to survey the scene, and the skipper sat down beside her. They had quite twenty minutes of quiet *tête-à-tête*, and to that extent placed Miss Pickersgill at a disadvantage.

'Isn't it a heavenly morning?' – or 'a ripping day,' as the case might be – was what they said; and 'I wonder will the breeze hold?' and 'Didn't you feel certain last night that it was changing for rain?' – conversation that had no literary value to make it worth reporting. However, it is not in words that incipient lovers explain themselves, but in the accompaniment to words played by furtive eyes and the corners of lips, and other instruments of nature inaudible to the outward ear. Myra's varying complexion confessed a lot of things, and the amount of intelligence in the horns of that moustache which had been waxed so carefully was wonderful. Indeed, it really seemed, thus early in the day, as if the die were cast. Both looked so handsome and felt so happy, and the weather and all the circumstances were so specially favourable to the development of kindly sentiments.

'I *am* so glad you were able to come,' the young man remarked, whenever they fell upon a pause, changing the emphasis to a fresh word each time. And the young woman put it in all sorts of modest but convincing ways that he was not more glad than she was. Oh, it was a heavenly morning, truly! And Mrs Pleydell and the crew were more and more careful to do nothing to mar the prospect.

But soon the fat aunt and excited cousins arrived, all in white, and as conscious of it as if dressed for a fancy ball, and it was time to make for the rendezvous across the bay. Thither were the yachts of all clubs converging in dozens and scores, like an immense flock of seabirds skimming the azure water, their sails like silver and white satin in the sun. As Bert Lawson steered his own, proudly convinced that she was queen of the company, he named his would-be rivals to his guest, keeping her so close to him that he had to apologise for touching her elbow with the tiller now and then. Occasionally he exchanged an opinion with the crew that the old so-and-so didn't look so bad, and they continually cocked their eyes aloft to where the blue ensign waved in the languid breeze. It wasn't every boat that could dip that flag to the new Governor – no, indeed!

'Isn't it a pretty sight?' the ladies cried to one another – and it certainly was. Even the prosaic shore was transfigured and glorious – in one place, at least. The St Kilda pier and the hotel, and the steep slope connecting them, smothered all over in green stuff and bunting, and packed with what appeared to be the whole population of the colony, was a striking spectacle as viewed from the sea. The most bigoted Englishman must acknowledge it.

'Oh,' exclaimed Fanny Pleydell, staring through a strong pair of glasses, 'I wouldn't have had you miss it for the world, Myra dear.'

'And yet I nearly did,' the girl replied, glancing at Bert from under her hat brim as he stood over her, intent on business. 'If mother had not been so much better this morning, I could not possibly have left her.'

The skipper ceased shouting to his too numerous men not to crowd the boat's nose so that he could not see it, and dropped soft eyes on his sister's friend. 'Dear, dutiful, unselfish little soul!' he thought. 'That's the sort of woman to make a good wife. That's the girl for me.' It was still not more than twenty minutes to eleven, and he had got as far as that.

But now Miss Pickersgill intervened. She put off from the gorgeous pier, which was not yet closed to the public, in the dinghy of a local friend, in order that the *Kittiwake* should not be burdened with its own. It afterwards transpired that she had engaged to grace the yacht of the local friend, and had thrown him over for Bert Lawson, having no scruples of pride against making use of him, nevertheless. She was a radiant vision in tailor-made cream serge, a full-blooded, full-bosomed, high-coloured, self-confident young beauty, with bold eyes and a vivacious manner, calculated to make any picnic party lively. As she approached, like a queen enthroned, all the male creatures hung forward to gaze and smile, Bert springing to the side to help her over – which was only what she expected and was accustomed to. And she jumped into the midst of the group around the cockpit, – four humble-minded admirers and one firm adversary, – chose her place and settled herself, nodding and waving salutations around, as if she were Mrs Bert already.

Myra's heart sank in presence of so formidable a rival. Myra was the daughter of a retired sea-captain in rather narrow circumstances; Lena's father was a stock-broker, and reputed to roll in money. She had fat gold bangles on her wrists, and a diamond in each ear. She lifted her smart skirt from a lace-frilled petticoat, and the serge was lined with silk. The dejected observer moved to make way for so unquestionable a superior. But Bert detained her with a quiet hand.

'Sit still,' he said. 'There is plenty of room.'

To her surprise and joy, she found he still preferred her near him. It was not money and gold bracelets that could quench her gentle charm.

And now the fun began. The yacht, with every stitch of canvas spread, set out upon her course, determined to be the first to salute her future commodore. There was just enough wind to waft her along with a motion as soft as feathers, as airy as a dream, and the heavenly morning, on the now wider waters, was more heavenly than ever.

'It's our day out, and no mistake,' quoth Miss Pickersgill, in her hearty way. 'Let's have a song, old chap' – to Bert – 'or do some thing or other to improve the occasion. What do you say, Mrs Pleydell?'

'I,' said the hostess cheerfully, but with tightened lips, 'am going to get you all something to eat.'

'And I'll go and help you,' said Myra, rising hastily.

'Oh, all right – go on; I'll keep 'em alive till you come back. Now then, tune up, everybody! I'll begin. What shall I sing, Mr Lawson?' with a languishing glance at him over her shoulder. '*You* shall choose.'

'I think you'd better whistle,' said Bert, whose eyes were on his sails, and his nose sniffing anxiously.

'All serene. I can do that too. But why had I better whistle?'

'Wind's dying away to nothing, I grieve to say.'

'By George, it is!' his young men echoed, in sympathetic concern. 'If we don't mind, we shall fall between two stools, and be out of everything.'

'What's the odds, so long as you're happy?' was Miss Lena's philosophic response. And they adopted that view. With every prospect of being ignominiously becalmed, out of the track of events in which they had expected to take a leading and historic part, they lolled about the deck and sang songs with rousing choruses – popular ditties from the comic operas of the day – and professed themselves as jolly as jolly could be.

'How fascinating she is!' sighed Myra Salter, listening from the little cabin to the voice of the prima donna overhead. 'I don't wonder they all admire her so much!'

'I am quite sure my brother does not admire her,' said Mrs Pleydell with decision. 'He thinks, as I do, that she is a forward minx – he *must*.' Bert's laugh just then came ringing down the stairs. In an interval between two songs, he and Miss Pickersgill were enjoying a bout of 'chaff' – rough wit that crackled like fireworks. 'Of course she amuses him,' said Fanny grudgingly.

'And isn't it lovely to be able to amuse people?' the girl ejaculated, envious still. 'She charms them so that they forget about the wind and everything. She is just the life and soul of the party, Fanny.'

'*I* think she spoils it, Myra. If we don't look out, we shall be having her serenading the Governor with "He's a jolly good fellow," or something of that sort. If she attempts to disgrace us with her vulgarity before him, clap your hand over her mouth, my dear. I shall.'

Myra laughed, and was somewhat comforted. But she still thought how lovely it would be to be able to amuse people and take them out of themselves. 'He would never be dull with her,' she thought sadly. 'I am so stupid that I should bore him to death.'

One of Miss Salter's unusual charms, perfectly appreciated by sensible Mrs Pleydell, and not overlooked by Bert, was a sweet humble-mindedness – a rare virtue in these days.

The first of several light luncheons was served on deck, without interrupting the concert. Between gulps of wine and mouthfuls of sandwich, Miss Pickersgill continued to raise fresh tunes, and the crew to shout the choruses, and the audience of fat aunt and simpering cousins to applaud admiringly. It was a case of youth at the prow and pleasure at the helm, and an abandonment of all responsibility. A dear little catspaw came stealing along, and hardly excited anybody. The yacht gathered way, and began to make knots again, faster and faster, but even that did not draw the light-hearted young folks from their frivolous pastime. Thanks to the syren of St Kilda, they had almost forgotten the errand they were on. It really did not seem to matter much to any one whether he or she met Lord Brassey or not; he had become an incident of the day, rather than its main feature.

Still, the eyes of the crew continually searched the horizon, and presently one man saw smoke where no one else saw anything, and out of that spot a faint blur grew which resolved itself into the *Aramac* with the Governor on board, and the

Ozone and *Hygeia*, its consorts. The three boats in a row advancing steadily, under all the steam they could make, were not unimpressive in their way, but the only thing the *Kittiwake* cared to look at was the lovely pillar of white cloud, shining like a pearl, which was recognised as the *Sunbeam* with all sail set. She was bearing off from the Government flotilla, dismissed from their company, superseded and discarded; but to yachtsmen's eyes she was a sort of winged angel, a spirit of the sea, and they but grubby mortals by comparison, common and gross.

'Why, why,' they exclaimed, with groans of regret, gazing on the fairy column as if that were all the picture, '*why* didn't they let him come up in her, and let us bring him? What does he want with a lot of cheap-jack politicians *here*? They just spoil it all.'

'It wouldn't be them if they didn't,' some one said, voicing a rather prevalent opinion. And in fact they were spoiling it rather badly on the *Aramac* just then, if all tales be true. They had not wanted Miss Pickersgill to show them how to do it.

It was past the hour fixed for the landing ceremonies – and the poor sun-baked crowds ashore would have been dropping with fatigue if there had been room to fall in – when Bert Lawson shouted 'Dip! dip!' to his brother, who held the ensign halliards, and was confused by the excitement of the moment. After all, the *Kittiwake* was first, and proud was every heart aboard when the cocked-hatted figure on the *Aramac's* bridge saluted her and the flag as if he had known and loved the one as long as the other. Every man and woman was convinced that he stood lost in admiration of her beauty and the way she was manœuvred. Bert brought her as close as was compatible with proper respect, and they all posed to the best advantage for the Governor's eye, Miss Pickersgill in front.

'*Now*, you fellows,' she panted breathlessly. 'All at once – "See-ee the conq-'ring he-e-e-ero" –'

But Mrs Pleydell's hand was up like a flash, and there was a 'Hsh-sh-sh!' like the protest of a flock of geese. The fair Lena was so taken aback that she nearly fell into the captain's arms. The captain did not seem to mind; his arm went round her waist for a moment almost as if it had the habit of doing it; and he whispered an apology that restored her self-control. At the same instant he signalled to the crew, and they burst into three great solid British cheers. Another signal stopped them from further performances, and the steamers swept by. The crisis of the day was over.

Then the *Kittiwake* turned and followed the fleet, and realized her remaining ambitions. She was back at St Kilda, with the yachts that had been lying there all the morning, by the time his great excellency, transhipped once more, arrived there. Through their glasses the ladies could see the procession of little figures along the pier, and the departure of the carriages after the guns had fired the salute; and they could hear the school children singing. When all was over, a sigh of vast contentment expressed the common thought, 'What a day we're having!' The turn of the landsmen had come, but no one at sea could envy them.

'Now we'll have a look at the *Sunbeam* as she lies,' said Bert, and then headed back for Williamstown.

'And we want some refreshment after what we have gone through,' said the hospitable hostess.

Luncheon was served for the third time, and subsequently two afternoon teas. The yachts, dissolving all formation, swam aimlessly about the bay, more like seabirds than ever, and took snap-shots at each other with their kodak cameras. Miss Pickersgill's singing powers failed somewhat, but she continued to chaff and chatter with the young men, breaking off at intervals to hail her friends on passing boats. Good-natured Fanny Pleydell laughed with the rest at the fun she made; the admiring aunt and cousins could not remember when they had been so entertained; and Myra Salter was satisfied at heart because Bert had never allowed her to feel 'out of it.' And so the happy day wore through. They had had seven hours together when they began to look for Lena's dinghy, and before separating they testified with one consent that they had never had a more delightful holiday, or, as Lena neatly phrased it, 'such a jolly high old time.'

'Then I'll tell you what we must do,' said the gratified host. 'Go out together – the same party, since we suit each other so well – on the sixteenth of next month. That's our opening day, Miss Pickersgill, as of course you know; and, with the Governor for commodore, it ought to be the best we've ever had.'

'All who are in favour of this motion,' chanted Lena, 'hold up your hands!'

Every hand went up at once, except Myra's. The shy girl looked to Fanny for an endorsement of the free and easy invitation, and Mrs Pleydell was knitting her brows. But soon she smiled consent, to please her brother, who, stealing behind Miss Salter unobserved, seized her two hands and lifted them into the air.

They imagined they were going to have their good time over again. They even anticipated a better one, though only of half the length. For whereas the wind had been too light on the 25th of October, it blew like business on the 16th of November, when it was of the last importance that it should do so. No more auspicious opening day had ever dawned upon Victorian yachtsmen. The Governor, who was *their* Governor for the first time in history, had consented to direct their evolutions in person. This alone – this and a good wind – assured laurels to the clubs of Hobson's Bay which all other clubs would envy them. The *Sunbeam* had been towed to the chosen anchorage; Government House was on board. All the swells, as Miss Pickersgill termed them, indigenous to the soil, would be lone and lorn at the races, because their Lord and Lady were away. If they offered their ears for a place in viceregal company, they could not get it. 'Aha!' said the yachtsmen one to another, 'it is our turn now.'

This time the *Kittiwake* took her own dinghy to St Kilda. She towed it along with her all the afternoon, as a brake upon the pace, which threatened to carry her beyond the position assigned to her in the wheeling line, for she was faster than the boats before and behind her. And so the services of local friends were not required on Miss Lena's behalf. Bert himself, in a very ruffled sea indeed, went off to the pier to fetch her. But not altogether for the sake of paying her special honour; rather, because it was most difficult to bring anything alongside to-day without bumping off fenders and on to new paint. He had had the kindest feeling for both girls during the past three weeks, but what little love he had fallen into was love for Myra Salter. He had just left her deeply in love with him. He had given her the card of sailing directions, taught her how to read the commodore's signals, and told her she was to be his captain for the day, as he was to be the crew's. Down in the small cabin, picking pecks of strawberries, with the assistance of the aunt and cousins, Mrs Pleydell's prophetic eye saw visions of an ideal home and family – that comfortable and prosperous domestic life which is the better and not the worse for having no wildfire passions to inflame and ravage it – and a congenial sister-in-law for all time. Myra lingered on deck to follow the movements of the tossing dinghy through the captain's strong field-glasses, also assigned to her exclusive use for this occasion. He had another pair – not quite so strong – for Miss Pickersgill.

Little did that young lady suppose that she was to play second fiddle for a moment. She wore another new dress and a ravishing peaked cap, much more becoming than the sailor straw. She smiled upon the skipper, struggling to hold the dinghy to the pier, as at a faithful bond-slave merely doing his bounden duty.

'It is our opening day!' she sang, as she flourished a hand to him. 'It – is – our – opening da-ay!'

'It is, indeed,' he shouted back. 'Made on purpose. Only I think we shall have too much of a good thing this time, instead of not enough. Wind keeps getting up, and we've reefed already.'

'Oh, it's stunning!' she rejoined, gaily skipping into the boat; she was a heavy weight, and nearly tipped it over. 'Let it get up! The more the merrier.'

'Yes, if there were going to be racing. I wish there was! We should just run away from everything.'

'Then let's race,' quoth Miss Pickersgill, as if commanding it to be done. 'Let's show the old buffer' – I grieve to say it was his sacred lordship she referred to – ' 'what the *Kittiwake* can do.'

Bert had to explain. It took him until they reached the yacht to make the young lady who looked so nautical understand what she was talking about. And after all she was inclined to be sentimentally hurt because he would not do such a little thing to please her.

The wind got up, more and more, showing that there was to be no monotonous repetition of the former circumstance. The *Kittiwake* danced and pranced as if the real sea were under her, and half a dozen dinghies trailed astern would hardly have made any difference. There was no sitting round the cockpit, as on drawing-room chairs, to flirt and sing; one side was always in the air, and the other all but under water, see-sawing sharply at uncertain intervals; and the ladies had to give their attention to holding on and keeping their heads out of the way of the swinging boom. Lena shouted to the men, who had to stick to business in spite of her, that it was the jolliest state of things imaginable, and said 'Go it!' to rude Boreas when he smacked her face, to encourage him to further efforts. But her five companions were more or less of the opinion that they had liked the first cruise better. The poor fat aunt was particularly disconcerted by the new conditions; she said she couldn't get used to the feeling of having no floor under her, and the sensation of the sea climbing up her back.

She was the first to say, 'No, thank you,' to strawberries and cream, and 'Yes, please,' to whisky.

Is there anything funny in having the toothache that people should laugh at the victim as at some inexhaustible joke? Ask the poor soul whose nerves are thus exquisitely tortured what *his* opinion is. He will tell you that it is one of the gravest elements in the tragedy of human pain; also that the heartless brute who sniggers at it ought to have thumbscrews put on him and twisted tight. Is there anything disgraceful in being sea-sick in rough weather, that those who don't happen to feel so at the moment should turn up their noses at the sufferers in contemptuous disgust? Emphatically not. It is a misfortune that may befall the best of us, and does, instead of being, as one would suppose, the penalty of a degrading vice, like delirium tremens. Why, even the *Sunbeam* was ill that afternoon – the first folks of the land, fresh from the discipline of a long and stormy voyage – which sufficiently proves the fact.

But when Myra Salter was observed to sit silent and rigid, with bleached lips and a corpse-like skin, it was with eyes that slightly hardened at the sight. Yes, even the captain's eyes! It is true he smiled at her, and said, 'Poor child!' and peremptorily ordered the useless stimulant, and was generally concerned and kind; but the traditional ignominy of her case affected him; her charm and dignity were impaired – vulgarized; and the flavour of his incipient romance began to go. Of course young men are fools – we all are, for that matter – and young love, just out of the ground, as it were, is like a baby lettuce in a garden full of slugs. And it is no use pretending that things are different from what they are. And if you want to be an artist, and not a fashionable photographer, you must not paint poor human nature, and leave the moles and wrinkles out. It is a pity that an estimable young man cannot be quite perfect, and that an admirable young woman should be unjustly despised; but so it is, and there's no more to be said.

Myra shook her head at the suggestion of whisky; only to imagine the smell of it was to feel worse at once – to feel an instant necessity to hide herself below. But Fanny Pleydell, coming upstairs at the moment when she was beginning to stagger down, caught her in her arms and held her back – a fatal blunder on Fanny's part.

'No, my dear, no!' she cried, on the spur of a humane impulse; 'you must *not* go into that horrible hole; it would finish you off at once. Besides, there isn't room for you; aunt and the girls are sprawling all over the place. Have a little spirits, darling – yes, you must; and keep in the fresh air if you want to feel better.'

She pressed whisky and water on the shuddering girl, and cruel consequences ensued. Bert turned his head away, and tried to shut his ears. Lena smiled at him in an arch and confidential manner. *She* was as bright and pretty as ever – more so, indeed, for the wind exhilarated her and deepened her bloom.

'I think,' she said, 'it is a great mistake for people who are not good sailors to go to sea in rough weather, don't you?'

Well, Bert almost thought it was. He was a very enthusiastic yachtsman, especially to-day, when he wanted the *Kittiwake* and all her appurtenances to be as correct as possible.

The drill was over, and the regiment of yachts disbanded. The *Sunbeam* had gone to a pier at Williamstown, and the commodore was receiving his new colleagues and entertaining them. The *Kittiwake* was off St Kilda, with her freight of sick on board. The aunt filled up one tiny cabin, the cousins another, and they groaned and wailed and made other unpleasant noises, to the amusement of a callous crew. Myra Salter, too helplessly ill to sit up without support while the boat rushed through the water with a slice of deck submerged, had sagged down to the floor of the cockpit, and now lay there in a limp heap, propped against Fanny's knees. She had not spoken for an hour, and during that time Bert had hardly noticed her. He had been devoting himself to Miss Pickersgill, so far as the duties of his official post allowed, as was only natural when she had become practically his sole companion, and when, as a lover of a good breeze and proper sailoring, she had proved herself so sympathetic.

Now he was rowing her home from the yacht to the shore. She sat facing him in the dinghy, with the yoke lines round her waist, and he could not keep his eyes from her brilliant person, nor keep himself from mentally comparing it with that sad wisp on the cockpit floor. She met his glance, and held it. They were both excited by the wind, the inspiring flight of the yacht, the varied interests of the opening day.

'Oh, it was splendid!' she exclaimed. 'Whatever the others may think about it, I know *I* never enjoyed myself so much in my life. And I *am* so much obliged to you for taking me, Mr Lawson.'

'You are the right sort to take,' replied Bert with enthusiasm; and he imagined a wife who would enter into his favourite pursuits like a true comrade. 'And I hope we shall have many a good cruise together.'

'It won't be my fault if we don't,' she said promptly.

'It won't be mine,' he returned. 'Consider yourself asked for every day that you'll deign to come.'

'What, for ever?'

'For ever.'

She looked at him archly, pensively, meaningly, with her head on one side. She was really very handsome in her coquettish peaked cap, and he reflected that she was evidently healthy and probably rich.

'You don't *mean* that, Mr Lawson?'

'I do mean it, literally and absolutely.'

'For every yachting day as long as I live?'

'For every yachting day, and every day that isn't a yachting day.'

She was so joyously flustered that she ran the dinghy into the pier. He had to catch her in his arms to prevent her going overboard. As there were people watching them from above, he could not kiss her, but he gave an earnest of his intention to do so at the first opportunity.

Of course she was the wrong one. He knew it no later than the next day, in his heart of hearts, though never permitting himself to acknowledge it, because he flatters himself that he is a gentleman. Equally, of course, he will go on to render his mistake irrevocable, and be miserable ever after, and make her so, from the highest motives. Already the wedding gown is bought, and they go together to ironmongers and upholsterers to choose new drawing-room furniture and pots and kettles for the kitchen. The marriage will surely take place when the bride has made her preparations, and anybody can foretell what the consequences will be. They will pull against each other by force of nature, and tear their little shred of romance to bits in no time. And then they will sink together to that sordid and common matrimonial state which is the despair and disgrace of civilization. She will grow fat and frowsy as she gets into years – a coarse woman, selfish and petty, and full of legitimate grievances; and he will hate her first, and then cease to care one way or the other, which is infinitely worse than hating. And so two lives will be utterly spoiled, and possibly three or four – not counting the children, who will have no sort of fair start.

And all because there was a bit of a breeze on the opening day of the season!

But such is life.

Marie Stanmore

In Wellington Was Consolation

1901

Jimmy McAndrew belonged to Dunedin, but something had happened down there which was to him more deplorable than the silting up of the channel, and he came up to Wellington in search of an off-shoot from the waters of Lethe, so that he might drink and forget. Consolation he knew there was none. He was but twenty-two, then, and probably had not heard of the wonderful cures affected by a physician named Time. These things put into more prosaic language mean that Jimmy had fallen in love with a married lady, who was given to flirting with young men of immature notions. Jimmy was of her last gathering, and had taken himself and his emotions with much seriousness, this being his first experience of the kind. At a certain stage of things McAndrew, senior, observing the folly of his son, casually offered him an advanced position in the Wellington branch of his business, but with considerable tact did not press the lad to accept. Bob Graham, a friend of Jimmy's, was told off to advise a removal from the scene of disaster. Graham and McAndrew, senior, smoked many pipes and drank many whiskies while arranging the plot, all of which was unknown to Jimmy, who worked right into their hands by accepting his father's offer. So it came about that a boat from the South landed him in Wellington one day, and a hansom took him to the house of a certain Mrs Russell in Thorndon. Mrs Russell was an old friend of his mother's, who from stress of circumstances was pleased to receive and chaperon well-referenced young men or maidens in the sanctity of her home for a monetary consideration. The McAndrews knew their son would be safe from the wiles of married Delilahs in that atmosphere when they arranged for him to board at Mrs Russell's.

On the morning after his arrival Jimmy walked along the Tinakori Road with the intention of getting down town to wire his mother of his safe landing. Mrs Russell had given him several directions about the way, but each one being more obscure than the other, he left the house knowing he must discover a way for himself. This he eventually did by crossing the earthquake-rent gully, and then sagaciously bailing up a letter-carrier for the rest. After sending his wire, he made for the beach and sat down to consider his case.

He was due to report himself at the office, but that could wait, he thought; for he wanted to have a little melancholy season all to himself before he took up the dreary burden of office graft again.

The tide was coming in, and a soft breeze was blowing off the water, and altogether conditions were conducive to sentimental reflection, and as he gazed dreamily towards Petone and the Rimutaka Mountains, beyond them came to him the vision of a woman in far off Dunedin. A Bible lay in his coat pocket. His mother had put it there when she bade him goodbye at Port Chalmers. She had thoughtfully marked several passages for his benefit, the seventh commandment, a line in the tenth, and a particular word of advice from Solomon to his son, which always has value because of that monarch's experience. Jimmy recollected the book, but the face of the woman in Dunedin came between it and him. He sighed. Mrs McAndrew had meant well, poor soul! For she was a good woman – just as good as a woman should be who has never had to work out intricate life questions for herself. Jimmy was a good son, and loved her it is true, but at present he loved that other woman quite a hundred times better. For of such things is a mother's harvest. As the memory of the woman down South troubled and saddened Jimmy, a girl came along the Esplanade, and catching sight of him, approached, and in a free and unconventional manner began to talk to him. She was a Miss Carre, an orphan, and a friend of Mrs Russell's, under whose care she had been left. Mrs Russell had obligingly supplied Jimmy with the young lady's history the previous evening, and being an old colonist, Mrs Russell was well versed in people's histories. This, many of them had as a grievance against her.

Miss Carre, it appeared, was the granddaughter of a noted Maori chief who had been on the side of the English during the war. His appreciation of the people who had come to dominate, led him to present his only daughter and a considerable dowry of land to a surveyor. Mrs Russell declared, furthermore, that all the surveyors in the early days married Maori ladies, and got land with their brides, thus convincing Jimmy that Providence must be on the side of the surveyor. A Christian church had baptized Miss Carre by the name of Josephine, but her mother's people corrupted this into Hoipini, and as such she came to be called by all her friends. Neither the young lady nor her story had interested Jimmy very much, because of the absorbing gloom of his own affairs; but now as he looked into her dark, handsome face, he began to recall the things he had heard of her. Other days these two would meet, always in a hap-hazard way down on the beach between office closing and dinner time. Thus Jimmy, finding Miss Carre sympathetic concerning his life and doings, confided his tragic love story to her. The Maori strain in the girl swiftly answered to anything in the form of reckless, lawless romance. She was astounded at Jimmy leaving Dunedin in such a lame, half-hearted fashion! Why had he not induced the lady to fly with him? Why had he left her with that wretch of a husband, when she must be pining her life away for her lover in Wellington?

Jimmy was rather taken aback! He was not at all sure that his lady love was pining her life away for him. Indeed he very much doubted it, and that was where the sting lay. Certainly she wrote him beautiful letters, and had promised that none of the other very young and foolish men, who dangled after her at dinners and dances, should ever take his place in her estimation; but his friend Graham had advised him to accept this kind of declaration with salt. Graham was close on forty, and not given to dealing in illusions, so Jimmy had unwillingly admitted that very likely the advice was good. Beyond his salary in his father's office, Jimmy had no visible means of support whatever, and though there were many things he had not yet thought out, he knew he could not take upon himself the responsibility of annexing another man's wife without having some capital to work upon. Besides there might be legal complications with the husband, thereafter, and he knew his father would make a fine fuss over that sort of thing in their family. Jimmy had not outgrown the influence of home opinions, which was well. There was a good deal of caution in the lad, more than his parents gave him credit for, but Hoipini of the eloquent voice, the big passionate eyes, and the strain of a former barbarism in her blood, made him promise to do things which his soul would have abhorred weeks ago down in misty, sleepy Dunedin. Without any more to do he was to take the lady he loved away from her lawful husband. If she declined to go, then of course she must be abducted. The pair were to sail off to the Fiji Islands or thereabouts. Hoipini was to supply funds for the undertaking out of ground rents in Wellington, which were to be in her own hands very shortly, for she was nearly twenty-one. Jimmy was much averse to being under an obligation to anyone, let alone a girl, he said, and so Hoipini suggested that he might grow kumeras or bananas after a while, in order to refund her money.

This idea settled the question, Jimmy thought, and one day he took a ticket to Dunedin as directed, and met Hoipini afterwards on the esplanade to have a last chat, and bid her good-bye. It was after six o'clock in the evening, and a fine soaking rain was falling. The conspirators did not appear to mind it in the least, as they sat huddled up in cloaks, sharing one umbrella, and whispering mysteriously. Both had forgotten about dinner. Time went on. Presently two hungry overtime men raced by to their evening meal.

'Fools,' said one, alluding to the pair under the umbrella, 'why, they must be getting drenched sitting there in the rain.'

'Devilish keen on one another, I should say,' replied the other.

Hoipini, oblivious of this brutality, was begging Jimmy to write, and keep her posted up in proceedings down South.

'You bet, I will,' promised he with much fervour, and then came a silence. Thoughts began to start through the young man's mind, quite new thoughts he imagined them to be. There was a good deal of latent poetry in Jimmy McAndrew, though he was of Scotch parentage, and consequently not reckless about change. The poetry was coming to the surface now. What a musical voice had this Hoipini! What a magnificent red under the brown of her cheeks! Was it true the lady down in Dunedin made up *her* complexion? Graham swore she did, but then he was a very cynical dog. Still *that* complexion was not be compared with –. Here the train of thought became derailed by the action of queer sounds beside him. Had Hoipini a cold? She stoutly denied having any such thing. Jimmy considered for a moment, and then spoke out.

'You are crying, Hoipini.'

'You great silly!' (This most contemptously).

'Hoipini, I don't believe you want me to go away with Mrs Matthews at all.' This from Jimmy with much conviction, probably born of hope.

'You *want* to go – then go!' Now this was most unfair of Hoipini, and Jimmy was indignant.

'Well, I'm hanged! And who is making me go?'

'Not *me*!' This being untruthful as well as ungrammatical. But Jimmy only noticed that a sob followed it.

'I say, Hoipini —.'

A pettish jerk, and a face turned away.

'Can't you turn your head till I tell you something?'

It was evident she could, for she did. Later on portions of a steamer ticket fluttered wildly into the darkened harbour waters, and two damp people stumbled breathlessly into Mrs Russell's abode, but they were smiling cheerfully in spite of the fact that one of them would have to go into explanations over things. Mrs Russell did not look pleased. No wonder, for the post office clock had struck eight-thirty.

'You can't beat change of air,' Graham remarked, as he handed back Jimmy's letter to his father applying for the parental blessing on his engagement. McAndrew, senior, chuckled and looked clubwards. They were close by, Graham understood, and nodded. So they entered. Once more those two drank a whiskey over Jimmy.

Mary F. Wright

A New Century Girl

1901

The early morning sun streams in at the open window of a large, airy room, containing a small bed; the furniture and appointments showing considerable refinement and a love of order.

Evidently a girl's room, from the dainty nicknacks, photographs bedecking the walls, neat little bookshelf and blue bowl of brown and gold galardias. Dumb-bells, golf-sticks, and boxing gloves gave another aspect to the room, and proclaimed it the abode of a very up-to-date young woman.

The blinds are drawn back, and the fresh, cool breezes blow in. A silvery alarum strikes, and a figure under the white curtain stirs; two large brown eyes open, and look at the clock in a lazy fashion. 'Five o'clock! Time to get up, and dreams are so sweet,' says a young voice sleepily.

However there is no help for it. Belle, the young *trainée*, fresh from the Christchurch Domestic School, is at her first place, with rich Mrs Brown, of Riccarton, and she has to prove that, after all, civilization has done something towards ameliorating domestic evils, by replacing the untrained uneducated, household servant of the nineteenth century by the cultivated, sweet, scientific young damsel, with the new modes of thought and action.

So Belle springs out of bed, and after a water, air, and sun bath, slips quickly into her clothes, and begins her morning duties.

Those clothes! They are the funniest, mouse-brown garments, and when donned make her look like a charming, athletic boy of fifteen. Her shapely limbs are encased first in an entire suit of Jaegers. She waits for a moment, and stands admiringly looking at herself in her skin-tight, dust-coloured underclothing. A mathematical eye could see no fault in her proportions. An artistic eye might have said her under-skin was too brown – the result of sun and air baths. Your beginning-of-the-new-century girl does not look – under her clothes – like a well-earthed stick of celery. She has the health tints of brown, and pink all over the limbs and body as in the face. Her outer clothes consist of a pair of knickers, brown stockings and shoes, a little close-fitting cap to keep the deep-tinted hair from getting dusty while she sweeps, for Belle is the Maid of all Work.

All the work to do? Impossible in a house where there are eight rooms and offices to be kept in order, and where the cook, also a *trainée*, arrives just in time to cook each meal, and departs immediately after, leaving only her handmaid behind to wash the dishes and saucepans!

What a lot has to be accomplished between the hours of six and eight, when breakfast is required to be ready, the rooms swept, dusted, arrayed with fresh flowers, bedrooms aired, and the hundred and one etceteras done.

But Belle works in bloomers, it must be remembered, and anyone who has seen the emancipated female move in these smart-looking, comfortable, unimpeding garments knows now that the poor nineteenth century woman was a martyr – a willing martyr, too, which is the worst of all martyrdom, as it is usually the most hopeless to prevent. They were martyrs, those weary-eyed, bent-backed domestic women of the past, martyrs to their own prejudices, and that most awful bugbear to the eternal feminine – a fear of ridicule.

A broom, a duster, a tray of china, all are so many gymnastic appliances which Belle handles with dexterity, acquired during years of training in the Domestic College, for in that wonderful new school, where the practical and technical have taken the places of the merely theoretical and experimental, Belle has been taught to do the smallest domestic duty with the least possible expenditure of physical and mental labour. No breakages – Belle would be ashamed to break, as that would show a flaw in her training, and prove that she was unworthy of the A.1. certificate by which she got her situation.

Belle's work did not take up all her day. The afternoons saw her on the lovely Avon in a little light canoe which she could hire for a few pence an hour. Nor was she always alone; sometimes another canoe kept her company, and sometimes she was to be seen in a double one with a long, lank youth, delicate, short-sighted, and full of book-wormy ideas of things in general and women in particular. This was Algernon Brown, the son of the house, whose young susceptibilities had been the only objection in Mrs Brown's eyes, when her worthy spouse, tired of the annoyances he had suffered at the hands of the typical nineteenth century handmaid, had suggested the experiment of the Christchurch Training School domestic.

'Why,' he asked plaintively, 'should we subscribe to that institution if we are not to get any benefit from it?'

'Think of Algernon, my love,' sighed his spouse; 'think if a good-looking *trainée*, a smart, stylish girl, were sent to us, he will be sure to succumb to the young person's charms.'

'Tut, tut, my dear, let the boy look after himself. Remember, domestic service is now a profession, and the domestic ranks with the lady doctor and the trained nurse, and is miles above the private governess, who is still in many instances in the position of the undischarged bankrupt – without a certificate.'

Belle arrived, and, as we have seen, Algernon proceeded to look after himself and her, too, by boating in the river, walking out, and playing golf with the smart stylish young person whom the Christchurch Domestic College had seen fit to confer on the Brown *ménage*.

What makes a man fall in love?

Half the time it is because he is suddenly brought face to face with the unexpected – the unusual – and Belle was still no common type. Physically she was handsome, though her face had not the pink and white dairymaid beauty admired in the middle of the last century, nor the purely intellectual advanced new woman's look that was the ideal of the latter days of the nineteenth century.

Intelligence and sound practical common sense characterized both her looks and actions, but there was the look of vitality, of animal well-being and health, of physique developed and unrestrained, which makes the lasting beauty in a woman. A young – a very young – woman may look well, 'spiritualized,' 'etherealized' by delicacy of health, but for staying beauty a woman must have healthy full-sized organs, and plenty of room in her outward frame to carry them about with her. A small waist, a narrow chest, beautiful? No; considered as much a deformity as a glass eye, a wooden leg, in these, beginning-of-the-twentieth century days.

Mrs Brown watched her 'chick' with anxious eyes, and one day confided her suspicions to her husband.

'Mr Brown, what did I say? Algernon wants to marry out Belle.'

'Eh, what? Well, she's a fine, good-looking, sweet-tempered girl, and knows how to make her home thoroughly comfortable, and will be a useful good wife, and a healthy mother.'

Alas! for Mr Brown's and Algy's hopes.

At that moment, whilst this discussion was going on in the Brown's household, a very crest-fallen youth occupied a seat in the double canoe. Belle had that moment firmly declined to paddle a double canoe through life with him. When in halting and bashful words he had placed his rather anæmic heart and his bony, neurotic hand at her feet, she had politely declined the offering. Pressed for a reason, she asserted that she could not possibly marry a man whose health was not perfectly robust. In her own mind she termed him a 'weed'. Very sweetly she advised him to go in for more muscular development, throw aside his books, turn farmer! Anything! But be a man, not a mere bundle of nerves!

At latest Algy was at the Agricultural College going through a course of gymnastics, and labouring with his hands rather than with his brains only, the result being considerable benefit to his chest measure, and to his physique generally. His forehead is no longer sicklied over with the pale cast of thought, and when he periodically weighs and measures himself, cheerfully noting his increasing proportions, he wonders whether Belle has found anyone yet to please her, or if she is waiting for him.

Jane Mander

A Stray Woman

1902

Dora Mortyn was lying back in a wicker chair on the balcony when she heard a cab stop in the street below. She went to the railing with that pardonable curiosity with which one gets infected in a boarding-house, and looking over, she saw the little figure in velvet and furs which had just paid its fare, and was tripping up the steps to the front door.

'Such a sweet little creature,' said Dora's friend, who came upstairs a few minutes later.

'Who?'

'The new arrival, Mrs Allen Manston. She has come to stay about a year, she says, while her husband puts up some batteries on the goldfields. She's so pretty, and has on such a dream of a travelling cloak.'

'Do you want to know what I think of her?' asked Dora that night, as her friend was brushing her hair.

'Yes, rather. I know your searchlight has been turned on her most of the evening.'

'Well, a vampire – you know Kipling's poem – she might have sat for Burne Jones' picture. She doesn't mean to be one; she only wants to be pretty and petted, but she would suck all one's vitality and give nothing in return; she is one of the women who would "never understand". She'll want plenty of attention, and feel very aggrieved if she doesn't get it, and she'll never relinquish one jot of it to other women. All the same she is a winning little soul, and will make one feel a real sympathy for her when she grumbles about a crease in her skirt, or a refractory hairpin, for such things are her poignant sorrows. And I think one would get rather fond of her. Indeed, I have quite a fancy for playing lady's maid to her, so that I might brush out her lovely fluffy hair, and hear her baby prattle in her serious moments!'

'H'm!' said her friend. '"A rag and a bone, and a hank of hair!" I suppose Kipling was right, and there *are* such women.

But did you notice the start she gave when you came in to dinner?'

'I? No. But I never heard her name before, and I am sure she can't know me.'

'She's watched you all the evening, though. She'll take to you, see if she doesn't, by the law of opposites.'

'I shouldn't wonder if she does. Those sort of people have always had a fancy for hanging on to me.'

'We'll get some fun out of her anyway,' said her friend. 'She'll want to shout us everywhere; she's just the sort of woman to fling about her husband's money.'

'And are we the sort of women who want it flung at us?' asked Dora.

'Not quite. But we'll play with our new toy, my dear. Why shouldn't we? It's all she wants.'

Dora Mortyn stood on the balcony beside her friend. A full moon was rising above some silver-tinged clouds in the east, and a beautiful long shimmer lay across Auckland Harbour in front of them. The two women revelled in the glory of it, and what was more, they both knew it without saying so.

From the room behind them came sounds of loud laughter, for Mrs Allen Manston was telling the fortunes of the men who clustered around her. At an extra loud peal Dora turned to her friend and smiled.

'What a merry little soul she is,' she observed, lightly.

'Er – yes. But it's a bit against the grain to see how readily our menfolk turn from our sensible conversation and rally round a frivolous toy like that,' answered the friend, a trifle bitterly.

'Oh, it doesn't take much to amuse men,' said Dora, with contempt. 'I remember once seeing a couple of nomadic town roosters – and you know how lean and woebegone town fowls can look – well, these two started to fight somewhere about the foot of Grey Street one evening. I assure you there was a stampede for the spot. From starboy to newspaper reporter, from loafer to University professor, they craned their necks round each other to get a glimpse of the blood-spattered champions. And they roared with laughter, and cheered as they might a man who had won the Victoria Cross. And we are fools enough to bury our individuality, and groom our bodies, to barter for the notice of such intelligence as that.'

'We do it, though,' said her friend, with a short laugh.

'Yes, and our hearts ache with a great bitterness when the new toy comes. My heart has ached because of a man for years, and you know it. I believe him to be a fine man, but I shouldn't wonder if he were here to-night he would be in there laughing at her idle chatter instead of being out here talking to us. What price virtue and brains? There are few men who want no more for all time.'

They were silent for some minutes, and then Mrs Allen Manston came out, and one by one, the men rose and followed her.

'Grand night,' said one man.

'Um,' said a second.

'Dear me, isn't it chilly?' said Mrs Allen Manston, and someone immediately went inside to get her a shawl.

'Aren't you cold, Miss Mortyn?' asked a third man.

'No, thanks. I like fresh air.'

'Oh, I do love moonlight on the water, don't you?' chirped Mrs Allen Manston to the company in general.

'Charming, isn't it?' said the man beside her.

The study of the moonlight proved so severe a tax upon their capacity for the beautiful that they soon went inside to play cards.

At half-past ten Mrs Manston rose, and began saying good-night.

'I must go in,' said Dora to her friend. 'I promised to brush her hair to-night. I think she wants to tell me something,' she added apologetically.

'It's so nice to have one's hair brushed,' began Mrs Manston, as she settled herself comfortably in a low chair.

'It's so nice to have pretty hair to brush,' said Dora warmly, as she held the shining golden ringlets.

Mrs Manston smiled contentedly, and the brushing went on.

'How gentle you are!' she said presently. 'You don't hurt me a bit, and my head is so tender. But then you are clever at everything.'

'Indeed. Who says so?'

'Oh, all the men here do. They are always saying Miss Mortyn says this, and Miss Mortyn says that. I wish I could influence men,' and she sighed with well-affected sincerity.

'My dear, we all influence men,' said Dora, not without a secret pleasure, because the men thought her opinions worth quoting.

'Oh, yes, of course. But you know what I mean!'

Dora didn't.

'It's so hard to manage men, isn't it?' Mrs Manston gazed with secret complacency at her pretty little foot, while her voice was perfect in its well-trained seriousness. Dora saw the bow on the pointed slipper, and smiled more at it than at the question.

'Yes,' she answered. 'Men require careful handling. We have first to consider the man, then his mood, and the circumstances, and a host of other little things. But what man won't be managed by you, eh?'

'Oh, it's Allen, my husband, you know; he always worries me.'

'Oh, your husband? Dear me! Then it's serious. He's the one person in the world you won't be able to manage.'

Mrs Manston started up with unexpected energy.

'Then you do know him!' she burst out.

'Know him! Of course I don't. I was only going on general principles, my dear. But what makes you think I know him?'

'I found him looking at a photograph once; it was of a woman, of course, and he had a look that nearly took my breath away!'

'Well, that's nothing. Men often do these little things. It is to them what lollies are to us. But what had the photo to do with me?'

'It was just like you; that is, you remind me so of the photo. And Allen looked at it so long, and he got such a fright when I touched him. I'm sure he doesn't love me. It's that horrid woman.'

'Who is like me? Thanks. Why you silly little goose, you can rest your mind about that. I've only given my photo to one man,' her face grew grave for a moment, 'and he was *not* Allen Manston.'

The child-like lips still pouted.

'But there's a woman all the same,' she said.

'Oh, nonsense! How do you know?'

'Well, he won't talk to me like he does to other women, and when I speak to him, he only says, "Um," and "Yes," and "Just so, my dear." He's so dull, so horribly dull.' The handkerchief was out by this time.

'But, my dear,' said Dora, sympathetically. 'Men can't all be jibbering idiots. It's most refreshing to meet a man who says one word at a time. But doesn't Mr Manston remember you when he's away?'

'Oh, yes, I suppose so. He writes to me every week, and he always carries a miniature of me on his watchchain, but that's not everything, is it?'

Dora wanted to throw her head back and laugh uproariously, but instead, she patted the curly head beneath her.

'Now what is it you really do want?' she asked soberly.

'Oh, I don't know. Allen never seems to notice me, you know. I – he – oh, I don't know what it is.' And she sobbed outright this time.

'Yes,' thought Dora, 'when a woman knows what she wants she can generally make a man see it too, but when her wants alter with her every mood, what has he to go by?'

'Men are so selfish,' sobbed Mrs Manston.

Dora looked over her.

'They are more self absorbed than we are, dearie, and they are born with a notion of grandiloquence, and a lord-of-creation air, but I don't think they mean to be selfish. When they are, we spoil them, we mothers, sisters, sweethearts, and wives.'

'That's just what I think. They're quite spoilt,' said Mrs Manston, cheering up.

'Well, we do it, you see,' said Dora. 'Instead of living so that they feel our good influence, and know their own unworthiness, we feed their self-love, and they live in a kind of reflected glory, imagining that their appreciation of our society is due to their own good taste.'

'Ye – es,' said Mrs Manston, hoping she understood.

'Let's see,' went on Dora, 'Mr Manston is coming to Auckland next week, for a short stay, isn't he? Well, suppose I take him in charge. I'll soon find out what's wrong with him, and settle your fears, eh? I'll tell you how to manage him. Now never mind the photograph and the strange woman, my dear. Every man has a little souvenir of that kind, just like we keep a faded bunch of violets in a scented envelope. Good-night.'

Dora Mortyn was just passing out of the dining-room into the entrance hall when a tall and handsome man entered the front door. At the sound of the step Dora turned, and as they met face to face their eyes flashed recognition and something more. Then for a moment their senses seemed to reel in company, for the one knew and the other feared that the long years had placed some insurmountable barrier between them.

'You here!' he exclaimed, in the low voice she had long ago learned to love.

'Mr Murray,' she murmured helplessly.

'No – not – Murray. I – I deceived you there. I – I am Allen Manston.'

Instantly she drew back her hand from his lingering clasp, and her face had mastered all emotion, and was calmly indifferent.

'Ah, then, I have the pleasure of knowing your wife, for I am a boarder here,' she replied carelessly.

At the word wife his face twitched and his lips set.

'I've no right to ask your forgiveness,' he said, stepping nearer her. 'But Heaven knows what I've suffered all these years! Only let me tell you before I go.'

Then came the sound of his wife's gay laugh on the stairs, and the next minute a dainty little figure in muslin and lace came tripping towards them.

'Your husband has just introduced himself to me,' said Dora, with superb self-possession.

'Oh, Allen darling, I thought you were coming to-morrow. How horrid and dusty you are!' And she put up her face to be kissed, while Dora looked on with a sense of cold indifference that astonished even herself.

As for the man, Fate was cruel to have put the two women there, side by side, for him to see in one short revelation what glory manhood had lost for want of the understanding that the right woman would so loyally have given.

'Come along, Allen, your room is upstairs,' said his wife,

putting her arm through his with a pretty show of possession. He cast one imploring look over her head at the woman he had lost, but he saw no sign of yielding there.

On the stairs they met another woman.

'That's Miss Mortyn's friend,' whispered his wife. 'They're both so clever, but I like Miss Mortyn best. She and I are quite chummy, you know.'

'But won't you let me explain, Miss Mortyn? Don't look like that. I know things can't be altered, but only give me a chance to make myself less hideous in your eyes.'

'You are not hideous in my eyes. And as I don't quite see the fun of dragging barbed wire across an open wound, I think we'll leave the explanation alone. It will serve no good purpose. In fact, I see nothing to explain. For a reason which you know, and I don't want to know, you changed your name once in your life when you were away from your home, and during that time you met me, and we became friends – no, more than friends. Then you had reasons for returning to your home in Australia. You married a pretty and charming girl, or – or perhaps you were married before you left? Then years afterwards we meet again. Hard luck, I admit, for one of us, or perhaps both of us. But as I happen to be within hearing of your wife's laugh, I can hardly feel any satisfaction in listening to an explanation of how you came to marry her instead of me.'

Allen Manston's hands gripped the balcony railing, and his dark eyes were fixed on the starlit sky with a feverish light. Love overwhelming was tearing at his heart and crunching its way into the strength of his manhood. And he knew all too well that the outward calm of the woman beside him was but a mask that hid as fierce a torrent as his own. And between them there stood the strongest barrier that Heaven or earth could make – a man's honour and a woman's virtue. He turned and faced her splendid courage, and bowed his head for very shame at his own dark thoughts.

'You must hear the worst,' he groaned. 'It was all my fault, my gross selfishness, my wretched craving for sympathy. I was married before I saw you. I revelled in your friendship, for it gave me what my starved soul needed, but I always meant to stop before it was too late.'

Her face whitened at his words, and for a moment her grey eyes blazed with a light that scorched him through and through, then it died down, and pity took its place.

'I am sorry,' she said simply. 'Sorry for us both, but most of all for you. As for me, all I need now is work, honest work, morning, noon and night; work that shall make a bed and a meal – the only things worth having; physical slavery that shall drug the memory and dull the senses. And I've tried it before, it's good medicine.'

'Is that all?' he asked hoarsely.

'All I need? Yes. But I shall have the past besides, and a bunch of dead violets.'

He passed his hand over his eyes, and then mastered himself with a supreme effort.

'You might prescribe for me too,' he said as calmly as he could.

'For you also, hard work, and loyalty to the woman you have sworn to honour. Never let yourself relax for one moment. Be to her, outwardly at least, all you think you could have been to me.'

There was a silence between them for some minutes, and then Mrs Manston's laugh came to them through the window.

Dora Mortyn turned to the man beside her. 'Let us put an end to this,' she said, in the same calm tones. 'You leave tomorrow morning. I shall not see you before you go. We may never meet again. It's not the first time in the world's history that a man and a woman have felt the foundations give way beneath their feet. We shan't sleep to-night, and we'll snatch an hour or two to-morrow night, but we'll recover our appetites in time. Now give me your hand, I think your wife is coming out to find me for I promised to brush her hair; and remember she is your wife, and that in all the world she is the one woman whose comfort you must study. Good-bye, Mr Manston.'

He seized her hand and kissed it passionately, but the words he meant to say choked in his throat.

'Light a cigar,' said Dora, imperatively.

Then there was a flood of light from the open door, and Mrs Manston's silvery voice broke the strain.

'Why in the world are you keeping Miss Mortyn out in the cold, Allen? Dora, dear, aren't you frozen?'

'I was just thinking of coming in and leaving Mr Manston to

enjoy his cigar in peace,' answered Dora, as she took the other woman's arm. 'I will say good-bye to you, Mr Manston, as I shall not be up when you go in the morning.'

A conventional handshake, and a swift, soul-searching look, and the show was over; but, as usual, the accounts had to be settled behind the scenes.

'And you've been telling Allen how to manage a woman – that is I. How good of you. I am sure he will notice what you say.' And Mrs Manston looked up gratefully at the solemn face behind her.

'I hope he will, my dear. But you may rest content about that imaginary woman. There is only one woman in the world for Allen Manston, and that woman he will always love and honour. Now good night,' and she kissed the smiling face that so innocently took her words to itself, and then walked steadily from the room.

At half-past ten the friend came in from the theatre, and strolled into Dora's room to tell her all about the play. But the sound of heart-breaking sobs came from between the pillows, and the friend beat a hasty and silent retreat, and sat in her own room for half-an-hour, trying to work it all out. Then, having devised some unostentatious sympathy for the morrow, she retired, to wonder for long why life held so many hushed chapters.

A year later Dora Mortyn got a letter, stamped Melbourne, from Mrs Allen Manston. At the end it said: 'You must have given some wonderful advice to Allen, he's really quite good to me now, and I don't feel quite such a little whipped girl when he's about. I told you he would mind what you said. Men always think more of the opinion of a stray woman they meet than of those they know best. Good-bye, remember me to all.'

G.B. Lancaster

Our Lady of the Plains

1902

A little dust-demon lifted itself lazily from the white cross-track, beaten out yesterday by the passing of a thousand sheep, and fled across the tussock with intent to reach the purple hill-shapes that hung on the horizon. But the dead heat caught it to smother it with the coming night; and resistlessly the slow silence over-crept the plain and lay there.

Crandeck's saddle-grip tightened ever so little with the sharp tightening of his heart-cords, and he whistled through parched lips.

For the power-charged stillness that fell away to the four wide corners where strange winds lived was unlovely to him, and unholy, and full of secretiveness. It was the sea without life, or movement, or regard. It was the empty beginning of the world before man moved over the face of it. And more truly than all, it was the far rimless, mysterious country that had clogged his feet through the dreams of many years, and he knew very certainly that it promised evil.

There was evil in the wild, sensuous smell of flax-swamp that rose to windward; and in the clump of stiff, wide-headed cabbage-trees that whispered together behind with a feverish tapping of dead fronds on bare grey trunks; and in the tussock that rolled out eternally before the stumbling hoofs, turning livid where the heavy sky stooped to meet it on the edge of the earth.

There had been yellow tussock below Harton through the slow day's grilling, and molten sky above; but he shook the stoop from his shoulders, and looked over the waste with the pride of the naturalized colonial. Then he began to say things such as were to Crandeck an utter weariness of the flesh and blatantly idiotic.

'She's a young country, I grant you, but she's got the biggest future of all Australasia. Canterbury mutton and beef – and – I tell you, Crandeck, I've my own idea about cropping these plains. Surface-ploughing first season, with —'

'Oh, darn!' muttered Crandeck, clacking his stirrup-irons wearily. He had no desire whatever to lay hands on the great unturned wealth of this dumb world. It was for Harton and the men of his breed to make New Zealand for the golden days to come, and for Crandeck himself – 'I am a sojourner, even as all my fathers were – not,' he said; 'an' I don't like it, Harton. I'll serve my year to Jamison because the pater has paid my premium – then I'll go away very swiftly, and never come back. I don't want to farm this ocean-farm. By Jove! I'd sooner dig up the New Forest with a toothpick! So there's my mind for you on that point. An' how much darker is it goin' to get before it's done, eh?'

Harton blundered into a smudge that was low manuka-scrub, and out into another that was sword-edged Spaniard. Then he soothed his mare into jaded submission to the unkindly will of things, sniffed the air that was suddenly tainted with the harshness of brine, and remarked that a sea-fog was coming up. 'When it will most certainly be darker than the hither-most pit, so we'll push along while there's any perspective left. Then I reckon we will have to wait.'

'Wait – here! What for? Day?'

'Our lady; she'll be lighting up directly. Look out, Crandeck; there's a dry creek!'

Crandeck followed through the stony unpleasantness with mixed ideas regarding the Virgin Mary, and stars and moons – or an occasional comet.

'Our who?'

'Jamison's daughter,' Harton's thick voice softened. 'Our Lady of the Plain, and the only woman for thirty-odd miles round, bar Jamison's housekeeper. You knew this, Crandeck?'

'The only woman!' said the man from England. 'Great heavens above! The only woman!'

Harton's saddle creaked. He was gathering himself for direct speech.

'She's only a baby yet, bless her! There are ten or a dozen fellows always knocking about Jamison's station, but –'

'I understand. All of 'em hate each other with an abiding hatred, and follow her round on their knees. I shall indubitably do likewise.'

'Hope you will.' Harton's tone was grim, 'and you'll get

lammed on the head with a shovel, or whatever's handiest. Our Lady is muscular. But – er – Crandeck, I wanted to say – that is – she doesn't know anything about – er – that sort of thing yet, you know, and we don't want her to. But if you're the man that's going to wake her out of her childhood, and – er – make her unhappy, by the Lord Harry, you'll have the lot of us on to you! It's just as well to warn you – er –'

'You always had a nice way of putting things,' said Crandeck, slowly. 'I should call you a tactful man, Harton, and I mean to talk to your Lady of the Plain as much as I jolly well please. When is that deuced light coming, anyway, and what is it? Hold up, you brute!'

'Lantern from a flagstaff on Jamison's hill. For the benefit of straying Israelites who used to peg out in Jamison's waterholes. There she goes! Keep it a bit more to starboard, and come along.'

The red eye drew them through the night by its steady, unwinking glare; Harton, biting his beard-corners in newly-awakened trouble, and Crandeck, saddle-worn and sulky to the verge of curses. A low-browed house reared itself blackly, and yellow streaming lights ate up the dark round many men speaking an uncouth language that was entirely genial and full of welcome.

In the following hours Crandeck learned that this talk was the shibboleth of the sheep-farmer and the run-holder. He watched some half-score lean, eager faces through the blue reek of tobacco smoke, the while he ached in all his softly nurtured young body, and doubted that the wisdom gained in a year's cadetting on Jamison's station would over-pay for the raw newness of a life lived on the level of strenuous fact.

For the speech of these men ran up and down the land as they hammered out the power of this strong country to be, and told of lawless deeds and the summary justice that came after, in straight words and very forcible.

A clean-faced boy, who owned some forty thousand acres of freehold, commanded the attention of the thickening smoke-reek.

'A dashed cattle-puncher, I tell you. He nailed forty of my calves, and banged 'em along with his own mob 'fore I could get on his trail. What? Certainly I'd know them, bang or no bang, though he swore they were his by all his gods, the brute! So I swore –'

'I'll be bound you did, Tony,' murmured Verenin, opening an eye.

'Tony, Tony! come out – quick. I've chased that weka into the koromiko bush by the tin fence, and you've got to catch him. Tony – is he asleep in there, boys?'

Jamison pulled out his pipe.

'Lassie, come here. Harton and Crandeck have – '

Our Lady came to the window with darkness behind her, and smiled on Crandeck.

'Did they give you any tea? Whisky and pipes? Oh, how silly! You'll have a head in the morning, you know. Vic always has a head when he comes back from Christchurch. You do, Vic, and it makes you shockingly cross, too. Wasn't he cross coming up, Crandeck?'

'There's never any sense in telling too much truth,' said Payne; 'has no one taught you that, my Lady?'

'You learnt instead,' said Our Lady, underbreath. 'I heard of it – no, it wasn't Tony or Dad. But I'm going to speak to you in the morning. Letters? Oh, who for? Wish some one would write me a letter!'

'I will, if you like,' said Verenin. 'You shouldn't laugh; I can. I won an essay prize at school once.'

'I 'spect they judged by weight 'stead of reading that year,' said Our Lady, with demure eyes on the bulky one. 'Hurry up, Tony. No, you shan't have a gun. You shot three chickens last time. Wait till I call for him. We-ka-a!'

The night where the young moon walked took them both, and later Crandeck went to his bed and was mystified. For the wide frank plains that had cradled Our Lady in freedom belonged to no world in which he had part, and the shadow of its silence lay on him with a horrible familiarity.

But in the grey-domed eternity of his dreams, swathed cabbage-trees stood in ranks behind a girl's figure that ran through the night, and called on a name that was his own. And he followed her unswervingly until Harton came and threw brushes at him and three boots, because it was breakfast-time.

Jamison's acres lay bare to the welter of sunlight and to all the winds that blew. For fences were not, neither crops nor trees; and kennelled boundary-dogs strung off the invisible line that severed the runs throughout the plains.

Our Lady made this matter clear to Crandeck when she came out to watch him sinking a post-hole, and to explain the uses of a 'bar' in clayey soil. Crandeck grew speedily blistered about the hands and the nape of the neck, and Our Lady sat under a sparse manuka bush, and laughed at him with clear, unabashed eyes.

'You'll learn; and everything worth learning hurts a bit – or it's not worth it – Q.E.D. Tony taught me that.'

'The logic or the fact?' Then Crandeck struck a stone that knocked a corner off the spade, and swore under breath.

'I think I found out the fact myself. Had to, you know. Dad won't let me ride with a saddle, and I had awful croppers before I could sit a young 'un. And Vic taught me to shoot with swanshot 'cause he said a girl ought to be as plucky as a man. And then there's the plain –' she flung out her arms to the golden tussock that ran in resistless following waves to the distance of her world – 'it hurts when it's lonely and grey in the evening, and crying out things that I can't quite understand, though I listen and listen. But it tells me lots. How to bear pain, you know; and what to say to the boys when they ask me for advice; and how to manage Pint-o'-Beer Dick when Dad gets angry and wants to thrash him.'

'Good Lord,' said Crandeck, standing upright with wrath on his forehead. 'What sort of a life – why doesn't your father send you to a school or a – a – anywhere out of this confounded desolation. It's no place for a girl.'

'If you say another word,' said Our Lady, with her eyes straight and hard on Crandeck, 'I'll thump you very much, Crandeck. It's no business of yours. I love the plain better than anything – except Dad, and I'll never go away from it. It's beautifuller than Revelations, because it's more than only words. And the tussock is like the sea of glass in Heaven, and when the mountains are all purple and scarlet and green they are like God's throne, and – and you're a beast, Crandeck.'

Crandeck stared.

'If Heaven isn't livelier than this place there's not much inducement for a man to become a Christian,' he said. 'I'd advise you not to try and make a convert by illustrating the Bible with your little corner of the world.'

'I don't want to forgive you for that,' said Our Lady, standing her ground with quivering lips; 'but I'll have to, because I called you a beast. I'll even tell you that you'd better put a bucket of water into that hole to soften it a bit. You're making a horrid mess of it.'

'Thank you,' said Crandeck, humbly, and went to the pump.

But he curbed his tongue through the days that came after, and played rounders and cricket with Our Lady, and hid his eyes carefully from her angrily-smothered tears when Tony brought his violin out into the full moonlight, and the very far ends of earth listened where the stars shone.

And the mantle of the rouseabout, and one who must obey fell on Crandeck's shoulders and chafed him. He learnt the inner mechanism of the thing that Jamison called work, and covered himself with shame by patiently sifting merinos and Lincolns into one and the same yard when Jamison had set him to drafting.

'An' that red-headed shepherdman o' yours grinned at me,' he told Our Lady. 'Said I'd got a lot to learn about sheep. Wish I'd asked him the origin of Jason's "Golden Fleece", anyway.'

'You don't know yourself,' said Our Lady, serenely. She was of necessity driving the lumbering tipdray through the stone-choked creeks and the unhandy litter of low scrub; for Crandeck wrought unrestfully with the clumsy, wide-mouthed tin of water, and the couple of stark sheep that slanted stiffly down with desire to upset it, and so guarded the three-days' meal for the boundary dogs.

'Don't I?' he retorted. 'Jason got his "Golden Fleece" from the Jews, like many an unlucky beggar since. I, too, was fleeced of all my gold in my college days.'

'You must have been an excessively mild sheep,' said Our Lady, and laughed. 'Cut off a forequarter of your relative for Rage. He's a most awfully hungry dog. And throw it on the far side of his kennel, or he'll go for you while you're filling his water-tin.'

Crandeck hacked scientifically at the red-blue rawness, and poured water without undue haste. Our Lady watched approvingly under her lashes.

'You're not a funk,' she said; 'and I don't think you're stupid either. I believe I'll like you, Crandeck.'

Crandeck looked at the browned, thin face and grave dark eyes, and the small, firm mouth; but the spell of the wide, dun plain was, as always, entirely hateful to him, and with the taste of it in his mouth, he answered her.

'It's confoundedly good of you, but I think you'll have to be quick about it. I mean to get away from here as soon as I decently can. It – it haunts me, this place. It's been alive before – and I was alive with it. You'll say I am talking abject rot, but – but –.'

'Yes?' she said; 'tell me. You mean that it's dead now, and that's why you don't like it?'

'Something of that sort, I suppose;' Crandeck cast wildly for words of sense. 'In this real thing it is beastly flat – and lonely – and silent, and – and unheeding, y'know. I've seen it before in dreams, or – er – mind's eye, or something, and I always hated it infer– very much. It hasn't got an edge to it,' he said, wrinkling his eyes in attempt to see it clearly; 'just clouds. But I know there's something beastly waiting behind them for me, and I know I'll see it some day. In the reality, probably.'

'I'm part of the plains,' said Our Lady, seriously; 'and I promise you that if I ever come into your dreamland, I'll pull away the clouds and let you see what's behind. It's easier to face anything if you know what it is, isn't it?'

Crandeck did not find it necessary to tell her that she was already an indissoluble part of the whole.

'Infinitely. But you may not always be here.'

'I shall,' said Our Lady, dragging away a handful of star-white manuka blooms as the dray crashed through the bushes. 'When I die I mean to be buried up under the flagstaff, where I light the lantern at nights. Then the plain can talk to me all the time, and p'raps I'll be better able to understand what it says. I'll come to you, though, if you can make me hear. But you'll have to shout loud, for there'll be such lots of interesting things to think of. Don't forget.'

'No,' said Crandeck; 'I won't forget.'

But when the day came for him to remember, the evilly-sweet scent of the wild manuka came too, and helped the memory. And in the added knowledge of the time it hurt him, as Our Lady had promised that all knowledge hurts the learner.

'And if you see the horrid thing in the flesh – oh, there's Tony. Shout, Crandeck! Shout loud. I want him.'

Out Lady bore on the green-hide reins, and under the flare of unshaded sun, the black smudge on horizon took substance, and grew the shape of a ridden horse.

Crandeck shouted without result until Our Lady stood on the seat beside him, and put her hands to her mouth so that her cry went out into the yellow ripple of distance.

The rider wrenched his horse about slowly.

'Doesn't seem in much of a hurry to see you,' remarked Crandeck.

'He isn't,' said Our Lady, composedly. 'He knows he's in for a jolly good scolding.'

Crandeck's eyebrows went up.

'By Jove! Does he let you wig him – what's he been doing?'

'I don't think,' said Our Lady, with dignity, 'that you've any right to ask those sort of questions, and I'm very sure you're not going to get an answer. This is between Tony and me. And when I lecture you I won't tell the universe either. Well, Tony; I'm going to walk back with you.'

Tony's half-broken colt sheered away from the cart in wrath, and Tony sat still, and frowned at the distant sparkle of roofs beyond the heat-quivered trail.

'Too far, I'm afraid; and – er – I want to see your father – I'm – er – in a hurry.'

'Dad's over at Kaiti Creek. It's no good, Tony. Drive on, Crandeck. You'll have to finish feeding the dogs by yourself.'

Tony's clear boy-face reddened as she dropped to the tussock. 'Well – if you will, I suppose you will. But you won't like it, My Lady. I'm not sorry, and you're not going to make me sorry.'

'You can clear, Crandeck,' said Our Lady; and Crandeck cleared with an inward amazement and an exceeding indignation that led him to ask straight questions of Harton on the very next day, when the answers super-added puzzlement and disgust.

Harton explained very simply that the inwardness of the wild young lives on the plains was known to Our Lady, both through the large, sweet wisdom that comes not with prayers nor fasting, and through the mouths of the men who came to her in their trouble of soul. 'Pint-o'-Beer' Dick was an Honorable, and a hopeless drunkard in his own right, and Payne's desire for this world's dross had stripped the title of honest man from him before he came over seas. But they stood to the pride to their manhood before Our Lady, and in her innocence she judged her 'boys' lives by her own straight standard of right and wrong, and incidentally held them from much unconsidered evil.

'Why not?' demanded Harton – he was re-boarding the side of a cowhouse, and his words came in sections – 'It can't smirch her – anything we'd tell her. What? Some bad lots, of course – but we shut 'em off pretty quick. An' there are times when a fellow needs the sort of help – 'nother man's no good – and, by George, she knows how to touch us up when we deserve it!'

It was becoming clear to Crandeck that – man being certainly made for hearth-love and the tending of a wife – it was natural that he should desire to take Our Lady away from this place, and to hedge her about with woman's gear, and the all-abiding serenity of an English life. He did not know this until he learnt that these other men considered that they held a claim to her.

'It's – it's iniquitous,' he said; 'it's – er – Jamison's a fool. She ought to be shielded from all this sort of thing. In England – '

'Don't talk piffle,' said Harton, driving a nail home with a steady ponderous stroke; 'and don't come to me for comfort if you let out those sort of ideas on Our Lady. We can't get along without her, and she can't get along without us. So you'd best take those sheep of yours and be off home, young man. It'll be a snorter of a night.'

Crandeck was filled with dividing thoughts as he tailed his half-dozen strayed sheep over the grey, crawling sea of wind-beat tussock, where the nor'-wester boomed and shrieked through the raw red autumn sunset.

He hated the plain and the life of it beyond words; and he hated the hidden horror that waited him – somewhere – somehow – in conjunction with it. Then he called himself a fool, and swore at his stiffened fingers and dust-brimmed eyes when they refused to help him give life and light to his pipe.

'It's an unholy place,' he said; 'and she loves it. But she will have to love me more.'

And he set himself to the teaching of Our Lady while the winter smote the whole present universe into a tingling vigour of frosty life, and made of the hills a gleaming crystal dazzle that took strange unearthly shapes under the white moon.

Crandeck learnt much regarding the grubbing of turnips, and the straining of wire-fencing, and all the unspeakable weariness of life on a sheep-station. He did some fair shooting in the ice-crisped flax-swamps when the westing was red sunk to pale green and opal, and the grey duck and heron came in to squabble about house-rents with blue-breasted, angular pukaki. He also wrote Home letters very often, and managed to deduct his voyage past and to be from the year of his bond to Jamison.

But he did not discover the one all-powerful thing which would have given him a lover's command over Our Lady, and neither did he know that he lacked it.

She shot with him on occasional evenings, and helped him stalk wekas and a stray wild pig through the manuka and tawhina scrub. And without doubt she was an excellent shot.

'You wiped my eye twice today,' he said, in the disgust that is lawful for a man at such times; and he swung the string of duck discontentedly. There were two brace of teal among them, and they had fallen to Our Lady's gun.

She climbed the little hill whereby the track led past the flagstaff to the house, and the bite of the clear air brought the red to her cheeks, and a laugh to her mouth.

'Doesn't it make you feel like a god or a demon?' she said; 'to have the power over life and death, you know – even if it's only exampled by something you kill to eat.'

'There's one god who shoots to wound – with a bow and arrow,' said Crandeck, with suddenly parched lips. 'Did you ever hear of him?'

'Of course; Vic taught me mythology. And he binds up the wounds with true lover's knots – which come undone quicker than any other. They are worst of all – except Granny's knots – oh, and Dad's "must nots", when he doesn't want me to do a thing. Take the ducks down to the kitchen, Crandeck; I'm going to light the lantern.'

No man dare lay hand on that flagstaff if it was not Our

Lady's will, and Crandeck slid over the frost-stiff tussock until he bumped into Harton with a force that unbalanced his temper.

It was growing to dusk among the cabbage-trees and rows of seeded gums that circled the house. Harton gripped Crandeck's shoulder, and spoke low with a gasp.

'Where is she?'

'Go and look for her,' said Crandeck, freeing himself sulkily.

'Shut up and listen then.' Harton's keen ear had caught the rattle of the rope through the sheave as Our Lady lowered the lantern. 'Jamison's dead. Shot himself over on our boundary-line. He's – he – didn't you know how things were going with him. Good God, man! Didn't you know? If you'd given me a hint I could – I might have saved – ' He was sobbing in his throat as a man sobs under the sudden grip of a numbing wound. But Crandeck knew that his sorrow was not for Jamison, and the knowledge irritated him.

'I can't tell her,' he said, 'I can't – can't! She'd hate me if I brought her such – oh, my poor little darling, poor little girl.'

'No; I suppose I'll have to tell her,' said Harton, tonelessly.

'You won't tell her that he – ?'

'D'you think I'm a brute? By all –' Harton's sudden fury dropped from him. 'Go on in, Crandeck. Tony's there, and Payne, but you might be able to help –'

They did not ask him questions when he brought Our Lady back to the house. Neither did they ask when they sat round the unlighted little room with its jovial comfort dumbly broken to the root of it by dim light of the dead man's chair.

By virtue of a half-sheet of paper run over in Jamison's unaccustomed scrawl the disentanglement of this thing had fallen on Harton. He smoked many pipes there with Our Lady's face before him in the darkness, and his brows furrowed over his sunken eyes.

A quick, free step came down the passage, and a door banged. Tony sprang up.

'Great Scott! Where's she off to? It's freezing hard!' He dragged the heavy table-cloth away with him, and ran out with it into the night. From the uncurtained window Crandeck saw him overtake a dark shape that blotted the starshine on the tussock hill; and increase its bulk by the winding of it in many folds of cloth.

'You didn't give her time to light the lantern,' he said; 'and she's gone to do it now. Wonder she can think of such things tonight. But, of course, Jamison wasn't such a tremendously good father to her.'

Payne had lit a candle that he might read the 'Field'; Harton looked at Crandeck in the light of it.

'If you want to break her heart you'll say that to her. The lantern was Jamison's idea. Isn't that enough for you?'

But it was given to Tony to possess clearer insight, and Our Lady, understanding, spoke to him out of her full heart.

'I mustn't forget the plain, Tony; not even for Dad. It would know, you see; and it's always been so good to me – and I love it so. Go away, Tony dear, and leave me just by myself. I can – understand better up here, and – and – oh, Tony, Tony, please go away.'

There was a solemn purity in the cold, still night, where the dried scrub cracked under the smiting frost, and in the soft, direct blaze of the Southern stars that drew the eye up from the world's rim to the mighty hithermost dome of the seventh heaven. It oppressed Tony and gave him fear, but he had the wisdom to know that it was best for Our Lady.

'Harton will come for you directly – he's going to stay a few days to see about – er – things, you know, and Crandeck is to do his work at Balclutha. He thought you'd rather not see him first, dear; but if –'

Our Lady lay face down among the frozen spines of the tussock, and she gave him to understand that she did not desire the presence of Crandeck, nor of any other man in all the world.

So the slow days dragged themselves into the past, and closed down the week with a cold, ink-black night and a mad lashing of rain on the roof.

Harton and Crandeck had sifted patiently through the seeds of Jamison's sowing, and had found many things that were ill therein. Therefore, Harton had called a meeting at Balclutha, and he told Our Lady's 'boys' all that was necessary for them to know.

'There's not a dashed penny left, and the station and stock

will have to go to pay part of the debts. I thought – I suppose we can make up the rest between us, eh, you fellows?'

'You bet,' said Verenin, stolidly; 'but what about Our Lady?'

'Don't believe she's a relative in the world. I don't know, unless – unless we send her to a boarding-school. She's only eighteen.'

There was a groan of mixed derision and pain.

'Our Lady! Harton, you cruel beast! Fancy ruling her into a dame-school. Besides, we can't manage without her.'

'I think you'll have to – now; can't you see that things must be different?'

'Suppose you'll marry her to some one – or to yourself,' said Payne with a sneer, and Harton got to his feet.

'Suppose you'd better shut up,' he said sharply. Then he looked at the others. 'We'll keep the home-block and Mrs Rooney, and Our Lady shall live there till we see how things turn out. And no man shall say a word of marriage to her or bother her in any way unless he gets the consent of the rest. We're all in this, and we're all answerable for her, eh?'

'Right–o,' said 'Pint-o'-Beer' Dick, 'Our Lady is ours in trust, and we'll take care of her – bless her! And you'll have the sale soon, Harton? There'll be a slump in sheep when they begin to send 'em down from the back country.'

Tony and Harton bought the land that the boundary-dogs had guarded, and gave them new places whereon to beat white, flint-hard circles from the level yellow. But all the plain was Our Lady's birthright, and she ran through the familiar ways of fern and scrub and cabbage-tree, and lighted the lantern for those strayed on the tracks that had passed to others, and so won through the bitter, solemn winter in the frost-bound silences to the sweet mutter of the spring wind, and the leagues of loosened yellow tossing to blue horizon.

Jamison's death had cast the bonds from Crandeck, but he waited still with Harton, until the sparseness of Our Lady's life lashed him beyond control, and he braved the assembly to tell them what he would do.

'I mean to marry her if she will,' he said; 'and I'll take her away from this place. It's an evil life for a girl, and – and I'll take her away from it. I don't care a hang what you fellows think about it, but it is only right that you should know first. You have done so much for her.'

Verenin swore in stolid fashion.

'I'm d—d if you're going to patronize us for it,' he said. 'She is Our Lady. But she ought to go – though, God knows, we will miss her.'

Harton stood at the window staring on the blue far hills where the flushed sunset moved.

'Yes,' he said slowly; 'it's not a life for a girl. She stays out half the night talking to the wind and the cabbage-trees and things. I've heard her; and the girlhood has gone out of her. She must go – and it must be you, Crandeck. We are all anchored here, and also – but does she love you, man?'

Crandeck was grasping the chairback, and his face was set. It is not an easy thing for a man – more especially an Englishman – to bare his soul before other men. But he recognized their right.

'I don't know; I think she will. She is so lonely, and – and I have waited –'

'It's best for her;' Harton spoke thickly; 'but, by Heaven, if you're not good to her, Crandeck –'

'It will take all you can give to make up for the old life,' said Tony, wisely.

Verenin opened and shut his fist reflectively.

'She's Our Lady,' he said again; 'and we'll be worse than mothers-in-law on to you, Crandeck –'

'Pint-o'-Beer' Dick saw the humorous side of this and laughed, whereat Crandeck swung round in wrath, and flayed him with hard words, thereby relieving his feelings immensely.

But it was Harton who rode over to Jamison's the following day, and spoke with Our Lady, for he knew her child-heart too well to think that Crandeck could win it by storm. He found her in the patch of manuka-scrub beyond the creek, and she raised grave eyes from her half-plaited stock-whip at his coming.

'You haven't been over for nearly a week, Vic. Why don't you? None of you come as often as you used to – and I'm so lonely.'

Harton was ever clumsy at words, but his love for Our Lady had taught him much.

'Better not, dear. We'd give all we've got to make you happy, and – and to take care of you. But there's only one way – one way, one of us can do it, dear.'

'Yes?' she asked, wearily.

Words were hard to come at.

'If – we all love you, My Lady, and you know it – if one of us married you, dear.'

Our Lady's hands gripped on the rough flax, and her eyes frightened Harton.

'I – oh, no, no! Not that! Never that! Oh, Vic – please don't make me marry you, Vic!'

Harton smiled a queer, twisted little smile.

'It is Crandeck, dear. He has loved you for a long while, and he wants to give you a happier life. We all think that it is best for Our Lady.'

She looked through the knotted, scant manukas into her world that she loved, and the sorrow on her still face hurt Harton's soul.

'Do you? Tony, and "Pint-o'-Beer" Dick and Mrs Rooney – and all of you?'

'Yes; and your father. I know he would have wished it, dear. Crandeck is a real good fellow –'

Our Lady stood up.

'I will try,' she said; 'but I can never love Crandeck like I do the plain, and I am not sure that you are right in thinking it best, Vic. Oh, it will hurt; but tell him I'll try, Vic.'

'He'd sooner hear that from yourself,' said Harton, and departed.

So Our Lady gave her free word to Crandeck, and would have taken it back when she knew the whole of its meaning, but that Crandeck would not.

'I told you that I hated the place and the beastly hidden thing in the dream-part of it,' he said; 'and I'm not going to wait here till its time is ripe. It might mean danger to you, dear heart; I seem to believe it does in my dream sometimes, and I'm blessed if I'll chance it any longer. So we'll go back to England, my own little love, and we'll be awfully happy, and not hear the wind calling out of those unspeakably dreary mountains any more.'

Our Lady drew back from his kiss.

'Do you think you quite understand?' she asked. 'I am part of the plain, and it is part of me. It is alive, and it talks to me, and I love it – better than I shall ever love you, Crandeck. I'll go with you because they all tell me there is – there is no other way. But it will be calling to me in the night, Crandeck; and I shall listen – and want to come back – always – always. Do you quite understand?'

'No, I don't, and I don't want to. You are a fanciful little lady, my sweetheart, and you will learn to love quick flesh better than dead earth. I'm going to teach you – and it'll be one of the things that don't hurt in the learning.'

But Tony knew better. He told Harton so as they rode home through the night, past the south-eastern corner of what had been Jamison's boundary, with the warm breath of the light nor'-west in their faces.

'Crandeck's a good enough sort of chap – but wood and iron can't assimilate, Harton, and we ought to have known it before. The plain is not even good arable land to him, and to her – neither of us know a tithe of what it is to her!'

'What in thunder are you driving at?'

'Have inanimate things soul-power over humans?'

'Bah!' said Harton; 'you're talking drivel.' But he smoked in painful thought until Tony jerked his colt back on its haunches wth a quick hand dropped to the other man's bridle-rein.

'Listen! That's her singing. Good Heavens! An' she's a full four miles from the house!'

Harton, peering with screwed eyes past the bare grey trunks of cabbage-trees, saw Our Lady's young, earnest face clear to the moon, and heard her words in the broad silence of the plain that listened to her.

'Good-bye, good-bye, dear wind of the red dawn and the evening! Good-bye, mountains – and smell of the flax – and the trampling nor'-westers. It is all done with and dead – Dear; did you know – did you know? No more yellow tussock for me; no more of the nights that we love – Dear; did you know – did you know? Oh! why did you teach me to love you? Good-bye! Good-bye! Good-bye!'

'She's mad. I'm going to put a stopper on this,' stammered Harton, preparing to descend.

'No, I'm dashed if you do;' Tony wheeled and led the horses

away with a strong hand. 'Let her alone. She'll belong to Crandeck to-morrow, and – and – and a jolly good thing, too! Did you see her face? She never looked like that for Crandeck. Tony – what is it? What does it mean?'

'It means,' said Tony, huskily, 'that we are fools, and don't understand. And we can't understand. She's just learnt what the love of a man for a woman is, and it can't touch her, because – because she learnt something bigger first.'

'Something – bigger? You don't – know?'

'No,' he said, unsteadily, 'I don't know. But it is. How much do we know about anything, after all? She knows more – and this d—d plain knows more. Look at it, Harton.'

Harton looked where the mighty bulk of it lay spread to the moon, with the great, regular movement of wind-stirred, whitened tussock, like breath that quickened the chest of a giant, and the stillness that is not placid, but tingling with curbed waiting about him.

And, for the first time, the threatening, unexplainable strength of the land that was old and wise beyond the knowledge of men, came down on him, and startled him.

'It's – it is the very devil,' he said. 'Thank the Lord she's going away to-morrow. Come on, Tony.'

He shook out the reins and went home at the gallop. But every sod that the hoofs cut from the turf seemed to sob at him in dumb live pain, until he loathed Tony for his words, and went to pace his room the night through; threshing out the limitations beyond which no human thought may stray with certainty, and finding no comfort therein.

Tony brought Our Lady a crown of white manuka-flowers for her marriage-day; and the sun was blazing and jubilant over a golden earth, and a blue sky, and a little group of men on the wide verandah surrounding a white frock that was Our Lady being married to Crandeck.

But when the Presbyterian parson, from forty miles away, had said all the 'Amens' and Crandeck stooped to kiss his wife before all her 'boys', the strong, assertive scent of the manuka irritated him to inexplicable jealousy.

'Take it off, sweetheart. You've nothing more to do with the plain and its belongings. You're mine now – mine, and nobody else's. Do you hear?'

'Confound you,' said Verenin; 'you needn't rub it in like that! He's so cocky, you fellows –'

'An' you'll write to us sometimes, My Lady? And I'll let you know how that turnip crop on the swamp turns out.'

'You've got my folks' address all right? Nottingham – shut up, Tony! Do you want to do all the gassing yourself?'

Payne brought up his four-in-hand with a whirl and a scatter of shingle and turf beyond the verandah, and Tony held Our Lady's hands very tight after he had helped her in.

'I'll look after the light. Be a brave girl, dear, and Crandeck will bring you back some day.'

'Yes,' she answered. But Tony turned away from her eyes, and choked over the shout that went with a burst shoe of Mrs Rooney's after the four-in-hand as Payne let out the whip.

By reason of a long day's work it was nine of the following evening before Tony rode over the two miles of tussock and swamp-flax to light Jamison's lantern. The dead manuka-wreath lay on the wooden verandah where Crandeck had flung it, and Tony's eyes were troubled as he climbed the little hill through the restless, windy dark.

At foot of the flagstaff he stumbled, and fell over something soft that gave to his weight without sound. He felt it with his hands. Then he knelt upright, and spoke to the march of triumphant wind that was the voice of the plain.

'Well – you've got her at last! You needn't make such a row about it, need you?'

The spurred boots that brushed the tussock over the hill-crest were Crandeck's, and it was Crandeck who said:

'Where is she? I know she's here. She left me – give her to me, Tony.'

Tony lit the lantern, and strung it half-mast. But he did not speak, and Crandeck asked no questions.

For, according to her promise, Our Lady had pulled away the clouds that rimmed the land of his dream, and behind them he saw her lie dead in the night under the flicker of Jamison's lantern.

Barbara Baynton

Billy Skywonkie*

1902

The line was unfenced, so with due regard to the possibility of the drought-dulled sheep attempting to chew it, the train crept cautiously along, stopping occasionally, without warning, to clear it from the listless starving brutes. In the carriage nearest the cattle-vans, some drovers and scrub-cutters were playing euchre, and spasmodically chorusing the shrill music from an uncertain concertina. When the train stopped, the player thrust his head from the carriage window. From one nearer the engine, a commercial traveller remonstrated with the guard, concerning the snail's pace and the many unnecessary halts.

'Take yer time, old die-ard,' yelled the drover to the guard. 'Whips er time, – don't bust yerself fer no one. Wot's orl the worl' to a man w'en his wife's a widder?' He laughed noisily and waved his hat at the seething bagman. 'Go an' 'ave a snooze. I'll wake yer up ther day after termorrer.'

He craned his neck to see into the nearest cattle–van. Four were down, he told his mates, who remarked, with blasphemous emphasis, that they would probably lose half before getting them to the scrub country.

The listening woman passenger in a carriage between the drover and the bagman, heard a thud soon after in the cattle-truck, and added another to the list of the fallen. Before dawn that day the train had stopped at a siding to truck them, and she had watched with painful interest these drought-tamed brutes being driven into the crowded vans. The tireless, greedy sun had swiftly followed the grey dawn, and in the light that even now seemed old and worn, the desolation of the barren shelterless plains, that the night had hidden, appalled her. She realized the sufferings of the emaciated cattle. It was barely

*'*Skywonkie*' *signifies weather-prophet.*

noon, yet she had twice emptied the water bottle, 'shogging' in the iron bracket.

The train dragged its weary length again, and she closed her eyes from the monotony of the dead plain. Suddenly the engine cleared its throat in shrill welcome to two iron tanks, hoisted twenty feet and blazing like evil eyes from a vanished face.

Beside them it squatted on its hunkers, placed a blackened thumb on its pipe, and hissed through its closed teeth like a snared wild cat, while gulping yards of water. The green slimy odour penetrated to the cattle. The lustiest of these stamped feebly, clashing their horns and bellowing a hollow request.

A long-bearded bushman was standing on the few slabs that formed a siding, with a stockwhip coiled like a snake on his arm. The woman passenger asked him the name of the place.

'This is ther Never-Never, – ther lars' place Gord made,' answered one of the drovers who were crowding the windows.

'Better'n ther 'ell-'ole yous come from, any'ow,' defended the bushman. 'Breakin' ther 'earts, and dyin' from suerside, 'cos they lef' it,' he added derisively, pointing to the cattle.

In patriotic anger he passed to the guard-van without answering her question, though she looked anxiously after him. At various intervals during the many halts of the train, she had heard some of the obscene jokes, and with it in motion, snatches of lewd songs from the drovers' carriage. But the language used by this bushman to the guard, as he helped to remove a ton of fencing wire topping his new saddle, made her draw back her head. Near the siding was a spring cart, and she presently saw him throw his flattened saddle into it and drive off. There was no one else in sight, and in nervous fear she asked the bagman if this was Gooriabba siding. It was nine miles further, he told her.

The engine lifted its thumb from its pipe. 'Well – well – to – be – sure; well – well – to – be – sure,' it puffed, as if in shocked remembrance of its being hours late for its appointment here.

She saw no one on the next siding, but a buggy waited near the slip-rails. It must be for her. According to Sydney arrangements she was to be met here, and driven out twelve miles. A drover inquired as the train left her standing by her portmanteau, 'Are yer travellin' on yer lonesome, or on'y goin' somew'ere!' and another flung a twist of paper towards her, brawling unmusically, that it was 'A flowwer from me angel mother's ger-rave'.

She went towards the buggy, but as she neared it the driver got in and made to drive off. She ran and called, for when he went she would be alone with the bush all round her, and only the sound of the hoarse croaking of the frogs from the swamp near, and the raucous 'I'll – 'ave – 'is – eye – out,' of the crows.

Yes, he was from Gooriabba Station, and had come to meet a young 'piece' from Sydney, who had not come.

She was ghastly with bilious sickness, – the result of an over-fed brain and an under-fed liver. Her face flushed muddily. 'Was it a housekeeper?'

He was the rouseabout, wearing his best clothes with awful unusualness. The coat was too long in the sleeve, and wrinkled across the back with his bush slouch. There was that wonderful margin of loose shirt between waistcoat and trouser, which all swagger bushies affect. Subordinate to nothing decorative was the flaring silk handkerchief, drawn into a sailor's knot round his neck.

He got out and fixed the winkers, then put his hands as far as he could reach into his pockets – from the position of his trousers he could not possibly reach bottom. It was apparently some unknown law that suspended them. He thrust forward his lower jaw, elevated his pipe, and squirted a little tobacco juice towards his foot that was tracing semicircles in the dust. 'Damned if I know,' he said with a snort, 'but there'll be a 'ell of a row somew'ere.'

She noticed that the discoloured teeth his bush grin showed so plainly, were worn in the centre, and met at both sides with the pipe between the front. Worn stepping-stones her mind insisted.

She looked away towards the horizon where the smoke of the hidden train showed faintly against a clear sky, and as he was silent, she seemed to herself to be intently listening to the croak of the frogs and the threat of the cows. She knew that, from under the brim of the hat he wore over his eyes, he was looking at her sideways.

Suddenly he withdrew his hands and said again, 'Damned if I

know. S'pose it's alright! Got any traps? Get up then 'an 'ole the Neddy while I get it.' They drove a mile or so in silence; his pipe was still in his mouth though not alight.

She spoke once only. 'What a lot of frogs seem to be in that lake!'

He laughed. 'That's ther Nine Mile Dam!' He laughed again after a little – an intelligent, complacent laugh.

'It used ter be swarmin' with teal in a good season, but Gord A'mighty knows w'en it's ever goin' ter rain any more! I dunno!' This was an important admission, for he was a great weather prophet. 'Lake!' he sniggered and looked sideways at his companion. 'Thet's wot thet there bloke, the painter doodle, called it. An' 'e goes ter dror it, an' 'e sez wot 'e'll give me five bob if I'll run up ther horses, an' keep 'em so's 'e ken put 'em in ther picshure. An' 'e drors ther Dam an' ther trees, puts in thet there ole dead un, an' 'e puts in ther 'orses right clost against ther water w'ere the frogs is. 'E puts them in too, an' damned if 'e don't dror ther 'orses drinkin' ther water with ther frogs, an' ther frogs spit on it! Likely yarn ther 'orses ud drink ther water with ther blanky frogs' spit on it! Fat lot they know about ther bush! Blarsted nannies!'

Presently he inquired as to the place where they kept pictures in Sydney, and she told him, the Art Gallery.

'Well, some of these days I'm goin' down ter Sydney,' he continued, 'an' I'll collar thet one 'cos it's a good likerness of ther 'orses – you'd know their 'ide on a gum tree – an' that mean mongrel never paid me ther five bob.'

Between his closed teeth he hissed a bush tune for some miles, but ceased to look at the sky and remarked, 'No sign er rain! No lambin' this season; soon as they're dropt we'll 'ave ter knock 'em all on ther 'ead!' He shouted an oath of hatred at the crows following after the tottering sheep that made in a straggling line for the water. 'Look at 'em!' he said, 'scoffin' out ther eyes!' He pointed to where the crows hovered over the bogged sheep. 'They puttywell lives on eyes! "Blanky bush Chinkies!" I call 'em. No one carn't tell 'em apart!'

There was silence again, except for a remark that he could spit all the blanky rain they had had in the last nine months.

Away to the left along a side track his eyes travelled searchingly, as they came to a gate. He stood in the buggy and looked again.

'Promised ther "Konk" t' leave 'im 'ave furst squint at yer,' he muttered, 'if 'e was 'ere t' open ther gate! But I'm not goin' t' blanky well wait orl day!' He reluctantly got out and opened the gate, and he had just taken his seat when a 'Cooee' sounded from his right, heralded by a dusty pillar. He snorted resentfully. "Ere 'e is; jes' as I got out an' done it!'

The 'Konk' cantered to them, his horse's hoofs padded by the dust-cushioned earth. The driver drew back, so as not to impede the newcomer's view. After a moment or two, the 'Konk', preferring closer quarters, brought his horse round to the left. Unsophisticated bush wonder in the man's face met the sophisticated in the girl's.

Never had she seen anything so grotesquely monkeyish. And the nose of this little hairy horror, as he slewed his neck to look into her face, blotted the landscape and dwarfed all perspective. She experienced a strange desire to extend her hand. When surprise lessened, her mettle saved her from the impulse to cover her face with both hands, to baffle him.

At last the silence was broken by the driver drawing a match along his leg, and lighting his pipe. The hairy creature safely arranged a pair of emu eggs, slung with bush skill round his neck.

'Ain't yer goin' to part?' inquired the driver, indicating his companion as the recipient.

'Wot are yer givin' us; wot do yer take me fur?' said the 'Konk' indignantly, drawing down his knotted veil.

'Well, give 'em ter me fer 'Lizer.'

'Will yer 'ave 'em now, or wait till yer get 'em?'

'Goin' ter sit on 'em yerself?' sneered the driver.

'Yes, an' I'll give yer ther first egg ther cock lays,' laughed the 'Konk'.

He turned his horse's head back to the gate. 'I say, Billy Skywonkie! Wot price Sally Ah Too, eh?' he asked, his gorilla mouth agape.

Billy Skywonkie uncrossed his legs, took out the whip. He tilted his pipe and shook his head as he prepared to drive, to show that he understood to a fraction the price of Sally Ah Too. The aptness of the question took the sting out of his having had to open the gate. He gave a farewell jerk.

'Goin' ter wash yer neck?' shouted the man with the nose, from the gate.

'Not if I know it.'

The 'Konk' received the intimation incredulously. 'Stinkin' Roger!' he yelled. In bush parlance this was equal to emphatic disbelief.

This was a seemingly final parting, and both started, but suddenly the 'Konk' wheeled round.

'Oh, Billy!' he shouted.

Billy stayed his horse and turned expectantly.

'W'en's it goin' ter rain?'

The driver's face darkened. 'Your blanky jealersey'll get yer down, an' worry yer yet,' he snarled, and slashing his horse he drove rapidly away.

'Mickey ther Konk,' he presently remarked to his companion, as he stroked his nose.

This explained her earlier desire to extend her hand. If the 'Konk' had been a horse she would have stroked his nose.

'Mob er sheep can camp in the shadder of it,' he said.

Boundless scope for shadows on that sun-smitten treeless plain!

'Make a good ploughshere,' he continued; 'easy plough a cultivation paddock with it!'

At the next gate he seemed in a mind and body conflict. There were two tracks; he drove along one for a few hundred yards. Then stopping he turned, and finding the 'Konk' out of sight abruptly drove across to the other. He continually drew his whip along the horse's back, and haste seemed the object of the movement, though he did not flog the beast.

After a few miles on the new track, a blob glittered dazzlingly through the glare, like a fallen star. It was the iron roof of the wine shanty – the Saturday night and Sunday resort of shearers and rouseabouts for twenty miles around. Most of its spirits was made on the premises from bush recipes, of which bluestone and tobacco were the chief ingredients. Every drop had the reputation of 'bitin' orl ther way down.'

A sapling studded with broken horse-shoes seemed to connect two lonely crow stone trees. Under their scanty shade groups of dejected fowls stood with beaks agape. Though the buggy wheels almost reached them, they were motionless but for the quivering gills. The ground both sides of the shanty was decorated with tightly pegged kangaroo skins. A dog, apathetically blind and dumb, lay on the verandah, lifeless save for eyelids blinking in antagonism to the besieging flies.

'Jerry can't be far off,' said Billy Skywonkie, recognizing the dog. He stood up in the buggy. 'By cripes, there 'e is – goosed already, an' 'e on'y got is cheque lars' night.'

On the chimney side of the shanty a man lay in agitated sleep beside his rifle and swag. There had been a little shade on that side in the morning, and he had been sober enough to select it, and lay his head on his swag. He had emptied the bottle lying at his feet since then. His swag had been thoroughly 'gone through', and also his singlet and trouser pockets. The fumes from the shanty-grog baffled the flies. But the scorching sun was conquering; the man groaned, and his hands began to search for his burning head.

Billy Skywonkie explained to his companion that it was 'Thet fool, Jerry ther kangaroo-shooter, bluein' 'is cheque fer skins'. He took the water bag under the buggy, and poured the contents into the open mouth and over the face of the 'dosed' man, and raised him into a sitting posture. Jerry fought this friendliness vigorously, and, staggering to his feet, picked up his rifle, and took drunken aim at his rescuer, then at the terrified woman in the buggy.

The rouseabout laughed unconcernedly. ''E thinks we're blanky kangaroos,' he said to her. 'Jerry, ole cock, yer couldn't 'it a woolshed! Yer been taking ther sun!'

He took the rifle and pushed the subdued Jerry into the chimney corner.

He tilted his hat, till, bush fashion, it ''ung on one 'air', and went inside the shanty.

'Mag!' he shouted, thumping the bar (a plank supported by two casks).

The woman in the buggy saw a slatternly girl with doughy hands come from the back, wiping the flour from her face with a kitchen towel. They made some reference to her she knew, as the girl came to the door and gave her close scrutiny. Then, shaking her head till her long brass earrings swung like pendulums, she laughed loudly.

'Eh?' inquired the rouseabout.

'My oath!' 'Square dinkum!' she answered, going behind the bar.

He took the silk handkerchief from his neck, and playfully tried to flick the corner into her eye. Mag was used to such delicate attentions and well able to defend herself. With the dirty kitchen towel she succeeded in knocking off his hat, and round and round the house she ran with it, dexterously dodging the skin-pegs. He could neither overtake nor outwit her with any dodge, so he gave in, and ransomed his hat with the 'shouts' she demanded.

From the back of the shanty, a bent old woman, almost on all fours, crept towards the man, again prostrate in the corner. She paused, with her ear turned to where the girl and the rouseabout were still at horse-play. With catlike movements she stole on till within reach of Jerry's empty pockets. She turned her terrible face to the woman in the buggy, as if in expectation of sympathy. Keeping wide of the front door, she came to the further side of the buggy. With the fascination of horror the woman looked at this creature, whose mouth and eyes seemed to dishonour her draggled grey hair. She was importuning for something, but the woman in the buggy could not understand till she pointed to her toothless mouth (the mission of which seemed to be, to fill its cavernous depths with the age-loosened skin above and below). A blue bag under each eye aggressively ticked like the gills of the fowls, and the sinews of the neck strained into *bassi relievi.* Alternately she pointed to her mouth, or laid her knotted fingers on the blue bags in pretence of wiping tears. Entrenched behind the absorbed skin-terraces, a stump of purple tongue made efforts at speech. When she held out her claw, the woman understood and felt for her purse. Wolfishly the old hag snatched and put into her mouth the coin, and as the now merry driver, followed by Mag, came, she shook a warning claw at the giver, and flopped whining in the dust, her hands ostentatiously open and wiping dry eyes.

'Ello Biddy, on ther booze again!'

The bottle bulging from his coat pocket made speech with him intelligible, despite the impeding coin.

He placed the bottle in the boot of the buggy, and turning to Mag, said 'Give ther poor ole cow a dose!'

'Yes, one in a billy; anything else might make her sick!' said Mag, 'I caught 'er jus' now swiggin' away with ther tap in 'er mug!'

He asked his companion would she like a wet. She asked for water, and so great was her need, that, making a barricade of closed lips and teeth to the multitude of apparently wingless mosquitoes thriving in its green tepidity, she moistened her mouth and throat.

'Oh, I say, Billy!' called Mag as he drove off. Her tones suggested her having forgotten an important matter, and he turned eagerly. 'W'en's it goin' ter rain?' she shrieked, convulsed in merriment.

'Go an' crawl inter a' oller log!' he shouted angrily.

'No, but truly, Billy.' Billy turned again. 'Give my love to yaller 'Lizer; thet slues yer!'

They had not gone far before he looked round again. 'Gord!' he cried excitedly. 'Look at Mag goin' through 'er ole woman!'

Mag had the old woman's head between her knees, dentist-fashion, and seemed to concentrate upon her victim's mouth, whose feeble impotence was soon demonstrated by the operator releasing her, and triumphantly raising her hand.

What the finger and thumb held the woman knew and the other guessed.

'By Gord. Eh! thet's prime, ain't it? No flies on Mag; not a fly!' he said admiringly.

'See me an' 'er?' he asked, as he drove on.

His tone suggested no need to reply, and his listener did not. A giddy unreality took the sting from everything, even from her desire to beseech him to turn back to the siding, and leave her there to wait for the train to take her back to civilization. She felt she had lost her mental balance. Little matters became distorted, and the greater shrivelled.

He was now more communicative, and the oaths and adjectives so freely used were surely coined for such circumstances. 'Damned' the wretched, starving, and starved sheep looked and were; 'bloody' the beaks of the glutted crows; 'blarsted' the whole of the plain they drove through!

Gaping cracks suggested yawning graves, and the skeleton fingers of the drooping myalls seemingly pointed to them.

'See me an' Mag?' he asked again. 'No flies on Mag; not a wink 'bout 'er!' He chuckled in tribute. 'Ther wus thet damned flash fool, Jimmy Fernatty,' he continued; '— ther blanky fool; 'e never 'ad no show with Mag. An' yet 'e'd go down there! It wus two mile furder this way, yet damned if ther blanky fool wouldn't come this way every time, 'less ther boss 'e wus with 'im,'stead er goin' ther short cut, – ther way I come this mornin'. An' every time Mag ud make 'im part 'arf a quid. I wus on'y there jus' 'bout five minits meself, an' I stuck up nea'ly 'arf a quid! An' there's four gates' (he flogged the horse and painted them crimson when he remembered them) 'this way, more'n on ther way I come this mornin'.'

Presently he gave her the reins with instructions to drive through one. It seemed to take a long time to close it, and he had to fix the back of the buggy before he opened it, and after it was closed.

After getting out several times in quick succession to fix the back of the buggy when there was no gate, he seemed to forget the extra distance. He kept his hand on hers when she gave him the reins, and bade her 'keep up 'er pecker'. 'Some one would soon buck up ter 'er if their boss wusn't on.' But the boss, it seemed, was a 'terrer for young uns. Jimmy Fernatty 'as took up with a yaller piece an' is livin' with 'er. But not me; thet's not me! I'm like ther boss, thet's me! No yaller satin for me!'

He watched for the effect of this degree of taste on her.

Though she had withdrawn her hand, he kept winking at her, and she had to move her feet to the edge of the buggy to prevent his pressing against them. He told her with sudden anger that any red black-gin was as good as a half chow any day, and it was no use gammoning, for he knew what she was.

'If Billy Skywonkie 'ad ter string onter yaller 'Lizer, more 'air on 'is chest fer doin' so' (striking his own). 'I ken get as many w'ite gins as I wanter, an' I'd as soon tackle a gin as a chow any day!'

On his next visit to the back of the buggy she heard the crash of glass breaking against a tree, then after a few snatches of song he lighted his pipe, and grew sorrowfully reminiscent.

'Yes, s'elp me, nea'ly 'arf a quid! An' thet coloured ole 'og of a cow of a mother, soon's she's off ther booze, 'll see thet she gets it!' Then he missed his silk handkerchief. 'Ghost!' he said breathing heavily. 'Mag's snavelled it! 'Lizer'll spot thet's gone soon's we get 'ithin cooee of 'er!'

Against hope he turned and looked along the road; felt every pocket, lifted his feet, and looked under the mat. His companion, in reply, said she had not seen it since his visit to the shanty.

'My Gord!' he said, 'Mag's a fair terror!' He was greatly troubled till the braggart in him gave an assertive flicker. 'Know wot I'll do ter 'Lizer soon's she begins ter start naggin' at me?' He intended this question as an insoluble conundrum, and waited for no surmises. 'Fill 'er mug, with this!' and the shut fist he shook was more than a mugful ''Twouldn't be ther first time I done it, nor ther lars'.' But the anticipation seemed little comfort to him.

The rest of the journey was done in silence, and without even a peep at the sky. When they came to the homestead gate he said his throat felt as though a 'goanner' had crawled into it and died. He asked her for a pin and clumsily dropped it in his efforts to draw the collar up to his ears, but had better luck with a hairpin.

He appeared suddenly subdued and sober, and as he took his seat after closing the gate, he offered her his hand, and said, hurriedly: 'No 'arm done, an' no 'arm meant; an' don't let on ter my missus – thet's 'er on the verander – thet we come be ther shanty.'

It was dusk, but through it she saw that the woman was dusky too.

'Boss in, 'Lizer?' There was contrition and propitiation in his voice.

'You've bin a nice blanky time,' said his missus, 'an' lucky fer you Billy Skywonkie 'e ain't.'

With bowed head, his shoulders making kindly efforts to hide his ears, he sat silent and listening respectfully. The woman in the buggy thought that the volubility of the angry half-caste's tongue must be the nearest thing to perpetual motion.

Under her orders both got down, and from a seat under the open window in the little room to which 'Lizer had motioned, she gave respectful attention to the still rapidly flowing tirade. The offence had been some terrible injustice to a respectable married woman, 'slavin' an' graftin' an' sweatin' from mornin' ter night, for a slungin', idlin', lazy blaggard'. In an indefinable way the woman felt that both of them were guilty, and to hide from her part of the reproof was mean and cowardly. The half-caste from time to time included her, and by degrees she understood that the wasted time of which 'Lizer complained was supposed to have been dissipated in flirtation. Neither the shanty nor Mag had mention.

From the kitchen facing the yard a Chinaman came at intervals, and with that assumption of having mastered the situation in all its bearings through his thorough knowledge of the English tongue, he shook his head in calm, shocked surprise. His sympathies were unmistakably with 'Lizer, and he many times demonstrated his grip of the grievance by saying, 'By Cli', Billy, it's a bloo'y shame!'

Maybe it was a sense of what was in his mind that made the quivering woman hide her face when virtuous Ching Too came to look at her. She was trying to eat when a dog ran into the dining-room, and despite the violent beating of her heart, she heard the rouseabout tell the boss as he unsaddled his horse, 'The on'y woman I see was a 'alf chow, an' she ses she's the one, an' she's in ther dinin'-room 'avin' a tuck in.'

She was too giddy to stand when the boss entered, but she turned her mournful eyes on him; and, supporting herself by the table, stood and faced him.

He kept on his hat, and she, watching, saw curiosity and surprise change into anger as he looked at her.

'What an infernal cheek *you* had to come! Who sent you?' he asked stormily.

She told him, and added that she had no intention of remaining.

'How old?' She made no reply. His last thrust, as in disgust he strode out, had the effect of a galvanic battery on her dying body.

Her bedroom was reeking with a green heavy scent. Empty powder boxes and rouge pots littered the dressing table, and various other aids of nature evidenced her predecessor's frailty. From a coign in its fastness a black spider eyed her malignantly, and as long as the light lasted she watched it.

The ringing of a bell slung outside in the fork of a tree awoke her before dawn. It was mustering – bush stock-taking – and all the station hands were astir. There was a noise of galloping horses being driven into the stockyard, and the clamour of the men as they caught and saddled them. Above the clatter of plates in the kitchen she could hear the affected drawl of the Chinaman talking to 'Lizer, who trod heavily along the passage, preparing the boss's breakfast. This early meal was soon over, and with the dogs snapping playfully at the horses' heels, all rode off.

Spasmodic bars of 'A Bicycle Built for Two' came from the kitchen, 'Mayly, Mayly, give me answer do!' There was neither haste nor anxiety in the singer's tones. Before the kitchen fire, oblivious to the heat, stood the Chinaman cook, inert from his morning's opium. It was only nine, but this was well on in the day for Ching, whose morning began at four.

He ceased his song as she entered. 'You come Sydiney? Ah! You mally? Ah! Sydiney welly ni' place. This placee welly dly – too muchee no lain – welly dly.'

She was watching his dog. On a block lay a flitch of bacon, and across the freshly cut side the dog drew its tongue, then snapped at the flies.

'That dog will eat the bacon,' she said.

'No!' answered the cook. ''E no eat 'em – too saw.'

It was salt; she had tried it for breakfast.

He began energetically something about, 'by-an'-bye me getty mally. By Cli', no 'alf cas' – too muchee longa jlaw.' He laughed and shook his head, reminiscent of 'las' a-night,' and waited for applause. But, fascinated, she still watched the dog, who from time to time continued to take 'saw' with his flies.

'Go ou' si', Sir,' said the cook in a spirit of rivalry. The dog stood and snapped. 'Go ou'si', I say!' No notice from the dog. 'Go ou' si', I tella you!' stamping his slippered feet and taking a fire stick. The dog leisurely sat down and looked at his master with mild reproof. 'Go insi' then, anybloo'y si' you li'!' but pointing to their joint bedroom with the lighted stick. The dog went to the greasy door, saw that the hens sitting on the bed were quietly laying eggs to go with the bacon, and came back.

She asked him where was the rouseabout who had driven her in yesterday.

'Oh, Billy Skywonkie, 'e mally alri'! 'Lizer 'im missie!' He went on to hint that affection there was misplaced, but that he himself was unattached.

She saw the rouseabout rattle into the yard in a spring cart. He let down the backboard and dumped three sheep under a light gallows. Their two front feet were strapped to one behind.

He seemed breathless with haste. 'Oh, I say!' he called out to her. 'Ther boss 'e tole me this mornin' thet I wus ter tell you, you wis ter sling yer 'ook. To do a get,' he explained. 'So bundle yer duds tergether quick an' lively! 'Lizer's down at ther tank, washin'. Le's get away afore she sees us, or she'll make yer swaller yer chewers.' Lowering his voice, he continued: 'I wanter go ter ther shanty – on'y ter get me 'ankercher.'

He bent and strained back a sheep's neck, drew the knife and steel from his belt, and skilfully danced an edge on the knife.

She noticed that the sheep lay passive, with its head back, till its neck curved in a bow, and that the glitter of the knife was reflected in its eye.

Mabel Forrest

The Housekeeper

1907

Frank Fort had had endless trouble with servants. His red-headed chum, Percival O'Dowd, said half in joke that he ought to try a housekeeper. O'Dowd thought it preferable to entertaining the notion of a wife. He said he would do it himself, but possessing only a selection which wouldn't carry a sheep to the acre and weighted by a substantial overdraft, he found it necessary to be his own housekeeper, cook, and housemaid, and he always spent from Saturday to Monday at Fort's station, which paid and was not in debt; consequently there was something worth eating to be had for Sunday dinner when there was no domestic upheaval on the tapis and a cook to cook it. O'Dowd, at home, lived mostly upon dried apples (which he always forgot to soak before cooking), and anything he could find about the place. It was quite a godsend to him when a passing traveller ate on the premises a water-melon he had stolen from a neighbouring cockie's, for later a melon vine clambered about the supports of the house on the spot where O'Dowd had been accustomed to throw his washing water, and it bore a few fine melons. Then the goats from the pub strolled over and ate most of the vine and trampled the rest. O'Dowd had meant to mend the fence round the house, but had gone to the township races instead. He was not in the best of spirits when he offered the advice about a housekeeper to Fort. He had lost money at the races. He always did. This time it was the bulk of a draft his mother had sent him from Ireland to keep Christmas on, and now the hot arid months before the New Year stretched out uninvitingly before him. He had meant to have a case of whisky and, perhaps, a housewarming on the strength of that money. He had intended to buy a new suit and renew his calls at Coolibar ridges, where brown-eyed Rosie Glanvers had just arrived home from boarding-school in Melbourne. But there!

The races were responsible. What did they want to hold races just at this time for? 'Sure, they ought to have more sinse!'

Frank Fort, or 'F.', as the district called him, laughed, and returned to the subject of the housekeeper.

'The devil always comes shaped like a horse to an Irishman, Percival,' he said, and smoked thoughtfully. 'I think I will get a housekeeper, though, someone over 40, eh? That wouldn't scandalise the community, would it?'

'Begobs! Say something over 50, and be on the safe side,' said Percival. 'Fair and forty, man. Forty's not old enough! She'd be coaxing you to make her Mrs Fort in no time!'

'My good fellow, you know I do not look at anything over 20,' answered Fort, looking sideways at Percival, who winced ever so little as he burnt his fingers with the match he held to the bowl of his pipe.

'My love is like a red, red rose!' sang Fort, and then stretched himself luxuriously in his hammock. 'Hit there yourself, O'Dowd?'

'Of course! I'm just the cut for a married man. I've such a fine property behind me. I could feed a wife on the fat of my neighbour's flocks. I certainly couldn't on my own! So it's a wife instead of a housekeeper you're thinking on, old man?'

'Not I! I was only joking. Seriously, O'Dowd, a man is a fool in my opinion to marry before he is 40, at any rate – if then! I am 30, and I want ten more years to kick up my heels in.'

'So it isn't Miss Rosie?' O'Dowd was looking out into the wide sun-dried garden, with its rows of trellised grape-vines.

'It isn't anybody!' Fort yawned comfortably, enjoying the certainty of his own heart-wholeness. 'Like a good chap, write out an advertisement for me for a housekeeper, middle-aged, unprepossessing appearance, etc., no encumbrances, not fond of Irishmen. Be sure to put that, Percy, or I'll have her falling captive to your bow and spear straight away.'

Percival drew out his notebook and scribbled down an advertisement, which answered the purpose more or less.

'"Wanted, housekeeper for station, middle-aged lady, without encumbrance." Does that mean children or husband? "Apply, stating salary required, etc." Now, Fort, how does that suit? I'm afraid you'd be after getting no replies if I put that in about the unprepossessing appearance. Most women are beauties to some men, and all are to themselves, bless 'em! Besides, if she came on those terms she would all the time be asking you if you thought brains weren't preferable to beauty any day, and I'm quite sure you don't think so.'

'Nor does any man, though they sometimes pretend they do. A pair of red lips against weighty grey brain matter! Ugh! What do we want women for except to look pretty at the heads of our tables and to wear the jewels we hang on them?'

'You're very young yet, Frank, very young,' said O'Dowd, shaking his head. 'What about your housekeeper-to-be, now?

'Oh, I grant you that class. The women who have to work and grow ugly in the doing! Poor devils! Yes, I grant you their use. Washerwomen and the like! And lady helps, etc. But I was thinking of the women we play with.'

'In short, the women with the higher destiny of amusing man?'

'Oh! don't get satirical, old chap. Have a whisky?'

O'Dowd drew the syphon to him. 'It's too d—d hot for argument,' he said apologetically.

By the next mail the advertisement for a housekeeper went down to the daily press in the city.

She was a success from the start.

O'Dowd, the pessimist, shook his red head. 'She doesn't look her age,' he said. She had given herself out to be 45, and her hair was grey all over her large shapely head. She had delicate lines about her mouth and a little furrow across her forehead. Percival allowed all that, which Fort made the most of, but her eyes were bright brown as Rosie Glanvers' own, only with the difference which we see between the young bird's, just peeping out of its downy nest, and the faithful collie's, who has watched long bitter nights, and yet not a collie exactly, for a collie's eyes have had all the wolf-dog domesticated out of them. The old wolf was still lingering in Mrs Armitage's eyes, O'Dowd said.

'You must have been looking pretty closely into them,' said Frank shortly, and Percival laughed in his whimsical fashion, and asked after the yellow rose, with a cunning smile, for Fort was trying to rear Cloth-of-Gold roses in his garden, a thing which the district had never accomplished yet. Some people said it was the fault of the soil, some said the want of the rain, some that the sun was too hot for the greater part of the year. But Mrs Armitage, who seemed to know everything, maintained that the roses loved the dry weather, and she put on her blue sunbonnet and cared for the cuttings herself. Everything in the house went like clockwork now. The German woman who cooked decided to stay, since there was a 'frau' to look after things. She never could get the 'Herr' to understand, and the housemaid said that she was a 'real lady'. She won the heart of the Scotch gardener by discovering herself as a countrywoman of his own, whose forefathers had let out crofts to his forefathers. 'It's a gran' old lowland family she cooms of,' he confided to the Boss, and Fort thought none the less of her for that. 'The district will talk,' muttered O'Dowd on the day she arrived. He never said it again. It was obvious that Fort was annoyed, and there was no further occasion to comment on what followed instanter.

The district talked itself blue, but after they met Mrs Armitage they invited her to their houses, and when she firmly and so sweetly excused herself they talked themselves red and pitied 'F.'. A tit-bit of scandal is such a blessing in the bush, where people have so much time to walk round it and examine it from all sides. Country air agrees with it when it might become stifled by other interests in the town, and it grows all the time.

O'Dowd still spent his Sundays at the station. The cooking was excellent, and he bagan to despise his dried apples and odds and ends of hastily-fried abominations, and to envy Fort. But, still, though he envied, he did not approve, and watched, figuratively speaking, from afar off. Mrs Armitage had beautiful hands, and she taught Fort to play cribbage, though he had never cared for cards.

'A nice game for two,' muttered O'Dowd in his moustache, and wished that he had not advised Fort to get a housekeeper. 'I never imagined one like her,' he added darkly to himself, which meant that he did not believe in housekeepers with beautiful hands. I think there was a good deal of dog-in-the-manger about Mr Percival O'Dowd in these days. The rose cuttings progressed wonderfully. Little green sprouts came out about the slim stalks, and one day on riding up to the station Percival was met by Fort with the news that there was a bud on one of the Cloth-of-Gold trees. They were 'trees' now, they had so waxed and grown great in the land under the care of the beautiful hands. 'It is quite a little triumph,' said Fort garrulously. 'Rose Glanvers has been trying to grow them ever since she came from school, and every slip she got died first go. Mrs Armitage has extraordinary luck with flowers.'

But, later on, Mrs Armitage refused to wear her laurels.

'It is Mr Fort, every bit as much as my care, that has pulled the roses through,' she said, smiling that charmingly aloof smile of hers. 'He is such a clever gardener!'

'And you are a very clever woman,' whispered O'Dowd to his serviette. Aloud he said: 'Ah! Mrs Armitage, when you smile on the flowers what would they be after doing but looking up?' She eyed him curiously for a moment. 'Always an Irishman, Mr O'Dowd,' she said, and passed him the butter.

'She's got my measure, all right,' said Percival to himself.

Then O'Dowd took to riding over to Coolibar ridges, and having long talks with Rosie. And somehow Rosie always brought the conversation round to 'F.' and 'F.'s' housekeeper.

'She must be a most interesting woman,' she said one day. 'But she is so hard to meet. Mother wrote and said she was sorry she was not strong enough to call, and would she drop convention and come here, but she never came.'

'Why don't you go over?' asked O'Dowd, wrinkling his freckled forehead under his red hair. 'It would be a kindness, and I'm the man for your escort any day.'

A little devil leaped in his heart. He did not want Fort to marry anybody, not only for Fort's own sake, for it might be as well for him to marry later on. Frank Fort, though his friend, was not the man he wished to give Rosie to. He must finish his wild oat sowing and settle down before Percival would like to see him take this little white heart to reign at the station. He had not much faith in Frank's loyalty to one woman. Nevertheless, Frank was his friend. He did not want to see Frank entangled with a woman with 'wolf eyes', especially one who was ten years at least his senior. Percival did not believe that Mrs Armitage was 45, but she was certainly older than Frank, and she was – oh! dash her! – she was a woman in a thousand to wind herself round a man's heart, in making herself necessary to him in a hundred ways. He would try a contrast of Rosie's freshness against the maturer beauties of 'F.'s' housekeeper.

Rosie rode over to call on Mrs Armitage, and, on being pressed by Fort, she stayed the night. Mrs Armitage played hostess instead of cribbage that evening. Percival watched, and was satisfied. Rosie was taken out by Frank to see the new flower on the rosebush in the moonlit garden. They were a long time admiring the flower. Mrs Armitage won O'Dowd's respect. She sat so still in her high-backed chair; the soft lace about her throat rose lightly to her even breathing, and she smiled and smiled bewilderingly. The Irishman felt the hot blood rising in his cheeks. He was a skunk to try to spoil this fine woman's little game, and after all . . . . But she looked up. He decided that he did not like her eyes. He pictured Rosie as a little white lamb astray in the forest, with a sleek wild creature following her up from tree to tree, never showing itself in the light, but stealing gradually nearer – nearer. . . . Mrs-Armitage yawned apologetically.

'Do you care about cards?' she said, leaning over and drawing the cribbage-board to her.

'She is going to teach me to play cribbage,' thought O'Dowd, and his pulses quickened ever so slightly.

By-and-bye the two moonlight strollers came in from the garden. Rosie was flushed. She put her hand on Mrs Armitage's arm when she said 'Goodnight', and called her 'dear'. O'Dowd frowned. Fort thought it very nice of her. He beamed affectionately on his housekeeper.

'I am going to ride home with Miss Glanvers early in the morning,' he said to Mrs Armitage when she returned from showing Rosie to her room.

'Tells her what he is going to do now!' said Percival to the little devil he kept on watch.

'She is a nice child,' said Mrs Armitage. The lamplight fell on her silver hair and fine head.

'She makes me think of a picture of a French marquise in the reign of Terror,' said Fort later, when the men were smoking on the verandah.

'Who? Rose Glanvers?' asked O'Dowd, wickedly. Fort smoked.

When Fort returned from his ride to Coolibar the following evening it was growing dark. Mrs Armitage was sitting in a rocking-chair on the verandah in a black dinner gown, the neck and arms filled in with fine black net, which revealed the firm beauty of her shoulders. In passing through the garden Frank had picked a full-blown rose from the sacred tree, and, as he swung up the steps, he held it aloft, shouting boyishly: 'Here! Prize to the victor! Te salutant, Caesar!' and he dropped on one knee, his spurs clanking on the verandah boards as he knelt before Mrs Armitage.

She laughed softly, leaning forward to take the rose.

O'Dowd, watching from the hammock where swung his long legs, noted how her hand hovered a moment over Fort's fair head.

'She'd be stroking his curls if I wasn't here,' he thought, and then said:

'Don't lose sight of the audience, F.'.

Fort jumped up and turned a laughing face to him. 'I knew you were there, you old thief! Well, watch the end of the play! There, do you remember Francis Barraud's picture in this year's Salon book – "A la sante de Madame la Marquise" – and the brutes crowding round the marquise, who sits with her proud frightened eyes on the rabble, and the dead body of her husband or lover – I do not know the story, I'm just imagining – on the floor behind her? Now, isn't she the moral of the marquise?' He held the yellow rose against Mrs Armitage's hair, without actually touching its soft masses.

O'Dowd raised his eyebrows till they encroached on his wide low forehead and almost touched his shock of red hair.

'Oh – yes–s,' he said slowly, choosing his words, 'but I don't remember that there was any rose in the picture; besides, Mrs Armitage does not look in the least afraid of the rabble – I presume you are the rabble, Fort, and I am the dead husband – or lover? I am sure I should like to be.'

Fort tossed the rose into the housekeeper's lap.

'I don't know if O'Dowd means to compliment us or not, Mrs Armitage,' he said lightly. 'You know he's only a mad Irishman! Well, I suppose I must be off to have a wash before the dinner bell rings!' And he went whistling up the hall to the bathroom.

Far away on the township road they could see the lights of

some teamsters' camp fires glimmering in the oncoming dark. In the garden there was a stirring of tiny hidden things that moved among the vines and grass. It was a still summer's night, and the bark of a dog at one of the station huts sounded near at hand. Mrs Armitage rose with a rustling of silken underskirts. O'Dowd had never seen her so fine. 'Keeps that for his final subjugation, I suppose,' he grunted to his familiar. To her he said:

'Fort is nothing but a boy in spite of his thirty years!' She nodded, looking past him dreamily.

'It's a pity we ever have to grow up,' she said, then turned to him and smiled, slowly. He had never imagined that her eyes could grow so soft.

'Do you think he will marry the girl?' she said.

For all the forty years he had spent in growing accustomed to the unexpected, O'Dowd was startled. He had never anticipated such frankness from her. Well, he would be equally frank. He took a step towards her. The dusk had blotted out the finger prints of the passing years from her forehead; he only saw her dark eyes shining through the gloaming.

'He will – if you will let him!' he said boldly.

After dinner the men smoked, to keep away the mosquitoes, in the corner of the verandah, and Mrs Armitage went to the piano. She played fairly well, though she owned to being out of practice. Once she glided into some Scotch airs, and Fort called out, 'Do you ever sing?'

For answer she struck the opening chord of 'When the Kye Come Hame.'

The light from the hanging kerosene lamp flooded her head and shoulders, and shone on the yellow rose pinned among her hair.

''Twixt the gloaming and the murk, when the kye come hame.'

Her voice was a little thin and worn on the high notes, but inexpressibly sweet and plaintive. It stole out into the garden, which was lit up now by the shining lances of the advance guard of the full moon, peeping red over the tree tops. It died away among the willows that fringed the creek. A black gin, passing along the station street, paused to listen; the men could see her standing a deeper shadow among the shadows outside the garden fence.

When the song came to an end, Fort thumped applause.

'Now something Irish for Percy,' he said, and she nodded, smiling over her shoulder at Frank. O'Dowd could see that her eyes were wet. She ran her fingers along the keys and began, 'I Saw from the Beach.'

O'Dowd leaned forward. Presently his pipe went out.

'Give me back, give me back the wild freshness of morning.'

Aye! The wild freshness of morning! O'Dowd's red head went into his long freckled hands. Fort listened with a complacent smile. 'The freshness of morning!' How she wailed her heart out for the unattainable! And Fort sat and smirked.

Percival was a lad again among the peat – a laughing, rollicking, dare-devil Paddy! He forgot the years of struggle with drought and misfortune – forgot that he had ceased to have any ambitions, and at a little over 40 had settled down to a hopeless outlook without a struggle. He remembered the blue-eyed colleen he had kissed and promised to go back to, and whom he had forgotten long ago. Ah – the freshness of the morning! This woman understood! She wanted the freshness of the morning to be given back to her again – and why? He looked across at his host's placid face. Because of this man before him, whose destiny it surely was to eventually settle down and marry Rosie Glanvers! Poor little Rosie! Poor Mrs Armitage! For a minute he forgave her the wild things that looked out of her world-wise eyes for the sake of the longing in her sweet voice. He wanted to kick himself – but, most of all, to kick Frank! Then the music ceased abruptly. Mrs Armitage rose and shut down the piano, and lowered the wick of the lamp. Fort noticed this with pleasure. He liked thought for little economies in women. It showed that they cared for men's interests. In a certain class of women one looked for extravagance. One did not expect to have to countenance it in one's housekeeper.

O'Dowd sat up and pushed forward a chair.

Mrs Armitage shook her head. She seemed tired.

'No. I am not coming out,' she said. 'Good night, Mr O'Dowd. Good night, Mr Fort. Are you going out with the musterers in the morning?'

'Yes,' said Fort, shaking the ashes out of his pipe over the edge of the verandah. 'Will you stay, old man,' turning to O'Dowd, 'and lend a hand?'

O'Dowd said that he would, and added, with half a sigh,

that he guessed that the selection could look after itself for a bit longer.

CHAPTER II

A faint rose-and-saffron dawn was stealing over the ridges when the musterers left the head station on the following morning. Shearing time was approaching, and the men would be busy from daylight to dark, and after bringing the sheep in from the pockets of the run. Soon the station would be surrounded by clouds of dust, and noisy with the yapping of the sheep-dogs and the whistling and shouting of the men as they encouraged the sheep to hustle into the yards adjoining the shed, and thence to the tender mercies of the penners-up and on to the shearing floor itself into the hands of Tommy, the novice, who was always wanting tar, and Billy, the ringer, who could do his hundred a day with practised ease, and who prided himself with being able to pink without snicking the sheep.

The early summer morning air was fresh and sweet with the scent of pale flowering things in scrub and scattered timber. The little lizards looked out from the crevices in the hardwood of the wool-loading stage, and some gaudy-winged parrots came down to drink at the creek, and rose with a whirr of wings, as the musterers splashed through the shallow crossing.

The sheepdogs ran laughing, red tongues glistening, and the men chatted and joked loudly, as they rode behind the Boss and O'Dowd along the swamp oak flats. Fort was whistling cheerily the tune of 'When the Kye Come Hame,' and O'Dowd was thinking deeply, with frowning brows. Suddenly he quickened his horse's pace to keep step with Fort's mare, and said,

'She's a fine woman, F., but not for you!'

'What the devil do you mean?' Fort was half amused, half annoyed. O'Dowd leaned forward in the pommel of his saddle to escape an overhanging bough, and answered,

'I mean your housekeeper, of course – one of the "poor creatures who have to work, and grow ugly in the doing." She's taking a long time about growing ugly, me bhoy!'

'I'd like to know what you're driving at!' was all that Fort said.

'Look here, F., I could have no ulterior object in what I am saying; rather it might play into my hands, if I had ever thought about taking a wife, for you to marry the housekeeper.'

'Damn you, sir!'

'Don't get your hair off, old man, so early in the day! For I'm going to have my say, anyhow! It's all very well, but you and Mrs Armitage have the house to yourself, and what with cribbage and yellow roses and French marquises – not that she's a bit like the girl in the picture to any man in his senses – and going on your knees and all that, you'll be in the deuce of a hole before long, and, as I have helped you out of other scrapes, I don't see why I shouldn't be allowed to speak the confoundedly interfering word in season to you – or any other young fool!' he added sotto voce.

Fort turned in his saddle, his eyes ablaze.

'You might think of the woman; your tongue is too easy about women!' he said fiercely.

'Yes, but no woman has ever been the worse for knowing me. Fort, can you be after saying the same?'

'Mrs Armitage might have been my mother!' said Fort sullenly, digging his spurs into the mare. She started and bounded aside, and he tightened the rein.

'Not in the course of nature. She's not a day over 40 – that's my belief – and wears well for that. Many a man has married a woman ten years his senior.'

'Well, what of that? You know I don't mean to marry anyone yet awhile.'

'But you are more than half in love with your housekeeper all the same.'

'What bally rot!'

There was silence between the two men, broken only by the jingle of bits and the creak of saddle leather, and then the overseer and two of the stockmen caught them up and began discussing a broken fence along the route, which a careless boundary rider had overlooked. But all the day Fort's forehead wore an unaccustomed frown, and when O'Dowd turned his horse's head toward the track which led to his selection, which forked from the home road to the station, Fort did not press him, as was his wont, to return with him for another night.

For all that, Percival's words had sunk deep, and the seed was sown on no barren ground.

A few weeks later Percival was in the township, trying to make arrangements about another loan from the bank, and to lay in some stores. He was seriously thinking of chucking the selection, and arranging about a caretaker, while he took a job of droving. A restlessness had been in his blood ever since that night when he had sat on the verandah at the station and listened to a woman's sweet voice yearning over the lost freshness of life's morning. Since Rosie Glanvers had come up a finished young lady from boarding-school, with her brown eyes and her dimples, it had been a sort of creed with O'Dowd that had he been in a position to do so he would have asked Rosie to be Mrs O'Dowd, but the utter impossibility of keeping even himself in comfort had sensibly debarred him from such a reckless step; and, more than that, the certainty that Rosie's heart was given to Fort had lately been borne in upon him. F.'s most trivial doings were of more interest to her than any feats Percival O'Dowd might possibly perform, and the quick wit of the Irishman was not likely to be mistaken in that direction. But now he asked himself, if he had inherited the impossible thousand a year, which he sometimes dreamed about, would he have laid it at Rosie's feet, even if she had had the bad taste to look favourably upon his red hair and freckles?

He could not say. He only knew that he was ill at ease, and that the wander-lust was in his blood.

As he loitered in the bar of the hotel, one of the men from Fort's came in. O'Dowd shouted, as was his custom, for all faces that he knew, and they passed the time of day.

'Heard about the Boss?' asked the man, winking above his glass. He knew perfectly well that O'Dowd had not been calling at the station lately, and much had been the speculation thereby occasioned in the men's hut. The most acceptable notion was that O'Dowd had been caught making love to the housekeeper, and that Fort had kicked him out. We like our stories spicy in Arcadia.

'No,' said O'Dowd shortly. 'How's shearing going on?'

But the man was not to be put off.

'Boss is goin' to be married,' he said. 'Blanky fool!' the whisky beginning to take effect on a head never very strong.

O'Dowd tossed a shilling on to the bar counter and strolled to the door.

So his words had been futile!

'Housekeeper's leavin'', said the man, following him to the door. 'Boss is goin' to marry Miss Glanvers?'

O'Dowd walked out into the street wondering. So it had turned out better than he had expected. He was immensely relieved, and marvelled a little at himself that he didn't feel more envious of Fort's good luck. But he had been accustoming himself to the idea so long. Poor devils like himself must grow accustomed to such things – to seeing their friends walk off with the plums, while the Dead Sea fruit remained their portion. Good luck to Frank! Dear old chap! Things would smoothen out now, and he must give them a decent wedding present out of that lately-arranged overdraft! Then he wondered when Mrs Armitage was leaving the station.

CHAPTER III

'Wasn't it kind of Mrs Armitage? Instead of coming to the wedding, as he wanted her to, she said she must stay and fix the house up with flowers and things, and have everything ready for us when we got home,' said Rosie, looking down and blushing prettily.

'When does she leave?' asked O'Dowd laconically.

'We expect to pass her on the road,' said Rosie. 'She wants to catch the morning's coach from the township. I hope I shall have a chance to thank her for all she did for Frank.' Rosie looked round for her new-made husband, as though afraid of losing him even for a moment.

Then the guests gathered round her to say good-bye, and wish her all the usual stereotyped things, wishes so often uttered, so seldom fulfilled. O'Dowd stood aside and speculated on many things, principally as to whether if he halted at the Half-way House this afternoon on his way home he should find Mrs Armitage there. He didn't fancy that the bride and bridegroom would pass her on the road. There were two roads – the higher and the lower – leading to Fort's station. He surmised that Mrs Armitage would have found out without much trouble from Frank as to which route he intended taking on the morrow, and would have decided that the black boy, who was to drive her to the township, should bring the buckboard the other way.

And so it turned out. Rosie forgot all about her before she reached her new home, and if Frank kept anxious eyes on the winding track she never noticed it. Thus does love make blind the brightest eyes.

When O'Dowd reined his horse at the sliprail before the slab-built Half-way House, he saw the station buckboard in the yard. He gave his horse to the knockabout, a disreputable-looking person, who only wore one brace to his patched moleskins, and who was reputed to be brother of a man of title at home, but who now scarcely remembered his own name, so long had he been in the mud, and stepped with a jingle of spurs on to the low galvanised iron-roofed verandah. The fat hostess came smiling to the door.

'It's rale good to see you, Mr O'Dowd,' she said. 'I s'pose as ye hev been to the wedding?'

O'Dowd said he had, and gave her all the details she craved, and then slid past her portliness into the coffee-room. Seated on the uncomfortable shiny horsehair sofa was the woman he wanted to see. She wore a black travelling hat and a light fawn dustcoat, and she had a large white motor veil tied under her firm chin. She was one of the few women past their first youth who can wear hats in lieu of bonnets without becoming hard of feature and stern of expression in the process. Her white ungloved hands lay idle in her lap. O'Dowd noticed how her wedding-ring slipped back as she held out her hand to him. He also was not blind to the hate in her stormy eyes, quickly veiled by down-drooping lashes. He noticed that her eyelashes were quite black. He did not believe that she was even 40, in spite of her silver hair.

'Isn't it hot to-day?' she said lightly. He liked her for not showing an ostentatious interest in the wedding.

'Yes,' he said, and, the landlady bustling in, he ordered some soda-water.

'Don't mind drinking whisky before me,' Mrs Armitage said, smiling, 'if you want to.'

That was the beauty of this woman. She liked men to be at their ease, but women who were too adaptable – the old carping spirit! He told himself that he was an evil-minded beggar!

But he refrained from the whisky. When the landlady, with much gasping and hard breathing, had unwired and opened the bottle for him, and had spilt some on the best green tablecloth, much to her chagrin, and departed to attend to the wants of a swagman who was thumping on the bar counter, O'Dowd leaned back in his chair and took a long look at Mrs Armitage. It was nice to see a woman who was always unruffled, whatever happened, even on the marriage day of the man she had meant to marry herself.

'You always look cool, anyway,' he said.

'I have travelled a great deal,' she said, with just a flicker in her eyes which made him think of wild forest creatures.

Percival rubbed his long hand thoughtfully over his red head.

'Aren't you tired of knocking about?' he asked, and then cursed himself for his mal apropos remark. He wondered what the station would look like without her, and how the yellow roses were getting on.

'I don't know,' she said. 'The charm of life – as, no doubt, you have found out long ago – is its variety!'

'One thinks that for awhile, but later one gets older and stiffer in the joints, I suppose, and it seems then that one stands by and envies one's friends their wives and homes, and the same dear old jog trot, where one always knows just exactly what is going to happen next!'

'Do we ever know that?' she said softly. 'Life is all one big surprise, until death comes, to most of us, as the greatest surprise of all.'

'And sometimes as the greatest good.' He looked out of the window on to the burning yellow-grassed plain, stretching out to miles of grey mirage, dancing like lakes of silver along the sky line.

And then, 'So you are off by to-morrow's coach?'

'Yes.' She looked out of the window now, away in the direction of Fort's station.

'Will you ever be coming this way again?' he asked lamely. There was something at the back of his mind, insistent but elusive, which he knew that he had come here to say, and he could not place it, or frame it in words, and yet he knew if he went away without saying it he would go desolate.

She smiled her strange smile and shook her head. 'I am on the wallaby again,' she said. 'Looking for work!'

'What a shame!' He reddened as he said it, knowing that but for him – perhaps she knew it, too. She looked at him steadily, and the old mystery of the untamed thing looked out of her eyes. The determined smell of boiled cabbage and salt beef came in to them from the back regions, where the fat lady was presiding. Presently the girl would come in to lay the cloth for their early tea.

O'Dowd, in a sudden flash of illumination, which made him reel, found what it was that he wanted to say.

'If you would marry me,' he said, 'I would chuck horse-racing and settle down; by Heaven I would! I'd work; wouldn't I just work for you!'

He rose and stood over her, trembling with the strangeness of his discovery and the boldness of his words. He knew that he had never wanted anything in his life as he wanted her answer.

Her beautiful hands still lay in her lap, the wedding ring slipping forward on the third finger of her left hand. O'Dowd found time to wonder what manner of man had placed it there, and room in his heart to hate him, ere she said:

'So it was six for Mr Fort and seven for yourself when you warned him against me!'

Silence, and the strong growing odour of cabbage water thrown out of the back door, and sinking slowly into the sun-baked earth of the yard.

A clink of glasses in the bar and a snatch of song from the swagman who was hurrying on with the knocking down of his fencing cheque. The raucous voice of a cockatoo, a pet of the landlady's, screeched, 'It's time to get the cows now, Jim, blast yer!' and they heard the rattle of china. The girl would be here in a few minutes to set the table.

'Is that all you can say to me?' said O'Dowd, reaching for his hat. He felt so hopelessly in the wrong. How was he to explain to her that he had never contemplated making such an avowal as he had spoken to her a minute ago. It had all come over him so suddenly, such a sweeping away of defences, such an overpowering rush of feeling – but she was not the woman to believe him. Treachery of the savage she might have understood, or the quick thrust and the struggle of the male for his mate, but not such subtleties of error as his heart and brain had made. No; she was not the woman to believe that this was unpremeditated.

She clenched her hands tightly, and her lips curled back over her strong white teeth. He quailed before the scorn in her eyes.

'Yes, I have one thing more to say,' she answered, bitterly. 'The last word between us. Go, and I pray that I may never have to look on your face again!'

The flop flop of the landlady's heavy slippers came along the creaking passage.

O'Dowd turned with no other word, and went out on to the verandah, calling to the knockabout to bring up his horse.

As he turned in his saddle to glance back at the Half-way House, its white roof glimmering in the sun, he saw Mrs Armitage come to the door and stand, looking after him.

How could he grudge her her triumph! It was fairly won.

So his last sight of F.'s housekeeper was the tall light-robed figure, framed in the rough wooden supports of the door, and her lips were smiling, smiling.

'You must come round the garden. We have made such a number of improvements, especially to the vegetable garden. Frank is taking such an interest in vegetables.'

Mrs Fort was a charming little matron in her wide hat and large white apron. When O'Dowd arrived to pay his formal call that afternoon she told him that Frank was out on the run, and that she had been making pie-melon jam all day.

'I burnt the first lot,' she said, confidentially, and then offered to show him the garden. They skirted the grape vine trellis, and went down the path by the peach trees, and Rosie screamed as they caught sight of a black shining body among the long grass by the tennis court.

'So careless of the gardener to leave the grass long just there. It is a regular harbour for snakes,' she said, as they paused near what had once been the bed where the yellow roses grew.

It was freshly dug over, and there was not a sign of the Cloth-of-Gold.

'You've moved the rose!' said O'Dowd, regretfully.

'Yes; wasn't it a pity. Frank' – in an injured voice – 'took it into his head that neither the gardener nor I understand roses, and he had them dug up and thrown away. I believe the man fed them to the cows! Wasn't it cruel? They did it one day when I was in the township. I cried when I came home. I felt so sorry for the poor things! And now Frank is having this made into a tomato bed. He said he hated the sight of the roses! Aren't men funny?' and she smiled wisely at her newly-acquired insight into the ways of the creature masculine.

O'Dowd was thoughtful as he rode home in the moonlight that night. Next week he was starting on a long droving job for the station, and he had several things to do before he turned in, but nevertheless he rode with slack rein, and let the horse choose its own pace.

Once he spoke his thoughts aloud.

'Rosie seems happy enough, anyway,' he said. 'But Frank . . . I wonder . . . If he didn't care, why did he root up the roses?'

Later as his horse, drowsing, stumbled and nearly fell, he leaned forward and patted its neck softly.

'Suppose you had slung me and broken my neck, old man, would it have been a loss to anybody? Jove! To think that I should live more than 40 years in the world and not have learned to mind my own business!'

And then through the silver-scented night he rode on alone, as he was to ride all his days.

Rosa Praed

A Happy Ending

1908

'Yes, I suppose it *must* have a happy ending!'

Miss Caroline Graffan, who was a writer of mildly sensational fiction, sighed as she re-scanned a letter addressed to her by the editor of *Brinton's Weekly*. She buttoned her cheap ready-made jacket in an absent-minded manner and pinned a faded Tam-o'-Shanter down upon her reddish locks which had already here and there a thread of grey. Taking up her well-worn woollen gloves and a stout note-book with a double-pointed pencil she went forth to seek inspiration by the sea. But first she tiptoed to the ground floor sitting-room where an old lady lay asleep, and thence to the top of the basement stairs where she called in a low urgent tone: 'Mrs Bishop!'

The landlady showed her ample form in the passage below.

'Going a walk, Miss Callie?' she inquired in a friendly, whisper and the little lady answered: 'Yes. I want to think out a story.'

'Another of 'em! Leonore's deep in the last. Is it for Australia?'

'No, for *Brinton's Weekly*. It's got to be a love-story with a happy ending.'

'Lor', Miss Callie, how you ever write love-stories with no practice of your own passes me. You ought to be enjoying a happy ending yourself by this time.'

Callie Graffan's sensitive face flushed. She answered with a touch of dignity: 'Will you please go up if mother should ring? I shall be back to tea.'

Across the square went the quaint little figure. The wind blew her reddish curls askew, tinged the tip of her small, upturned nose and gave a watery look to her eyes. They were nice hazel eyes, fringed with thick brown lashes – the best feature in the thin face which Nature had meant to be piquant and which had grown only pathetic. As she turned the corner,

Callie encountered the landlady's daughter, absorbed in a pink journal. Leonore looked up.

'I just 'ad to see how *The Girl Who Loved Him* is going on, miss. It's beautiful. But you won't deprive her of 'im at the last? You'll give 'em a happy ending?'

Miss Callie nodded, but her smile was rather wistful.

Leonore read with avidity all the stories that appeared under the pseudonym of *Lura Lynn*, and was proud of the secret which she had confided to her young man at the newspaper shop that *Lura Lynn* was really Mrs Bishop's lodger, the shabby little lady who kept a blind mother upon her literary earnings, and whose stories even went as far afield as Australia. That, alas! was no proof of world-wide popularity but was indirectly due to the fact that Callie's father had once held a cure in the Lura district in Leichardt's Land. She did not remember much about Australia, but it was to the breath of the bush that Callie owed a certain human note in her otherwise commonplace productions. The ring of the pseudonym she had chosen happened to strike the editor of *The Leichardt's Land Chronicle* one day while glancing through the pages of *Brinton's Weekly*, and induced him to skim a story of hers which otherwise he would have passed unnoticed. This led to Callie contributing most of the fiction required for the *Chronicle* at a humble rate of payment. She eked out her hard-working existence at Weirgate, whence all the young men of her class went away to seek fortune and wives, and where no suitor ever came to woo. None, at least, had ever wooed Miss Callie, who was an old maid at thirty-two, bravely facing destiny, but longing vaguely for romance that never was realised except on paper.

'It would be so much easier to write love-stories,' she thought, 'if only I knew what it was to be loved!'

Now she looked down the sunlit, shadow-flecked road which wound along the cliff. A row of pretentious villas bordered it, in the gardens of which bulbs were springing. The turf at the sides had started into new green under the sharp March winds, and a lark rising as she passed soared to the blue sky, singing as though its throat would burst.

'He seems to have a happy story to tell,' murmured Callie. 'I wish he would tell it to me.'

She turned aside into a shelter facing the sea where at this hour she was generally sure of being alone. Here she began to jot down a few desultory notes for her work. Some of the pages of her note-book, however, being loose, fluttered out of her grasp and the wind carried them to a little distance. Callie was just about to dart in pursuit when she became aware that the shelter had another occupant. A huge, long-limbed man in rough grey tweeds lounged out from the other side. Callie glanced at him curiously. He was over six feet and had the loose-jointed build of the backwoodsman. His skin was browned to a coppery hue, the dark beard slightly frosted at the sides. His fresh, strong look recalled to her dim memories of men with stock-whips, clad in moleskins, who used to ride up to her parson-father's homestead.

The stranger raised his cap, drawling in a distinctly Australian twang –

'Wo-a there! *I'll* round 'em up and yard 'em.'

With a stride of his long legs he pinned the sheets by the point of his stick and handed them to her in clumsy fashion. Callie thanked him and sat down again, but he paused in tentative fashion.

'Excuse me,' he remarked; 'I'm a bit bushed. Not long home, you see. Are you a resident in this place – miss?'

The last word appeared a kind of afterthought. Callie stopped fixing the errant sheets and looked up dubiously.

The gentleman – for clearly he was a gentleman, if an unpolished specimen – raised his cap and repeated his question, adding apologetically, 'Out in 'Stralia when a chap's off the track he don't wait to be introduced.'

'I know,' said Callie, with a comprehending nod; 'I've been in Australia.'

'That's first-rate.' The giant seated himself beside her with the air of having found a long-lost brother. 'Are you 'Stralian, miss?'

'Not really. My father was out there a few years and I happened to be born in Leichardt's Land.'

'Wa-al na-ow! *I'm* from Leichardt's Land. Your father a squatter?'

'No; a clergyman.'

The giant made a rueful grimace.

'I don't take much stock in missionaries – the worse for me, perhaps. See here, miss – ever been bushed in these parts?'

'No,' replied Callie, amused. 'I've lived in Weirgate since I was ten years old, when we came to England. And that's more than twenty years ago.'

He scrutinised her with some care.

'It would be about that,' he observed frankly, and poor Miss Graffan blushed with such warmth at the remark that she began to look far less than her age. But the stranger seemed entirely unconscious of having erred.

'Can you tell me,' he went on, 'whereabouts to find a young lady I'm after?'

'A young lady!' repeated Miss Graffan.

'It's like this,' and the giant leaned forward, ready on the instant to confide his difficulty. 'I'm on her lay, but I've come to a dead end and dunno where to dig. Her name is Lura Lynn.'

'*Lura Lynn!*' Callie stared at him with wondering eyes. 'What do you know of Lura Lynn?'

'Just what her writings have told me. I've read most of 'em in *The Leichardt's Land Chronicle*, and they took my fancy. I looked up the editor and got him to give me all the information he would about the young lady which only amounted to this, that she mailed him her stories from Weirgate. Ever read any of 'em?'

Callie modestly confessed that she had.

'I ain't what you'd call a booky chap,' continued the stranger, 'but it's my opinion that Lura Lynn's stories are as good as you'd get. Of course I can see she don't know much about Australia, but you read 'em in the bush o' nights with the chance of a black's spear whizzing into camp, native dogs howling for all they're worth, with maybe a morepork or a curlew screeching, and only the clank of your horse's hobbles – ne'er another white man within fifty miles, you know, miss – well, then, Lura Lynn's stories set a lonely chap thinking of what a comfort a nice woman would be to him – a sweet-faced girl, soft and dainty, the sort a man would like his mother to have been – the sort that other fellows, when they've luck, pick up over here for wives. That's what I've come for.' The giant thumped a hairy fist upon his sinewy grey-clad knee. 'I don't mind telling you, miss – that's what I've come for.'

'That's what you've come for!' echoed Callie, bewilderedly. The giant gave a sheepish laugh.

'Ah! I've come to marry Lura Lynn – if she'll have me. I've come fourteen thousand miles on the chance.'

Miss Graffan drew in her breath sharply.

'But you don't really know what she's like!'

'Don't I?' The stranger laughed again, this time with more assurance. 'I know she's the girl for me, if she'll only take me on. I can guess pretty much what she's like from her stories, and I've made a picture of her in my mind. She's handsome of course, and young. Spruce, well-set-up, tall; a good figure, showing off her frocks – I like to see women prink, and I'll make it easy for her. I'll dress her up to the nines. But she must be a smart girl and know how to get round me – all chaps enjoy being wheedled when it's nicely done – a 'cute, clever girl, clean-shaped to her finger-tips. That's Lura Lynn according to my notions. You're acquainted with her, I take it?'

'Ye-es,' faltered Callie, startled into candour.

'Well, you shan't tell me if I'm right about her, I'll find out for myself. All I ask is – where can I meet her?'

Callie's eyes were fixed on the heaving sea. Wild thoughts surged in her meagre bosom. Her starved heart thrilled to this strange romance. She longed to lend herself to the joy of it – even for an hour. When the man found out that she was Lura Lynn he would be bitterly disappointed of course, but she shrank from telling him. She wanted to snatch at the vicarious satisfaction this poor little passing experience might afford her. She fancied that it would not be quite so difficult afterwards to grind out love-stories.

'Are you serious in what you said?' she breathed slowly.

'Just about,' he answered bluntly. 'I'm here to ask that girl if she'll come along with me and go shares in my show.'

'And what is your show?' inquired Miss Graffan, putting on her tiny touch of dignity.

'Two thousand square miles of grazing country and ten thousand head of cattle at – say, two-punten a head all round, and five thousand for horses and plant. Tot it up, miss. That's my show. But first we'll have as big a spree as she dear old pleases – globe-trot, or take our time in this country. It's good enough for me. All I want is – my wife!'

Callie gazed thirstily at the grey sea. The thought of what a bright happy fate hers might have been were she herself only different, brought a rush of tears to her eyes. Bending down to hide them, she noticed her old serge skirt, her shabby gloves, her worn opossum-skin tippet. She hated them all, she was ashamed of them all – the more so because, rough though the man seemed, she saw that he was very well tailored. At that moment he pulled out of an enormous pocket-book a card which he handed her. It had never occurred to her to doubt him, but the ring of his voice was convincing.

'That's my name,' he said – 'James Bostock – and my address. The Lura's my district, you know. Our Agent-General and the Directors of The Leichardt's Land Bank are my references. I'm putting up at the hotel yonder. Now will you give me the address of Miss Lura Lynn?'

Callie had been considering rapidly and had made up her mind. She spoke decisively, but with a sympathetic smile.

'I can't do that without Miss Lynn's permission, but as she's a friend of mine I could tell her anything you wish. She's away just now.'

The giant's face fell. Then he responded cheerfully –

'Right-oh! I only want to act on the square. Look here – let you and me be chums, Miss –'

'Graffan,' put in Callie.

'Let's be chums, Miss Graffan, if you'll honour me. You'd make a very good mate. You're the sort that understands a chap's mind.'

Callie flushed deeply. Looking closely at her, James Bostock discovered that she had very pretty eyes.

'The game's up to you,' he said, 'only recollect I'll be there when my turn comes. Meanwhile I'll lie low till you tell me she's back. But mum's the word to her. I can do my own courting.'

'So I should imagine,' smiled Callie, flushing more deeply than ever as he bent over her. 'But please don't say anything about Miss Lynn to anyone else. I'm sure she wouldn't like it.'

'No need – now I've told you. Reckon I was in luck when I stumbled on this shanty. What! Going already?' he exclaimed disppointedly, as Callie rose. 'Can't I walk with you?'

'If you like,' said Callie, rather breathlessly; 'I must get home to tea. My mother and I live close by in Henrietta Square.

Mother's blind, or I'm sure she'd be pleased to see anyone from Leichardt's Land,' added Miss Graffan, in a most demure manner.

'Let me come and yarn to her a bit. I'm no end of a hand at yarning. And I can make first class tea – *and* toast. You try me,' said the giant, so persuasively that Callie tucked her note-book and her scruples securely out of sight.

'Very well, you may come. But not a word about Lura Lynn – mind.'

It was Leonore who betrayed the secret a fortnight later. She was engaged in animated conversation with her young man at the newspaper shop one afternoon when James Bostock looked in, bent on purchasing the last number of *Brinton's Weekly*.

Leonore had a copy outspread on the counter before her and she was warmly discussing the progress of affairs of the heart in the case of *The Girl Who Loved Him* as compared with those of the writer, commenting on these last with considerable shrewdness. James Bostock heard enough of her remarks to send him speeding up the street. He took the road along the cliff and soon reached the shelter where he knew that at this hour he should find Callie Graffan. There she was in the place where he had first seen her – her two-pointed pencil in her hand, but she was not writing. Her gaze, grown subdued and tender, wandered dreamily over the sparkling sea. The spring sunshine was reflected in her face. There had been some attempt at smartening up the old serge coat and skirt. She wore a new Tam-o'-Shanter, a fresh lace scarf and a knot of violets in her breast. Bostock's quick, comprehensive eyes took in every line of her as he approached. He was thinking how different she was from his preconceived notion of Lura Lynn. She heard him coming and the loveliest wave of colour rose and spread over her thin cheeks. Then as she lifted her face a scared look came into her eyes, for there was something in his that alarmed her.

She closed her note-book carefully, placing the pencil inside the rubber band.

'There's no use in your doing that,' he cried harshly. 'I know all about your scribbling.'

He bore down upon her, his great arms swinging, his coppery features tense, his honest eyes seeming to shoot lances at her.

'You've deceived me horribly,' he began.

Callie went very pale, for now she knew that he knew. Then her little form braced itself. She laid the note-book on the seat beside her. So the end had come! She had meant to meet this moment with dignity, but she could only answer in a broken, girlish way –

'Yes, I have, I know. And so would you, if you'd been me.'

'Oh! I would – would I? And please – why?' said he. He was close to the bench now and stood looking down at her, fierce, insistent, and yet oddly triumphant.

A long sobbing breath came up from the bottom of Callie's surcharged heart. She made a strenuous effort to control her trembling lips.

'Why!' she cried passionately. 'Because I'd written plenty of love-stories, but never lived one. And I wanted to know exactly how you felt about me – the me that you thought I was. I knew that you'd find out the truth soon enough, but I couldn't bear to disillusion you – I – oh!' – she struck her hands vehemently together. 'I've had so little in my life. Don't grudge me this one fortnight.'

Her voice dropped. Tears started from under the thick brown lashes and travelled rapidly down the small, convulsed face. Pity kept the big man silent. He sat down beside her awkwardly but she would not look at him. Her hands were clenched. The small thin shoulders heaved.

With the tip of his large finger he ventured to raise one of those irrepressible curls that stuck out under the Tam-o'-Shanter.

'Oh! you poor little thing! You poor little dreaming, desolate thing! Do you know I think you've got the cunningest hair I ever set eyes on, and the sweetest, dearest, little face. Want to know how *I* feel? Well, I feel as if I've no use at all left for that Lura Lynn – not the one I fancied – that is, if Callie Graffan will take a rough Bush chap on. Ain't half good enough for her, though. But say, Callie darlin' – will you go shares in that show of mine, and let's have a real good time together?'

She turned swiftly now and looked up at him, startled

beyond words, wildly incredulous, but thrilling with joy. Her amazed cry was stifled in his breast as he wrapped his long arms round her.

'That Lura Lynn would never have worked out,' he said consolingly. 'She was a deal too fine. An old Bushwhacker like me wants a chum – a mate – just what you'll be, Callie.'

Half an hour later a small, flushed person emerged from the shelter of those strong arms and made a sudden dash at the neglected note-book and pencil.

'Na-ow – na-ow, you've done enough o' that,' he cried. 'We're not going to waste any more time over other folks' love-stories. Going to live our own, remember. Come along right home and tell your mammy she's got to think about shifting camp.'

'Oh! wait one moment, James – just one moment. Let me get a note – or two – before the feeling goes.'

'What feeling?' he asked, puzzled.

'Oh, I didn't tell you. I could not get this story right. But *now* I know! Oh, James! life's just beautiful if one can have a happy ending.'

Sumner Locke

When Dawson Died

1910

One day Old Man Dawson took to his bed and refused to budge even when the tongue of his wife oscillated at double the usual swing. He said he was going to die; so, after arguing the point with him, she said he could; and daily the family waited, believing that the old man really meant to do as he said. They knew by experience that he seldom went back on his word; and the novel situation of having him do a thing that was altogether foreign to them held them in an excitement worthy of a more stimulating cause.

Two of the girls used to stand over the skim-buckets and commune as to the future development of things. They wondered if Mum could run the show without Dad, or if Will would be deputed boss. They felt certain there would be fire somewhere – Will was wayward and Mum always did rule the old man. Annie, the elder girl, was not bad looking – someone had told her that four years ago at the local show; Annie remembered that day because it had never come again – and she felt she deserved a better fate than the daily fowl-run and the skim-buckets. There never was enough water to wash the buckets properly; and the old man said the yard dam wasn't to be used for waste water. Perhaps when he'd been dead a bit they might use it when they liked. Mary thought perhaps they might sell out and go to the town; and the chance of seeing a bit of life like that pictured in the coloured catalogue that a through traveller had presented them with two years ago was a moment of exquisite pain to them. That day the buckets looked different; they had got twice the amount of slushing during the debate; and Mum was sleeping off a war that she and the old man had had that morning over changing the mattress. The old man wouldn't move for a moment, and the woman had howled in grief at the unturned straw bed.

One of the boys who attended to the special department of pigs suggested at dinner that the doctor had better see the old man, whereat the woman smashed two plates over his head in passing.

'D'yer think old Mill's goin' inter harness again to-day?' she said wrathfully.

'I kin ride the Yonk for 'im,' protested the small attribute.

'No, yer can't,' bellowed the woman. 'Wen I was bad with Flora he was twenty minutes too late. D'yer think we want 'im comin' late again?'

'Is father goin' ter die ter-day?' came from the end of the board table, where the second last edition of the family was blowing bubbles into a cup of yesterday's skim.

'Go and ask 'im!' shouted his mother in return. Then she slapped the nearside of her fourth, who was dabbling fingers in a flat tin of milk and pushing the dead flies under to see if they would rise again. 'Take yer dirty 'ands outer that dish. If yer father *did* die, all that milk'd be wanted for the comp'ny comin' round.'

'Kin we invite Jack, Mum?' This from the promoter of the milk bubbles, with wide eyes on his parent.

'Can't invite no one!' snapped the woman.'And don't you go talking about it, neither – he mightn't go for years yet; I don't want no bakin' and things for nothin'.'

Annie looked at her confidant of the milk-buckets; and a telegraphic anticipation shot in a telepathic way from mind to mind. After dinner the two girls looked out their Show dresses of four years ago, and decided that if company came to call there would be something doing, and maybe that Mr Walker, of Horse Gully, might come along. They had passed him on the road once, and he had said good-day; and they had giggled fit to kill themselves.

When the eldest of the tribe got home that night he was told to 'swaller his tea quick 'cause the old man was dying and had some work he wanted doin' before he died.'

Also the last three numbers of the male portion of the family were instructed from the depths of the blue-grey blanket bed, where the head of the family lay sunk in his own iniquity, to fetch home some of the cattle which had strayed into a paddock ten miles away. The old man said he didn't want a summons before he died – the brutes better be branded or earmarked in the morning – he'd like to see it done at once. And so it was –

with the pruning knife and a jab of kitchen salt to stop the blood.

About five o'clock next day the general family had assorted themselves round the place. Some of the boys had gone to the paddock dam to wash. The woman had thought it wiser, in case of anything happening; and after consulting the old man he had agreed to allow them to use the dam water, and the boys had raced there, shouting with the inflated lungs of young Australians well in condition.

The second eldest boy was nailing the prop-roost in the shed where the fowls shared a rest with the milk cans. A board served as a protecting lid for the milk, and some of the older birds roosted there in a crouched attitude, and squawked tones of melancholy into the coming night. Will, the elder, was secreted with his father. The old man spoke from the uncovered pillow of faded dress material:

'What'd yer do? Did yer catch Miller?'

'Yes. I got 'im. Fourteen quid for the bull.'

'That's a better deal – gimme the paper. Did he sign it?. . . And the bull's gone?'

'I'm thinkin',' went on William, 'that them young heifers could go this next trip. No good keepin' them?'

'What's the price?' wheezed the old man.

'Dunno,' said Will. 'I'm puttin' a lot on Johnson's chance there. I'll see him ter-morrow.'

'Maybe,' said Mr Dawson from the bed-well. 'I'd like to know what's doin' with them before I'm under.'

'Yes, I'll get fixed for Narragoon ter-morrow. Ye'd better have a sleep now.'

When he had gone out the old man turned his face to a slit of window where the blind had been looped aside and nailed tight. The blue vapour was settling on the hills right out, and to him looked like white mists. He rubbed his hands over his eyes, but still he saw it; then he called suddenly to the woman, and she came in with a light.

Half an hour after, the dark had come. The boys hadn't returned from the bath in the dam, and the two girls were down at the sheds still talking. Across the yard the voice of the woman burst like a cannon on the right. She called the entire family by name, and, getting no answer, wailed in a mournful tone that ended in a break of bad temper:

'Carn't yer answer, Will? Where are yer? Yer father's dead! Annie, Annie!'

Across the paddock the shriek rent; and animals that sought to sleep raised languid eyes towards the house. The girls came from the shed as Will turned in the door, rushing past the woman roughly. She waited.

'Yer'd better go down and bring yer brothers out've the mudhole,' she said in a flurry. 'Tell 'em their father's dead; and they'd better hurry if they want to see 'im warm.'

The girls began to run, and the woman lit the kitchen lamp and began tidying up the place a bit. Presently the general troop rushed in, breathless.

'Is 'e in bed, Mum?'

'Did yer think 'e was in the fowlhouse?'

Then they pushed into the bedroom; and an awesome silence dropped over everything.

Never before, in their mean existence, had they known such a thing! Absolute calm was on each face, calm that was due to a great wonderment. The lamp shed a weak sort of glow that reached across the old man's face so that it was outlined against the coarse pillow. It was ghastly in the half-light; and round the room the family stood, waiting as if some great phenomenon was about to burst upon them.

'Better put out the lamp,' began the woman, dropping into a frightened calm after her storm of temper. 'No good wastin' kerosine.'

Will was hanging half over the bed. He was sorry the old man had gone before he had fixed up about the cattle. He'd have liked to have brought that bit of business off first.

'Get outer here,' said the woman, in a stifled, strange voice. 'He ain't going to do nothin' more.'

One by one the family turned in the silence; but a sudden disturbance from the bed, together with a shriek from the woman, brought them back with a turn, and a new look in their faces.

''E's movin', I declare!'

Will came again to the bed; and the eyes of the old man suddenly blinked in the dim light.

'Ain't gorn yet?' said the woman, bringing the lamp nearer, while the family climbed about the bed with wary whispers.

The old man sat up. He stared at his fourth child quite squarely.

'Take your dirty feet off the bed,' he said in a strong, vibrating voice. Then he turned to Will. 'Not this time, son; I'm going to get up. Want to look at them heifers – think – they're – worth more'n Johnson will – pay for 'em. Where's me boots?'

In the interval, when the family simmered down into their normal state, the old man could be heard giving Will a hundred injunctions about the place.

In the kitchen the woman and the girls were putting up an amount of hurry and work in preparation of the tea. The woman's tongue got loose again.

'Just as I said. 'E never knows 'is own mind one minute; put that bacon back in the pot, Annie. 'E's sure to be fit for a big feed after dyin' so long. Lord! I never seen 'im so white in 'is natural before. Just as well 'e never died ter-night; them heifers wants fixin' up, and Will don't understand – besides, it ain't good buryin' in this hot weather – no rain fer a month by the look of things.'

The old man shuffled through the kitchen, his bootlaces trailing on the floor.

'Joanna, where's the tin dish?' he said, turning at the outer door; 'ain't 'ad a wash since I took bad.'

'Annie, tip that milk inter the bucket an' give your father that dish,' said the woman, glaring dubiously at him. 'Hurry up, too; he wants to wash the death off of him before we sets down.'

And Old Man Dawson, well washed, sat down once more at the family board and discussed the profits of the coming season.

Henry Handel Richardson

Death

1911

. . . den vanskelige död. *Niels Lyhne*

Mary Christina was going to die. – For sixty years, come March, she had been an inhabitant of the earth, and had suffered her full share of life's vicissitudes: she had passed from girl to woman, had loved and been loved, had borne children and tended children, had watched young faces lose their youth, and harden, and grow unbeautiful; she had cared for graves; had resigned herself, in the course of years, to the creeping on of age: she had wept, and laughed, and been indifferent, mostly indifferent, as is man's way; but now she was going to cease to be, and nothing would please her, or sadden her, or leave her merely cold, again.

She knew what was coming, before anyone else; for she had had a presentiment; so, at least, she called it, one grey November afternoon, when, with icy hands outspread, she crouched low over a fire from which she could derive no heat.

That day, while a sharp wind was causing the last, tattered leaves to whirl madly on their stalks, Mary Christina had journeyed to a distant quarter of the town. Her business done, she entered a crowded conveyance. As she sat and let her eyes range over the row of faces opposite her, faces worn with toil, and reddened with exposure to the wind, she said to herself: 'My God, how ugly people are!' But, in the same breath, a small, inner voice rebuked her: 'Be thankful to be among them, Mary Christina! What if you were never out of doors again?' To which, elliptically, she made answer: 'Better now than in spring, when things are freshening up.'

Mary Christina was going to die.

That night, the hour being come, she took off for the last time the wrappings in which the world had known her, and, with as little covering as she would ever again need, lay down between the sheets that witness the incoming and the outgoing of mortals.

But the lying down and folding of the hands is not enough; it is no such easy matter as that to die. The way out of life is as darkly mysterious as the way in.

Thus, after having ever been one of those stoics who look upon illness as a moral failing, to which it is dishonourable to yield; after having borne her casual ailments as mutely as a suffering animal, Mary Christina now began to fling about on her bed, in such a manner that every one within call was needed to restrain her; and to utter shrill, shameless cries, which echoed through the house. Beads of moisture rolled from her forehead and made round spots on the sheets, or splashed the hands of those who held her.

A stranger, summoned in haste, sat beside her bed. Before him, a scrupulous, womanly reserve dropped like a rent veil.

The well-known faces of her children – children now in the eyes of Mary Christina alone – hung over her. Hand after hand sought hers, sweat-bedewed; and from the lips of the youngest broke man's most human cry: 'Oh, mother . . . mother!'

But though these, of all living creatures, had been in Mary Christina's thoughts ever since they had come into the world; though she had watched, night for night, till she knew their eyes closed in sleep, harassed by the fears that only a mother knows: though, up to the last, her love had thrown out a thousand arms, to safeguard them on their divers ways; she was now as indifferent to them as to the several strangers who moved round her bed. And the withdrawal of her warm affection seemed, to those who had been used to shelter beneath it, like the first significant victory gained by death over life.

For Mary Christina, the centre of existence had shifted: henceforth, her desire was only to herself. First came the idolatrous attention demanded by her body – this strong, personable body, still ablaze with energy, and resolutely desirous of living. It was made the object of a religious care; untiring were the endeavours to ward off the inevitable. The minutest variations in the heat of the blood, in the pulsations of the heart, were verified and controlled. Hitherto, she had lived unconscious of her vital functions; now she, too, shared the palpitating interest in their course. For all these things, now of a morbid importance, were possible disarmers of the great enemy, of the griping, gutting pain, to repel which, was her chief concern. This came at intervals. It began somewhere in the distance, far away, drew rapidly nearer, darkening the bed with the shadow of its wings; it hovered over her, circling like a vulture, she lying defenceless and terrified; then, with one swoop, it descended and settled on her, plunging beak and claws into the shuddering flesh. She looked at those about her with wild eyes, dumbly imploring them, praying to them, as to gods, to shield her from it: but they did nothing. It tore at her, sick and faint with anguish; the muscles of her body twisted into knots; she heard her own shrieks rend the air.

For longer than eight long days she fought this fight, returning time and again to the encounter, in which, each single time, she left more of her strength. Little by little, however, the force of her struggles declined, and the hope that had sustained her, the hope of once coming off conqueror, died out. She still swallowed, with avidity, the bitter draughts that were held to her lips; she submitted, gladly, to the importunate services of the nurse, which broke in, by night and by day, on her hard-won rest; she still gave desperate battle, when the agony sucked at her; but it became a mere blind instinct to live, without faith in the issue. – And the watchers round the bed began to avoid her eyes, in which, at moments, the death-secret was legible.

For eight days and over, she disputed each inch of ground, and those whose lot it was to stand and look on, felt the limits of human endurance strain to breaking-point. Then, however, a change was visible. The pain still wrung her, in savage bouts; but Mary Christina did not answer to it, as at first: her nerves were losing their fine power, both to feel, and to interpret the feeling. She ceased to resist so ardently, let the anguish engirdle her, do its worst. Now that her nerves were drowsier, too, she was able, the moment she ceased to suffer, to sink into repose; a tranquil, twilight state, on the borderland between sleeping and waking; and the experiences of a lifetime had numbered no goodlier pleasure than this: the wishless well-being that follows on a vanishing pain.

Her dark hair, fine as silk, was gathered loosely round her head; iced cloths were strapped to her brow; her large, worn hands lay folded on the sheet. The watchers stifled their own flickering hopes, and gave up asking her how she did; for she could hardly bring herself to return a pressure of the hand: all else was immaterial to her, so long as the agony was kept at bay, and she not roused from her present sweet reprieve. They moved on tip-toe, fearful of disturbing her; for they believed she slept. But she was not asleep – as one saw, who bent more nearly over her: the dark pupils were fixed, beneath the half-fallen lids, like the unclosed eyes of one already dead.

In these benign moments, when her torture slackened, Mary Christina lay and let pictures pass before her – pictures, fragments, flashes – of the life which, until now, had been hers; and, compared with this intensely personal past, which had its rise in mistiest morning memories, even her children seemed unfamiliar to her – the chance associates of an hour.

Fifty years ago!... The walls of the room expanded, then fell in, like the sides of a card house. It was a wide and sunny square; before an old-fashioned house with a shiny brass knocker, under a pale-blue English sky heaped with bulbous masses of cloud, a group of children played. One had hair of a light, flaxen colour, which flapped to her waist-line, floated behind her as she ran. She was the wildest and merriest of all; she threw the ball highest; she caught it most surely as it came to earth again. In a spirit of wantonness, elated by her own skill, she threw it so high and so far that it did not return: it had gone over the wall of a neighbouring garden. They were not allowed to enter this garden; the ball, her ball, of which she had been so proud, was lost for ever, and through her own folly. She sat down on the steps, and wept bitterly. Her playfellows, unable to comfort her, stole away....

Years had passed. Overhead, a lowering grey sky; which was yet no greyer than the flat stretch of earth beneath. Snow was in waiting, but, so far, only a few detached flakes had fluttered down. On a hard-frozen pond, people were skating; a young girl stood at the edge, and followed their bird-like dartings and skimmings. She wore a scarlet hood on her head. Seen against the prevailing dullness, this hood burnt like a flame. Two young men passed, swinging their skates; one turned to look at her, and she caught an admiring word. He had bright, merry eyes. She reddened; then, obeying an impulse, took to her heels and ran, never pausing till she had crossed the home threshold. Too big for such frolics, they rebuked her; but she only smiled at them in return, not grasping what they said. Her thoughts were singing; life seemed suddenly to mean undreamed-of wonders – the unravelling of a magic coil...

And again the years moved forward. It was summer now. The sun went down, huge, flamboyant, in a violet-streaked sky. At the bottom of a tangled old garden, in a thicket of raspberry-bushes, she stood with heaving breast, striving to repress tears of shame and disappointment. Throughout the afternoon, he had seemed to avoid her, had kept at the side of her friend. Now, she made as if she were gathering fruit; but the basket on her arm was empty: she stared unseeingly at the streaky red and gold of the western sky. While she stood thus, a world of bitterness in her young heart, a hand was laid on hers, and a kind voice said: Mary Christina ... I missed you ... I came to look for you ... The little fancy basket dropped from her nerveless fingers, dropped among the bushes; and there it was left, to lie and rot. How foolish of her it had been to forget that basket! It was made of green straw; had a pretty twisted handle. Why had she never gone back to look for it? – what had blotted it from her mind? Did it still lie, where it had fallen – a shapeless, sodden mass? Or had strange hands recovered it? ... Who lived now in the home of her girlhood? Did other young lips meet beneath the flames of the evening sky?... other feet tread the familiar paths, whence hers had for ever passed?...

The sick woman stirred uneasily, and moved her head. It was deep night; the house was still, the room sunk in shadow. The darkness oppressed her; she tried to look about her, and moaned. At the sound, a soft-footed Sister of Mercy rose from out a patch of gloom, and bent over her, presenting a cup to her dry lips: as she drank, Mary Christina's fixed and feverish eyes met the stiff white linen of wimple and bands. The draught soothed her; at once her lids half-closed again; and the watcher shrank back into the corner from which she had sprung.

Before she had reached it and sat down again to her beads, Mary Christina seemed to hold a living child in her arms, gathered two tiny feet into the cup-shaped hollow of her hand. A fire burnt in the grate; wine-red curtains were drawn against a night of lashing rain. Out on the highways, and in the storm-swept fields, these icy rain-stripes spelled a shuddering desolation; within, in the safe, warm room, husband and wife knelt to examine each soft line and curve of the miracle that was theirs. – Surely there was no better joy than this joy! . . . See! – how his hand grasps mine! He listens . . . he smiles! Never was such a child born before! . . .

Another turn of the wheel, and the babe was cold to the touch: she stood, pressing a little dress to her face, and eating her heart out, with vain regret. How she had struggled, and rebelled! She had then believed that no after-grief could equal this grief for the little dead child, (so long since become one with the earth it lay in); for this faint life-spark, of which all but herself speedily forgot the existence. It had not been so; many a greater grief had overtaken her: with the passing of the years, it sometimes seemed as though sorrow's bowed and grey-veiled form would never again quit her side. She had learned that it is easier to see a child die, unspoiled, than to watch it change, grow hard, betray its soul; had even come to rely on death, as on the fundamental stay of life – the bed-rock, beneath loose and shifting sands.

But after this last precise vision of the waxen babe that awaited her in the land of shadows, the memories came crowding thick and fast; she could not follow each singly to an end. The later years, too, had been so like, one to another; and they had flashed past with a dizzy quickness: one day she had been thirty, and it seemed only on the morrow that she was sixty – an old woman stretched out to face death. With the far-reaching sight granted to dying eyes, she lay and looked back at the confused pattern of her life, as at some richly-worked arras, and surveyed it; but without emotion. Now, the many happenings that composed it, struck no answering chord in her; and it passed belief to think that she had once been stirred to the depths of her soul by them. In this hour of profounder knowledge, she saw that they had only been dreams and shadows – delusive images that had tricked her brain. Nothing of them had persisted; nothing been real or lasting: her hand had caught the frayed edge of no perdurable garment. The wonders had been a chimera; the evils, too. And their hold upon her had been a imaginary one: her inmost self, the vitalest part of her, had remained unmoved by them, and unharmed. She had not striven in mortal combat; for there had never been a combat to engage in. That was still another illusion – perhaps the greatest of all. Life, tapped at its core, stripped of its rainbow gauds, meant – she knew it now – a standing dumbly by, to let these dream-things pass. Now that she was done with it, with life and living, and could view it as a whole, she saw that this was what it came to; one was never really of it; it only seemed so, at the moment. One's soul held aloof, shy, proud, chill, while past it bore an unsubstantial pageant of varying places, and their accompanying ghosts. Sometimes, these shapes held out their arms to us; sometimes, we stretched yearning hands to them. For a brief suspense, there appeared to be an entanglement; then, one or other yielded, and the procession went on as before. Love had no more reality, no more enduring-power, than the lover's arms; the dream-child we reared, changed and passed; joy passed and pain, and the windy excitements of the day. – And memory, turning on the steps of death's threshold, for a last backward look at the sun-tipped mirage, could impossibly distinguish one transient image from another. Now, they all seemed alike; they *were* alike: there had been no real difference between them. Joy and grief, love and hate, rapture and despair, were, in very truth, one and the same – the thin, blue spire of smoke, that ascended from a phantasmal fire.

And having achieved this ultimate wisdom, the dying woman was lapped by a great peace: not again would she choose to be ŏf life. Now, she asked for rest – only rest. Not immortality: no fresh existence, to be endured and fought out in some new shadowland, among unquiet spirits; but deep, deep rest, with the heavy brown earth flattened down above her, and every wish stilled at last. Without substance, without meaning, it had all been an idle beating of the air; but it was over now; and she thanked God that it was so. Never again, the laceration of a sunset, the agony of a fading autumn day! Only sleep; the sleep of nothingness: an eternal forgetting ....

She lay and let death's torpor steal over her, dimly noting its progress. But towards evening, when the cold blue eastern shadows fell, she made the instinctive effort of the dying: sought to flee the unfleeable, while there was yet time.

'I will get up and go away ... far away.'

She was raised in her bed and propped by loving arms; then

laid down again; for she was unable to support the weight of her own body: her head, all a-tremble, sank from side to side, like a top-heavy flower on its stalk. – And the sensation of sinking, of being sucked under by a current she could not stem, began anew. It was as if she were caught and swept round in a whirlpool: for a time she would ride high, on the same level; then came the dizzy, downward drop, and she was by so much nearer to the black, serpent-like, central shaft, so much farther from the blue roof of the sky. Down . . . down . . . down! – a giddy whirl towards the horrors of the dark; and so it would go on, in ever-contracting circles, till the awful moment when she whirled no more, and when the churning waters met, with a crash like that of thunder, above her head.

Then, the vertigo ceased, and a merciful weakness came to her rescue. Her thoughts, drawing to an inseparable tangle, escaped her, and were reabsorbed in the Supreme Thought, from which they had primarily come forth. Though her eyes remained open, doctor and nurse no longer hushed their voices when they spoke of her: for them, she was already numbered among those mute or inarticulate things, which, because they cannot make protest, are held insensible to hurt and affront.

Life ebbed lingeringly, unwillingly. A muddly pallor overspread her face; her breath came snortingly; the pinched nose strained upwards. But the heart beat on, throbbing through the dead body till long after midnight.

Then this, too, ceased.

The weeping watchers retired, with the sense of relief in their breasts that accompanies death accomplished; and the withdrawal of their lamentations left a great vacancy in the room. The black-robed woman who remained, raked out the embers of the fire, and pushed back the chairs from the bed. On the eyes of the thing that had been Mary Christina, she laid two squares of damped muslin; and, as she did so, she made fervid intercession with the other Mary – the Gracious Namesake of this poor soul that had gone unblessed into the darkness. The coverings decently stretched and folded, she turned out the gas, and set a night-light in a glass of water. – It threw living shadows on the wall.

Katherine Mansfield

The Woman at the Store

1912

All that day the heat was terrible. The wind blew close to the ground – it rooted among the tussock grass – slithered along the road, so that the white pumice dust swirled in our faces – settled and sifted over us and was like a dry-skin itching for growth on our bodies. The horses stumbled along, coughing and chuffing. The pack horse was sick – with a big, open sore rubbed under the belly. Now and again she stopped short, threw back her head, looked at us as though she were going to cry, and whinnied. Hundreds of larks shrilled – the sky was slate colour, and the sound of the larks reminded me of slate pencils scraping over its surface. There was nothing to be seen but wave after wave of tussock grass – patched with purple orchids and manuka bushes covered with thick spider webs.

Jo rode ahead. He wore a blue galatea shirt, corduroy trousers and riding boots. A white handkerchief, spotted with red – it looked as though his nose had been bleeding on it – knotted round his throat. Wisps of white hair straggled from under his wideawake – his moustache and eyebrows were called white – he slouched in the saddle – grunting. Not once that day had he sung 'I don't care, for don't you see, my wife's mother was in front of me!' . . . It was the first day we had been without it for a month, and now there seemed something uncanny in his silence. Hin rode beside me – white as a clown, his black eyes glittered, and he kept shooting out his tongue and moistening his lips. He was dressed in a Jaeger vest – a pair of blue duck trousers, fastened round the waist with a plaited leather belt. We had hardly spoken since dawn. At noon we had lunched off fly biscuits and apricots by the side of a swampy creek.

'My stomach feels like the crop of a hen,' said Jo. 'Now then, Hin, you're the bright boy of the party – where's this 'ere store you kep' on talking about. "Oh, yes," you says, "I know a fine store, with a paddock for the horses an' a creek runnin' through, owned by a friend of mine who'll give yer a bottle of whisky before 'e shakes hands with yer." I'd like ter see that place – merely as a matter of curiosity – not that I'd ever doubt yer word – as yer know very well – *but*...'

Hin laughed. 'Don't forget there's a woman too, Jo, with blue eyes and yellow hair, who'll promise you something else before she shakes hands with you. Put that in your pipe and smoke it.'

'The heat's making you balmy,' said Jo. But he dug his knees into his horse. We shambled on. I half fell asleep, and had a sort of uneasy dream that the horses were not moving forward at all – then that I was on a rocking-horse, and my old mother was scolding me for raising such a fearful dust from the drawing-room carpet. 'You've entirely worn off the pattern of the carpet,' I heard her saying, and she gave the reins a tug. I snivelled and woke to find Hin leaning over me, maliciously smiling.

'That was a case of all but,' said he, 'I just caught you. What's up, been bye-bye?'

'No!' I raised my head. 'Thank the Lord we're arriving somewhere.'

We were on the brow of the hill, and below us there was a whare roofed in with corrugated iron. It stood in a garden, rather far back from the road – a big paddock opposite, and a creek and a clump of young willow trees. A thin line of blue smoke stood up straight from the chimney of the whare, and as I looked, a woman came out, followed by a child and a sheep dog – the woman carrying what appeared to me a black stick. She made frantic gestures at us. The horses put on a final spurt, Jo took off his wideawake, shouted, threw out his chest, and began singing, 'I don't care, for don't you see...'. The sun pushed through the pale clouds and shed a vivid light over the scene. It gleamed on the woman's yellow hair, over her flapping pinafore and the rifle she was carrying. The child hid behind her, and the yellow dog, a mangy beast, scuttled back into the whare, his tail between his legs. We drew rein and dismounted.

'Hallo,' screamed the woman. 'I thought you was three 'awks. My kid comes runnin' in ter me. "Mumma," says she, "there's three brown things comin' over the 'ill," says she. An' I comes out smart, I can tell yer. They'll be 'awks, I says to her. Oh, the 'awks about 'ere, yer wouldn't believe.'

The 'kid' gave us the benefit of one eye from behind the woman's pinafore – then retired again.

'Where's your old man,' asked Hin.

The woman blinked rapidly, screwing up her face.

'Away shearin'. Bin away a month. I suppose yer not goin' to stop, are yer? There's a storm comin' up.'

'You bet we are,' said Jo. 'So you're on your lonely, missis?'

She stood, pleating the frills of her pinafore, and glancing from one to the other of us, like a hungry bird. I smiled at the thought of how Hin had pulled Jo's leg about her. Certainly her eyes were blue, and what hair she had was yellow, but ugly. She was a figure of fun. Looking at her, you felt there was nothing but sticks and wires under that pinafore – her front teeth were knocked out, she had red pulpy hands, and she wore on her feet a pair of dirty 'Bluchers'.

'I'll go and turn out the horses,' said Hin. 'Got any embrocation? Poi's rubbed herself to hell!'

'Arf a mo!' The woman stood silent a moments, her nostrils expanding as she breathed. Then she shouted violently, 'I'd rather you didn't stop – you *can't* and there's the end of it. I don't let out that paddock any more. You'll have to go on; I ain't got nothing!'

'Well, I'm blest!' said Jo, heavily. He pulled me aside. 'Gone a bit off 'er dot,' he whispered, 'too much alone, *you know*,' very significantly. 'Turn the sympathetic tap on 'er, she'll come round all right.'

But there was no need – she had come round by herself.

'Stop if yer like!' she muttered, shrugging her shoulders. To me – 'I'll give yer the embrocation if yer come along.'

'Right-o, I'll take it down to them.' We walked together up the garden path. It was planted on both sides with cabbages. They smelled like stale dishwater. Of flowers there were double poppies and sweet-williams. One little patch was divided off by shells – presumably it belonged to the child – for she ran from her mother and began to grub in it with a broken clothes peg. The yellow dog lay across the doorstep, biting fleas; the woman kicked him away.

'Gar-r, get away, you beast . . . the place ain't tidy. I 'aven't 'ad time ter fix things to-day – been ironing. Come right in.'

It was a large room, the walls plastered with old pages of English periodicals. Queen Victoria's Jubilee appeared to be the most recent number – a table with an ironing board and wash tub on it – some wooden forms – a black horsehair sofa, and some broken cane chairs pushed against the walls. The mantel-piece above the stove was draped in pink paper, further ornamented with dried grasses and ferns and a coloured print of Richard Seddon. There were four doors – one, judging from the smell, let into the 'Store', one on to the 'back yard', through the third I saw the bedroom. Flies buzzed in circles round the ceiling, and treacle papers and bundles of dried clover were pinned to the window curtains. I was alone in the room – she had gone into the store for the embrocation. I heard her stamping about and muttering to herself: 'I got some, now where did I put that bottle? . . . It's behind the pickles . . . no, it ain't.' I cleared a place on the table and sat there, swinging my legs. Down in the paddock I could hear Jo singing and the sound of hammer strokes as Hin drove in the tent poles. It was sunset. There is no twilight to our New Zealand days, but a curious half-hour when everything appears grotesque – it frightens – as though the savage spirit of the country walked abroad and sneered at what it saw. Sitting alone in the hideous room I grew afraid. The woman next door was a long time finding that stuff. What was she doing in there? Once I thought I heard her bang her hands down on the counter, and once she half moaned, turning it into a cough and clearing her throat. I wanted to shout 'Buck up,' but I kept silent.

'Good Lord, what a life!' I thought. 'Imagine being here day in, day out, with that rat of a child and a mangy dog. Imagine bothering about ironing – *mad*, of course she's mad! Wonder how long she's been here – wonder if I could get her to talk.'

At that moment she poked her head round the door.

'Wot was it yer wanted,' she asked.

'Embrocation.'

'Oh, I forgot. I got it, it was in front of the pickle jars.'

She handed me the bottle.

'My, you do look tired, you do! Shall I knock yer up a few scones for supper? There's some tongue in the store, too, and I'll cook yer a cabbage if you fancy it.'

'Right-o.' I smiled at her. 'Come down to the paddock and bring the kid for tea.'

She shook her head, pursing up her mouth.

'Oh no. I don't fancy it. I'll send the kid down with the things and a billy of milk. Shall I knock up a few extry scones to take with you ter-morrow?'

'Thanks.'

She came and stood by the door.

'How old is the kid?'

'Six – come next Christmas. I 'ad a bit of trouble with 'er one way an' another. I adn't any milk till a month after she was born and she sickened like a cow.'

'She's not like you – takes after her father?' Just as the woman had shouted her refusal at us before, she shouted at me then.

'No, she don't; she's the dead spit of me. Any fool could see that. Come on in now, Els, you stop messing in the dirt.'

I met Jo climbing over the paddock fence.

'What's the old bitch got in the store?' he asked.

'Don't know – didn't look.'

'Well, of all the fools. Hin's slanging you. What have you been doing all the time?'

'She couldn't find this stuff. Oh, my shakes, you are smart!'

Jo had washed, combed his wet hair in a line across his forehead, and buttoned a coat over his shirt. He grinned.

Hin snatched the embrocation from me. I went to the end of the paddock where the willows grew and bathed in the creek. The water was clear and soft as oil. Along the edges held by the grass and rushes, white foam tumbled and bubbled. I lay in the water and looked up at the trees that were still a moment, then quivered lightly, and again were still. The air smelt of rain. I forgot about the woman and the kid until I came back to the tent. Hin lay by the fire, watching the billy boil.

I asked where Jo was and if the kid had brought our supper.

'Pooh,' said Hin, rolling over and looking up at the sky. 'Didn't you see how Jo had been tittivating – he said to me before he went up to the whare, "Dang it! she'll look better by night light – at any rate, my buck, she's female flesh!"'

'You had Jo about her looks – you had me, too.'

'No – look here. I can't make it out. It's four years since I came past this way, and I stopped here two days. The husband was a pal of mine once, down the West Coast – a fine, big chap, with a voice on him like a trombone. She'd been barmaid down the Coast – as pretty as a wax doll. The coach used to come this way then once a fortnight, that was before they opened the railway up Napier way, and she had no end of a time! Told me once in a confidential moment that she knew one hundred and twenty-five different ways of kissing!'

'Oh, go on, Hin! She isn't the same woman!'

'Course she is . . . I can't make it out. What I think is the old man's cleared out and left her: that's all my eye about shearing. Sweet life! The only people who come through now are Maoris and sundowners!'

Through the dark we saw the gleam of the kid's pinafore. She trailed over to us with a basket in her hand, the milk billy in the other. I unpacked the basket, the child standing by.

'Come over here,' said Hin, snapping his fingers at her.

She went, the lamp from the inside of the tent cast a bright light over her. A mean, undersized brat, with whitish hair, and weak eyes. She stood, legs wide apart and her stomach protruding.

'What do you do all day?' asked Hin.

She scraped out one ear with her little finger, looked at the result and said – 'Draw.'

'Huh! What do you draw? – leave your ears alone.'

'Pictures.'

'What on?'

'Bits of butter paper an' a pencil of my Mumma's.'

'Boh! What a lot of words at one time!' Hin rolled his eyes at her. 'Baa-lambs and moo-cows?'

'No, everything. I'll draw all of you when you're gone, and your horses and the tent, and that one' – she pointed to me – 'with no clothes on in the creek. I looked at her where she wouldn't see me from.'

'Thanks very much! How ripping of you,' said Hin. 'Where's Dad?'

The kid pouted. 'I won't tell you because I don't like yer face!' She started operations on the other ear.

'Here,' I said. 'Take the basket, get along home and tell the other man supper's ready.'

'I don't want to.'

'I'll give you a box on the ear if you don't,' said Hin, savagely.

'Hie! I'll tell Mumma. I'll tell Mumma' – the kid fled.

We ate until we were full and had arrived at the smoke stage before Jo came back, very flushed and jaunty, a whisky bottle in his hand.

''Ave a drink – you two!' he shouted, carrying off matters with a high hand. ''Ere, shove along the cups.'

'One hundred and twenty-five different ways,' I murmured to Hin.

'What's that? Oh! stow it!' said Jo. 'Why 'ave you always got your knife into me. You gas like a kid at a Sunday School beano. She wants us to go up there to-night, and have a comfortable chat. I' – he waved his hand airily – 'I got 'er round.'

'Trust you for that,' laughed Hin. 'But did she tell you where the old man's got to?'

Jo looked up. 'Shearing! You 'eard 'er, you fool!'

The woman had fixed up the room, even to a light bouquet of sweet-williams on the table. She and I sat one side of the table, Jo and Hin the other. An oil lamp was set between us, the whisky bottle and glasses, and a jug of water. The kid knelt against one of the forms, drawing on butter paper. I wondered, grimly, if she was attempting the creek episode. But Jo had been right about night time. The woman's hair was tumbled – two red spots burned in her cheeks – her eyes shone – and we knew that they were kissing feet under the table. She had changed the blue pinafore for a white calico dressing jacket and a black skirt – the kid was decorated to the extent of a blue sateen hair ribbon. In the stifling room with the flies buzzing against the ceiling and dropping on the table – we got slowly drunk.

'Now listen to me,' shouted the woman, banging her fist on the table. 'It's six years since I was married, and four miscarriages. I says to 'im, I says, what do you think I'm doin' up 'ere? If you was back at the Coast, I'd 'ave you lynched for child murder. Over and over I tells 'im – you've broken my spirit and spoiled my looks, and wot for – that's wot I'm driving at.' She clutched her head with her hands and stared round at us. Speaking rapidly, 'Oh, some days – an' months of them I 'ear them two words knockin' inside me all the time – "Wot for," but sometimes I'll be cooking the spuds an' I lifts the lid off to give 'em a prong and I 'ears, quite sudden again, "Wot for." Oh! I don't mean only the spuds and the kid – I mean – I mean,' she hiccoughed – 'you know what I mean, Mr Jo.'

'I know,' said Jo, scratching his head.

'Trouble with me is,' she leaned across the table, 'he left me too much alone. When the coach stopped coming, sometimes he'd go away days, sometimes he'd go away weeks, and leave me ter look after the store. Back 'e'd come – pleased as Punch. "Oh, 'allo," 'e'd say. "Ow are you gettin' on. Come and give us a kiss." Sometimes I'd turn a bit nasty, and then 'e'd go off again, and if I took it all right, 'e'd wait till 'e could twist me round 'is finger, then 'e'd say, "Well, so long, I'm off," and do you think I could keep 'im? – not me!'

'Mumma,' bleated the kid, 'I made a picture of them on the 'ill, an' you an' me, an' the dog down below.'

'Shut your mouth,' said the woman.

A vivid flash of lightning played over the room – we heard the mutter of thunder.

'Good thing that's broke loose,' said Jo. 'I've 'ad it in me 'ead for three days.'

'Where's your old man now?' asked Hin slowly.

The woman blubbered and dropped her head on to the table. 'Hin, 'e's gone shearin' and left me alone again,' she wailed.

''Ere, look out for the glasses,' said Jo. 'Cheer-o, 'ave another drop. No good cryin' over spilt 'usbands! You Hin, you blasted cuckoo!'

'Mr Jo,' said the woman, drying her eyes on her jacket frill, 'you're a gent, an' if I was a secret woman, I'd place any confidence in your 'ands. I don't mind if I do 'ave a glass on that.'

Every moment the lightning grew more vivid and the thunder sounded nearer. Hin and I were silent – the kid never moved from her bench. She poked her tongue out and blew on it as she drew.

'It's the loneliness,' said the woman, addressing Jo – he made sheep's eyes at her – 'and bein' shut up 'ere like a broody 'en.' He reached his hand across the table and held hers, and though the position looked most uncomfortable when they wanted to pass the water and whisky, their hands stuck together as though glued. I pushed back my chair and went over to the kid, who immediately sat flat down on her artistic achievements and made a face at me.

'You're not to look,' said she.

'Oh, come on, don't be so nasty!' Hin came over to us, and we were just drunk enough to wheedle the kid into showing us. And those drawings of hers were extraordinary and repulsively vulgar. The creations of a lunatic with a lunatic's cleverness. There was no doubt about it, the kid's mind was diseased. While she showed them to us, she worked herself up into a mad excitement, laughing and trembling, and shooting out her arms.

'Mumma,' she yelled. 'Now I'm going to draw them what you told me I never was to – now I am.'

The woman rushed from the table and beat the child's head with the flat of her hand.

'I'll smack you with yer clothes turned up if yer dare say that again,' she bawled.

Jo was too drunk to notice, but Hin caught her by the arm. The kid did not utter a cry. She drifted over to the window and began picking flies from the treacle paper.

We returned to the table – Hin and I sitting one side, the woman and Jo, touching shoulders, the other. We listened to the thunder, saying stupidly, 'That was a near one,' 'There it goes again,' and Jo, with a heavy hit, 'Now we're off,' 'Steady on the brake,' until rain began to fall, sharp as cannon shot on the iron roof.

'You'd better doss here for the night,' said the woman.

'That's right,' assented Jo, evidently in the know about this move.

'Bring up yer things from the tent. You two can doss in the store along with the kid – she's used to sleep in there and won't mind you.'

'O, Mumma, I never did,' interrupted the kid.

'Shut yer lies! An' Mr Jo can 'ave this room.'

It sounded a ridiculous arrangement, but it was useless to attempt to cross them, they were too far gone. While the woman sketched the plan of action, Jo sat, abnormally solemn and red, his eyes bulging, and pulled at his moustache.

'Give us a lantern,' said Hin. 'I'll go down to the paddock.'

We two went together. Rain whipped in our faces, the land was as light as though a bush fire was raging – we behaved like two children let loose in the thick of an adventure – laughed and shouted to each other, and came back to the whare to find the kid already bedded in the counter of the store. The woman brought us a lamp. Jo took his bundle from Hin, the door was shut.

'Good-night all,' shouted Jo.

Hin and I sat on two sacks of potatoes. For the life of us we could not stop laughing. Strings of onions and half-hams dangled from the ceiling – wherever we looked there were advertisements for 'Camp Coffee' and tinned meats. We pointed at them, tried to read them aloud – overcome with laughter and hiccoughs. The kid in the counter stared at us. She threw off her blanket and scrambled to the floor where she stood in her grey flannel night gown, rubbing one leg against the other. We paid no attention to her.

'Wot are you laughing at,' she said, uneasily.

'You!' shouted Hin, 'the red tribe of you, my child.'

She flew into a rage and beat herself with her hands. 'I won't be laughed at, you curs – you.' He swooped down upon the child and swung her on to the counter.

'Go to sleep, Miss Smarty – or make a drawing – here's a pencil – you can use Mumma's account book.'

Through the rain we heard Jo creak over the boarding of the next room – the sound of a door being opened – then shut to.

'It's the loneliness,' whispered Hin.

'One hundred and twenty-five different ways – alas! my poor brother!'

The kid tore out a page and flung it at me.

'There you are,' she said. 'Now I done it ter spite Mumma for shutting me up 'ere with you two. I done the one she told me I never ought to. I done the one she told me she'd shoot me if I did. Don't care! Don't care!'

The kid had drawn the picture of the woman shooting at a man with a rook rifle and then digging a hole to bury him in.

She jumped off the counter and squirmed about on the floor biting her nails.

Hin and I sat till dawn with the drawing beside us. The rain ceased, the little kid fell asleep, breathing loudly. We got up, stole out of the whare, down into the paddock. White clouds floated over a pink sky – a chill wind blew; the air smelled of wet grass. Just as we swung into the saddle, Jo came out of the whare – he motioned to us to ride on.

'I'll pick you up later,' he shouted.

A bend in the road, and the whole place disappeared.

Blanche Baughan

Pipi on the Prowl

1912

Pipi was very happy. To an indifferent observer, it is true, the little mummy-like old Maori woman, bundled about with a curious muddle of rag-bag jackets and petticoats, and hobbling along the high-road on crippled bare brown feet, might have presented a spectacle more forlorn than otherwise. But then, what does the indifferent observer ever really see? That grotesque and pitiful exterior was nothing but an exterior; and it covered an escaping captive: it clothed incarnate Mirth. For Miria had gone to town, and Pipi, one whole long afternoon, was free!

She chuckled as she thought of Miria – Miria the decorous, Miria the *pakeha* coachman's wife, Miria, who wore tan shoes. Miria did not like her grandmother to go roaming at her own sweet will along the roads; she did not even like her to smoke; what she did like was to have her squatted safe at the *whare* door, holding on to little Hana, whose kicking really began to be painful, and looking out that little Himi did not get hold of the axe and chop himself to bits. She had left her like that half an hour ago; probably she imagined her to be still like that – submissive, stationed, and oh, how lack-lustre, how dull! Well, Pipi might perhaps be a little *porangi* (crazy) at times, but she was never anything like so *porangi* as that. How lucky that Ropata's wife was a trustworthy crony! How fortunate that the babies could neither of them speak! Pipi smiled, and showed her perfect teeth; she took out, from deep recesses of her raiment, her treasured pipe, and stuck it in her mouth. *E! Ka pai te paipa!* – a good thing, the pipe! There was no *topeka* (tobacco) in it, to be sure; but who could say whence *topeka* might not come, this golden afternoon? To those newly at liberty all the world belongs. And, like stolen waters, stolen sport is sweet. No urchin who, having safely conveyed himself away at last out of earshot of mother or teacher, bounds breathless to the beloved creek where 'bullies' wait the hook, knows more of the mingled raptures of lawlessness and expectation than this old great-grandmother Pipi did, out upon the high-road, out upon the hunt!

Although it was midwinter, the afternoon was warm – there is never really cold weather upon that sheltered northern coast. The road ran right round the head of the league-long harbour, and showed a splendid view; for the tide was in; every cove and inlet was full, and the sinuous, satin-blue sheen of the water reflected with the utmost fidelity every one of the little long, low spits, emerald-turfed and darkly crowned with trees, that fringed, as with a succession of piers, the left-hand shore; while the low, orange-coloured cliffs of the fern-flats opposite burned in the brilliant sun like buttresses of gold. But what was a view to Pipi? Her rheumy old brown eyes sought but the one spot, where, far down the glittering water-way, and close to the short, straight sapphire line that parted the purple Heads and meant the open sea, the glass of the township windows sent sparkles to the sun. The township – seven miles away, and Miria not there yet! *Ka pai!* Pipi was ready for whatever fish Tangaroa might kindly send her on dry land, but meanwhile freedom, simple freedom, mere lack of supervision, was in itself enough; and happily, happily she trudged along, nodding, smiling, and sucking vigorously at her empty pipe.

Before very long she came to the river – the sinister-looking river, black and sluggish, that drains the valley-head. In the swamp on the other side of the long white bridge, dark *manuka*-bushes with crooked stems and shaggy boles, like a company of uncanny crones under a spell, stood knee-deep in thick ooze; some withered *raupo* desolately lined the bank above. Even on that bright day, this was a dismal place, and the *raupo*, with its spindly shanks and discoloured leaves fluttering about them, looked lamentably like poor Pipi. *Poor* Pipi, indeed? Dismal place? Huh! what does a fool know?

With brightened eyes, with uncouth gestures of delighted haste, out across the bridge scurried Pipi, slithered down into the swamp, clutched with eager claws at a muddy lump upon the margin, and emitted a deep low grunt of joy. Old snags, quite black with decay, lay rotting round her, and the stagnant water gave forth a most unpleasant smell. But what is foulness when glory beckons through it? Squatting in the slime, her tags and trails of raiment dabbling in and out of the black water, Pipi washed and scraped, scraped and washed, and finally lifted up and out into the sunshine with a grin of delight, a great golden pumpkin, richly streaked with green. The glint of its rind had caught her eye from the other side of the bridge. Evidently it had fallen from some passing cart, and rolled down into the swamp. It was big; it was heavy; it was sound. The goodness of this pumpkin! the triumph of this find! Pipi untied one of her most extra garments, tied the treasure securely in it, slung the bundle on her back as though it had been a baby, and went on.

From the river, the road runs straight uphill, through a cutting between high banks of fern and gorse, with a crumbly crest of *papa* clay boldly yellow on the full blue sky. The road is of yellow *papa* also, and unmetalled, and rather heavy. Pipi grunted a good deal as she toiled up it; and about halfway up stood still to get her breath, for the pumpkin, precious as it was, lay like lead upon her frail old shoulders. Why! at the very top of the bank, glaring in the sunshine against the yellow *papa*, what was that? A white paper only, with nothing in it – or a white paper parcel? Steep as the bank was, go she must, of course, and see; and up, pumpkin and all, she climbed. Aha! Something inside. What? . . . Bread; and, inside the bread? Jam; thick, sweet, deep-red jam, very thick, very sweet, *very* good!

Next to tobacco, Pipi loved sweet things. She did not expend much pity upon the school-child that, heedlessly running along the top edge of the bank that morning, had lost its lunch and spent a hungry dinner-hour; neither did the somewhat travelled appearance of the sandwich trouble her. She scrambled down again on to the firmer footing of the road, and there she stood, and licked and licked at the jam. Miria's face, if she had caught her at it! Oho, that face! – the very fancy of its sourness made the tit-bit sweeter. The bread itself she threw away. Her stomach was not hungry, Miria saw to that; but her imagination was, and that was why this chance-come, wayside dainty had a relish that no good, dull dinner in the *whare* ever had. Sport was good to-day. First that pumpkin, now this jam! *Ka pai* the catch! What next?

She resumed her journey up-hill, but had no sooner reached the top than she suddenly squatted down on the bank by the roadside, as if at a word of command, with next to no breath left in her lungs, but hope once more lively in her heart – for here, surely, advancing to meet her, was the Next – a tall young *pakeha* woman, with a basket on her arm. Only a woman. That was a pity, for there was the less chance of *topeka*; still, what had that kit got in it?

Pipi knew all about strategical advantages by instinct. She sat still and waited on her hill-top as her forefathers had sat still on theirs, and waited for the prey. Soon it came; a little breathless, and with footsteps slackening naturally as they neared the brow, just as Pipi had foreseen. Yes, she would do, this *pakeha*, this pigeon; she would pay to be plucked. She was nicely dark and stout; she smiled to herself as she walked; and such good clothes upon the back denoted certainly a comfortable supply of *hikapeni* (sixpences) in the pocket.

'Tenakoe! Tenakoe!' (greeting!) cried Pipi, skipping up from her bank with a splendid assumption of agility, as the stranger came alongside; and extending her hand, expanding her smile, and wagging her wily old head, as if this strange young *pakeha* were her very dearest friend in all the world. And the bait took! The *pakeha*, too, stretched forth her hand, she, also, smiled. A catch, a catch to Pipi the fisher! Let us, though, find out first how much she knows, this fish ... Not to speak the Maori tongue means not to read the Maori mind, so:

'E hoa!' says Pipi leisurely, *'E haere ana koe i whaea?'*

Good! it is all right. The *pakeha* stands still, laughs, and says, 'Oh, please say it in English!'

She is ignorant, she is affable, she is not in a hurry. She will do, this nice young *pakeha*! Pipi translates.

'Where you goin'?'

'I am going – oh, just along this road for a bit,' says the girl vaguely.

Pipi considers. 'Along the road,' in the stranger's present direction, means back towards home for Pipi; it would surely be a pity to turn back so soon? A fish on the line, however, is worth two in the water; also, after the feast is eaten, cannot the empty basket be thrown away? In other words, as soon as ever it suits her, cannot she pretend to be tired and let the stranger go on alone? Of course she can! So Pipi says, 'Me, too,' and, turning her back, for the time being, upon the enticement of the open road ahead, goes shambling back, hoppity-hop, down the hill again, at the side of her prey. She shambles slowly, too, by way of a further test, and, see, the girl instinctively adapts her pace. Excellent! Oh, the pleasantness, the complaisance, of this interesting young friend! Pipi takes hold of her sleeve, and strokes it.

'Ah, the good coat,' she cries, with an admiration that she does not need to assume. 'He keep you warm, my word! My coat, see how thin!' and she holds out for inspection a corner of her topmost covering, an old blouse of faded pinkish print, phenomenally spotted with purple roses. It is true that she has the misfortune to hold out also, quite by mistake, a little bit of the layer next beneath, which happens to be a thick tweed coat; but this she drops immediately, without an instant's delay, and it is well known that *pakehas* have as a rule only pebbles in their eye-sockets – they see nothing; while their ears, on the other hand, are as *kokota*-shells, to hold whatever you please to put in. 'I cold, plenty, plenty,' says Pipi accordingly, with a very well-feigned shiver. 'How much he cost, your good, warm coat?'

'Why, I don't quite know,' replies the *pakeha*. 'You see, it was a present; somebody gave it me.'

'Ah, nobody give poor Pipi,' sighs Pipi, very naughtily. Is it a good thing or not, that two of the Colonel's old flannel shirts, Mrs Cameron's knitted petticoat, and Miria's thickest dress, all of them upon her person at that moment, have no tongues? 'Nobody give *kai* (food) even. What you got in your big kit?' she asks coaxingly. '*Plenty* big kit!'

'Ah, nothing at all. Only air. It's just cramful of emptiness,' says the girl, sadly shaking her head. 'What you got on your back in the bundle there? Plenty big bundle!'

It is useless, of course, to deny the existence of so plain a fact as that pumpkin. Why had not Pipi had the wit to hide it in the fern?

'On'y punkin,' she says, with a singular grimace, expressive at first of the contemptibility of all the pumpkin tribe, then changing instantly to a radiant recognition of their priceless worth, for her mind has been

Stung with the splendour of a sudden thought.

'He *fine* punkin, big, *big* punkin,' she cries, and then, munificently, 'You give me coat, I give you this big, big punkin!'

She exhibits her treasure as one astounded at her own generosity.

The *pakeha*, however, seems astounded at it, too.

'Why!' says she, 'my coat is worth at least three thousand pumpkins.'

Perhaps it is? Pipi tries to imagine three thousand pumpkins lying spread before her, with a view to assessing their value; but, not unnaturally, fails. Ah well! Bold bargaining is one weapon, but tactful yielding is another.

'*E!* You give me *hikapeni*, then, I give you punkin.' She concedes, with an air of reckless kindness, and a hope of sixpence-worth of *topeka* to be purchased presently on the sly from Wirimu, the gardener.

But 'I don't care much for pumpkins,' says the stupid *pakeha*. 'And I haven't any *hikapeni*,' she adds. The stingy thing! A fish? Why, the creature is nothing at all but an empty cockle-shell not worth the digging. And Pipi is just thinking that she shall soon feel too tired to walk a single step farther, when, suddenly producing a small, sweetly-familiar-looking packet from her coat, 'You like cigarettes?' inquires the *pakeha*.

'*Ai! Homai te hikarete! Ka pai te hikarete!* (Yes! Give me a cigarette! I do like cigarettes),' cries Pipi, enraptured, and the *pakeha* holds out the packet. Alas! there are only two cigarettes left in it, and manners will permit of Pipi's taking only one. This is very trying. 'You smoke?' she asks innocently. The girl denies it, of course, as Pipi knew she would: these *pakeha* women always do, and Miria, their slavish advocate and copyist, declares they speak the truth. Vain words; for, in the hotel at Rotorua, has not Pipi seen the very best attired of them at it? Moreover, why should this girl trouble to carry cigarettes if she does not smoke, herself? Plenty stupid, these *pakeha* women! Plenty good, however, their cigarettes, and greed (oh Miria!) overcoming manner, '*E!* you not smoke; you give me other *hikaret*', then,' she says boldly.

This miserable *pakeha*, however, proves to be as a pig, that, full of feed, yet stands with both feet in the trough – she only shakes her head, laughs sillily, and mutters some foolish remark about keeping the other for somebody else she might meet. Ah, well, never mind; Pipi has at least the one, and she would like to smoke it at once and make sure of it, but 'No right!' she says plaintively – she means 'no light'; she has no matches, and no more, it appears, has the *pakeha*. Boiled-headed slave! How, without matches, can she expect anybody to smoke her cigarettes?

'Perhaps this man has some,' suggests the *pakeha*, pointing to the solitary driver of a wagon coming down the hill behind them. She explains the predicament, and the man, with a good-natured smile, pours out half a boxful into Pipi's up-stretched palms, and drives on. Ah, and perhaps he had *topeka* with him, too, real, good, dark, strong *topeka* in a stick; and, had Pipi only been wise enough to wait for him, and let this miserable person go by, she might by now, perhaps, have been having a real smoke. As for this *hikarete*, by the smell of it, Hana, aged thirteen months, could smoke it with impunity. No coat, no *kai*, no *hikapeni*, one *hikarete* of hay – Huh! the unprofitableness of this *pakeha*!

'You go on!' says Pipi, with an authoritative gesture. They have got as far as the bridge, and she squats down by her swamp. All that long hill to toil up again, too!

But behold, the black-hearted one at her side says, actually, 'Oh, I'm in no particular hurry. I think I'll sit down a bit, too,' and does so. Now, who that has found the *riwai* (potato) rotten wants to look at the rind?

Worse and worse – who can grow melons in mid-air, drink water without a mouth, or strike a match without something to strike it on? . . . What now? Here is the *pakeha*, in reply to this reproach, sticking out her thick leather boot right into Pipi's hand – an insult? She would kick the *hikaret'* out of it? Not so, for her eyes are soft . . . Swift as a weather-cock, round whirl Pipi's mobile wits.

'E hoa!' she cries with glee. 'You give me the *hu* (shoe)? Poor Pipi no *hu*, see! I think *kapai*, you give me the *hu*.'

But the *pakeha* only shakes her head vigorously and laughs out loud. Is she *porangi* quite? No, not quite, it seems, for, taking a match from Pipi's hand, she strikes it on the clumsy sole, and lo! a flame bursts out. Pipi can light her *hikaret'* now, and does so, coolly using the *pakeha's* skirt the while, as a breakwind, for she may as well get out of her all the little good she can. And now, how to get rid of this disappointment, this addled egg, this little, little cockle with the big thick shell? Aha, Pipi knows. She will do what she has done so often with the prying Mrs Colonel Cameron – she will suddenly forget all her English, and hear and speak nothing but Maori any more. That will soon scrape off this *piri-piri* (burr). What shall she start by saying? Anything will do; and accordingly she mechanically asks again in Maori her first question, the question she asks every one. 'You are going, where?' But, O calamity! This time, the *pakeha*, the ignorant one, not only understands, but answers – and in the same tongue – and to alarming purpose!

'*E haere ana ahau ki a Huria* (I am going to Judaea),' she says. And Judaea is the name of Pipi's own *kainga!*

'*Ki a Huria!* and you know to speak the Maori!' she exclaims, startled into consternation.

'Only a very little as yet,' replies the girl. 'But Miria is teaching me.'

'Miria! which Miria?' cries Pipi, in an agony of foreboding.

'Why, Miria Piripi, Colonel Cameron's coachman's wife – *your* Miria, isn't she?' says this monster, with a sudden smile. 'She has told me about you, often.'

The truant who should suddenly see his captured 'bully' pull the hook out of its jaws in order to plunge it in his own, might very well feel as Pipi felt at this frightful moment. True enough, she had often heard Miria speak of the *pakeha* lady who came to visit Mrs Cameron and was 'always so interested in the natives'; and with the greatest care she had always kept out of her way, for Pipi had her pride – she resented being made into a show. And now — !

'Yes, and I have often seen you, too, though you may not have seen me,' pursued the relentless *pakeha*. 'You, and little Hana and Himi. Where are Hana and Himi now? I shall be sure to tell Miria I've met you,' she finished brightly.

Alas, alas for Pipi's sport! The fish had caught the fisher, and with a vengeance. She collected her scattering wits, and met the *pakeha's* eye with a stony stare, for she came of a princely race; but cold, too, as a stone, lay the heart within her breast.

The heart of the *pakeha*, however, had also its peculiarities. For all she was a *pakeha*, clad in a fine coat, wearing boots, and carrying cigarettes about with her only by way of Maori mouth-openers: for all this, her heart was the heart of a fellow-vagabond. It understood. She *had* heard Miria, and Mrs Cameron too, talk of Pipi; but with a result of which those superior speakers were not conscious. How often she had silently sympathised with the poor old free-lance kept so straitly to the beaten track of respectability; how often she had wished for a peep at Pipi *au naturel*! And now she had got it; and she meant to get it again. She could not help a little mischievous enjoyment of the confusion so heroically concealed, but she took quick steps to relieve it.

'Well, I must go on,' she said briskly, rising as she spoke. 'Take the other cigarette, Pipi, and here's a shilling for some *topeka. E noho koe* (good-bye)! Oh, and, Pipi, don't let's tell Miria yet that we've met, shall we? It will be so nice for her to introduce us properly some day, you know!'

Pipi was game. *'Haere ra'* (good-bye) was all she answered, unemotionally. But she could not help one gleam of joy shooting out of her deep old eyes, and Lucy Willett saw it, and went on with a kindly laughter in her own.

That night, when she had rolled herself up in her blanket, and lain down on the *whare* floor (she disdained the foppishness of beds), Pipi glowed all through with satisfaction. Miria, on coming home, had found her seated, patient, pipeless, before the fire, Hana and Himi one upon each knee, both intact, both peacefully asleep; and had been so pleased with this model picture, as well as with the size of Pipi's pumpkin, that she had indulged her grandmother with schnapper for supper. And Pipi had found that pumpkin; she had harvested red jam from a fern-bank; she had had one cigarette to smoke, and with another had been able to encourage Ropata's wife to future friendly offices. More than that, she had had time for one blessed pipeful of real Derby, richly odorous, and in her most initimate garment of all could feel now, as she lay, safely knotted up, the rest of a whole stick. Nor was even that all. By some extraordinary good management that she herself did not quite understand, she had eluded the hook as it dangled at her very lips while yet she had secured the bait; and she had an instinctive, shrewd suspicion that, in cleverly causing the eye of the *pakeha* to wink at guilt, she had made sure of more patronage in the future. Who could tell? Perhaps, some fine day, that good thick coat, even, might find its way to Pipi's back. *Taihoa* (just wait)! Meanwhile, what a good day's sport!

Mary Simpson

The Salvage Sale

1926

I was heading for the Savings Bank with my few coins. They had to be deposited before the haughty officials there closed the doors at three, or 'No Funds' would be written against me. En route a sign over the old drill hall caught my eye:

FIRE! FIRE! FIRE!
Swindells' Salvage Sale!
Booming Bedrock Bargains!

I recollected that Swindells' warehouse had been devastated by fire, and he was selling off here. Having great decision of character, therefore, I without hesitation swerved from my course, and plunged into the structure where bargains boomed.

It was hot in those temporary premises. It was crowded with flustered women. Half a dozen prams stood within the door, the claims of the babies sacrificed to the mothers' lust for burnt merchandise.

On stepping inside I was immediately entangled with a red cobra or sea-serpent marked with irregular streaks of black. On inspection this reptile turned out to be an unwinding 'bolt' of red sateen. The fires had licked it, and the hose had watered it with tears. An early shopper had seized the end of the 'bolt', and, gripping it tight, had gone round and round the building looking for someone to tell her its bedrock price, and, as she went, the 'bolt' had revolved drunkenly in the corner, reluctantly paying out its hawser of sateen. After winding in and out of the fast-arriving buyers, getting under loaded tables, and climbing over the cash-desk with the cobra still by the head, the bargain-hunter had fainted from exhaustion, and the snake had escaped her. It was in this that I was now enmeshed.

Looking hopelessly at the unreachable bargains, I and others struggled in its tight embrace. The red sateen went gaily in and out of the dun-colored crowd, knitting us together in an intricate pattern, like a new kind of maypole dance. The more we fought for release, the tighter grew our bonds, till at last

Swindells, jun., came with shears and snipped us free. Then, trampling the sateen serpent underfoot, we rushed the bargain-tables. I gained the penny haberdashery with a bound, but that woman with the purple toque who sits opposite me in church was ahead of me. We are instinctive enemies, though we rub shoulders and digest the same sermons weekly. We know each other not, yet hate each other well. This Pharisee snatched what I was after – gent.'s tarnished sleeve-links at one penny per dozen sets. Had I been a cave woman and obeyed my instincts, I would have smitten her on the purple toque with a club, but discretion was ever the better part of my valor. So instead, I stooped, and, 'mid the scuffle of human hooves round the haberdashery, deftly wound about the ankles of my enemy a mile or so of braid which had fallen to the floor. Thus, having hobbled her where she stood, I blithely got a start of her to the next 'throw-out.'

Long tables supported. by trestles were stacked with men's wear. Suits for 7s. 11d. Burburrys, once 55s., now 5s. Certainly, the fire had eaten away the Burburrys' shoulders, but what matter? Further on were rainproofs without skirt parts. The two remnants neatly joined together would make a seasonable garment for Father to wear to the city.

But recollecting my mission to the bank, and knowing my surplus cash to be infinitesimal, I reluctantly left the Burburrys at 5s. to the affluent, and forged my way through the myriad of women to those benches running right round the sides of the building, where shirts, reduced to cinders and ashes, could be had for threepence. With these I hoped to protect my men-folk from the coming snap of winter.

I fought in that scrum with fair success, securing at times as much as three-quarters of a shirt at once. Among these wrecks I unearthed a white vest – just the thing for Father to wear to bowls. Intact it was, its purity unsmirched, not a button missing. How came it there? But it was not for me to answer that question. I stowed it under my arm along with the rest of the loot. After that my luck turned, the neckband or the ankle part of a pyjama being my only haul.

Thank Heaven, I am not as some gamblers! I know when to stop. So, wiping heat and cinders from my face, I struggled for the pay-desk with my bargains, there to have them wrapped up.

'The lot one shilling,' I said casually. Swindells counted them.

'Two tennis shirts, in pieces,' he gabbled; 'one narf tail pieces, two pairs o' sleeves, and – why? Wot's this?' He held up the white waistcoat.

'It's a vest,' I said.

'A ves'!' he squealed. 'Clean fresh goods! See the mark! Three and eleven-pence – and you want it for threepence! D'you want to make me bankrup'?'

'It was among the threepennies,' I insisted doggedly. But Swindells, his usual oily urbanity scorched off, refused to see eye-to-eye with me. The thief actually snatched the vest from me and pitched it among the 'wet onlys.'

Robbed of my one bargain, I threw the shirt-tails at him, and, staggering to the four-foot-high bench that encircled the walls, leaned heavily upon the charred goods there. Presently I felt something catch my ankles. Peering down, I discovered beneath the bench whereon I leaned another world. Women were crawling about on all-fours, clearing tracks for themselves, over and through a mass of burnt underflannels which Swindells had thrown there to be sold in sixpenny armfuls.

It was they who had interfered with my ankles, evidently taking even those for salvage.

It looked nice in the gloaming of that underworld. I could see it but dimly. It was walled in by the skirts of bargain-hunters, who were raking over the remnants on the bench which formed its roof. I joined them, and soon learned the lay of the country, the outstanding feature of which were the hummocks or mounds of flannel about which the submerged grovelled.

It appeared, on investigation, that the heaps of burnt underwear consisted of shirts and pants whose 'middles' had been licked away by the flames. The garments had then fallen in halves. Swindells or his assistants had thrown their heads and tails in opposite directions, afterwards raked them together again, churned them all about with sticks, had added flannels with the fronts burnt away and pants with the seats missing, then tossed in a flavoring of charred pyjamas seasoned with singlets minus sleeves, added a pinch of braces 'to taste,' and mixed well.

And a pretty pot-pourri they had made of it.

I joined the burrowing, creeping humans who infested this

mixture like rats sliding about in a sewer. One almost expected to meet the shade of Victor Hugo, in which case I would have carolled 'Fancy meeting you!'

It was exciting sport in the half-light among the charred and tindery underwear – almost hidden from sight as we were by the serried rows of above-world shoppers, kicked and trodden on at times by their intruding toes. It was almost as thrilling as hunting big game to drag from the heap of rubbish half a shirt, and then track its tail down the maze of salvage to the dead finish. I could feel my face stiffen into an inscrutable mask, my eyes narrow, and my speech, when I indulged in any, grow cynical and cutting. I have not worshipped Sherlock Holmes for nothing. Like human bloodhounds, having portion of a garment, we scented the missing fragment down, following every clue, and making the capture, only to find the quarry in the hands of some blackened trader who, having started with the shirt's tail-piece, was working backwards along a chain of evidence, in search of the neck and shoulders.

Placards announced that we could have as much as we could hold for sixpence. I quickly collected a decent bundle of divorced trouser-legs, and hung them, scalp-wise, at my belt. The 'tops' I found later, being put up at private auction by a syndicate as 'patching'. When the syndicate became aware of me and my 'scalps' they offered me my weight in gold – that is to say, in charred socks, for them. We came to terms, and I, swollen out on all sides by my new acquisition, padded heavily and silently on like an elephant.

I was determined to make the entire round trip of the underworld, for I had just found a set of buttons, and if intrepid courage counts for anything, I was going to have the button-holes.

So I 'all-foured' off. A gentle melancholy soon developed in me – a not uncommon symptom, I found on enquiry, due no doubt to the semi-darkness, to the chill from the water-sodden salvage, and to the vague fear that one would never get out of that living tomb alive. Added to this, a tender regret that, literally wallowing as we were in bargains at bedrock rates, we should not be able to get away with more than sixpenn'orth of it. All, however, were not of fine fibre. Some coarse, practical creatures, clutching at bargains which turned to dust and cinders in their grasp, did the round trip of the underworld in double-quick time, switchbacking over the hummocks like large, unwieldy birds amongst tree-tops. They gathered their rubbish on the wing. There was one devastating traveller with a stout cord arranged in a slipknot attached to her waist. In this she strangled each rag that came her way. In her hands she carried a dozen celluloid collars with which she rasped the ears of all gropers she passed. Someone asserted that a white flag should save us from this vulture; but she had not even a military sense of honor, and in one of her rounds she caught me by the throat with a crook-handled umbrella she had found somewhere nor'-nor'-east, and left me for dead south of hummock 19.

Another type travelled stealthily, like stalking cats. One such I met. I had just rounded a hillock of wet flannels in search of that set of buttonholes, when my eyes met the yellow glare of another pair. It was she, the antagonist whom I had tied up with braid at the penny haberdashery; and clutched to her chest was a strip of calico with buttonholes in it!

I have always sensed the feline in that woman, and my instinct was correct. Snarlingly we drew apart. She bristled up her hair, licked her lips, and growled 'Gr-r-r-r —.' Between us lay a bathing-suit. She grabbed one leg. I grabbed the other, and, obeying an impulse, thrust it rudely in her face. She stuck her claws in it. I braced my back to the hummock and my feet on her bunions, and pulled for the victory. Then the 'neck-to-knee' gave way. I did a double back somersault over the mound. I never saw her again. The breakaway had been so sudden that she disappeared headlong down an abyss of shirting.

When some good Samaritan had peeled my hat from my head, forced by the impact over my ears, I regained consciousness. But, alas, my set of shirt-buttons was lost, and someone had robbed me of all my socks. But I still had my bag of small coin, and at that I rejoiced. I could feel its leather handles across my palm among the braces, sleeve rings, and other rubbish I was carrying home to Father.

By degrees the hilly character of the place became trodden to an uninteresting level, and in consequence much of its delightful mystery was lost. Instead of popping on friends around corners, we met frankly in the open like trampling elephants, and compared our pickings. I saw our Sunday-school superintendent's wife kneeling and gazing into a tangle of trousers, which suggested a picture of 'Man Dancing', by a Cubist artist. The kneeling one, after greetings, murmured something about collecting for 'the poor'. She lied. I have since seen the superintendent in one of Swindells' 'slightly damaged'.

By-and-bye, I wearied, and – fatal sign! – began to doubt the value of my bargains; I never seemed able to collect the things I needed – hadn't the knack of it, somehow. What use could Father find for a little boy's nightgown? I asked myself. Yet I hesitated to throw it overboard. And my precious bag of coins worried me dreadfully. Suppose I lost it? Every few minutes I had to reassure myself of its safety by feeling on my wrist for its handles, among the dozen neckties, the three scorched Derby hats, and the smoking-jacket which I had added to the loot.

After a while I found myself having a heart-to-heart talk with an utter stranger on the merits of some other stranger called Alf. I think that in the half-light my gossip had mistaken me for Alf's aunt, or possibly she thought I was his grandmother. So I sat still. And it just proves how wasted is all effort, for, while I sat quiescent and listened, that good old soul grovelled for and piled upon me the halves of boys' flannel shirts. (I had mentioned when first we met among the neckbands that I needed flannel.)

So now she went prosing and piling me with pieces. Said she: 'You see, Alf's a good lad, only 'e drinks an' plays two-up. (Here's a nice bit o' flannel now – make a nice little . . .) An' 'e knocks 'is poor ole father about. ('Ere's another flannel, not much burnt, only the neck gone, an' the sleeves an' one shoulder. See?' She holds up the charred thing. 'An' 'ere's a front breath,' she adds. 'If we can only find the back breath now, an' the other lorst bits, you're right – a good flannel for 2½d. – tha's right, can't get 'em no cheaper than that.) An', as I was sayin', if Alf would have give up darnce-'alls an' stop robbin' 'is brother's money-box 'e – ('Ere's the buttons.).' She grovelled her length away – five feet – and had to be drawn back by the heels.

But I suddenly rebelled. I was sick of her, sick of the smell of fire engine and smoke, sick of my scheme of building winter clothing out of embers, sick of her pointless tale about the Alf I didn't know and didn't want to. So I adroitly turned my whole accumulation of shirt ends and burnt holes over her, and ignoring her hoarse cries for mercy, crawled rapidly out of the inferno. As I regained the crowded, chattering upper world I heard the Town Hall clock booming three. I limbered up and fled like a battery of French artillery to take up my position at the bank counter. Arrived there (the bank is only round the corner), I unloaded my loot with a flourish and felt for my handbag. I found the handles only! The bag itself was gone. I pictured it reposing in the sixpenny bundle of some thief of the underworld at Swindells' Salvage Sale.

Jean Devanny

The Perfect Mother

1927

Mrs Macdonald and Mrs Leitrim were friends. But Mrs Leitrim was a thorn in the side of Mrs Macdonald because of her exceeding righteousness.

Mrs Macdonald was an easy-going soul, buxom, not too big, not too tidy, either, but full of rosy goodnature. Everybody loved her.

Mrs Leitrim was a commanding woman. Strikingly handsome in a blonde way, meticulous of speech and not sparing of it; a managing woman, superior. Everybody admired her.

The two women were close neighbours in the mining town of Millerton, West Coast. Mrs Macdonald's husband was a miner; Mrs Leitrim's the company's head clerk. An 'accountant', Mrs Leitrim styled him. This vocational distinction gave the latter woman an advantage over Mrs Macdonald to start with. Not that Leitrim made more money than Macdonald. He did not make as much. Mike Macdonald was a 'pillar' man, one of the 'royals', who knew just about all there was to know about scientific mining. But clerking was clean, refined and a one-shifted job. Mrs Leitrim was not 'messed about' with changing mealtimes, disturbed nights and the other incidentals to weekly changes of shift, as Mrs Macdonald was. She found it easy to be tidy and methodical. She had only two children, too, to Mrs Macdonald's four.

Mrs Leitrim was not aware that she was a thorn in her friend's capacious side. She would have been hurt had she known it. For she was fond of Mrs Macdonald; had no intention of making comparisons and no wish to do so. She could not help her own orderly existence and was very broad-minded and tolerant (except in one direction) besides. She was an intellectual. Before her marriage she had participated in the political agitations of New Zealand. Without attaching herself to any definite party aspect, she had been known as a sincere and implacable agitator for reforms, chiefly in regard to woman and child welfare. Her single life from childhood onward to the time of her marriage had been crowded with incident, riotous with colour, flaming with the fires of a daring and courageous self-expression. A 'career' had been open to her. She had been considered the coming woman, and yet – for love of a man and desire for a child she had pushed aside ambition and settled down.

At this time she had two baby boys, two beautiful baby boys.

She had told Mrs Macdonald of her pre-marital ambitions; of what they had meant to her – everything in the world worth living for – till love had come and with it visions of and cravings for motherhood.

'Yes,' she would say. She talked such a lot she was bound to repeat herself a good deal. 'I loved the public life. I lived for it. I felt that I was fitted – without boasting, Mrs Macdonald, really, without boasting, I felt that I was fitted to do great things in politics.'

'Of course you were,' Mrs Macdonald would put in obligingly and admiringly. 'Of course you were. Everyone knows how wonderful you were. You can do great things yet if you want to. You didn't die when you married –'

'No, no!' Mrs Leitrim would interrupt. Like all great talkers and doers, she thought other people's opinions quite irrelevant to a discussion. 'No, no. I don't want you to misunderstand me.' (There was no use at all in Mrs Macdonald trying to interpose to the effect that she did not misunderstand.) 'I've quite given it up. I made my decision. It was public life or private life and I chose private life.'

'But, my dear, you didn't die when . . .'

'No, no, Mrs Macdonald! I have no intention of ever going back to it; at least, not till the children are grown up. A mother's duty lies with her children.' Mrs Leitrim would whisk off her pince-nez, flourish them, wipe them and plant them firmly on her classic nose again. 'Now, you mustn't misunderstand me, Mrs Macdonald. I don't regret it in the least and never will. I adore my children –' Here Mrs Macdonald would insist on pushing in:

'Of course you do, my dear. All mothers love their children.'

'But what I mean, Mrs Macdonald, is that I don't take my motherhood lightly. I realize the responsibilities of the parent; especially of the mother. Those responsibilities quite preclude the possibility of politics for me until the babies are grown up.

But I don't regret it! Oh, no! I adore them!' And Mrs Leitrim would quite shame poor Mrs Macdonald with her correct speech and manner in regard to the children. Her:

'Do you want attention, darling?' and the child's: 'Yes, please, Mummy dear,' made Mrs Macdonald blush for her own:

'You little devil, messing round the place. I've half a mind to rub your nose in it.'

But she liked her admirable neighbour very much. She was not at all jealous of the perfection which was the thorn in her side because of her husband's attitude towards it.

The Macdonalds had been comfortable enough before the Leitrims settled next door a year before this time. Mrs Macdonald had muddled along in her happy-go-lucky way; letting the children go a tiny bit dirty if she felt disinclined to clean them; running up bills at the grocer's while she wasted the money on pretty clothes of which she took no care; playing tennis, going to the pictures, and dances; having a good time, in fact, as she considered it. She still had her 'good time'. But after the Leitrim's perfect household had been established next door Mike Macdonald's complacent, amiable forbearance of his wife's frivolous, easy-going ways had gradually changed. He was a quiet, home-loving sort himself, very fond of the children.

Leitrim had set him carping at his wife. Leitrim was not too clever, not commanding; not superior in any way and he realized it and could never be grateful enough to his wife for marrying him. He sounded her praises to all and sundry; descanted on her housewifely virtues, her economy, her cleanliness and orderliness, but most of all on her Perfect Motherhood. And all his praises were deserved, as everyone about could see. Macdonald was always about. Leitrim and he were as friendly as the two women and most of their spare time was spent gossiping. Result, that Mike began to poke his nose into his wife's business, as she expressed it; began to make unpleasant remarks about women that could not stay in their homes, that thought more of dancing and gadding about than of their children. But Mrs Macdonald never got nasty. She would laugh in her soft, chuckling way and say something like:

'Oh, well, Mike, I know I'm not perfect. You'll have to put up with me as I am.' Even when he got to making straight-out comparisons between her and Mrs Leitrim, Mrs Macdonald felt no animus against her neighbour and little against him. A little fitful exasperation was the extent of her reaction to his criticisms.

'Mrs Leitrim is a big woman,' she would usually say at these times, not being very versatile in her ideas. 'She's big. I'm only an ordinary woman. She's clever and intellectual. I'm not.'

'You can learn,' he would argue. 'And you don't need to be intellectual or clever to clean up a house and wash the kids. Or to stay home from dances either. Mrs Leitrim won't go out dancing and leave her kids till three o'clock in the morning like you do. It's not right.' Once she asked Mike, apropos of Mrs Leitrim's perfect motherhood:

'Do her children love her any more than mine do me, Mike?' He had to answer: 'No,' to that but made it as sulky as he could. For Mrs Macdonald's children adored their mother, who let them play in the dirt with other children as dirty as themselves, was reasonable about naughtiness and always generous in regard to lollies. Mike added after a pause, during which his wife had hummed a tune pleasantly as though his admission had settled everything:

'But her children love her, too, don't they?'

'Yes, they love her. Anyone would love her,' she put in in a burst of generosity, 'I love her. She's lovely. But you can't make me over into a Mrs Leitrim, Mike. I'm all right. I enjoy my life.'

'So does she. She's happy in her home and children and husband.' Baffled, his wife went on undressing the children, slapping one here, swearing mildly at another there, at the same time as she dressed herself for a dance.

'Get cleaned, Mike, and come with me,' she urged. 'Come and have a bit of fun. What's the use of digging your own grave? The kids will be all right. You're getting Mrs Leitrim on the brain. You'll be in love with her next.' He smiled shamefacedly at that and muttered:

'Don't talk rot. You know very well I only want my wife to be as good as another's.' She stood in the door and regarded him quizzically.

'Your wife's all right, Mike. She's happy. Are you coming?'

'No!' he snapped petulantly. So she went to the dance alone, had a jolly time and tumbled into bed at two in the morning.

Mike brought her in a cup of tea when he got his own breakfast at seven, after which she got up, drowsily. The children had long been out on the road in their night-clothes, shouting, quarrelling and playing. When Mike passed Leitrims' on his way to work it soured him to see their two little boys washed and dressed and their mother out sweeping the rocky yard floor.

'Good morning, Mr Macdonald,' Mrs Leitrim called out briskly. (Mike's wife would have said: 'Hallo, there!')

'Good morning. You're up early as usual.'

'Well, it is not that I dislike my bed. The children drag me out.' Mike went on his way thinking how handsome she was. Leitrim ought to be proud.

The one subject on which Mrs Leitrim was not broadminded and tolerant was that of sex. She had married at thirty. Being splendid looking she had been much sought by men, but, as she often told Mrs Macdonald, though she had liked men very much and was really quite passionate – yes, she would freely admit she was really a passionate woman – she had preserved her moral character; she had kept men in their place.

'Of course, Mrs Macdonald, I don't presume to criticize others. I don't want you to misunderstand me. I realize that human nature is human nature and that some poor things are weak. We can't all be cut of a pattern. I don't take up a hard attitude on the matter, Mrs Macdonald. Oh, no! But there must be a limit to toleration in the interests of the race. Laxity must not be allowed to degenerate into licence. If you had only seen what I've seen around the jazz halls in Wellington and Auckland you would realize the necessity for limitations. This filthy jazz!'

Mrs Macdonald, who had seen quite a thing or two around the tin huts of the miners, who had let Mike get her 'into trouble' in the first place and had more than one innocent skeleton in her cupboard in regard to sex since, always felt particularly at a disadvantage on this subject. Not embarrassed. Oh no. She was too naturally philosophical for her conscience to be pricked by the other's preachments and predications. Everything was all right so long as it was all right, was her motto, and she was all right. Only she could never find anything satisfactory to say about the matter. And this was the only subject that Mrs Leitrim ever invited her to give an opinion on, strange to say. She thought at times it was rather funny how Mrs Leitrim harped so much on certain aspects of sex; for instance, marital infidelity; denouncing it, expansively, and yet there seemed always a question in her tone and words. Her extremist animadversions – she got passionate on the subject at times – would be accompanied by a sort of straining demand by her eyes for confirmation by Mrs Macdonald. The latter felt this but could not understand it. She would murmur:

'Yes, yes, I suppose you are right, my dear. You're always right. But what I say is: live and let live. We've only got one life.' Which kind of remark seemed to rouse impatience in Mrs Leitrim. One day she became almost bullying in her efforts to make her friend agree with her.

'Live and let live, yes, Mrs Macdonald, but you must admit that the mother who doesn't put her children first, before all things, is the lowest kind of person?'

'I don't see how it affects the children,' Mrs Macdonald answered mildly.

'Oh, it must! You can't hide these things, Mrs Macdonald. Look at my two darlings, my two beautiful boys.' Mrs Leitrim had one on her knee and the other standing beside her in Mrs Macdonald's kitchen. 'Suppose I took a lover? Could I be the same mother to them? To my beauties?'

'Well, I don't know much about these things,' the other said uncomfortably. 'You are too – too real. You make so much of everything.'

'Oh, if a thing has to be done it ought to be done properly.' Was there a feverish note in Mrs Leitrim's voice? Mrs Macdonald looked at her. She looked nervous, a condition which was altogether ridiculous in her. 'No, Mrs Macdonald. A mother can't love her children and man too. The two things act one against the other. The good mother must be wrapped up in her children. When I think of these two wonderful bodies that I have created, that I gave up my life for. – Now don't misunderstand me! I gave it up willingly; I deliberately made my choice, and I don't regret it. No, not for an instant. I don't regret it.' There was more than nervousness in her voice now; – hysteria. She pressed her boy to her breast and showered kisses on his upturned face.

Mrs Macdonald was positively startled.

'But children are a tie, aren't they, Mrs Macdonald? A great tie. I see why nature made the mother-love so strong.'

Now it is irrefutable that the intuitions of the simple ordinary woman are the strongest kind of intuitions. Mrs Macdonald's timid mind here made a leap to an astounding conclusion, though she had never heard of psychology, never heard of complexes, of inhibitions. And on the strength of her impulsive understanding she asserted herself.

'Now look here, my dear,' she said firmly. 'You're making a hash of your life with your fool ideas. Look at me. Ain't I happy. Aren't my children happy and healthy? I'm not a passionate woman; I could go along for ever without seeing a man; Mike's mostly a nuisance to me. But more than once I've had another man. It just came my way and I took it. And I'm no worse for it either. No one's any the worse. Now you just put that in your pipe and smoke it.'

Mrs Leitrim stared with wide-open eyes. Then she burst into tears, rose hurriedly, took one child by the hand and the other under her arm, cried hysterically:

'You've done a bad thing to-day, Mrs Macdonald; I depended on you; I trusted you and now you've done a bad thing;' and almost ran out of the house.

Mrs Macdonald cried too. 'Oh the poor soul! The poor soul!'

Thereafter, when Mike carped and sulked and made comparisons she smiled indulgently. She even tidied up a bit, to oblige him. Until his nagging got so intense and constant as to seriously threaten her domestic life. Mike had Mrs Leitrim on the brain, it seemed, though he mentioned her name less and less. Mrs Macdonald began to cry a little and she went out more than ever. She discovered a temper in herself and kept it no secret from Mike. She had the back-blocks woman's habit of talking to herself and now as she went about her housework she muttered disjointedly.

'Yes, he's in love with her and doesn't know it. – He's bothered and worried because he doesn't know what's the matter with him. – Thinks he wants me to be clean and tidy and stay home when what he really wants is her. – He hardly ever comes to me now, at night. – He's got her in his mind all the time and the best he can do is to try to make me act like her –' And so on.

But she never allowed the other woman to suspect, nor did she enlighten Mike as to her conclusions. She had her pride.

Mrs Leitrim had been different to her friend ever since that day of disclosures. Not less friendly, but different. A little more superior in her manner, perhaps; obviously an unconscious attitude, and less discursive. She tabooed the subject of sex completely. More assiduously than ever she devoted herself to her children.

They had a friend, the Leitrims, a gentleman from Christchurch, who often stayed with them for a day or two. Mrs Leitrim had informed Mrs Macdonald that 'Jarvis' was an old companion of hers before her marriage. In fact, he had greatly desired her for his wife but had behaved like a brick when she chose Leitrim. And Leitrim was awfully decent about things. He quite understood that a friend was a friend and heartily welcomed Jarvis to their home. Jarvis would have been a better match, she agreed with Mrs Macdonald. He had a good business. In fact it was his business that really brought him over the Island to the Coast. But then, she had been awfully keen on Leitrim. And she did not regret it. Oh, no!

After this friend's visit she had been in the habit of running across and chatting intimately to Mrs Macdonald of the talks she had had with Jarvis. His visits meant so much to her. He had been a part of the old busy life; part of the turmoil; the chase, the fight. Mrs Leitrim's fine eyes would flash and her nostrils quiver at the sound of the very word 'fight.' Sometimes she would close those eyes and seem to listen like a huntsman awaiting the horn.

But when Jarvis came again, stayed two days and went, she kept away from her friend; pointedly avoided her eyes when she had to come outside. Mrs Macdonald was usually at the back door or not far from it. And for some intuitive reason the latter did not go over to Leitrim's. She did not know why. Usually the two ran back and forth haphazard, in the homely manner of the hospitable West Coast. And Mrs Macdonald was puzzled to catch a glimpse now and again of Mrs Leitrim at her window, staring across at her friend with a white straining face. Even from a distance Mrs Macdonald could feel the question in her look.

As the only topics of interest in the New Zealand mining towns are the doings of one's neighbours, Mrs Macdonald began to think seriously about Mrs Leitrim; to worry a bit; even to wish that she would leave the place. She felt a bit sorry for Mike too, now, and ceased to cry in secret.

'The big boob,' she thought with contemptuous good-nature, having Mike's tousled red head and ugly thick features in mind. 'To fall for a woman like her. She hardly knows he exists. She's not in our class.'

But Mrs Leitrim came back in a day or two her old charming self.

'I see you've had your friend to visit you again,' said Mrs Macdonald.

'Yes, Jarvis was over on business. But I don't think I shall have him to stay any more, Mrs Macdonald. After all, it is hardly the thing for a married woman to have a man staying in the house when she is alone. And Harry could not stay away from work, of course. I don't want you to misunderstand me or think me straitlaced. I'm not. It would be inexcusable for a woman of my advanced trend of thought to be prudish or intolerant, but – really, the children must be considered. It is my duty as their mother not to risk my good name. I can't run the risk of having the neighbours talking. And in these places –. You know what these places are for scandal, Mrs Macdonald.'

'Why, good God, yes! Of course they scandalize! Why shouldn't they? What else is there to do? But they don't mean anything by it. There's nothing in it. But as for you! Having a gentleman friend come to stay with you for a day or two! Why, nobody even dreamt of saying a word! Nobody even thought a thing about it! Bless my soul! What ever put that into your head? Making too much of everything again! If it were me, now, or any of the others like me, but you can do as you like, my dear. And anyhow, you didn't die when you –'

'No, no!' There was a distinctly tired note in Mrs Leitrim's voice. 'I didn't die when I married. But I am one of those people who must do things thoroughly, Mrs Macdonald, if they do them at all. I won't risk the merest suspicion falling on my children's mother. I told Jarvis not to return. Surely you think I did right, Mrs Macdonald?' The questioning note was urgent, the straining demand for agreement.

'I think you're a damn fool,' said Mrs Macdonald shortly. 'Children indeed! What your children want is a human being for a mother, not a blooming iceberg or an autom – autom – what the devil is the word? How long do you think you'll last out in a place like this? If you ask me, you're a nervous wreck now. And you that big and fine and strong. You're a fighter, you are. You want fight, and when you can't get fight you want man.'

Mrs Leitrim jumped, positively jumped.

'Oh! How dare you, Mrs Macdonald? I've – I've done with you! I'll – I'll never speak to you again! You're a bad woman!' She picked up her children, her two beautiful boys, one in each arm and made for the door. Her voice was high-pitched; tears rained down her face. 'I trusted you! I – I depended on you, Mrs Macdonald, and you've talked like a wicked woman! I'm done with you!' She flew across the yard and slammed her own kitchen door behind her. Mrs Macdonald sat very still for a long time. She was upset, too. Then:

'I wonder what she depended on me for,' she muttered.

The next day came out brilliantly fine. The sun, which was always close to the mining camp stuck onto the yellowish-white clay of a mountain top, seemed bent on giving its inhabitants a foretaste of hell. The clay cracked with the heat and scorched the eyeballs with its ferocious glare. The tennis court, cut out of a clay bank, was unthinkable. Yet Mrs Macdonald felt that she would rather not stay close to her neighbour. She did not know what attitude to adopt towards Mrs Leitrim should they both be outside at one time. There was no rancour in her for the harsh words spoken. She suspected hidden fires and suffering of a sort she could not understand. She would have ignored the previous day and gone on as before but she was at sea in regard to the other woman's temper. Impossible to stay inside all day. Indoors beneath the corrugated iron roof would be torture in the heat. She hated to think of her two oldest children in school. Eventually she decided to take the two little ones a mile down the hill to the manuka clumps which grew there in the better soil and sit in their shade and read while the children played about. It would be a heavy climb back with the drag of the children upon her and Mike would have to put up with an improvised tea, which he hated. However, neither drawback weighed much with her so away she went immediately after lunch. Mrs Leitrim had not showed herself.

The afternoon wilted away slowly and Mrs Macdonald drowsed in the shade of the manuka. Not altogether comfortably, for her mind would return to the friend who must be broiling up above. She kept tangling the heat of the sun with Mrs Leitrim's nature, somehow. The whitish glare of the earth with her glimpses of Mrs Leitrim's staring, pallid face at her window in the days after Jarvis had left. The broken-backed clay of the mountain with the rents in Mrs Leitrim's commanding calm wrought by her astounding hysteria. Heat! The mountain seemed to wobble, to totter with it, emasculated to the point of exhaustion. And in Mrs Macdonald's fancy Mrs Leitrim tottered too. Once she dozed off, but awakened sharply with the feeling real as life upon her that Mrs Leitrim's hand had clutched at her; her voice had wailed for help; her eyes had strained for answer to a question. She got up and shook herself and wished it were time to go home.

About four o'clock her buxom, soft body panted back to her door. She was tired out. The heat was still intense, though it had lost the sweltering quality. The sky was further away and faintly blue, presaging the cool of the night. Mrs Macdonald hated that camp just then. Her amiable spirit was tired as her body. She was not used to mental stress. She was red in the face; the children cried, tired out, too, and her stomach recoiled at thought of the tough steak she had to fry for tea. But nevertheless her eyes swept her neighbour's house for sign of Mrs Leitrim. She would go over after tea and put her foot down on this nonsense. Wicked, indeed! There would be no living in the place if neighbours took to quarrelling. She was glad to see the two little boys playing about in the yard. Shut in, of course. A young girl friend was sitting on the front doorstep, too. Mrs Leitrim was not visible.

At sight of her the girl jumped up and went inside. Mrs Macdonald clumped wearily into her kitchen and dropped into a chair. She must hurry and light the fire. Mike would be home in a minute. Her oldest boy ran in.

'Hallo, Mum! I say, Mrs Leitrim's gone down the hill by herself. Went a couple of hours ago on the trucks.'

'What!' For Mrs Leitrim to go anywhere without her children was astounding. Even the child thought so. 'What! By herself?' But here the girl came to the door. She had an envelope in her hand which she held out to Mrs Macdonald.

'Here. Mrs Leitrim told me to give this to you.' She watched

Mrs Macdonald curiously as she took the letter and opened it. The easy-going woman began to read with wonder in her face but she had hardly time to read a line before she dropped it as though it had stung and cried out a sharp 'Oh!'

The girl leapt to pick it up and inquisitively spread out the sheet but the woman snatched at it and said sharply:

'Run outside, you two. I've got to get my tea on.' The girl went slowly, plainly manifesting her itch to get her nose into that letter. At the door she turned and said craftily:

'Mrs Leitrim was crying when she went away.' Her tone invited questions. But Mrs Macdonald shut the door in her face.

That letter!

When she had read it she quietly laid it down upon the table and went out and brought in some sticks. She set the fire and lit it. But when she reached to lift down the steak from the nail on which it hung in the porch she missed it, blinded by the gush of tears which ran down her face. The meat smelled. That mattered nothing; it always did in the summer; some vinegar water would fix that. But Mrs Macdonald brushed her tears aside so as not to miss any of the maggots in the creases; Mike had a peculiar and ridiculous antipathy to meat which had been blown. She hurried to get them all off before he came. She did not want to be crying when he came, either. A little flare of malicious satisfaction, the tiniest flare possible, shot up in her when she thought of Mike, but was gone almost before she realized it. She had a wish, somehow, – it must have been her pride – not even to appear to crow over Mike. She wanted to act as though Mike had never mentioned Mrs Leitrim to her, nor given a thought to her perfections.

Men! A lot they knew about women! And the less they knew the better. She had sense enough not to poke her nose into Mike's jaunts into Westport. As long as things were all right they were all right. But that poor soul! Despite herself Mrs Macdonald was crying when Mike came in. The two oldest children were with him, crowding him, chattering volubly.

'Here,' he said at once to his wife. 'What's this the kids are saying about Mrs Leitrim? That she's gone down the hill and left a letter for you?' He stared at his wife's hot, wet face.

'Send them out, Mike,' she said.

'Why?' But he told them to 'shunt,' nevertheless, and when

they disappeared took the letter from his wife with a half-ashamed, bullying eagerness. His face as he read that letter was a study. If his wife had been a malicious woman she would have felt amply recompensed for the botherment he had caused her. Mike was too naive to hide his emotions; his blank dismay and consternation. And his – yes, and his jealousy, too. He read it and stood there grimacing, thinking his funny faces a grin, and the paper fluttered to the floor.

Mrs Macdonald gave him one glance and then busied herself round her frying-pan, but her tears flowed faster than ever and she knew that she was crying for Mike, for her poor old Mike.

He grunted, coughed and tried to speak, becoming aware of his wife. To give him respite she said casually:

'You'd better get the coal in, Mike. Tea won't be long.' He took up the butter box they used for a scuttle and went outside. When he returned he was mad; plain mad. His jealousy had come uppermost and he vented it in the form of virtuous denunciations. The only form possible to him. His wife knew that he was still quite unconscious of his real condition. He was sincere enough.

'So she's gone, ay?' He dropped the coal-box with a thud. 'Gone to her precious Jarvis, who'll take her away to America. America!' He seemed to be struck to the heart with realization of the distance between him and America. He stood beside his wife with hanging, limp arms and dropped jaw, his eyes peering from under his bushy red brows, following Mrs Leitrim to America. He looked like a child in pain.

'Oh, Mike!' Mrs Macdonald said. Then threw the apron she had donned over her head and cried loudly.

'Now don't you cry for her!' He almost bawled. 'I won't have my wife crying for her! A mother! A fine mother! A perfect mother! By God! And she's gone to a man and left them!'

'No, No! Mike! It isn't the man she's gone for. It's the politics, the life. I always told her she wanted fight.'

'Well, isn't it the same thing? Hasn't she left them?' He marched around the room with hunched shoulders and pugnacious jaw, trying to rid himself of his mortification by shouting it at his wife. His panegyrics of Mrs Leitrim's perfect motherhood and housewifery had been eloquent and intense, but had never touched the oratorical altitudes reached by the floods of abuse and invective her perfidy now provoked from him. He picked the letter off the floor and flourished it, picking out phrases here and there.

'And she calls my wife – my wife, mind you, Rosie – her best and dearest friend. I don't want her sort calling my wife her dearest friend. She can get her friends in America, where she's going with Jarvis. My wife's a decent woman.'

A dangerous light began to creep into Mrs Macdonald's eye. Her tears were properly dry now, swallowed up in the flood of Mike's rhetoric. She watched him and thought of lots of things, but mostly of Mrs Leitrim's strained, questioning look and of her:

'I depended on you, Mrs Macdonald.' Mike smote the letter with his hand. A good hard-working hand, never meant to pull the ropes of domestic finesse, and continued:

'She couldn't stand it any longer, couldn't she? My wife can stand it and so can other women. And she knows "you'll take care of my babies, Mrs Macdonald, you are so good and true and so perfect a mother." My God! My wife to take her kids and keep them! I'm to keep her kids! while she gallivants to America with Jarvis! Politics!' Mike metaphorically spat. 'Well, her kids can go to hell where she's gone. —' But here Mike stopped. He was compelled to stop by the flat of Mrs Macdonald's hand across his mouth. She was no longer the amiable, easy-going soul; no longer the soft tolerant looker-on; but a woman inflamed to do battle for her sex; the faithful and understanding fighting for her friend. She faced him like a splendid virago, and Mike's bitterness and broken love was smitten out of his simple soul by her greatness in this, the supreme moment of her life.

For it is to each according to his station. Heroines of history may garb their thoughts in heroic words, and high-flown ladies in times of stress find a language befitting the dignity of their place. Mike and his wife belonged to the mines, and their talk furnished all that they needed. It was ugly at times and usually coarse, but —.

Mike lost nothing of the loveliness that lay in the core of his wife's strident, passionate outburst.

'You shut your mouth! Shut your mouth! You're always yapping, yapping, yapping, about something you know nothing about! You shut your mouth and get over to Leitrim's and get those kids! Do you hear? Get over and get them and then wait for him!'

(Leitrim worked till five o'clock.)

And when Mike had gone Mrs Macdonald heaved a great sigh and trembled a little. Then she turned to the stove and took the tough steak off it. It still smelt a little, the meat, but she thought it would not be so bad if she put plenty of tomato sauce in the gravy. And as she dealt out each one's portion, six pieces in all, she subsided back into her old soft, lollopy sweetness and murmured:

'Oh, well, two kids won't make much difference.'

Katharine Susannah Prichard

Happiness

1927

Nardadu, grandmother of Munga, was singing as she gazed before her over the red plains under blue sky. Singing, in a low wandering undertone, like wind coming from far over the plains at night:

'Be-be coon-doo-loo
Multha-lala coorin-coorin . . . '

She was sitting beside the stockyard fence in the offal of a dead beast. There had been a kill the night before. A stench of blood and filth flowed through the air about her. On an old hide rotting in the sun, a little lizard lay quite still. Nardadu plucked over a length of entrail and set it aside. She reached for another, grey-green, and dark with blood.

A small squat woman, with broad square features, wide jawbone, short hair in greasy strands packed with mud and bound by a dirty white rag, she sat there singing, and picking over all that was left of the dead bullock. A gina-gina, blue for a length, almost black with dust and grease, showed her bony legs and feet. Her face all placid satisfaction, the black sticks of her arms and fingers swung backwards and forwards, disturbing flies. Flies clung at the sunken wells of her eyes; but she plucked on over the mess of blood and dung, singing:

'Be-be coon-doo-loo, coon-doo-loo,
Be-be, be-be coon-doo-loo,
Multhalala, la-la, lala, lala,
Coorin-coorin, coorin-coorin.'

Across a stretch of ironstone pebbles the buildings of Nyedee homestead were clear in the high light of early morning. There were trees round the long white house with verandas where

*'Cuddle your nose into my breast
And know happiness.'

John Gray slept and ate with his women and children. Megga had planted the trees long ago, the tall dark ones, those bushes with curds of blossom, and the kurrajongs whose leaves were light green and fluttering just now.

Megga had ridden and worked with John when he first camped by Nyedee well. Tall and gaunt and hard, she had cooked in the mustering and droving camps, driven men and beasts through long dry seasons. Eh-erm, she drove John. He was still her little brother.

Half a mile away, Nardadu could see every plank and post of the veranda; white hens stalking across it; harsh green of cabbages, onions, turnips surging beside the big windmill; the mill, its wheel and long fine lines ruled against the sky; and the little mill on mulga posts with gauge stuck out like the tail of a bird. Kinerra and Minyi came out from the house for water. Slight, straight figures in dungaree gina-ginas, they moved slowly to the little mill. But it was out of order: would not give water except in a high wind.

White hens scattered and flew before Megga as she came along the veranda, Meetchie behind her, John after them both. A shrill screaming and flow of women's voices reached Nardadu; the throb and deeper reverberation of John's voice, as he came between the women, throwing a word or two before him. Small and stiff as chalk drawings her people had made on rocks in the hills, John and the two women rocked and moved with sharp little gestures before the house.

Nardadu knew what it was all about. She had heard that screaming and quarrelling of women and the anger of John's voice so often before. She smiled to herself and went on with her singing. Winding and rumbling through her, on and on it went, the eerie, remote melody. Nardadu remembered her mother singing that song. It did not belong to Nyedee people. Nardadu had brought it with her to Nyedee from beyond those wild tumbling hills which stood on the edge of the plain, northeast. Her mother had sung the little song to Nardadu when she was a cooboo. Nardadu had sung it to Beilba and Munga. Always it came fluttering out of her when she was pleased or afraid.

She was pleased this morning to have found something she could cook in the ashes of her fire to satisfy the hunger of Munga when he came in from the dogging. All the men of the uloo had been out trapping dingoes while John was away. But John was home again, and the men would be in soon. The old, high, four-wheeled, single-seated buggy in which John had come from Karara station, with Chitali and old Tommy, still stood red with dust, out before the shed. Horses which had drawn the buggy, rough hair streaked and matted with dust and sweat, were feeding beneath the acacias and mulga, beyond the stockyards.

The little windmill would be mended. There would be the good smell of meat roasted on ashes, in the evening air, down by the uloo. When the men had eaten, talk would be made of dingoes: of wild dogs caught, or too cunning for any trap. Wongana would make a song about a dingo, clicking kylies beside his camp-fire. There would be singing: singing and sleeping in the warm, starlit darkness.

On other stations Nardadu knew, men of the camp would not have gone dogging and left their women at the uloo. Wiah! A curse threaded the words of her song. But Nyedee was not like other places. John Gray left the uloo to the ways of the uloo. Megga? Eh-erm – Nardadu guessed Megga was responsible for that. By her will it was, John did not drink whisky until his legs would not carry him; or take a gin even when old men of the camp sent her to him.

Nardadu did not understand how a woman came to have such power with a man that her will should be stronger than his. But Megga – Nardadu understood something of her and her will, having lived so long with her. Had she not made men of the uloo even wear wandy-warra, and the women grass and leaves from a string round their waists, before there were gina-ginas or trousers and boots on Nyedee? But that John should come under her will so, John who was a man of men? Nardadu clucked and threw out her hands in the native gesture of surprise.

Master he might be of all the country which lay before her old brown eyes, from the wedge of red and yellow purple-riven hills along the west, to those wild and tumbled timbered ridges north and east, beyond which stretched the country of her people and the buck spinifex flats, away and away inland. Yet John he was to her: John the all-powerful to be sure, giver of food and clothing, whose anger and boot you avoided; but who laughed and made fun with you, good-humouredly, when all went well with him.

She had come through the gorge of Nyedee hills with him, how long ago? Nardadu could not count beyond three. 'Plenty years,' she would say it was since John Gray had first brought cattle through the gorge of Nyedee hills, over there where the great koodgeeda's eyes made a pool of fresh drinking-water. Trembling, she remembered the great silver lidless eye in the shadow of dark rocks. How it had flashed at her, glimmered from beneath the water when she went down with her jindie! They had camped quite near, and Wagola, her man, had sent her down to the pool for water because he said the koodgeeda would not hurt a gin. He had made her sleep on the side nearest the pool, too. How terrified she had been, plenty years ago, when she first came to Nyedee with John Gray!

Wagola, her man, had been speared over there on the range by one of her own people. Wagola's brother claimed her. She had grown Beilba then; and Munga was Beilba's son. Her eyes wavered to the creek gums and burying-ground of the uloo, railed places and mounds covered with bark and branches. Her voice had the shrill anguish of wailing for her daughter.

Now she was an old woman, had bulyas on her hands, and led the women's singing in the corroborees. She had no husband to concern herself about, only Munga, her grandson, who put up her low humpy of boughs and hide. And the cows. Nardadu was cow-woman on Nyedee, drove the milkers from their night wandering on wide plains where the windgrass was yellow, and acacias, in their young green, stood against hills blue as the dungaree of a new gina-gina.

While a coolwenda was putting his slow melodious notes across the vast spaces of hill and plain, and stars were still in the sky, she went scurrying after the cows, and brought them through the Two-mile gate to the yards, red heifers and calves, a huge white cow who charged whenever she got a chance, and the old red bull, lumbering and sulky. Nardadu ruled the cows. A drab gnomish figure in dirty gina-gina and the old felt hat which had been Wagola's, she shambled swiftly over the stones, banging two tins to make the cows hurry: proud of herself, of being on the strength of the station, old woman though she was, cow-tailer.

She had not been away since first she came to Nyedee. She had never been pink-eye; but then none of the Nyedee people went pink-eye. Other tribes came to pink-eye on Nyedee every year. There were corroborees, and youths for hundreds of miles about were made men in the widespreading scrub of mulga and minnerichi which stretched to the foot of the dog-toothed range.

The hut of mud-bricks, baked in the sun, on the place where Nyedee homestead now stood – Nardadu had helped to build that. After its walls were up Megga had not ridden out with the men. She had stayed at the hut to watch the sinking of wells, raising of windmills and stockyards. Every plank was set under her eyes: the windmills, with their great wheels and wedge tails of blue-grey iron, stretched taut against the sky.

Then camels bringing stores and sheets of ribbed iron had come over the creek! Again and again they had come, the great beasts, so savage and evil-smelling, yet led by a little stick through the nose and rope reins, bringing more and more sheets of iron and painted wood, flour, sugar, tea, gina-ginas; trousers, boots and hats for the men who went riding with John, pipes, tobacco and boiled lollies. Such days they were, great days of bustle and excitement, from the first fluting of the butcher-bird before stars paled in the eastern sky, until the sun went away behind the back of the hills.

The first room of mud-bricks was kept for a kitchen and the new house grew out from it, with verandas, doors, wire cages for rooms. Megga had sent old men, women and children from the uloo to gather white clay in a creek bed, miles away, and had showed them how to paint the house. But to Nardadu, it still seemed, that the long white house among trees had reared itself by magic on the floor of the dead sea. Far out across the plains she had seen a mirage lying across it, reflections of a house in the sky, and had sung her song as a movin against evil, any evil magic could do an old woman by stealing her wits, when she was minding cows by herself, far away from her kin and the uloo of her people.

Megga herself had worn white clothes when the house was finished. The gins washed them, hung them out to dry and pressed them smooth with irons made hot in the fire. She had gathered about herself, too, china dishes and pots which broke when you dropped them, bringing down Megga's wrath as nothing had ever done.

Then the chickens came. Small fluffy creatures Megga had loved and tended until they were neat white hens, which if a dog killed – eh-erm, there was hell to pay.

Nardadu remembered the killing of one of those hens by Midgelerrie, her own dog, a brindle kangaroo hound, as dear to her almost as Munga. There was no better hunter on Nyedee; but he had pounced on and devoured one of those hens. Lowering, Megga, she remembered, had sent John out with his gun and he had shot the dog. John had told everybody in the uloo he would shoot any dog if it ate Megga's hens; but Nardadu had never forgiven Megga for the shooting. She did not blame John. He did as he was told.

Nothing had been the same on Nyedee since the chickens came. Nardadu believed that Megga's hens were the cause of all that went awry on Nyedee afterwards. Nardadu's was not the only dog John shot because he had eaten one of Megga's hens. The uloo bore Megga a grudge because of her hens, and the dogs John had shot for eating them.

It was beyond anything natural to men and women, Nardadu had decided, the way John and Megga lived in their new house among the trees, with an abundance of food and clothing, shade from the sun and shelter from the rain. They looked about them with pride and contentment. John strutted out from the house to the stockyards and blacksmith's shop, and stretched reading on the veranda when he was not away mustering, or on the road with bullocks for market. Megga cooked, sewed, watched over her china and sat on her chairs, teaching girls from the uloo to scrub, polish, make gina-ginas for themselves. Only two of the youngest gins were allowed into the house, after they had scrubbed their heads and bodies all over with soap and water, every morning, and put on fresh dresses. Other women from the uloo were permitted to sweep round the veranda, in turn, or to help with the washing; but that was all. And always there were new sheds going up, sheds for harness and tools, a butcher miah, shade miah for the hens even.

The station was growing and prospering. John and Megga were growing old with the station; but still, there were no children on Nyedee except children from the uloo who played about the stockyard and woodheap sometimes. Down at the uloo they were concerned about it. The old women suggested that both John and Megga should be advised to take a mate. But Megga, it was agreed, was beyond the age of childbearing.

The men asked John why he did not get a woman. They did not understand his not having a woman except his sister, who was not a wife, to live with him. John laughed and said he had been too busy making the station to think about a wife and family. Men of the uloo believed what he said. They had seen him so often, after a day's hard riding, eat, and sleep as soon as he rolled in a rug beside his campfire. They understood he had thought of nothing but his station and cattle for years.

But the seasons were good. It rained – how it rained that year! It had not rained since on Nyedee as it had rained then. Nardadu herself, and all the other old women in the camp, had gone down to the creek and beaten it back with green branches when the muddy water swirled over its banks towards the uloo. They had been busy patching their huts to keep the rain out. Grass was green on the plains in a day or so; thick and deep in no time. The cows grew fat. Nardadu clucked with pleasure over their milk and calves, thick-set and sturdy. Megga, busy and masterful, directed everybody and everything, looking stouter, more good-humoured, every day. Since the hens and chickens had come, she seemed to have nothing left to wish for.

John went off mustering after the rain, taking all the boys, two or three gins and most of the horses with him. The grass and herbage everywhere made him gay and light-hearted. He talked now and then in easy familiar fashion with Chitali and the boys as he rode along; or when they camped for the night, he by his fire, they by theirs, at a little distance.

They were chasing breakaways in the back hills when the boys came on tracks of wild blacks from the other side of the range. Nyedee boys said these were cousins of theirs. John Gray visited the camp, talked to the old men, and in the evening when Nyedee boys were sitting singing round the camp-fire of the strangers, a young gin was sent to John Gray's camp by way of courtesy to an honoured guest.

Nyedee boys marvelled when she did not return, immediately, as others had always done from John Gray's fireside.

And in the morning, John had presented the old men of the camp with pipes, tobacco, and a couple of blankets.

Somehow Megga heard of it. The boys talked when they got

back to the uloo. They told their women and the old men, who chuckled, laughing, and smelling what was to follow.

Megga had been angry with Minyi for breaking a cup. Minyi, to make her angrier and to take her mind off the cup, had told Megga of the gin John kept by his camp-fire that night in the Nyedee hills. Megga was furious. The girls heard her talking to John about it. John had been angry, too, angry and sulky. He walked up and down the fence for hours afterwards. For many nights, he walked the fences, morose and restless. Out on the run it was just the same, the boys said, John did not sleep as he used to: threw wood on the fire half the night, and walked about.

The blacks watched him fight out his trouble. They knew well enough what was the matter with him. His mouth took a hard line. Nardaḍu had seen John striding backwards and forwards at night, sombre and angry as her old bull when he went moaning and bellowing along the fences, separated from the herd. John scowled at everybody who spoke to him during the day. He could not break the habits Megga had imposed on him; would not drink more whisky than he did usually, or have gins about him. But after he had been south with cattle that year he brought back the kurrie.

She was with him in the old high buggy he had driven over from Karara in; and John looked as pleased with himself as Megga had looked when the new house sat, all built-up and whitewashed, on the plains. He had got what he wanted.

And Megga! Nardadu saw Megga's face, as though by lightning, so bleached and stiff it was. Megga had not known John would bring this other woman with him to Nyedee. He kissed Megga and said:

'I've got a surprise for you, Meg. This is my wife.'

Megga did not speak, while the other laughed, saying in a high, singy voice:

'My name's Margie!'

John went on, as if he had done something as much for Megga's sake as his own:

'It was getting a bit lonely for you, Meg, with no white woman to talk to. You and Margie'll be company for each other.'

Nardadu could see and hear them still as if they were

corroboreeing before her. Megga, fat and dumb, in front of the girl on slight, bare-looking legs; Meetchie – which was the uloo's way of saying 'Mrs Margie' – in her light frock and hat, holding a red sunshade: John between them, proud and pleased with himself.

They were delighted with the kurrie at the uloo; delighted and excited by her light, brightly coloured dresses, patterned with flowers; her necklaces, high-heeled shoes, the songs she sang, and the tookerdoo she gave them, sweet stuff covered in brown, sticky loam. John himself stepped with a jaunty kick and swing as he walked; his eyes laughed out at you. Nardadu gurgled and chuckled after him, and men of the uloo were very satisfied. Nobody worked very much in those days; and John was easy to get on with. He went about whistling in a queer, tuneless way. Nardadu had even heard him trying to whistle her own little song:

'Be-be coon-doo-loo, coon-doo-loo . . .'

How the gins laughed, and he with them, though Nardadu blackguarded him furiously when he took her calves off their milk too soon, so that the kurrie should have plenty of cream and milk in her tea! Black tea was all the gins ever tasted. But the chatter and giggling round the woodheap where they drank their tea and ate their hunks of bread and meat and jam when it was suspected why John was concerned about milk for the kurrie!

He was angry if Nardadu did not drive the cows through the Two-mile gate. Useless to explain she was afraid of the narlu who haunted the mulga thickets beyond the gate: the narlu who had led Wagola from the tracks and hunting-grounds of his people, along the dog-toothed range. John laughed and joked with her good-naturedly enough; but he would have the cows taken where the grass was good. To be sure, he had sent Munga to mind the cows with her, and such days they had been for Nardadu and her grandson, out there on the wide plains, yellow with wind-grass, or in the dove-grey mulga thickets, under blue skies, she teaching Munga how to pick up tracks, and the movins against evil spirits and bullets; to find water, snare bungarra and dig for coolyahs.

Good days! Only in Megga's face the satisfaction faded; and

the kurrie became wan and sickly in the hot weather. Nobody saw her during the day; but in the evening, when the sun had gone down behind the hills, she wandered about the veranda and garden. Wandered, wailing and complaining about the heat, the dust-storms, flies and mosquitoes. Up and down she walked: wept and lamented.

John was very tender with the kurrie in her weakness and sickness; as kind as he knew how to be, trying to soothe her when she cried: 'Take me away from this dreadful place, John. I loathe it. Life here, it's so bare, and hard and ugly!' although it hurt him to hear her talk like that about Nyedee. Nyedee, with its wells and windmills, comfortable homestead, garden and bathrooms! What more did a woman want?

Against Megga, though, he would hear no word of complaint. She was mistress of her brother's house: had always been: would always be, he said. She cooked, was storekeeper, accountant, provisioned the parties of well-sinkers, fencers, musterers, rationed the blacks, and saw the gins kept the house clean and in order. There was nobody like her. Two men could not do what she did. She knew every well and windmill and what stock they carried. Megga must go on as she had always done. Meetchie could never do what she did, but she was his boogeriga, his little green parrot, his love-bird.

When Meetchie went away to have her baby the days flowed on at Nyedee as they had always done. Long, quiet days, filled by the riding out, or riding in, of John and the boys with cattle or horses: the arrival and departure of gangs to repair windmills, sink new wells, make fences, while Megga baked bread, prepared the meals, salted meat after the first day of a kill, figured in her account-books, sewed, worked in the garden, read and slept.

Meetchie came back with her baby, bringing cretonne dresses and sweets for the gins. There was a new, older more obstinate look on her face. She did not wail so much or sing so often; but soon the end of the house was regarded as hers and the baby's.

Within a few years there were three children in those rooms at Meetchie's end of the house: one a girl with hair the colour of the tasselled mulga blossom, a little, fleet, wild creature who watched the plains for dust of John's horse when he had been away and ran to meet him when the gins cried: 'John comin'!'

No horse on Nyedee would have let John take the child on his saddle, or have stood while she flew up by his stirrup; but always John dismounted to meet his daughter, gave his reins to one of the boys, and, catching her up in his arms, carried her home on the back of his neck, his face as childishly joyous as hers.

But Megga and Meetchie barely spoke to each other. Years only deepened the animosity between them, although Megga loved the children as though they were her own; and Meetchie knew she loved them.

As Nardadu looked at it, the house seemed to be cramped down over one of those dark, slimy, fungus growths which poison the air about them. At the uloo, when the women quarrelled and fought together, their shrieks drifted away; bad feeling was lost in a day and forgotten. But there, in the house, misery and bitterness crouched and clung. You knew they were about when you went near the place and saw the women: Megga's face set to her contempt and repressed indignation: the young wife's face moody and resentful.

For ten days' tramping there was no other building like this John had made in the bed of a dead sea: no other house under those wide, blue skies: no other white women to talk to each other but those two.

John left the house to the women as much as possible. He was out on the plains and in the hills for weeks at a time. The shadow lifted from his face as soon as he was out of sight of the homestead, although he cried out in pain and anger sometimes as he slept under the stars.

The conflict which had been going on for years took a step forward when the kurrie seized Megga by the throat with her fierce white hands and would have crushed life out of her had not John come between them. Then Megga had gone to live in the old store-room near the creek.

Meetchie said she could do all Megga had done. She would cook, manage the housekeeping, order stores, provision the camps, feed the blacks. For months she worked to convince John she could do as well as Megga; but she could not. She had neither strength nor liking for what she had undertaken: she struggled on, overburdened, distraught, screaming at the hens and the gins, losing her soft young beauty, becoming almost insane in her weariness and discontent. John took as much as possible out of her hands. But bread would not rise, store-orders were forgotten, tucker-bags lost. He was cross and impatient. Why couldn't Meetchie have left Megga to run the place as she had always done? The station could not afford to have its work messed up in this way.

And Megga, living alone in her hut by the creek, sat gazing over the plain, day after day, strong, capable hands idle before her; the light gone out of her eyes. Deprived of her work, what had she to live for? She had given everything she had to the station, helping it to grow. She had reared and trained it, as she had John. And the seasons were going from bad to worse. Would it ever rain again? She could see, and John knew only too well, how he would need her to relieve him of all the little odd jobs he did now round the homestead, in the dry season ahead. He would have to be out on the run, moving cattle from well to well, wherever there was a picking, all through the blazing heat and dust storms.

Nardadu could hear them talking over at the house, Megga, Meetchie and John. Their voices came to her, clashing and clanging against each other.

'Your sister means more to you than I do!'

'What is it you want?' John's voice was surly and menacing. 'Meg has left you the house. You want her to clear off of Nyedee, is that it?'

Meetchie made a long wail of grievances. Megga was always interfering, setting the children against their mother, and the gins would only do as she said. Meetchie had told Kinerra to catch and kill a hen for the children's dinner, and Megga had said no more hens were to be killed. It was always the same. If Meetchie told the gins to do one thing and Megga told them to do another, they obeyed Megga. 'Either she goes or I go!'

'Turn my sister out for you?' John shouted. 'Not on your life! She went to the hut of her own accord. But further she shan't go.'

John had left the house and was striding across the red earth and ironstone pebbles towards Nardadu.

Beside the little windmill Kinerra and Minyi, who had been listening to and watching the quarrel, turned to get water. There was no wind; the mill-fans hung motionless; Kinerra, climbing wooden stays of the mill, swung the wheel; Minyi pumped, and filled the fire-blackened kerosene buckets. Two slight, straight figures, buckets on their heads, the girls moved slowly back to the house.

John walked to the shed before which the buggy was still standing. Nardadu had her affections, superstitions. They stirred as she watched John coming from the house towards her. His back was straight: he swung along with as steady, direct steps as when she had first known him, although his body had thickened and swelled in the white moleskin pants and faded blue shirt beneath. But the face under his wide hat-brim, fatter, redder, was sullen and heavy now: the blue of his eyes, burned deeper for the years out there on the plains working cattle under bare skies, held only passion and defeat.

The beat of his heels and spurs, as they clicked on the pebbles with a little silver tinkling, made Nardadu shiver. She remembered she should have been away beyond the gates with her cows: that John would shake his fist and yell angrily, if he saw her. Her song quavered into a queer, gurgling laughter.

But John did not see her. He was calling Chitali and old Tommy, who had driven over from Karara with him.

Nardadu listened. John told the boys to put horses in the buggy again.

When the buggy drew up before the house Meetchie hurried forward and climbed into it. John lifted the children in beside her. He took the reins and they drove away, Megga, standing on the veranda, watched them go. Nobody called to her. The buggy whirled off in dust.

'Wiah!' Nardadu muttered, getting to her feet. Her instinct, sure and sensitive, told her Megga had won, and lost, in the fight which had been going on so long in John's house. Megga had got back the place and work which were hers and driven the kurrie off.

But John had brought the kurrie to Nyedee because he wanted a kurrie. And there were the children. Had he not loved and played with his children as men of the uloo loved and played with their children?

More than ever now, he would wander along the fences at

night, like that sulky old bull from the herd: his face turn to Megga as it did this morning: misery and bitterness crouch under the long, white house, with its back to the blue, wild hills.

Against the sky-film, thin, clear blue, soft as the ashes of mulga and minnerichi, dust moved.

A cry rose in Nardadu's throat. She watched that dust grow against the sky and the edge of mulga scratching the sky. The tagged tail of horsemen swept out from it. Men of the uloo were returning from the dogging.

They swerved in a wide curve towards the stockyards, young horses before them. Nardadu could see Munga in charge of the packhorses: Munga on his white horse, ginger with dust, packhorses before him. The bay mare, a bucket lashed to her back, made for the troughs, and Munga, after her. The swing-in of dark, slender legs and flying tails through red mist of dust; bodies of men and horses joined, free-flying, galloping; all wildness and grace! Nardadu exulted. The horseman her Munga would be! And how pleased with the meat she had to feed him from her fire that night, as though he were a man!

The song of her gladness trembled, ranged its high minor notes and went wandering out to Munga:

'Be-be coon-doo-loo, coon-doo-loo,
Multha-lala coorin-coorin.'

Myra Morris

Sun

1928

Annie had lived most of her life underground, like a mole. At half-past eight every morning she caught a cable-tram into the city. It went a circuitous route, round smutty-walled factories and clusters of squalid-looking houses and little shops. It passed the tawny Yarra where the masts of ships huddled together like tall young forest trees, and lost itself in the mazes of the city.

She worked in a sweet-shop, run by two oily Greeks. You had to go down stone steps under the pavement to get to it. It had a strange, sweet, away-from-the-earth smell. There was a soda-fountain at the back of the marble counter. Everything was cold – the slabs of marble, the nickel taps, the glass jars full of rich brown chocolates, the square white tables at which people sucked their drinks through straws.

Annie was pale-faced, with prominent blue eyes, and she had long fine hairs growing on her chin. Her hands were white, too – unhealthily white, like the belly of a fish. It was no wonder she was so white; she had known practically no outdoor life. All day she stayed in the little shop, serving drinks, and weighing out sticky chocolates. At six she went home in a crowded tram, had her meal with her mother and two brothers and washed up in the stuffy kitchen, with its foetid sink that was nearly always out of order. After that, if it were warm she sat on the veranda, watered the tiny lawn and wind-blown flower-beds, or went for an aimless walk along the seafront. Sometimes the band would play in the rotunda, and she and Pearl Drew, the girl next door, would sit and listen to 'Ain't She Sweet?' and 'Muddy Waters' with an intensity of boredom. If it were cold she would go round the corner to the pictures, or stay by the fire working eyelets round the necks of night-dresses and camisoles, which she still wore, along with the high-boned corsets that gave her an unfashionable bust.

During the week-ends things were much the same. On a Saturday afternoon she would turn out her tiny bedroom with painstaking deliberation, do odd jobs about the house or sew.

Sometimes of a Sunday morning she would go to church and kneel in the pew carefully, so that the toes of her best shoes should not be turned up. In the afternoon she and Pearl might go down to the beach and sit in the shade of the sea-wall, watching the couples pass. They watched with cold, resentful eyes, muttering stories about the looseness of men, and the foolishness of young girls who would not let them alone.

Her own days were uncoloured by the thought of any man. She wove no bright romances about herself. Passion was as far away from her as the moon. She might have been completely sexless. Hers was a dull, spiritless life, with one week the same as another. Twenty-four, she had known nothing different. If she had thought about it she would have realized that most other girls did not live exactly as she did; but she was too apathetic, too stifled by the narrowness of her life to think about anything.

Sometimes as she crossed the street she would see the sun lying warm and yellow along the pavements, and gilding the tremulous tops of trees. She would feel it on her shoulders, like a hot hand laid there, and get into the shade quickly. The sun made her feel faint and head-achy. She wondered how people could sit out in the sun. It wasn't natural.

Once, in the middle of a fine spring morning, a customer clattered down the stone steps and bought some chocolates. There was a faint indefinable smell of straw about him.

'It's bright and sunny outside,' he said, with the easy talkativeness of the country-bred man. 'It does you good to feel the sun burning clean through you.'

'I don't like it – the sun,' said Annie, 'I've not been used to it. It makes me feel sick.'

'You're not alive,' said the man jovially, stuffing the bag into his pocket. 'Sun 'd warm you up and make you come alive, Miss.'

She knew it wouldn't do all that, but you certainly did want warming up. You shivered down in the cold shop, and your feet had no feeling in them. Even when the sun was warm in the street it was chilly down there. And winter was well over. The wind had a fugitive warmth in its breath. The fruit-blossoms, startlingly pale against black stems, were all finished. The sea at the back of the house was the filmy blue of delphiniums. Summer was coming on tentatively.

When Annie thought of the heat she thought of her sister Kate

– big and fat and good-natured; married to a man for whom she had cooked on a cattle-station south of Lake Eyre. A desolate place it looked in a picture – flat as a meat-dish, her mother said; a boundless plain, feathered lightly with meagre scrub and streaked with long, dry creek-beds.

One day a letter came from Kate. Kate had extra work to do, she said, and had been very 'poorly.' Sometimes she didn't know how she was going to get through, what with one thing and another. She wondered if Annie would come along for a little while before the weather got too hot.

Annie's mother put it to her at dinner. Annie was terrified because it was something outside the ordinary routine of her life. She would be called on to show initiative perhaps. Then she looked out of the window and saw the pale sun flooding the street. She remembered the feel of it, and was touched by a vague, inexplicable excitement.

'It'd do you good,' said her mother, wiping a hot plate with her check apron, 'You look peaky. The sun 'd liven you up.'

The same, in a way, as the customer had said: 'The sun will make you come alive.'

She thought of it in the night, and decided for it with a queer, breathless feeling, as though she had made a great, unalterable resolution. She counted over her underclothes carefully: as her mother had said, you never knew when you might have an accident.

She left a few days later by the Adelaide express, then by train and coach up to Merri Merri, Tom's place. The coach was empty, but it was hot inside. The sun was all about her. It beat down on the horses' backs, and a steaming odour came from them. It pressed down on the leather of the seats, and created a smell, acrid and pungent. She thought that she must smell that smell all her life. The plains lay around her, lifeless and incredibly remote, with the sky touching their edges. She looked curiously at the scant vegetation – tufted low scrub that grew close to the earth, wild geranium and grey salt-bush. A creeping plant with a large yellow flower ran along the ground, but she thought that the flower was not so yellow as the sun. She could see *that* brimming over, spreading in little pools on top of the ridges – golden, like some of the drinks she had served in the shop.

At Merri Merri she got out. The house was decrepit and

wooden, with wide, shady verandas and a lot of white posts. Kate was down at the gate. She looked older and was withered. Her eyes were puckered up in her face, and there was an air of lassitude about her. Big Tom, talking to the driver of the coach, was the colour of dust.

Annie walked up the path, insisting on carrying her suit-case; nervously eager to please, vaguely frightened because she was thrown out of her usual way and didn't know what was the next move. The sun beat down on her shoulders. She stood and put her palms out, as though she could hold it like water.

'What is it?' asked Kate carelessly.

'The sun,' said Annie, with an indrawn breath, 'It's real, somehow – like a person.'

'Oh, it's nothink,' said Kate, 'We get used to it.'

In the living-room another man sprawled over a broken chair. He had lazy, blue eyes and black, curling lashes that gave him an impudent look.

'Pat Gilligan,' said Kate, in her off hand way. 'He's got a place of his own over the ridges, but he's helping Tom with some cattle. How did you leave mum? Is that kitchen sink mended yet?'

Annie answered at random. She was vaguely afraid of Gilligan, who later sat at the table with them. She hated men. They'd get nothing from her, anyhow – not them! It might have minimized her discomfort had she known that he was thinking:

'Lord! What a wash-out!'

During the days that followed she was mostly in the house, helping. From the door she could watch out over the shimmering plain; watch the thin mulga and acacia dancing in lacy lines, and the barren, undulating country stretching away to the horizon, where it seemed miraculously to be drawn up into the air. Sometimes she would go and stand out in the heat, and it would give her a queer, excited feeling, though Tom told her not to go without a hat. She was beginning to like Merri Merri, though it took some getting used to. Kate and Tom laughed at her and made her embarrassed.

'She's a born old maid,' said Tom one day, and he kissed her slyly.

Kate laughed, and she ran out surging against this outraging of her shy womanhood. But, outside, Gilligan, who had watched from the veranda, laughed lazily, and she fled in a sudden agony of shame.

It grew hotter at Merri Merri. Kate was prostrated, and most of the work fell to Annie. But there was always time to stand at the door and dream as she had never done before, looking out, with her hands on her hips, her pale eyes touched with clear, whitish light. Now her mind was full of colourful, chaotic imaginings. She thought of things that frightened and appalled her; things sensuous and beautiful, like roses in summer gardens, music over water and men's voices singing deeply. She had never been touched by these before. She was passionately aware of something in her that was struggling to come out; something that had to do with the blazing sun and a hunger for happiness and – Pat Gilligan. She would find herself staring at him against her will, longing, yet fearful, that he would turn round and look at her. But Pat Gilligan slouched over the saddle all day, and had little enough to say to her – at least, until the wheezy gramophone was left at the house by one of the men. They danced on the veranda of an evening then.

'What, never learned to dance?' he exclaimed. 'Poor kid!'

Because he loved music almost without reservation and the beauty of body rhythm, he taught her out on the rough-boarded veranda, with infinite patience, laughing good-naturedly when she stumbled and drew away shrinkingly from his too-tight hold.

It was the beginning of a fragile enchantment for Annie. She began to think of him deliberately through the long, hot, lonely days when Kate was lying down. She would watch out for his blue shirt, blotted faintly in the dust that rose from the dry earth. That hunger for happiness took an insidious hold of her. . . . It was the sun, the sun, the sun! It was making her come alive, as the man in the shop had said it would. Out under the empty sky she would still try to catch it in her hands so that she could almost see it dripping through her fingers like sticky, golden honey. She felt that a new soul had been born into her body.

'She's different, she is that!' Tom said.

How different only Annie knew – freed from the intolerable high-boned corsets, and taking pains with the disfiguring hairs on her chin.

'It's like as if I'm drunk', she told herself one fiery day when

Tom had ridden over to a neighbouring station. 'And when you're drunk you're likely to do things you wouldn't when you're sober.'

She put a little rouge on her face, and felt sorry for Kate, lying inert on the bed racked with neuralgia.

'I'll do now with some aspirin,' said Kate wearily after the evening meal. 'Tom won't be back to-night, so I'll get to sleep early. You needn't come in again.'

It was stifling in the house. Annie crept out of her little bedroom with an ugly crepe kimono fastened decorously over her petticoat. Gilligan, who had come in late, was sprawled on the veranda, smacking insects against his face.

She let herself down gently into a chair, conscious of him, though he had made only a vague, meaningless movement. She could smell the warm, passionate smell of flowers. It was lonely out there. She felt herself unwanted, lonely. She groped fumblingly after some tangible comfort. She wanted something to happen – she hardly knew what. She began to cry softly, for no reason at all.

'Better go to bed,' said Gilligan kindly, from the shadows.

He leaned forward, his hands planted squarely on his knees, his eyes seeking her. Poor little thing! She was making him feel a bit that way himself.

'I don't want to go to bed,' she said in a stifled voice, 'It's too hot, and I'm sort of frightened.'

'What of?'

Gilligan sounded bored, but there was a comforting quality in his soft, Irish voice. He realized that she was a woman, soft and sweet, and obviously a little more than interested in him. His senses became suddenly more alert. A hard life this, leaving no room for women. . . . But when one came under your notice like this – he remembered Annie's pale eyes, pretty in a pleading sort of way, and tried to catch a glimpse of them as she struggled for an answer.

'I dunno,' said Annie stupidly, 'Things.'

She began to cry afresh; easily, like a very young child.

Gilligan stirred in his chair. Few men can bear to see a woman cry, and something rose up in his heart and made him hot to comfort her. He felt a little of the love that all men keep for all women, and which needs only a touch to spring to life.

'Come over here,' he said awkwardly.

His hands groped for hers in the dark and held them warmly. He smelled the cheap, penetrating scent of roses as she leaned against him.

In the silence they could hear the dry pods of the creepers bursting like mimic pistol shots. Down by the waterhole the frogs were calling dolorously apart and together. The darkness seemed to flow on and on.

'Don't let us go in,' said Annie breathlessly. 'Stay like we are for a bit.'

In the morning she woke, beset with a crowding sense of shame. Memories of the night poured in upon her. What had she done? Allowed a man to kiss her, make violent love to her, talk as though she were almost as free and easy as one of those loose flappers she and Pearl Drew had talked about! True, she had held herself very stiffly at first, fighting against that deadly feeling of inertia, but she had let herself rest against his chest after. She remembered the feel of his stubbly cheek against hers. Soft, delightful things he had muttered; calling her his little Irish rose, and saying that he must have been blind because he hadn't noticed her before. She clenched her hands nervously. What of it? She didn't care! She was glad he had kissed her – like that. She supposed they would drift into marriage. She loved him, and that was a fact.

The sun beating hotly outside the kitchen windows seemed to sting her into a new knowledge of herself and him. She hadn't been like that when first she had come to Merri Merri. She had altered unbelievably.

'You done it, you done it!' she muttered exultantly, shaking her fist up to the hot ball of sun.

Yes, that was it all right. She couldn't explain, but it was as though the sun had roused her up to do battle for herself. She had 'come alive.' She felt that she could not wait until Gilligan got back from the ridge to which he had ridden out early. But when he came he found her depressed by a message that had come. Her mother was ill. She must go at once. The coach left in the morning. She could not wait any longer.

'Don't worry,' said Gilligan, in his lumbering way. 'You'll come back. If you don't, I'll go across to Melbourne – see? Got a brother in the skin-line there. We're going to git married after – see?'

He was a little astonished himself at the swift turn of events and inclined to be dubious about that Irish impulsiveness that had led him to the point where he now stood. But she was a nice, soft little thing, and he supposed he was in love with her. Anyhow, a man had to marry some day.

Annie whimpered a little as she went off. Passionately she longed to stay. Some deep-down resentment surged within her when she thought of her mother and the city. The sun was coming down like a sheet of golden water. In it danced grotesquely the figures of Kate and Tom and Pat Gilligan.

Two months later Gilligan walked down the stone steps into the sweet-shop. He saw Annie at once. She looked pinched and cold, and looked at him vaguely, as if she did not remember him; or as if, if she did, it was an unpleasant remembrance. Something in his heart fell a little. She seemed nervous and distant, and he had come a long way to see her. Annie, in her absence, had become more precious to him than he had imagined possible. He had invested her with a thousand unknown qualities.

'It's me,' he said with a foolish, uncomfortable grin. 'I've come to take you back, Annie. Remember what you promised? You never wrote, but I still take it it's going to marry me you are.'

She polished a glass nervously, her quick, jerky movements reminding him of a rabbit's. He could see where the hard line of her corsets showed through her silk blouse.

'We were silly,' she said, speaking in a fretful voice. 'I never. . . .'

There was a faint hostility dawning in her pale eyes. Gilligan stared at her uncomprehendingly.

'Then you never meant,' he began stumblingly.

'Oh, I dunno,' she said in a sullen voice, 'I must have been different at the time. Up there, I mean. I couldn't go on with it now – ever. I don't want to get married – ever. That's a fact. I'm not made that way.'

He looked at her, struggling for understanding. He remembered that night on the veranda when she had cried. If she hadn't. . . .

'For the love of Mike!' he said heartily, 'It was you yourself that gave me the lead. If you'd 'a left me alone, I. . . .'

She stopped him with a little cry.

'I dunno,' she said sullenly, 'It must 'a been the sun, up there!'

'The sun!'

He frowned at her, his curling lashes sticking into the flesh round his eyes. And all at once it dawned on him that it was distasteful to her even to look at him.

A customer had come in, and she was moving about with an air of efficiency, squirting a pinkish liquid into a glass. He had the feeling that she was happy doing that, that she would never do anything else.

'Well, good-bye,' he said awkwardly, from the foot of the steps.

'Good-bye,' she called swiftly, her face lightened with a look of relief.

Well, he was gone again. That was good. She would never understand what had got hold of her up there. It made her hot and ashamed to think of it. Phew! It was cold down here. She rubbed her hands together. A little pale glint of sun came goldenly through glass. She blinked, and it was gone. Hateful that hot sun up at Merri Merri! There was something wicked in it. Well, she was glad she had to come home.

She turned to the nickel taps with a new air of escape.

'Strawberry-ice, one. That's one shilling, please.'

Notes on Authors

LADY MARY ANNE BARKER (1831–1911) was the wife of a British officer who died in 1861. She remarried and with her husband, Frederick Broome, came to New Zealand in 1865. *Station Life in New Zealand* (1870) and its sequel *Station Amusements in New Zealand* (1873) describe her life on a Canterbury sheep run. 'The Shepherd's Story' is taken from *A Christmas Cake in Four Quarters* (1872), an account of her Christmasses in different lands, where it is presented as a short story orally told.

B.E. BAUGHAN (1870–1958) wrote a quantity of poetry but is best known for her collection of stories about colonial life *Brown Bread from a Colonial Oven* (1912) which, with their sharp witty observation, mark the move away from the love-story conventions of the nineteenth century.

BARBARA BAYNTON (1857–1929) began life as the daughter of a bush carpenter in New South Wales and ended it as the wife of an English lord. Only a few of the intervening years were devoted to writing; the rest to collecting husbands and, subsequently, opals and antiques, while alternately living in England and Australia. The six stories in *Bush Studies* (1902), source of 'Billy Skywonkie', are, however, regarded as some of Australia's best. Baynton also published a novel, *Human Toll* (1907).

ADA CAMBRIDGE (1844–1926) came to Australia in 1870 with her clergyman husband. Soon she was writing for local newspapers and magazines to supplement the family income. Besides her extensive contributions to periodicals, she had eighteen novels published in England and three volumes of poetry. Yet she died poor. 'The Wind of Destiny' comes from her collection *At Midnight and other stories* (1889). Cambridge's *A Marked Man* (1890) has recently been reprinted by Pandora Press; her *The Three Miss Kings* (1891) by Virago.

CLARA CHEESEMAN (1852–1943) was the author of a novel *A Rolling Stone* (1886), an article about early Australasian writing 'Colonials in Fiction' (*New Zealand Illustrated Magazine*, 1903) and probably more untraced stories like 'Married for his

Money', published in the *Australian Ladies Annual* (1878). She is typical of the genteel school of women writers.

ELLEN CLACY (c. 1830–?) paid a brief visit to Victoria during 1852–53. After returning to England she published her delightful account of this trip, and *Lights and Shadows of Australian Life* (1854), a two-volume collection of novelettes and stories, including 'An Agreeable Mistake'.

JEAN DEVANNY (1894–1962) has re-emerged in the last few years with re-publication of her novel *The Butcher Shop* (1926). Active in the Labour movement in New Zealand, she became a communist on moving to Australia in 1929 and all her writing evidences strong political commitment. She wrote more than twenty novels and one book of short fiction, *Old Savage and Other Stories* (1927) from which 'The Perfect Mother' comes.

MABEL FORREST (1872–1935), a Queenslander, published a great deal of poetry and prose in Australian periodicals between 1900 and 1930. She became best known in the 1920s for her alliteratively-titled novels such as *Gaming Gods* (1926) and *White Witches* (1929). 'The Housekeeper' first appeared in the *Sydney Mail* and was collected in *The Red Kangaroo* (1907).

G.B. LANCASTER (1874–1945) was the pseudonym of Mrs Edith Lyttelton, who was born in Tasmania and spent part of her childhood in New Zealand. She wrote a quantity of stories, set in both Australia and New Zealand, and also thirteen novels. She was widely known as a writer in her time, and stories under the name G.B. Lancaster would be advertised as attractions in new journals. 'Our Lady of the Plains' appeared in the *New Zealand Illustrated Magazine* 1902.

SUMNER LOCKE (1881–1917), a Queenslander, wrote plays and a novel set in the USA but was best known for her three very popular selection books. She died soon after giving birth to the playwright and novelist Sumner Locke Elliot and was the original of 'Dear One' in his *Careful, He Might Hear You* (1963). 'When Dawson Died' first appeared in the *Lone Hand* for August 1910 and was reprinted in *Mum Dawson, 'Boss'* (1911).

MARY J. MANDER is better known as Jane Mander (1977–1949). Her best known work is the novel *The Story of a New Zealand*

River (1920). She was born near Auckland and grew up in the country, but left New Zealand in early adulthood for Australia, New York and England, a progress reflected in her novels. 'A Stray Woman' (published in the *New Zealand Illustrated Magazine*) is a very early story, but its subject, the disappointment of marriage, is a familiar one in her novels.

KATHERINE MANSFIELD (1888–1923). The best known of all New Zealand's writers, Katherine Mansfield remains monumental in our past. Although the most famous of her later stories are set in New Zealand, the early New Zealand stories, 'The Woman at the Store', 'How Pearl Button was Kidnapped', 'Ole Underwood', are closer to her unrefined materials and therefore less remote from the fledgling literature she left behind.

MYRA MORRIS (1893–1966) was born in Victoria and brought up in the Mallee district. Though once regarded as one of Australia's finest short story writers, her work is now largely forgotten. Besides her collection, *The Township* (1947), she published two volumes of poetry and three novels. 'Sun' was inlcuded in *Australian Story Book* (1928).

ROSA PRAED (1851–1935) was born in Queensland but married an Englishman and left Australia for London in 1875. A prolific and extremely popular writer, Praed published over forty novels, besides collections of stories and volumes of reminiscences. Several of her novels are being reprinted by Virago and Pandora Press. Her collection *Stubble Before the Wind* (1908) included 'A Happy Ending'.

KATHERINE SUSANNAH PRICHARD (1883–1969) was born in Fiji while her father was editor of a local newspaper. As a child she lived in Tasmania; later in Melbourne and Perth. Like many of the other women represented here, she began her literary career as a journalist. Her twelve novels include such Australian classics as *Working Bullocks* (1926) and *Coonardoo* (1929). She also produced several collections of short stories and poems, an autobiography and many plays, mostly unpublished. 'Happiness' first appeared in the *Bulletin* for 10 December 1927.

HENRY HANDEL RICHARDSON (1870–1946) was born Ethel Florence Lindsay Richardson in Melbourne but left for Germany at the age of eighteen to study music. Marriage, and her later switch to a literary career, ensured that she remained an expatriate. She is best known for her novels, *Maurice Guest* (1908), *The Getting of Wisdom* (1910) and the historical trilogy *The Fortunes of Richard Mahony* (1930). 'Death' first appeared in the *English Review* in 1911.

MARY SIMPSON (1884–?), a Victorian who wrote under the pseudonym 'Weeroona', contributed to many Australian magazines, including the *Bulletin* and the *Australian Journal*. 'The Salvage Sale' comes from her only collection, *Tell-Tale Stories from the Bulletin* (1926).

MARIE STANMORE published 'In Wellington Was Consolation' in the *New Zealand Illustrated Magazine* in 1901. Nothing else by her has come to light and no biographical information was published.

TASMA was the pseudonym of Jessie Couvreur (1848–97) who came to Tasmania as a young child. Besides uncollected journalism, stories and sketches, she published *A Sydney Sovereign and other Tales* (1889) and six novels. The best known of these, *Uncle Piper of Piper's Hill* (1889) will shortly be reprinted by Pandora Press. 'Barren Love' first appeared in the annual *Hash: A Mixed Dish for Christmas* (1877).

W.W. seems to have succeeded in making her life as mysterious as her tales. An undated letter in the Moir Collection, La Trobe Library, is signed 'M.H. Fortune' and was probably written between 1905 and 1910. In it she complains of failing eyesight and increasing difficulty in selling her now rather old-fashioned stories. Despite her years of writing, she was obviously living in extreme poverty. Morris Miller lists *The Detective's Album: Tales of the Australian Police by W.W. Reprinted from the Australian Journal* (Melbourne, 1871) as the first collection of detective stories printed in Australia. 'The Evidence of the Grave' appeared in the *Australian Journal* for September 1870.

MARY J. WRIGHT contributed 'A New Century Girl' to the *New Zealand Illustrated Magazine* in 1901. No other work of hers has appeared. Like Marie Stanmore, she was probably one of the large body of occasional women writers who published in monthly magazines.

Acknowledgements

The editors and the publishers are grateful to the following for permission to reproduce stories in *Happy Endings*:

'A Stray Woman' by Jane Mander. Reprinted by kind permission of Rangi Cross and Richards Literary Agency.

'Our Lady of the Plains' by G. B. Lancaster. Copyright Margaret Joan Garrett (née Lyttleton), 1945.

'Death' by Henry Handel Richardson. Reprinted by kind permission of Curtis Brown Ltd on behalf of the estate of Henry Handel Richardson. Copyright the estate of Henry Handel Richardson.

'The Perfect Mother' by Jean Devanny. Copyright the estate of Jean Devanny.

'Happiness' by Katharine Susannah Prichard. Permission courtesy of the copyright holder, Ric Throssell, c/o Curtis Brown Australia Pty Ltd.

Cover painting: 'Study: Girl with Poppies', 1986, by Grace Joel, reproduced by kind permission of the Robert McDougall Art Gallery, Christchurch, New Zealand.

Every effort has been made to establish copyright in these stories. Any information leading to further identification of the writers in this volume would be welcomed by the editors and the publishers.